Praise for Marta Perry
and her novels

"Beautifully written with a perfect balance of
story elements and true romance."
—*RT Book Reviews* on *Since You've Been Gone*

"Ms. Perry is a master at telling powerfully
emotional and spiritual stories."
—Diane Risso, *RT Book Reviews* on
Promise Forever

"Marta Perry creates her characters marvelously,
and expresses her faith in such a subtle,
nonpreachy way that sometimes you're hardly
aware that it's an inspirational piece. You're
too busy enjoying the story, feeling for the
characters, and feeling more connected with
God. Very well done, Ms. Perry."
—Lisa Ramaglia, *Scribes World Reviews* on
A Mother's Gift

"Four stars for *A Father's Place*. Marta Perry is
synonymous with sweet, loving romance!"
—*RT Book Reviews*

MARTA PERRY

Since You've Been Gone

The Doctor Next Door

Love Inspired

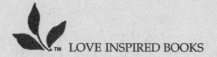 LOVE INSPIRED BOOKS

ISBN-13: 978-0-373-68885-2

SINCE YOU'VE BEEN GONE AND THE DOCTOR NEXT DOOR

SINCE YOU'VE BEEN GONE
Copyright © 1999 by Martha Johnson

THE DOCTOR NEXT DOOR
Copyright © 2000 by Martha Johnson

www.LoveInspiredBooks.com

Printed in U.S.A.

CONTENTS

MARTA PERRY

has written almost everything, including Sunday school curriculum, travel articles and magazine stories in twenty years of writing, but she feels she's found her home in the stories she writes for the Love Inspired line.

Marta lives in rural Pennsylvania, but she and her husband spend part of each year at their second home in South Carolina. When she's not writing, she's probably visiting her children and her beautiful grandchildren, traveling or relaxing with a good book.

Marta loves hearing from readers and she'll write back with a signed bookplate or bookmark. Write to her c/o Steeple Hill Books, 233 Broadway, Suite 1001, New York, NY 10279, e-mail her at marta@martaperry.com, or visit her on the Web at www.martaperry.com.

SINCE YOU'VE BEEN GONE

Therefore, as God's chosen people, holy and dearly loved, clothe yourselves with compassion, kindness, humility, gentleness and patience. Bear with each other and forgive whatever grievances you may have against one another. Forgive as the Lord forgave you. And over all these virtues put on love, which binds them all together in perfect unity.

—*Colossians* 3:12-14

This book is dedicated to my parents,
Joe and Florence Perry,
with love and gratitude.
And, as always, to Brian.

Chapter One

Emily Carmichael's twin sons raced down the soccer field, David struggling to keep up with Trey as he always did. David's jersey had come out of his shorts, flapping around his knees like a skirt, and his glasses slid down his nose. The soccer ball rolled toward him, dazzling white against green.

"Kick it, David. Kick it!" Trey shouted.

Emily held her breath. Just this once, if David could only succeed…

He swung his leg, missed and sprawled on the turf, his glasses flying.

Emily's nails bit into her palms. She couldn't run to him, no matter how much her heart ached. That would violate the macho code of third-grade boys. The ball and the players surged on toward the goal, leaving him behind. Trey ran a few steps, hesitated, then turned and came back to his brother. Emily breathed again as he helped David up.

"At least you won't have to get him a new pair of glasses. Looks like Trey found them."

Emily turned to smile at Lorna Moore. "That would only be the fourth time this year."

"One of the costs of sports they don't tell you about when you sign your kids up."

A golden leaf from the trees that fringed the field drifted into Emily's lap. She held it for a moment, mind absently registering the soccer mom conversation taking place around her...car pools, school schedules, dancing lessons...

"Have you heard?" a breathless voice behind her asked. "You know who's back in town? Nick O'Neill!"

Emily's fingers tightened, crumpling the leaf. The name broke through the smooth surface of her day like a shark in a trout pond.

She struggled to keep her face impassive, her eyes on the game. Unfortunately, what she was seeing wasn't the group of eight-year-olds. It was Nick's face the way she'd last seen it fourteen years ago—angry, accusing, betrayed. The familiar spasm of guilt caught her.

"I don't know how he has the nerve to show his face in Mannington again."

The comment floated through the autumn air, pitched just loudly enough to reach Emily. Sooner or later someone would ask her directly. They were too intimidated to question her father-in-law, so they'd ask her.

James Carmichael, benevolent dictator of Carmichael Mills, major employer in this small Pennsylvania town, was enough to intimidate anyone. He ruled his mill the way he'd once ruled his son and now tried to rule his son's widow. Only economic necessity had forced him to consider sharing his power through the merger with Ex Corp.

Emily brushed the remnants of the leaf from her tan slacks. Since Jimmy's death four years ago, she'd taken his seat on the mill's board of directors, not that her formidable father-in-law allowed anyone else to do much directing. At least he kept her informed about company business…in this case, that Nick O'Neill, of all people, was coming to town as Ex Corp's representative.

"Well, Emily, aren't you going to tell us? Is it true that Nick O'Neill is back?" Margaret Wentworth leaned forward to rest an elegant hand on Emily's lawn chair, the slightest hint of malice glinting in her eyes.

She should have known it would be Margaret who asked. Wentworths had lived in Mannington almost as long as Carmichaels had, and Margaret had once believed Jimmy Carmichael was hers for the taking.

Emily tried to smile. "Ex Corp is sending him to manage the merger with the mill. I don't know any more than that."

"You mean you haven't seen him yet?" Margaret's arched brows lifted. "My husband saw him walking down Elm Street just this morning."

Please don't let her bring up the past, Lord. Please. It's buried, isn't it?

"We thought perhaps he was coming to see you. You're such old friends." Margaret planted the barb and smiled.

"I haven't seen him." That almost sounded as if she cared. "He'll probably be too busy with the merger to look up old acquaintances."

"Not just acquaintances. You and Nick were quite the item back in high school, weren't you?" Margaret laughed lightly. "The town bad boy and sweet little Emily, the doctor's daughter. How could anyone forget that?"

The smile felt as stiff as cardboard on Emily's face. She could almost hear the indrawn breaths as everyone waited for her response. "I'm sure people have better things to do than worry about people I forgot a long time ago. Do you remember all your old boyfriends, Margaret?"

Anger flashed in Margaret's eyes. Emily bit her lip. She hadn't meant it as a reference to Jimmy. She considered apologizing, then realized that would make matters worse.

Margaret turned away with a brittle laugh, and Emily's hands unclenched. Apparently she'd been kidding herself. Memories were long in a town like Mannington. They certainly stretched back fourteen years.

Guilt flickered again. Her past was returning to

haunt her, in the shape of the man she'd never forgotten.

What was she thinking? Of course she'd forgotten Nick. And would again. He'd be here for a few weeks, and then he'd leave and everything would return to normal.

A little shiver went down her spine. She knew why Nick was supposedly coming to Mannington. But given what had happened between him and the town—between him and Emily—she couldn't believe that was his only reason.

The whistle blew, ending the game, and the twins rushed toward her. She shoved thoughts of Nick's return to the back of her mind and stood to meet them.

"Good game, guys." She ruffled Trey's hair, put a hand on David's shoulder.

"We almost won, Mom." Trey, ever the optimist, gave her the grin that one day would break girls' hearts. "Next time we'll do it."

"Next time we have to play the Tigers," David pointed out. "They're a lot better than we are." He kicked disconsolately at a clump of grass, and Emily knew he was seeing the ball he'd missed.

"Well, we just have to get better." Trey said it as if nothing could be easier. "When we get home, we'll practice. You'll see. Everything's going to be great."

For an instant, Emily envied him his optimism. She'd like to feel that way about the changes Nick O'Neill and this merger might bring to town.

No, that was impossible. But it should be possible, even easy, to avoid the apprehension roused by the thought of seeing him. She just had to avoid seeing him at all.

Nick leaned back in his chair, stretching, and rested his hands on the papers he'd been studying. He'd been a long time putting himself in a position of power over Carmichael Mills. Now that he'd gotten here, he fully intended to savor it.

He frowned down at the file on his desk. Preliminary, and way too sketchy. When he met with James Carmichael, he'd demand a full accounting. And for once in his life, Carmichael wouldn't be able to call the shots. Nick would enjoy that moment. He needed to prepare, but concentrating proved difficult.

Sound drifted through the window—kids' voices, somewhere outside. He could have been isolated from that if he'd chosen to stay in a motel, but that wasn't the way he'd wanted to come back to Mannington, staying in a cheap motel room like a traveling salesman.

For a lot of years he'd imagined returning. He'd pictured himself walking into one of the big houses on Elm or Sycamore, the kind of place where he hadn't been welcomed fourteen years ago.

He shook his head at the ridiculous dream. But he couldn't deny the pleasure he'd felt at leasing the old Findley house, fully furnished, for his stay.

The window he'd opened to let in some crisp autumn air was also letting in what sounded like World War III. Only two kids, by the voices, but they made enough noise for twenty. He'd have to close the window.

The curtain billowed, and a soccer ball flew through the window, bouncing twice on the Findleys' Oriental rug.

That generated silence outside. Nick reached for the ball, rolling it across the carpet, and listened.

"You kicked it. You go get it." The speaker was young and male.

"I'm not going in." Equally young and male, but scared.

"Well, somebody has to. We can't leave a brand new soccer ball in there. Besides, it has our initials on it."

Nick flipped the ball over. A childish hand had printed a *D* and a *T* in black marker next to the logo. He grinned, half-expecting a small figure to bounce through the window next.

"Can't we ask Mommy to do it?"

"Mom said to leave the new neighbor alone." It sounded as if the speaker took a deep breath. "All right, David. I'll do it. You boost me up."

Nick reached the window just as a small figure wobbled precariously against the sill, some four feet off the ground.

"Looking for this?" He held up the ball.

A pair of brown eyes focused on him, then

widened alarmingly. The boy—no, boys, one on the other's shoulders—swayed backward, about to fall into the Findleys' azalea bush. Nick lunged through the open window and grabbed the kid just as he fell.

"You okay?" He leaned across the sill, setting the boy onto the grass, then glanced from one to the other. And did a double take. Twins—identical twins Both looking at him with scared brown eyes. He grinned. "It's all right. I don't bite. Are you okay?"

"Yes, sir." The window climber got his composure back first. "I—we're sorry. We didn't think anybody was home."

"We just wanted our ball." The other one's voice trembled.

"This ball, you mean, David?" He ventured a guess that David wasn't the window climber and got a scared, awestruck look in return. "How do I know it's yours?"

"I—I—because…" He ran out of steam.

The other one grinned. "He's kidding, David. He knows it's ours. We're the only ones here."

Nick flipped the ball around. "Okay, I guess *D* is for David. What's *T* stand for? Timmy?"

The boy shook his head. "Trey." He straightened, holding out a small, rather dirty hand. "James Allen Carmichael the Third. Only, everybody calls me Trey."

James Allen… These were Emily's kids, staring at him with Emily's golden brown, vulnerable eyes.

For an instant he couldn't say anything at all. Then he realized the boy was still holding his hand out. He shook hands gravely, first with Trey, then with David.

"Nice to meet you. I'm Nick O'Neill."

The name didn't seem to mean anything to them. The old man must have told Emily he was coming, but she obviously hadn't mentioned it to her sons. Well, why should she? He was ancient history as far as she was concerned.

Just as she was to him. He wasn't the kid he'd been fourteen years ago, and Emily Forrest—no, Carmichael—didn't mean a thing to him. Not one single thing. The score he'd come back to Mannington to settle was with the old man, not her.

"Are you a friend of Professor Findley?" David had apparently decided Nick wasn't a monster waiting to eat soccer balls and unfortunate little boys.

"Not exactly. I'm just renting his house while he's away. Do you two live around here?"

"Over there." Trey pointed across the back lawn. "Our backyard bumps into this one. Professor Findley didn't care if we ran in his yard sometimes."

David nudged his twin. "Only when he wasn't home. That's what he said. Only when he wasn't home."

"Well, he isn't home, is he?" Trey planted his hands on his hips and glared at his twin.

"N-no." David frowned. "But Mommy said not to bother the new neighbor."

"We're not bothering him, exactly." Trey smiled at Nick. "Are we bothering you?"

"The soccer ball…" David apparently served as conscience for both of them.

"That's okay." Nick tossed the ball out the window to them. "Tell you what. How about if I come out and kick the ball around with you? I could use a break."

Trey's eyes lit up. "Would you?"

"We're not exactly *good*," David added.

Actually, Nick should be planning his meeting with Carmichael. But the lure of seeing Emily's boys a bit more was irresistible. He shoved the sweet, heart-shaped face out of his mind. She'd be a woman now, not the girl he remembered—the girl who'd let him down and broken his too-susceptible seventeen-year-old heart.

Nick swung his legs over the sill and ducked under the sash.

"Are you coming out the window?" Trey blinked at him.

"Why not?" He dropped lightly to the ground in the Findleys' flower bed.

David eyed him. "Mostly grown-ups don't climb out windows."

"Why do you suppose that is?"

Trey shrugged. "'Cause people would talk about them, I guess."

People will talk. Yes, he definitely was back in Mannington again. Emily had used that phrase to put up barriers between them more than once. It had been years since he'd felt the urge to do something just so people would talk, but he felt that way now. The town had that effect on him.

"Will people talk about me playing soccer with you?"

Trey looked doubtful. "Maybe."

"Good. Let's do it." He grabbed the ball. "Bet I can dribble clear to that lilac bush before you can steal the ball."

He started across the grass, weaving through fallen leaves no one had raked, the boys racing after him. He didn't make it halfway before Trey, face intent, eyes narrowed, ducked in front of him and swiped the ball away. Looked like it had been too many years since he'd had time for a game of soccer.

He chased Trey and the ball, managed to steal it, lost it again when David charged into him. For several minutes they dodged each other across the grass. Crisp autumn air chilled his throat, stiff muscles came alive and a nearly forgotten exhilaration surged through him.

Kids probably felt like this all the time. They hadn't gotten so busy that play turned into exercise, one more chore to fit into an impossible day.

Trey wasn't skilled, but he was fast, stealing the ball and grinning. David tried valiantly, but he couldn't seem to coordinate running and kicking. Maybe it was the glasses that kept sliding down his nose. Nick resisted the urge to push them back up for him.

"I got it, I got it!"

Trey ducked around him, shouting. David went for the ball and barreled into Nick's legs. He tried to untangle himself, lost his balance and saw the ground coming at him. The three of them ended in a breathless heap, dry leaves rustling.

"I didn't know tackling was part of soccer."

He looked up at the sound of her voice. She stood between him and the sun, and light streaked her soft brown hair with gold.

His breath caught in his throat, as if he'd been hit by a three-hundred-pound tackle instead of a small boy. The depth of his astonishment stunned him. In all his plans for what would happen when he came back to Mannington, he'd left something important out of the reckoning. He hadn't thought he'd feel anything when he saw Emily again.

Emily's heart seemed to be beating somewhere up in her throat. It was a wonder she'd gotten the words out at all, let alone that they'd had just the right casual, unshaken tone.

She had a crazy desire to laugh. No, she could hardly convince herself she wasn't shaken by seeing Nick O'Neill again.

Remnants—that's all the feelings were that flooded her. Bits and pieces of memories she thought she'd forgotten had surfaced, but she could control them. She could be just as cool and detached as she'd promised herself she'd be if she ran into Nick.

Nick disentangled himself from the twins and rolled to his feet. Tall, muscular, a stranger. Not much there of the boy she'd once known. They were meeting again as old acquaintances, that was all.

He looked down at her, those incredibly dark blue eyes unsmiling. "It's been a long time." He held out his hand, and for the life of her, she couldn't move. His mouth twitched. "Or were you thinking it hasn't been long enough?"

"No, no, of course not. It's nice to see you again, Nick." She put her hand in his, felt his fingers curve warmly around hers. Her palm tingled for an instant.

Nick's dark, winged brows lifted. Black Irish, that was what people had said he was, hair like black silk contrasting with the deep, deep blue of his eyes.

"Is it nice to see me? Somehow I have the feeling that Mannington doesn't exactly welcome the returning prodigal."

"You're not exactly that, are you?" She drew her hand away, pulling her polite, social manner around her like a cloak. "I don't think you can blame people for being a little apprehensive. No one understands exactly what this merger might mean to the town." Surely he remembered how rumors flew in a one-industry town. Would the merger bring prosperity or layoffs? No one was sure, and everyone cared.

"Only natural for people to be a little distant?" Something faintly mocking showed in the curve of his mouth. "No lingering prejudice against me, for old times' sake?"

The words she'd overheard at the soccer game flashed through her mind. People still thought of Nick as the rebellious, angry boy who'd left town under a cloud. They wouldn't be easily convinced by the cool, composed armor he wore now.

"I'm sure no one even—" She stopped, unable to produce a polite social lie with his skeptical gaze on her and very aware of the twins watching, eyes wide.

His smile turned a shade warmer. "Some things never change. Sweet Emily still can't say a bad word about anyone, can she?"

She felt her cheeks warm, although why it should be an insult to be called sweet she didn't know. "You'll find lots of things have changed," she said, evading the personal comment.

"Not you." His eyes swept her. "You still look about fifteen."

She glanced down, realizing she wore her oldest jeans and a tattered sweatshirt. Why, oh why, did he have to catch her this way? She'd intended their meeting, if there had to be one, to take place at the mill, in a pleasant, professional arena where it would be easy to remind herself that she was a grown woman.

She forced a smile. "I see you've met my boys."

And what was he doing in her yard, anyway, playing with her sons? She stifled a ridiculous impulse to send the boys inside, as if they needed protecting.

"Yes, we've met." Nick grinned at what seemed to be a warning look from Trey. The twins had been up to something, obviously. "I'm renting the Findley house while I'm here. The boys were showing me how much I've forgotten about soccer."

"I thought football was your game." The words brought a sudden vivid image of Nick, grinning and triumphant after a touchdown, searching the stands for her. She remembered meeting his gaze, almost speechless with joy that, of all the girls who'd yearned for him, he'd chosen her.

"You played football?" Trey's face lit up. That was his dream, one she kept trying to redirect into something that seemed safer. "What position?"

"Wide receiver." Nick shook his head. "I was a lot faster in those days."

"Wow. Could you…"

"Trey." She would stop that before it started. "Mr. O'Neill is here on business. He doesn't have time for games."

Nick's eyebrows lifted. "How do you know what I have time for?" His eyes teased her in a way that was so familiar, it captured her breath.

He'd looked at her like that before, said something very like that the first time they'd talked, when she'd come shyly up to him after football practice, assigned to get an interview for the school paper, sure he'd brush her off, or worse, think she was like the other girls who made excuses to talk to him.

"I…well, I don't, but I assumed Ex Corp didn't send you here to play soccer." *Remember why he's here. Don't let the past interfere.*

"They like their executives to stay fit. Don't you think I can use the exercise?" His eyes, half laughing, half challenging, dared her to assess him.

"I'm sure you can get a temporary membership at the gym," she said primly, trying not to notice the way his white sweater clung to his broad shoulders.

"But this is much more fun, Emily." His gaze warmed and his voice lowered on her name as if they were the only ones present.

Her blood seemed to be singing through her veins, and there must be something wrong with her vision, because she couldn't separate the man he was now from the boy she'd once loved.

The man's emotions seemed kept under tight rein, as if they couldn't be trusted in polite society, but she still saw signs of the boy—reckless, heedless, appealing. She didn't think he'd changed all that much, except that *appealing* wasn't the word any longer. *Dangerously attractive* said it better.

She took a steadying breath, then looked at her sons. All right. Nick might have awakened memories of the girl who'd once loved him, but she intended never to be that vulnerable again. And if that meant turning herself inside out to avoid him while he was here, that's what she'd do.

"Time to get washed up for supper, boys. Thank Mr. O'Neill for playing with you."

Trey grimaced, then held out his hand in the formal manner his grandfather insisted upon. "Thank you, sir."

"It was fun," David added. Then her shy son startled her by grinning at Nick as if they were old friends. "Come play with us again."

Nick shot her a look that said he knew exactly how little that pleased her. "I'll try." He smiled. "If your mother says it's okay."

"Mommy…"

Emily shooed them toward the kitchen. "We'll see. Go on now."

When they'd gone inside, she turned back to Nick, to be met with a skeptical look.

"We'll see? Was that what your father said fourteen years ago when he found out you were dating me?"

The memory of the confrontation with her father still hurt, but she had no intention of letting Nick know that.

"It was so long ago, I'm afraid I don't remember." She held out her hand with a formality that would have met with her father-in-law's approval. "It was nice seeing you, Nick. Maybe we'll meet again while you're in town."

The warmth of his grip made her doubt the wisdom of the gesture. He smiled, his fingers curling around hers. "Oh, I'm sure we will."

She tugged her hand free. "You'll be busy with the negotiations."

"Aren't you a member of the board of directors?" His tone suggested he wasn't too impressed.

"That doesn't mean much where my father-in-law is concerned. I'm sure he's the one you'll be dealing with."

"Really?" His dark brows lifted. "That's not the impression he gave me."

She could only stare at him. "What do you mean?"

"I talked to Carmichael on the phone earlier." Nick paused. "He said he planned to deputize you to give me the grand tour of the mill and see that I have what I need. According to him, we're going to be spending a lot of time together." He smiled, a hint of mockery in his eyes. "It'll be just like old times, Emily."

Chapter Two

The shock in Emily's eyes took Nick by surprise. Apparently she hadn't known what Carmichael planned. Suspicion blossomed quickly. What exactly was that crafty old man plotting? Did Carmichael think he could somehow turn the long-ago relationship between his daughter-in-law and Nick to his advantage?

His mouth tightened. If Carmichael thought that, he was wrong. There was nothing left of those feelings, nothing but a minor resentment for the way Emily and he had parted. He was past the age to be nursing a broken heart over something that happened so many years ago.

He forced a smile. "I take it Carmichael didn't confide in you."

"No." Her smile looked just as forced as his. "I'm sorry, but I—" She stopped, absently snapping a dead flower head from the chrysanthemums and then looking up at him. "If you remember him at all, you'll remember that James Carmichael likes to run things his own way."

Remember? Oh yes, he remembered, all right. "Even with his son's widow?"

Her smile took on a rueful tinge. "Especially with his son's widow." She shook her head. "I'll talk to him. I'm sure this is something he should do himself. He can't expect me—" She broke off the sentence, those golden brown eyes distressed.

"To work with an old boyfriend?" He finished for her.

She brushed a strand of hair back from her face, fingers tangling in it. All in an instant he remembered how her hair felt, silky strands as fine as a baby's curling around his fingers.

Whoa, back off. He wasn't a kid anymore, and he wasn't going that route again. And he certainly wouldn't let a few raw memories distract him from what he'd come to Mannington to do.

"I doubt he even knows we once dated." Emily sounded as if she was trying to convince herself. "I'm just not the best person for the job, and this merger is important not only to us, but to the whole town."

She looked so upset that he found himself wanting to do or say anything to wipe that expression from her face.

"It's okay, Emily." He resisted the impulse to

stroke the frown from between her brows. "I'll talk to Carmichael. You're too busy with those boys of yours to spend the next month shepherding me around."

The troubled look faded from her eyes as she glanced toward the house, her expression softening. "They do keep me busy."

He followed the direction of her gaze. A porch stretched across the back of the white Victorian, looking as if it badly needed a fresh coat of paint. It was cluttered with bikes, bats and other kid stuff. The twins had left the back door open, and the noise of a lively altercation floated out.

"Sounds like they need a full-time referee."

"They squabble constantly." She shook her head. "I keep telling myself it's their age. But if anyone else dares to pick on one of them, they merge in an instant."

The intensity of the love in her voice rattled him. She hadn't changed—that had been his first thought—but now he realized it wasn't true.

The girl he'd left behind had been tentative, vulnerable, with an eagerness to please everyone shining in those golden-brown eyes. She'd matured into a woman—soft, strong, assured. Probably the only place she was still vulnerable was in her love for her sons.

She was looking at him, and he had to say something. "They're nice kids. Look a lot like you, don't they?"

She smiled. "Everyone says so. I see Jimmy in them a bit."

He didn't want to remember how he'd felt when he learned she'd married Jimmy, his one-time friend. "I was sorry to hear about his death."

"Thank you." Emotion darkened her eyes for just a moment. "It's been a long time, I guess. Over four years."

"Do the twins remember him?" *Do you still grieve for him, Emily?*

She shrugged. "Little flashes of memory, I guess. They don't really talk about it much. For them, it was half their lifetimes ago."

"I suppose they're a real comfort to Carmichael."

"I…" She looked wary suddenly. "Yes, I guess so. He's never been the bouncing-them-on-his-knee sort of grandparent, though."

He tried to picture that rigid autocrat in the role and failed utterly. "No, I guess he wouldn't be." As he remembered it, Jimmy had been scared to death of his father, always trying nervously to live up to the old man's expectations and failing most of the time.

Emily bent to pick up the gardening gloves and trowel she must have abandoned when he'd invaded her space. A warm flush mounted her cheeks. "I shouldn't have said that. He's fond of the boys. And pleased that there's a James Carmichael the Third to carry on the name."

Then it hit him. The cost of his revenge would be

higher than he'd anticipated, and it was one Emily and her children would pay. If he succeeded in what he'd come to Mannington to do, there wouldn't be a mill for Trey and David to inherit.

He pushed the thought away with a spurt of anger. This didn't have anything to do with Emily's kids. Jimmy had undoubtedly left them very well provided for. In the long run, this didn't have anything to do with the old man's money, either. The revenge he had in mind would hit James Carmichael where it hurt, in his pride and in his power.

Emily glanced toward the house again. "It sounds as if I'd better get in there and calm things down." She hesitated, then smiled. "It was good to see you again, Nick."

That smile swept right through him, riding a surge of memories. He wanted...

Before he could move or speak, she turned and was gone, crossing the back porch, the screen door slamming behind her. He had to suppress the urge to follow her.

Frowning, he started back across the lawn. He'd have to work harder at shutting down his feelings. Remembering Emily the way she'd been—worse, being attracted to Emily the way she was now—didn't fit into his plans at all.

He had to concentrate on his business with Carmichael. And probably the only way he could accomplish that was to stay as far away from Emily as possible.

He kicked at the soccer ball the twins had forgotten, then tossed it toward the house. It shouldn't be that hard to steer clear of Emily, not since she obviously wanted exactly the same thing.

"Macaroni and cheese!" Trey shouted, running into the kitchen from a trip to the bathroom to, Emily hoped, wash his hands.

"I love macaroni and cheese, Mommy." David slid onto his chair, his expression blissful.

She suppressed a twinge of guilt over taking the easy way out when it came to supper. She'd been too distracted after that unexpected encounter with Nick to be creative in the kitchen.

"David, it's your turn to ask the blessing."

The three of them joined hands around the table, and Emily's heart warmed at the feel of those little hands in hers. *Lord, help me to be the parent they need.* Her silent prayer added to David's recitation of the blessing. *Guide me to do the right things for them.* Nick's face flickered in her mind. *And help me to—*

She stopped, biting her lip. To what? It hardly seemed right to ask God to help her avoid Nick.

"Amen," David said.

"Macaroni!" Trey scooped up the serving dish before his brother could reach it. He sniffed the aroma, smiling.

"Vegetables, too," she warned, passing him the green beans.

He gave her a serious look. "Are you sure macaroni isn't a vegetable?"

"Positive." She wouldn't let herself smile. Trey was too quick to take advantage of his ability to charm her. In that, he was very like Jimmy.

"I like him," David said around a mouthful of macaroni.

She glanced at him, startled, then realized he was talking about Nick. She suppressed a sigh. It would be too much to hope they'd forget so entrancing a new friend quickly.

"Was Nick a good football player, Mom?" Trey looked thoughtfully at the lone green bean on his fork.

"Mr. O'Neill," she corrected.

"He said we could call him Nick."

"He came out the window," David said breathlessly.

For an instant she could only stare at him. "What?"

"He came out the window. When we…" David stopped, obviously struck by the realization that he was heading in a dangerous direction.

"Blabbermouth," Trey muttered.

"All right, out with it." Emily put her fork down. "Exactly how did you meet Mr. O'Neill?"

David's lower lip began to tremble. "We didn't mean…"

"We were kicking the soccer ball. Practicing so we'll get better, like you said we should." Trey's voice was filled with a righteousness that made her instantly suspicious. "We couldn't help it."

"Where exactly did the soccer ball go?"

Trey drew a circle in his macaroni. "You know the window in the Findleys' den?"

"Trey! You didn't break a window!" What an introduction that was for Nick...but she should be a lot more worried about the Findleys' window.

He shook his head. "It was open, and the ball just popped in."

"We didn't mean to, Mommy," David added.

She closed her eyes for a moment. Well, it could have been worse. She opened them. "I hope you apologized."

"We did," Trey said quickly. "He said it was okay. Then he said he'd play ball with us."

"And he came out the window," David said again.

That had obviously made an impression on David. She could only hope he wouldn't try to imitate Nick's behavior.

"Was that—" She hesitated. She didn't want to pump her sons. On the other hand, she really wanted to know something. "Was that before he knew who you were, or after?"

Trey frowned, as if trying to remember.

"After," David said. "Remember, Trey, we talked about our initials on the ball, and he asked our names."

"After," Trey agreed. "You didn't answer, Mom. Was he a good football player?"

"Very good." She could almost hear the cheers. "I remember there was talk of a big college scholarship for him."

"Where did he go? Who did he play for?" Trey's eyes rounded.

"He…didn't." She shook her head, trying not to remember those last few painful days. "He moved away."

"But didn't he still play football?"

Most of the time she thought Trey's persistence was a good quality. Not now. She got up, carrying her plate to the sink, suddenly not hungry.

"I don't know, Trey. We lost touch after that." Lost touch. What a nice way of putting it. "Get busy eating now. I know you both have spelling words to work on. I want to hear you practicing."

An hour later the dishes were done, and the sound of a spelling drill issued from the twins' bedroom, interrupted by sporadic giggles. Emily walked slowly into her own room, then closed the door.

The back window, with its ruffled white Cape Cods, looked out toward the Findley house. She stood for a moment, staring out. Then, feeling a little ridiculous, she pulled the shade.

The small box was in the back of her sweater drawer in the double dresser. She felt for it, then pulled it out and lifted the lid.

Nick's class ring. She picked it up. The gold was still bright after all these years, the letters still sharp and clear. Why not? It had hardly been worn. Nick had given it to her the night of the autumn dance. And the next night—

She closed her eyes against the memory, but it wouldn't go away…

"I told you that boy was no good." Her father had been ready to leave for an evening call at the hospital, doctor's bag in his hand. He'd paused at the door, then come back to touch her shoulder lightly, pity mixing with the anger in his eyes. "I'm sorry, Emily. Sorry you had to be hurt by this."

She shook her head, unable to speak, her throat choked with tears. Then she managed to get the words out. "But nobody's proved Nick was involved. You can't blame him."

"Flynn O'Neill is a thief." Her father's hand tightened on her shoulder. "Somebody else had to be involved. He couldn't have pulled it off alone. Who would it be but the son? They haven't been in town long enough to involve anyone else."

"Nick wouldn't…" Fresh tears stopped the words.

He sighed. "Emily, I don't have time for this now. Those O'Neills should consider themselves lucky Mr. Carmichael agreed to let them leave town again, instead of pressing charges against them."

He started for the door, then turned back once more. "I want your promise, you hear? Promise me you won't speak to that boy again." His face darkened.

"Bad enough that everyone in town knows you were dating him. Don't make things worse for either of us."

A doctor's family had to be above rumor, above scandal. That had been drilled into her from the time she could talk.

"I promise, Daddy."

"Good girl."

Usually those words soothed her. That time they hadn't worked.

Her father had gone then, leaving her to her tears. But that hadn't been the end, not that night. There had been worse to come. She twisted the ring in her fingers.

"Emily, you can't believe this!" Nick had stood on the back porch, in the shadows, hand pressed against the screen door, the rasp of crickets forming a chorus behind his words.

"Please." Emily sent an apprehensive glance across the lawn. "My father made me promise not to talk to you. If anyone sees us I'll get in trouble."

He slapped his palm against the door frame, his lean face angry and frustrated. "Come out and listen, then. You don't have to talk. Come out or I'll make enough noise that the whole neighborhood will know I'm here."

She felt like a badminton birdie, swatted back and forth between two rackets. Her father, Nick… She shoved the door open and slipped onto the porch. "Only for a minute…."

The fierce pressure of Nick's mouth cut off the words. For a moment she resisted, then her arms went around him just as fiercely. She clung to the hard strength of his shoulders. She couldn't let him go; she couldn't!

When his mouth lifted, his face was as tear-wet as hers.

"Nick." Her voice trembled. "You didn't do it, did you? I know you didn't."

His hands grasped her shoulders, fingers biting. "I'm no thief. And neither is my dad. You ought to know that!"

"I do, I know it." Even as she said the words, doubt flickered in her mind. Oh, not about Nick, never about Nick. But what did she know about Flynn O'Neill? That he looked angry, that he scared her a little the one time she'd met him, that people said he was a transient, a troublemaker…

Maybe Nick sensed what she didn't say. He held her away from him, eyes darkening. "Do you know? Are you sure about me?"

"Nick! Of course I'm sure!" She pulled his hand to her lips, pressing a kiss against it. "I know you'd never steal."

He drew her back against him, and his breath was hot across her cheek. "Then go with me. Now, tonight. I can't lose you, Emily. I love you."

"Go…go with you?" Her mind could hardly comprehend it.

"My dad's headed for New York, but we don't have to go with him." Nick's words gained momentum, as if they could carry her along on the tide of his energy. "We can go to Maryland. We can get married there. I'll get a job, I'll take care of you."

"Married." She hardly heard the rest of it. Run away with Nick, leave her father to face the gossip, the sly looks…

Nick caught her chin, forcing her to look at him. Slowly, so slowly, she saw his love die, drowning in the deep blue of his eyes.

"You do believe it."

"No!"

His mouth twisted bitterly. "Last night you said you loved me. I thought you were the one person in this crummy town I could count on. Or did you just want this?"

He snatched the class ring she wore on a chain around her neck. The fragile links pressed coldly on her skin and then snapped, the ring coming away in Nick's hand.

"Don't!"

She reached for him, but it was too late. He spun away from her, flinging the ring across the lawn.

"Your ring…"

"I don't want it." His gaze was contemptuous. "Just like I don't want you. You're like all the rest of this town. Have a nice life, Emily."

Before she could speak the light came on in Mrs.

Dailey's kitchen next door. She sent a scared glance that way, sure she'd see old Mrs. Dailey peering out between the lace curtains, but no one was there.

She turned back to Nick, tears choking her, but he'd gone, cutting across the dark lawn the way he'd run down the lighted football field.

And now he was back. Emily looked soberly at herself in the dresser mirror, then down at the ring in her hand. Nick didn't know she still had it, of course. He probably wouldn't believe that she'd spent hours that night on her hands and knees in the wet grass with a flashlight, the search made more difficult by the tears clouding her vision. Well, he never would know.

Guilt swept over her again, familiar guilt. Oh, not that she hadn't gone with him. That would have been wrong. They'd been way too young—too young to have any sense of what marriage involved. But somehow...

She shook her head for the girl she'd been. She'd let him go away thinking she'd turned against him, too, just like the rest of the town. She'd hurt him, and the memory of that still had the power to make her ashamed.

But it was too late to mend that with Nick now. He wouldn't believe her, and if he did, he wouldn't care.

If she'd learned anything from the feelings Nick had roused, just by seeing him again, it was that she couldn't afford the emotional cost of being around him. And that meant she had to talk to her father-in-law as soon as possible. She had to convince him that she was the last person in the world who should be put in charge of Nick's visit to Carmichael Mills.

Chapter Three

"It will just be a moment, Mrs. Carmichael." Martha Rand, James Carmichael's longtime secretary, gave Emily a cool smile across the desk that barricaded the inner sanctum at Carmichael Mills.

They'd known each other for years, but once Emily had become Mrs. Carmichael it hadn't occurred to Martha to call her anything else.

She smiled back, repressing the urge the woman gave her to be sure her hair was neat and her blouse tucked in. "I'm not in a hurry."

She wandered across acres of broadloom to the wall of photographs that made a focal point in the outer office. At least, she wasn't in any hurry as long as she saw her father-in-law this morning. Saw him and convinced him that someone else had to take on the job of escorting Nick O'Neill through the coming weeks.

A mostly sleepless night had convinced her of the wisdom of avoiding Nick for the rest of his stay. Incredible, to think seeing him after all these years could spin her emotions just as he had fourteen years ago. Maybe her instincts told her that, in spite of his sophisticated veneer, Nick was still a restless, reckless wanderer, just like his father.

Incredible, too, to realize that half the people in town remembered her relationship with Nick, and that still more identified him, however hazily, with the theft from the mill. The series of phone calls she'd fielded the evening before had shown her that.

Oh, no one had come right out and asked for the gossip on Nick O'Neill's return, or asked how she was taking it. The variety of excuses for calling had been remarkable, but that's all they'd been—excuses.

People cared, she told herself. Cared about her, cared about her boys and cared about the future of this town.

She focused on the turn-of-the-century photograph of the original mill, with Jimmy's grandfather standing in front of his workers, the red brick mill looming protectively behind them. That image symbolized what the mill meant to all of them. Without the mill, Mannington might just dry up and blow away.

"Mr. Carmichael will see you now, Mrs. Carmichael."

If Martha Rand heard anything strange about that

sentence, she didn't indicate it. Emily nodded to her, grasped the gleaming brass knob and pushed open the door to the private office.

Her father-in-law, rising behind the massive mahogany desk, inclined his head with a hint of a frosty smile. "Good morning, Emily."

"Good morning." Entering this room always made her feel the same as she did entering the principal's office or being hailed by a policeman—sure she'd done nothing wrong, but vaguely guilty anyway.

James Carmichael remained standing until she'd taken the chair across from him, then sat down, his back ramrod straight. He might be older, thinner, his mane of hair whiter than the first time she'd seen him, but his presence hadn't diminished in the slightest. He lifted a silvery brow.

"I'm surprised to see you at the mill this early. Is something wrong? Is James all right?"

Her fingers tightened on the carved wooden arms of the chair, and she forced them to relax. Her father-in-law's concern was always for his namesake first. He never called the boy by his preferred nickname, Trey, and never seemed to recognize that he played favorites. He must visualize Trey sitting behind that desk someday, as if her son couldn't possibly dream of anything else. Maybe, if they were lucky, the merger would take the pressure off her son to be what Jimmy hadn't been.

"Both the boys are fine. I've come about something

else." She took a steadying breath. "I understand you want me to take charge of Nick O'Neill's visit."

If she didn't know it was impossible, she'd almost believe wariness flickered in those icy blue eyes. Ridiculous. James Carmichael was always in control. He had nothing to be wary about.

"Where did you hear that?"

She could only hope her cheeks weren't flushing. "I ran into him yesterday, and he mentioned it. Did you know he's renting the Findley house?" And if you did, why didn't you warn me?

"I believe he did mention it when we spoke on the telephone." His expression indicated complete disinterest in where Nick stayed.

She was getting sidetracked, always a dangerous weakness when talking with her father-in-law. She had to stick to the point and make him see this was wrong.

"Is it true? Do you expect me to work closely with him while he's here?"

"Someone from the family should." Her father-in-law always said *"the family"* as if it were in capital letters.

She took a deep breath and tried to remember that she was a grown woman who was allowed to have opinions of her own. "I'd really rather not do it, if you can make some other arrangements." That didn't come out sounding as definite as she'd intended.

"Not?" Her father-in-law frowned at the unfamiliar response. People didn't generally say no to him. "Perhaps I should have consulted you first, but naturally I assumed you'd be willing to do whatever is needed to make this merger go smoothly. For the sake of your sons, if nothing else."

The comment hit where it hurt. James always managed to find other people's weak points. With her it was her boys. What did he imagine Nick's Achilles' heel to be? She veered away from that thought, unwilling to examine it.

"Of course I want the merger to go well. But I'm not the right person to be working with Nick."

Was it possible he didn't know about, or didn't remember, her association with Nick? He always seemed so isolated from the rest of the town, alone in the mansion on the hill.

Her father-in-law rested thin, elegant hands on the pristine desk blotter. "On the contrary, I believe you're just the right person. After all, you and O'Neill were once…good friends."

So he did know. From Jimmy?

"All the more reason why I shouldn't be involved. You must see that it creates an awkward situation for both of us." She held her breath, willing him to understand.

"For two old friends to work together? It seems the perfect solution."

Her heart sank at the finality in his tone. "But I don't know enough about the mill's operation."

She hoped she didn't sound as desperate as she felt. Maybe she wasn't being entirely rational about this, but she didn't care. "He'll want to know technical details I can't tell him."

He waved a dismissive hand at that argument. "He'll have access to any records and any employees he requires. Your job will be to take him around, introduce him to people, make sure things run smoothly. And, of course, to represent the family."

"But something as important as the merger—won't he expect your personal attention?" She'd never actually argued with her father-in-law, but this hovered dangerously close, and it gave her a queasy sensation in the pit of her stomach.

"What Nick O'Neill expects is of no concern to me." His voice flattened on the words, and his gaze fixed on her icily.

"As the representative of Ex Corp…"

"Exactly." His lips thinned. "You can't imagine I'd tolerate his presence for a moment if it weren't for that."

No, he hadn't forgotten anything about Nick. "If you asked, perhaps Ex Corp would send someone else."

His gesture silenced her. "Impossible. We can't afford the time that would take." He stood up, walked to the window and stared out at the sloping roof of the mill. She could almost sense the intensity of his gaze. She knew, as everyone did, how much the mill meant to him. The mill his father had built, the respect of his workers, the admiration of the town... They were all linked for him.

He turned to face her. The autumn sunlight that poured through the panes wasn't kind. It picked out the shadows under his deep-set eyes, the lines around his mouth. He was always pale, but now his skin looked almost waxen.

"I had hoped you'd do this without argument, Emily. But I can see I'll have to explain."

There wasn't an explanation in the world that would make her want to involve herself with Nick again, but she nodded.

"No one is to know this." He frowned. "Dr. Forsyth tells me that my heart condition is more serious than he first believed. It looks as if I'm facing surgery, and even that may not help."

Her breath caught, a prayer forming in her mind as his words penetrated. She started from her chair, wanting to go to him, but then sank back again. James Carmichael neither expected nor welcomed signs of affection.

"I'm sorry." She swallowed hard, wishing she could comfort him. "I didn't realize. Why didn't you tell me?"

"I didn't think you needed to know."

No, of course not. He'd never relied on anyone else in his life. Her heart filled with a pity she didn't dare express. He wouldn't want that, either.

"But shouldn't all this business about the merger be postponed until you'll well again?"

"No!" He swung to face her. "That's exactly what we can't do. The negotiations had already begun when I found out. You know as well as I do that the mill isn't going to survive without the new business Ex Corp can bring. If they learn of my health problems, the advantage to them would be enormous." He smiled thinly. "I can imagine the rejoicing that would take place if they thought I was in a position of weakness. And that's why no one must know."

"But…"

"No one, Emily. My illness makes it crucial that the merger be completed." The lines in his face deepened. "In a situation like this, one can only trust family. If Jimmy were alive, he'd know how to deal with it. My son had a natural head for business."

Her heart contracted. *Please, Lord, don't let him ever learn the truth about Jimmy. It would hurt him so much.*

"I have to depend on you to take charge of O'Neill. I don't trust anyone else to represent our interests." He didn't sound as if he had much confidence in her ability, either. "Do you understand?"

She understood. The burden of protecting the family was being placed squarely on her, and it wasn't one she could refuse. She nodded slowly.

Her father-in-law leaned on the desk, taking a

shallow breath. "Whatever you do, you can't let O'Neill suspect anything is wrong with me." He seemed to be holding himself upright by sheer force of will, and his gaze bored into her. "If he knew, he would be like a shark smelling blood in the water. He'd have no mercy at all."

She wanted to argue that Nick wasn't like that, but she bit back the words. How did she know what Nick was like now? He wasn't the boy he'd been, and she wasn't even sure she liked the man he'd become. He still had that reckless, dangerous edge, and now he had the power to go with it.

But like it or not, they'd be spending a lot of time together in the next few weeks. And she'd have to find a way of dealing with that.

"I'll take care of it," she said firmly. "You can count on me."

The phone rang as Nick started to leave the house. He turned back, picking up the receiver with an impatient movement.

"O'Neill."

"Hey, buddy, how's the prodigal's return going?" Josh Trent sounded considerably more cheerful than Nick felt.

"They haven't exactly welcomed me with open arms." He leaned against the table, Emily's face flickering through his mind. He banished the image and pictured Josh instead, leaning back in his chair in the corner office, the New York skyline dominating the huge windows behind him. "Don't worry. That won't keep me from doing my job. Do you doubt it?"

"Never," Josh said promptly. "But old hometowns can be tricky."

"Mannington wasn't my hometown." Come to think of it, he'd never had anything he'd call a hometown, not the way his father liked to wander. Maybe once he'd dreamed Mannington could be that, but Emily and this town had taught him how wrong that was. "Is that all you called to bug me about?"

"Not exactly." There was a thump as Josh's feet probably hit the floor. "Heard an interesting rumor I thought I'd pass along to you."

Nick's attention sharpened. Josh had an enviable ear for pertinent rumors where business was concerned. "Something about Carmichael Mills?"

"Something about Carmichael himself." Satisfaction crept into Josh's voice. "Nothing concrete, just vague rumblings that maybe this merger is more important to him than he's made it sound."

"Why?" The word snapped as his blood started pumping.

"Don't know." He could almost hear the shrug in Josh's voice. "Just a slight hint of desperation someone picked up. You'll have to ferret it out. Any divorce in the offing? Any family scandals about to break?"

Again he saw Emily's face and was astonished at

the anger that surged in response to Josh's careless words.

"Nothing that I can see. But I'll keep my eyes and ears open. Thanks, Josh."

"Anytime, buddy. After all, what's good for Ex Corp is good for all of us, right?"

"Right." Or so the powers that be would have him believe. "I'll be in touch."

Nick stood for a moment with his hand on the receiver. Rumors about Carmichael's motives could be just that. Or they could mean something that would give him an edge in the negotiations.

If there was anything, he'd find it and he'd use it. After what Carmichael had done to his father, he didn't deserve anything else.

His jaw tightened. "Vengeance is mine, saith the Lord," but to his way of thinking, that vengeance wasn't coming along fast enough. If God's will was at work anywhere in this situation, it must be in the fact that he'd been put in a position of power over James Carmichael. And he intended to be sure Carmichael was paid back for every bit of grief he'd caused.

Emily didn't figure into this at all, and it was time he stopped picturing her face and hearing her soft voice whenever the Carmichael name came up. He was here on a mission, and he intended to accomplish it. He wouldn't let any long-buried feelings for Emily get in the way. Remembering how she'd sided with the town against him should be a good antidote.

As he got into the car, he found himself taking an unplanned glance toward her house. He slammed the door. Emily was proving difficult to ignore. Which meant that his resolve to stay as far away from her as possible was the right one. Now he just had to keep it.

The mill hadn't changed in the last fourteen years—that was his first thought when he pulled into the parking lot. Faded red brick of the original structure contrasted with the cement block of the newer section. Biggest building in town—it had always been, and he supposed it still was—lurking over every other structure like some hungry creature. It was a testament to the influence James Carmichael wielded.

Late marigolds bordered the walkway leading to the offices. Nick started up the walk, glancing toward the chain-link gate that lead to the workers' entrance. That was the entrance his father had always used. He'd never, to Nick's certain knowledge, walked in the front door.

Striding quickly, Nick pushed open the glass door, hand on its Carmichael Mills logo, and stepped into the marble-floored hallway. And promptly saw the one person he'd told himself he wanted least to see. A surge of pleasure told him his emotions weren't in sync with his brain.

"Emily." He glanced around the hallway, empty except for the two of them. "Were you waiting for me?"

Her smile seemed the slightest bit forced. "Yes. I wanted to show you the office we've arranged for your use while you're here." She turned, her quick movement ruffling the golden-brown hair that brushed her shoulders. "This way."

He followed her down the hallway, his business instincts aroused. What was behind this development? He'd been sure yesterday that she'd do almost anything to get out of leading him around.

His gaze traveled from the top of her hair, muted under the fluorescent light once they were away from the windows, to the neat pumps that were a far cry from the scuffed sneakers she'd worn the day before. In fact, everything about her seemed designed to be as different as possible from the windblown woman he'd found looking down at him.

Brown and white tweed jacket, neatly tailored brown skirt—this wasn't the Emily he remembered. This was a well-dressed, polite, efficient stranger.

"Are you working at the mill?" He'd assumed the board of directors' position strictly an honorary thing.

Emily's swift pace slackened. He fell into step with her, and she looked up at him.

"Media relations—I'm in charge of media relations and publications." She smiled. "It's only part-time. We don't usually have much need for media relations, but what there is, I do."

"I thought you wanted to be a teacher." He frowned back into the misty past.

She seemed surprised that he remembered. "I was for a while. But when the boys were born I wanted to stay home with them. And after Jimmy's death, it was even more important to be with them."

"So your father-in-law came to the rescue." He hadn't meant the comment to be sarcastic, but it came out sounding that way.

Emily's chin lifted. "I do my job."

Now he'd insulted her. "I didn't mean…"

She stopped, then swung open a door. "I hope this will do. If there's anything else you need, all you have to do is ask."

He followed her into the office, but his mind wasn't on the stacks of files or the desktop computer. "All I have to do is ask you?"

She glanced up, her topaz eyes a little surprised, a little defiant. "Yes. Ask me."

"I thought you were going to talk your father-in-law into having someone else be my escort while I'm here."

"Yes, well…"

She hesitated, and he thought he detected a faint flush on her cheeks. It brought on a perverse desire to tease her.

"Well, what? Did you change your mind about spending time with me, Emily?"

The flush deepened, turning her skin to peaches and cream. "I certainly don't mind spending time with you. In a business capacity."

He lifted an eyebrow. "I guess that tells me where I stand."

"I didn't mean it that way."

The flash of anger in her eyes startled him. At fifteen she'd never been angry, just anxious to please. She *had* grown up.

"Sorry." He wasn't—not really. Everything that made her different from the Emily he remembered made what he intended easier. "Look, I just meant that I know when we parted yesterday, you intended to beg off this job. What changed your mind?"

She shrugged, turning away. He put his hand on her arm to turn her attention back to him. Her gaze dropped, startled, to his hand, and he realized this situation made her as uncomfortable as it made him. But he didn't want to let go.

"Come on, Emily. What's going on?"

She looked up at him, wary at first, and then a rueful smile broke through. "Nothing really. It's true I thought someone else would do a better job of this, but my father-in-law wants me to do it."

"And is your aim in life to please him?" Anger roughened his voice, surprising him. Why? Because the girl he'd cared about was now tied, irrevocably, to his enemy?

She studied him for a moment, those golden eyes wide. "No, I wouldn't say that. But he is my children's grandfather, and I'm employed by the mill. I owe him something."

Anger carried him to the phone. "Well, I don't." He picked up the receiver. "What's his extension number?"

"Nick, please." She looked at him with a concern that spun the years back, so that he saw again the girl he'd once loved.

The realization jolted him like a kick to the heart. Whoa, back off. You can't let yourself feel this.

"Sorry, Emily." He lifted an eyebrow. "The extension?"

"Four eleven." She frowned. "Honestly, Nick, I'm all right with this. I'd rather you didn't say anything to him."

"Mr. Carmichael, please," he said to the anonymous female voice on the line. "Nick O'Neill speaking."

"I'm sorry, Mr. O'Neill. Mr. Carmichael is gone for the day."

His grip tightened on the receiver. He was primed to have a confrontation with the man now, over anything. "Will you tell him I wish to speak with him as soon as possible?"

"I'm afraid I can't." He thought he detected a note of satisfaction in the woman's tone. "Mr. Carmichael has gone out of town for a few days. It won't be possible for me to reach him until Monday at the earliest. Will that be satisfactory?"

No. "Very well. I'll speak with him then."

He hung up, turned to face Emily. Had she known this already?

"What is it?" Judging from the apprehension in her face, she hadn't.

"Your father-in-law is unreachable until Monday." He realized he still had a death grip on the receiver and deliberately relaxed his muscles. Never let them see you sweat, he reminded himself. Not even Emily. Especially not Emily.

"I'm sorry." She gave him that rueful smile again. "Looks as if you'll have to make do with me in the meantime."

Suddenly he knew what it was about being with Emily that made him so uncomfortable. It wasn't those flashes of the girl she'd once been, distracting as they were. Being with her brought back memories of the boy he'd been fourteen years ago—angry, un-accepted, always on the outside looking in.

He straightened. He wasn't that boy any longer, and if he had to remind himself of that twenty-four hours a day while he was in this town, he would.

"All right, Emily. You win." He held out his hand. "For the time being, I guess we're going to be partners."

Chapter Four

Emily hesitated for a long moment, feeling as if she were about to leap off the high dive board with no assurance there was water in the pool. Then she put her hand in his.

His grip was warm and strong and altogether too much a reminder of the boy she'd once loved. She pulled her hand away as quickly as possible, hoping that her cheeks hadn't flushed. Crazy to feel anything at the touch of someone who meant nothing to her anymore—someone she'd work with for a few brief weeks and then forget. Unfortunately it had been one thing to agree to this partnership in her father-in-law's presence, and quite another when she was this close, this alone, with Nick O'Neill.

She didn't have a choice, she reminded herself.

"Well." She backed off a step and bumped into the desk. "What would you like to do first?" Preferably something that got them out of this small office. "A tour of the facility?"

Nick's eyebrows arched, and she suspected he knew exactly what she was thinking. Then he nodded.

"That's fine. Give me the grand tour, Emily." He swung the door open. "I'm sure you'll be able to answer all my questions."

That meant he thought she couldn't, that he thought her job at the mill was a piece of make-work created by her father-in-law to give her a paycheck. Her lips tightened. Thank goodness no one knew just how much that paycheck meant to her. She strode quickly through the doorway. She'd show Nick O'Neill just how competent she was.

"Where would you like to start? Fiber processing? Yarn warping?"

For just an instant she thought he was surprised at something, either her willingness to show him around or the fact that she even knew the names of the various departments. Then his eyes narrowed.

"Let's start with the dyeing department."

She met his gaze blankly for a moment, and then she understood. "Isn't that where…?"

"Where my father worked." His tone was even, but a tiny muscle in his jaw twitched, and Emily knew exactly what that meant.

She swallowed, not sure whether she was more dismayed by the fact that she could still read him so well or the realization that this was not just a job to Nick.

She had to say something. She couldn't just ignore his reference to Flynn O'Neill.

"How is your father?"

In anything, his jaw grew tighter. "He died last year."

She stopped, turning to face him, her hand going out to him automatically. "Nick, I'm so sorry. I know how close you were."

For a moment she thought he'd take her hand and respond to her sympathy. Then he turned away. "Is it down that way, or has it moved?"

So her sympathy wasn't welcome. Maybe that wasn't surprising. Any hope she'd had that Nick had forgiven and forgotten died. He was angry, still carrying a grudge over the wrong he thought had been done to his father. Angry with the town, probably still angry with her. That hurt more than she'd expected.

"That department hasn't moved, but we need to stop and get hard hats before we go onto the manufacturing floor." She forced herself to concentrate on the job at hand. "And masks, if you want to go into Dyeing."

He gave a curt nod. "Lead the way."

Once they were equipped, she pushed open the heavy door, settling the mask in place over her nose and mouth. Fabric dyeing wasn't nearly as noisy as the rest of the plant, but the overwhelming odors more than made up for that.

Nick stopped just inside the door, his eyes assessing the huge, high-ceilinged room. What was he thinking? He should be checking out the modernized equipment and the safety gear every worker wore. But she suspected he wasn't seeing that at all. He was picturing his father at work here and probably remembering how that had ended.

People had noticed them, and Emily caught the antagonism in several glances. Just as Nick hadn't forgotten, others hadn't, either.

Nick's dark blue eyes were intense above the mask. "Looks as if people know who I am."

"You know what small towns are like." She tried for a light note. "There are no secrets."

His winged brows lifted. "About anything?"

The several secrets she guarded rested uncomfortably. "Well, I suppose there might be a secret or two somewhere. But surely you didn't expect your arrival to be one of them."

"No." Even under the mask, she could see his jaw tighten. "I guess the return of Flynn O'Neill's son would be news."

She should have anticipated the bitterness in his voice, but it took her by surprise. Her first impulse was to reach out to him, but she stamped it down. He hadn't welcomed her sympathy a moment ago, and he wouldn't welcome it now. In that respect he had more in common with James Carmichael than he'd like.

"I meant that people know about the merger," she said carefully. "This is still a one-industry town.

Everyone has a stake in what happens to the mill. I'm sure they're not thinking about anything else."

He looked at her for a long moment, eyes skeptical. Then he shrugged. "Okay. Let's get on with it."

They went from department to department. Everywhere people greeted her; everywhere Nick was eyed with either wariness or suspicion. If it bothered him, he didn't let it show.

By the time they finally reached the clamor of Shipping and Receiving, she'd begun to relax. This was going to be all right. There had been that bad moment when Nick told her about his father, and people certainly hadn't been welcoming, but they'd gotten through this with a minimum of effort and, better yet, no personal involvement at all.

"Shipping and Receiving." Her gesture took in the yard, busy with trucks coming and going. "Do you want to check out the warehouses at this end?"

He shook his head, as if he'd lost interest once they were away from the section where his father had worked.

"I've seen enough for the first time through. Let's get back to the office."

She nodded. As she turned, her heel caught on the hose that snaked across the concrete. She stumbled, arms flying out for balance.

Nick's arms went around her, strong and steadying, bringing a flood of memories. She pulled herself free, feeling the betraying warmth in her cheeks.

"Are you all right?"

"Yes. Thank you." That didn't sound very gracious, but it was all she could manage. Two unpleasant truths stared her in the face as a result of this little expedition. Nick hadn't forgiven or forgotten what had happened to his father here. And worse, the feelings she'd once had for him still lay under the surface, ready to be triggered by the slightest contact.

Emily was still wrestling with the situation when she arrived at the school to pick up Trey and David. The usual row of car-pool moms lined the walk or leaned against cars, waiting for the final bell to sound. Lorna Moore waved and started toward the curb, her wiry red hair bouncing with every step. Emily got out, smiling, and joined her. Talking to Lorna would give her a welcome respite from the question of Nick's return.

"Hi, Em." Lorna did an exaggerated double take at the sight of Emily's business suit. "Whoa, you look dressed to kill. What's going on?"

Emily shrugged. "Business meeting at the mill." She glanced at her watch. "I was afraid I'd be late."

"So? It wouldn't hurt our kids to wait for us once in a while, would it?"

"I'd like to see the day when Lorna Moore wasn't on time for something." She smiled. "You were born with a clock in your head. Admit it."

Lorna leaned against the fender of Emily's car,

raising her face to the afternoon sun. "Actually, I think I was tardy once, sophomore year. Remember when I had that big crush on Coach Fosdyke? I hung around the gym too long and didn't make it to homeroom on time. Ruined my perfect record."

Lorna sounded sincere, but the sparkle in her green eyes belied the complaint, and Emily grinned. But before she could reply, Lorna checked her watch and looked toward the double doors of the brick elementary school. "Okay, we have time. Give me the scoop."

"Scoop?"

"On Nick O'Neill. You don't think I've forgotten, do you?" Lorna screwed her freckled face into something resembling a look of adoration. "Dreamy. That's what we called him in high school, or something equally repulsive. So, how's he turned out?"

She should have known she wouldn't get through this day without someone asking that question. Better it was her best friend than someone else.

"If we were fifteen again, we'd still call him dreamy, I guess."

Lorna lifted an eyebrow. "And now? What does he look like to a grown-up woman?"

She shrugged, leaning against the fender next to Lorna. She tried not to let the image of Nick's face form in her mind. "Taller. Older."

"Come on, give." Lorna poked her. "You might get away with that with some people, but not me. What's he really like?"

"I'm not sure." That was the truth. She searched for words. "Attractive. Very attractive. But he seems almost…I don't know, closed in. As if he's got a defensive wall up, and nobody's going to get past it."

Lorna considered that, head tipped to one side. "Well, I guess he might still be bitter. I mean, he was practically run out of town."

"It wasn't that bad," she protested, knowing in her heart it was true. "Anyway, that was a long time ago."

"You don't forget the hurts you got when you were in your teens." Lorna frowned. "I could list every breakup, every bad grade, every time I was stood up. Couldn't you?"

"I guess." The image of Nick's anguished face wouldn't be banished.

"So, what are you going to do about it?"

"Me?" She turned a startled face toward her friend. "What do you mean?"

Lorna's eyes sparkled. "Well, here he is again. You haven't forgotten. He hasn't forgotten. Maybe you ought to see if the sparks are still there."

"Lorna! I'm not looking for romance—you know that. And certainly not with Nick O'Neill, of all people. He's here on business, remember?"

"Just because he's here on business doesn't mean he can't mix in a little pleasure." Lorna nudged her. "How long has it been since you were out on a date? A year? Maybe it's time you threw a little of that caution to the wind."

"I don't intend throwing any caution to the wind, thank you very much. And certainly not with Nick O'Neill, of all people."

Lorna eyed her. "Why not? What's wrong with him?"

"Nothing." She wasn't about to tell Lorna her totally irrational fear that Nick would let his bitterness about his father affect everything he did in Mannington. "It just wouldn't be suitable, that's all."

"If you ask me, Emily Carmichael, you're a little too worried about what's suitable and what's not."

"I didn't…" The school doors burst open, letting out a deluge of children and saving her from finding an answer. "Here come the kids. I'll see you later."

But the subject of Nick O'Neill wasn't exhausted yet, she discovered when she got her own two separated from the herd and into the car.

"Mommy!" Trey bounced on the back seat. "Guess what?"

"Seat belt, Trey," she reminded. David was already buckling his.

Trey wiggled, impatient, and fastened the seat belt. "Okay, it's fastened. Guess what?"

"What?" She glanced at him in the rearview mirror as she started the motor.

"We have a soccer game tomorrow. And this time we're going to win, I just know it."

"Not unless we get a lot better before then."

Trey ignored his brother's mournful prediction.

"And it's only three more days until the fair starts, and we get to eat funnel cakes, and go on the rides and see the animals. Coach said if we win the game with the Tigers, he'll buy all of us a candy apple at the fair. So we have to win, we just have to!"

"If we don't get a lot better…" David began again.

"We're better," Trey said firmly, and Emily smiled. It was as if she had her own Eeyore and Tigger in the back seat.

"I know you're improving," she said tactfully. "I think David means that maybe you're not quite champs yet."

"But we are getting better." Trey wiggled. "Maybe Nick will practice with us again today. That would help."

Her heart gave a little lurch at his name. "Now, boys, I don't want you pestering Mr. O'Neill."

Trey looked hurt. "We wouldn't pester. We'd just ask him if he wants to play, that's all."

"No." That came out more sternly than she intended, and she softened it with a smile. "That's not fair, Trey. He might be busy, and he wouldn't want to turn you down."

"But Mom, if we don't ask, how will he know we want him to play?"

Amazing how logical Trey could sound when he wanted something. "No, Trey, I mean it. You can't ask. If he wants to play, I'm sure he'll come out."

"But Mom…"

She gave him her best mom look in the rearview mirror, and he subsided. She could only hope his mind wasn't busy with ways to circumvent her decision.

Nick frowned at the financial report he'd brought home from the office, trying to force himself to concentrate on the rows of figures on his laptop. Unfortunately, Emily's face kept getting between him and the screen.

She'd become quite a woman; he couldn't deny that. He'd assumed that job of hers at the mill had been so much fluff, but he'd been wrong. She knew an amazing amount about textile manufacturing for someone who'd always wanted to be a teacher.

Always? How did he know what Emily had always wanted? He was basing a lot on the knowledge he'd gained in the few months he'd lived in Mannington. A few months was all he'd had before the roof fell in, and at that it had been longer than he and his father had stayed some places. Flynn O'Neill always had been afflicted with wanderlust, always seeing some wonderful new horizon that had to be explored.

He shoved himself away from the computer and walked to the window. He ought to be thinking about work, not reminiscing about the past. Emily had a new life; he had a new life. And speaking of her life, he'd have expected the twins to be pounding on his door by now. He had halfway promised another soccer session.

He lifted the curtain aside, seeing movement, and then grinned. Trey and David were kicking the soccer ball back and forth. They were also staying very carefully on the very back edge of their property line. Emily must have given them orders about staying in their own yard.

Was she worried about disturbing him? Or was she concerned about letting her boys get too close? The very thought gave him a strong desire to go out and play.

Without giving himself time to think about it, he crossed to the French doors and went outside.

The twins spotted him as he crossed the lawn toward them. They stopped, Trey holding the ball, and looked at him with identically hopeful expressions.

"Hi, guys."

"Hi, Nick." Trey spoke quickly, and David gave him a shy smile.

Then they didn't say anything. They just stood, looking from him to the soccer ball.

He had to work to suppress a laugh. Emily's boys listened to her; he had to give her that.

"Practicing?" he asked.

Trey nodded. "We have a game tomorrow after school."

"With the Tigers," David added, the corners of his mouth drawing down.

"Sounds like those Tigers might be pretty tough."

"We're as good as they are." Trey bounced the ball.

"Well, almost as good." He paused. "We just need to practice some more."

That was obviously his cue. "Want me to practice with you?"

Trey grinned, tossing him the ball. "If it's not too much trouble."

"If it's not bothering you," David said.

"No, it's not bothering me." Now what had happened to his intention to spend the rest of the day working? Well, he'd be better off after a short break. A man needed a break, didn't he? It had nothing to do with the fact that these were Emily's kids, and that he saw her face every time he looked at them. "Let's start with moving the ball."

They dribbled their way back and forth across the two yards. His feet slid on a patch of wet leaves, and he resolved to get some raking done later. The boys should have a practice area that didn't contain any built in hazards.

Emily's yard wasn't much better, he realized as Trey kicked the ball in a flurry of leaves. He'd have expected her to have a lawn service to take care of little things like that. Someone who'd married into the Carmichael dynasty ought to be able to afford life's little luxuries.

"Get it, David," he shouted.

David went manfully after the ball, but Trey beat him to it. David stopped, breathing hard, and put his hands on his knees.

"It's okay." He patted the boy's shoulder. He had forgotten how little an eight-year-old was. "You'll get it next time."

David nodded, pushed his glasses up and charged after the ball again.

A movement at the back window of Emily's house caught his eye, and he stumbled. Emily was watching them from behind the curtain. Why didn't she come out? Maybe she'd had enough of him for one day.

Somehow the thought gave him a little additional energy. He raced after the boys, shouting encouragement as if he'd been coaching soccer all his life.

"Way to go, David. Steal it! You can do it!"

David charged for the ball in response to his words. Trey, hearing him coming, turned to see where he was, and David ran right into his elbow. There was a thud Nick could hear from several feet away. David sprawled flat on the grass and lay there motionless.

"David!" Nick's heart pounded as he raced toward the child, berating himself. He shouldn't have pushed, he should have been more careful….

"Hey, buddy, are you okay?" He knelt beside the boy, sliding his hand under David's shoulders and lifting him.

David's eyelids fluttered. Before he could speak, Emily swooped down on them, snatching him away from Nick.

"David? David, talk to me, honey. Are you all right?"

Nick heard the panic in her voice and reached out a reassuring hand.

Emily brushed it away, eyes blazing. "What have you done to my son?"

Chapter Five

Emily couldn't mistake the reaction in Nick's eyes at her sharp words—hurt, swiftly masked. Biting her lip, she focused on her son.

"I'm okay, Mommy." David rubbed his forehead, blinking his eyes as if to hold back tears. He pulled away from her. "I'm not a baby."

"Of course not." Nick's voice sounded casual, but his hand gently smoothed the hair away from the red lump above David's eye. "What say we let your mom put some ice on that? That's what sports trainers always do."

David sat up a little straighter. "I guess. If you think so."

Nick grinned at him. "That's what I'd want, if it was my head." He held out his hand to David.

Something inside Emily seemed to melt as her son's small hand tucked confidently into Nick's large one. No matter how hard she tried, she couldn't be both a father and a mother. Sometimes a boy just needed a man, and it looked as if this was one of those times.

"One ice pack, coming up." She led Nick and the boys into the kitchen, trying not to hover. "Trey, get me a plastic bag for the ice, please."

She had to stop overreacting to every bump and bruise. Most of the time she could hide her concern from the boys, but sometimes it just spurted out. When she'd seen David lying motionless on the ground...

Enough. David was fine, and she'd made an idiot of herself. She handed the ice bag to David and looked at Nick. Right now she needed to apologize and then see him on his way.

"Sorry. I'm afraid I overreacted."

"No problem." His deep blue eyes hid his feelings from her. He reached out to settle the ice more firmly on David's head. "Okay now, sport?"

David nodded. His attention riveted on Nick's face as if what he thought was the most important thing in the world. "I'm okay. We'd better go practice some more."

Before she could protest, Nick intercepted her.

"I could use a drink first. Soccer's thirsty work." He settled into the ladder-back chair at her kitchen table as if he belonged there.

Emily's gaze clashed with his, and she suspected

he knew exactly what she was thinking. She didn't want her sons looking to him instead of to her. She didn't want him to be a part of their lives. She didn't even want him in her quiet, orderly kitchen, filling it up with his disturbing masculine presence.

But short of being rude in front of the boys, she couldn't do a thing about it. She turned to the refrigerator. "Iced tea or fruit juice?"

He smiled. "Just cold water, please."

"For me, too, Mom," Trey said quickly, and David nodded.

It looked as if her sons had a new hero. She found it disconcerting to see them look at Nick with that adoring expression, because she'd probably once worn one very similar.

She filled the glasses, dropped ice in them and set them on the table. If Nick were reading her glance, he'd know it was telling him to drink his water and go home.

He smiled, then lifted the glass in a silent toast.

Trey put both elbows on the pine tabletop. "We're getting better, aren't we, Nick?"

"Sure thing."

"I bet we'll beat the Tigers tomorrow." Trey wrapped both hands around his glass, his expression speculative. "Our game is at four o'clock in the park, you know."

"Trey." Her tone was warning.

He shrugged, putting on the righteous expression

he did so well. "I'm just saying, Mom. That's all. It's okay to just say, isn't it?"

Nick's gaze met her rueful one over her son's head, and his eyes filled with amusement.

"Tell you what, Trey. If I get finished with work by then, maybe I can stop at the game. Okay?"

Trey grinned. "Okay."

David removed the ice bag from his forehead. Thank goodness the lump had gone down. "I can play tomorrow, can't I, Mommy?"

"We'll see. Are your glasses still in one piece?"

Nick picked up the pair David had plopped on the table. "I think so." He straightened the frames a little. "Looks like this guy could use a pair of sports glasses."

"Sports glasses?" She had the sinking feeling this was something she should have known about and hadn't.

"Your optometrist should be able to do them. They won't fly off or break so easily."

"They look dorky," Trey said.

"Hey, I'll have you know I never looked dorky in them."

Trey blinked. "You wore them?"

Nick nodded. "Nothing wrong with using the right equipment for your sport. You think Olympic athletes worry about how they look when they're setting records?"

"Can I, Mom?" David seemed convinced, either by Nick's say-so or the mention of the Olympics.

This was undoubtedly something her insurance wouldn't cover, but she'd scrape up the money somehow if it meant keeping David a little safer.

"I'll give Dr. Morton a call in the morning."

"All right!" David grinned, and he and Trey exchanged high fives.

She caught Nick's gaze on her and refused to meet it. Was he wondering why she'd hesitated? At moments like this she'd love to have someone in whom she could confide about her financial worries. But to tell anyone would be to betray Jimmy's weakness, and she couldn't do that. Not even Lorna knew, and Nick was certainly the last person in the world she'd tell.

"Well, we've probably kept Nick long enough." She got up from the table.

"But Mom, we wanted to practice some more." Trey's lower lip came out. "The Tigers…"

"Yes, we know all about the Tigers, but I need to get supper started, and I'll bet Nick has work to do."

Her glance demanded his agreement, but he just smiled.

"Actually, I'm caught up. But I am hungry. Why don't all of you go downtown with me for some pizza?"

"Pizza!" Trey shot off his chair. "I love pizza!"

"Especially pepperoni," David added. "Could we have pepperoni?"

"Wouldn't be a pizza without it," Nick said. "Well, Emily?"

"I don't think…" Her mind raced, trying to find an acceptable excuse.

His dark eyebrows arched. "Afraid to be seen with me in public?"

"Certainly not." Not afraid, just reluctant to stir up any more talk. Somehow she knew what Nick would think of that as a reason. "We'd be happy to join you. Dutch treat, of course."

He smiled as if he'd taken her acceptance for granted all along. "We'll see about that."

Nick followed Emily and the boys from the car toward Luigi's Pizzeria, wondering just exactly what she was thinking at this moment. The stiffness about her spine suggested she didn't like the situation but was determined to brave it out.

He wasn't sure why it had seemed so important to push her into this dinner. He could tell himself he wanted to do something to bring smiles to those two little kids, but he knew that wasn't it. Or at least, that wasn't all of it.

Emily had always been so concerned with what everyone thought—her father, the other kids, the whole town. He had a hunch that concern still existed, and it both frustrated and annoyed him. Why did she care so much? And how would the town react to seeing Emily and her kids out with the black sheep who'd come back to disturb its serenity?

The luscious aroma of melting cheese curled

through the screen, luring them inside. Nick pushed open the door. The boys bolted for a table by the front window.

Same round tables with their red-and-white-checked tablecloths, same jukebox blinking in amber and green, same worn speckled tile on the floor. Even the prices looked the same, and he couldn't help smiling.

They'd come here after the football games, a whole crowd of kids, raucous and celebrating. And Luigi had given them an extra pie on the house because they'd won.

"What'll it be?" He leaned over the table where Emily was dissuading Trey from pulling half a dozen napkins from the metal holder. "Two large, one pepperoni and one plain?"

"I don't think we can eat all that."

He grinned. "Speak for yourself. I'm ravenous. What do you like to drink with it?"

David slid off his chair. "I'll help order it. I know what Mommy and Trey like."

He could tell by Emily's expression that this was unusual for her shy son, and the thought gave him a surprising amount of pleasure. He put his hand on the boy's shoulder, and the sharp angle fit into his palm.

"Good enough. We'll take care of the ordering."

Luigi himself came to the counter to take their order, his white apron stretched what seemed impossibly far around an expanding middle.

He looked at Nick and beamed. "Nick O'Neill! I heard you were back in town. I told Maria, I'll bet anything Nick comes in for pizza. That boy always loved my pizza."

"Never found any to match it." Ridiculous, to be so happy at the first genuine welcome he'd encountered in Mannington. "So, how are you doing, Luigi? Business good?"

"So-so." His pen poised over a pad. "What's for you tonight?"

Nick gave him the order, and David chimed in with requests for colas for himself and Trey and an iced tea for his mother. What, if anything, did Luigi think about him buying pizza for Emily and her boys? Was he remembering old times, too?

They carried the drinks back to the table, with David concentrating hard, obviously determined not to spill a drop. Nick grinned at him when they were safely deposited on the table.

"Good job, David." He slid into the chair next to Emily.

Memories assailed him like so many charging tackles. Emily next to him after a game, her golden brown hair brushing his shoulder each time she moved. The way her eyes lit with shy pride when she looked at him. The way it had felt, being a local hero after so many years of drifting from town to town.

Local hero. Something bitter rose in him at the words. Good thing he'd enjoyed that, because it hadn't lasted long. James Carmichael had seen to that, with his determination to get rid of the man he considered a troublemaker. And Emily had gone right along with what the town decided to believe.

"Nick?" Trey's voice was questioning, and he realized the boy must have spoken more than once.

"Sorry, Trey. I was thinking about how good Luigi's pizza is. Did you know that your mom and I used to come here for pizza after football games when we were in high school?"

"All of us did," Emily said quickly, hurt and anger warring in her eyes at his pairing of their names. "Your daddy, too."

Nice work, O'Neill. Let your bitterness spill over onto innocent kids, why don't you?

"That's right." His thoughts raced for a way to make amends. No matter what he felt about Emily or her father-in-law, he couldn't say things that might hurt her kids. "Your dad and I played football together, you know. He loved pepperoni pizza just like you do."

Emily's gaze seemed to measure him for a long moment, as if asking what kind of a man he'd become. He stared back, half ashamed, half defiant.

What do you think, Emily? Whatever I am, this town made me.

The pizza arrived, fragrant and steaming, served by Luigi himself, who hovered over Nick until he took the first bite and pronounced it as good as he remembered. By the time Luigi headed back to his kitchen, beaming, Emily was engrossed in helping the boys get their slices and dissuading Trey from burning his mouth on hot mozzarella.

He watched her with her sons, still feeling a lingering shame over his hasty words. She was so gentle with them—that quality hadn't changed from the girl he remembered. But she had a maturity he hadn't anticipated when he'd thought about seeing her again.

She'd grown up. She wasn't stuck in the past, the way he sometimes felt he was. She'd gone on after he left—gone to college, coped with her father's death, married Jimmy.

Had they been happy together? He suddenly knew that was the question he really wanted to ask. Had Jimmy made her happy enough to forget her first love?

He must have. After all, they'd had their boys to bind them together. Now, every time she looked at them, she must think about Jimmy. Jimmy's image would have pushed his out of her heart a long time ago.

Trey put down a half-eaten slice. "Did you know that the fair is next week, Nick? We're going to go."

"And eat funnel cakes," David added.

"And candy apples."

"Seems to me you two are concentrating on your stomachs a lot." Emily reached across the table to hand David a napkin.

"Growing boys do that." Nick tried to remember what he'd been like at that age and couldn't. He couldn't even remember where he and his dad had lived then.

"Tell me about it." Emily smiled at him. Apparently he was forgiven for his careless comment. "These two both had to have new jeans when school started."

"Mom said she couldn't afford us if we grew any faster," Trey said.

Emily's gaze darted toward him, then away. "I didn't really mean that, Trey. I was just kidding."

"Anyway, Nick's lucky." Trey led the conversation determinedly in the direction he wanted it to go.

"Why am I lucky? Because I don't have to buy new jeans?"

Trey grinned. "No! Because you came to town in time for the fair. You're going, aren't you?"

The fair, with another set of memories from the fall he'd spent in Mannington. Another set of memories that included Emily.

He looked at her and caught the full impact of that anxious, golden-brown stare, as if her thoughts mirrored his. That look seemed to pierce right through the protective armor of his achievements and success, right to the boy who'd never quite fit in. It left him vulnerable, and vulnerable was the last thing he'd intended when he'd returned to Mannington.

"I think I'll probably be too busy for that, Trey," he

said quickly. "I've got a lot of work to do before I leave."

This time for good. He needed to keep reminding himself of that. He'd come here to even the score. Once that was accomplished, he'd leave and he wouldn't be back. And until then, it might be safer to avoid any more situations that brought back memories.

Emily tiptoed across the darkened bedroom. She adjusted the quilt Trey had kicked off, then slipped a book from under David's hand. She'd begun to think they'd never settle. She'd come to their room twice to tell them to get to sleep, and both times they'd wanted to talk about Nick.

She slid soundlessly from the room and paused in the hall, rubbing the throb that had begun in her temples. From the moment she'd heard Nick was coming back to town she'd known this wouldn't be easy. She just hadn't anticipated how difficult it would be.

Hand skimming the worn-smooth railing, she went back downstairs. If she went to bed this early, she'd be guaranteeing herself a restless night's sleep.

Why, Lord? She seemed to be continuing a conversation that had already begun. *Why did Nick come back? And why am I experiencing such confused feelings about him? Is there something You have for me to learn in all this?*

The telephone interrupted her thoughts, and she answered it reluctantly.

"Emily."

Her father-in-law's voice caught her by surprise.

"I thought you were out of town." She sank down in the armchair by the phone, massaging her forehead.

"Out of town? What made you think that?"

"Well..." Then she remembered. "I believe Martha told Nick that you were unavailable until Monday."

"Only to him." His voice was dry. "However, I don't intend to come to the office tomorrow. Will you stop by the house on your way in?"

"Of course." She wanted to ask why, but knew better. If he wanted to discuss whatever it was on the telephone, he'd have said so.

"In the morning, then." He rang off abruptly, as he always did.

Emily sat for a few minutes staring at the phone. She didn't want to see her father-in-law. She also didn't want to see Nick again. But it didn't look as if she had any choice about either of those things.

The Carmichael mansion sat at the very top of Maple Street, surrounded by the lesser homes of Mannington's other wealthy families. The house was a superb example of Italianate style, so they said, but it had always seemed cold to Emily, and she found her steps slowing as she approached the glossy black front door.

Her father-in-law had suggested she and the boys move in with him after Jimmy died. It had been all she could do to soothe his ruffled feathers when she'd refused.

But she couldn't have brought the boys here; she just couldn't. They were uncomfortable enough on their visits. She couldn't imagine what they'd have been like growing up in such cold, formal surroundings. She knew only too well what it had done to Jimmy.

She lifted the brass knocker, then let it fall. Lorna walked in and out of her in-laws' house as if it belonged to her. She'd be hard put to do that here, where the doors were always locked.

Once inside the cool marble foyer, Emily followed the uniformed maid to the library. Her father-in-law leaned back in a desk chair that was similar to the one in his office at the mill.

"Emily."

His gaze seemed even cooler than usual. She slipped into the chair opposite him.

"How are you feeling today?"

"Fine." He brushed away the question. "I want to talk to you."

"Is this about the merger?"

"No." He fingered the heavy pewter paperweight on the pristine blotter. "This is about you. I understand you had dinner with Nick O'Neill last night. You and my grandsons."

A shiver slid down Emily's spine at his tone. "We went for pizza together. He'd been helping the boys with their soccer."

"Soccer?" His silver brows lifted. "How does he even know them?"

Emily suppressed a wave of exasperation. He really did ignore anything that wasn't of concern to him or the mill. "You'll recall he's renting the house behind mine. That makes him difficult to avoid."

Her father-in-law frowned. "I wasn't suggesting you avoid him. But I had hoped…"

He didn't finish the sentence, but his wishes were fairly evident. He wanted her to see Nick every day, but expected that the twins would be kept away from him.

She wanted to say that he was the one who'd put her in this position, but it didn't seem fair to point that out.

For a long moment he stared at the paperweight, turning it over and over in his long fingers. "Perhaps it's for the best," he said, so softly she had to strain to catch the words.

"I don't know what you mean."

He shook his head, smiling faintly. "Nothing. It's nothing. I just wanted to ask how things have gone with O'Neill. What information has he requested thus far?"

Even as she went over the time she'd spent with Nick at the mill, she wondered. James Carmichael never did anything without a reason. Why was it "just as well" that the twins had made a friend of Nick?

His attitude toward Nick worried her nearly as much as Nick's attitude toward him. And that was quite a lot.

Chapter Six

Emily hurried into her own office, eager for a few moments alone to compose her thoughts before seeing Nick. What was in her father-in-law's mind about this merger and the role Nick played in it? She couldn't begin to guess.

The vague apprehension lingered on the edge of her consciousness as she took care of several routine matters. When she started going through her appointment book for the third time, she took a stern look at herself.

She was procrastinating—that was what she was doing. She was putting off the moment at which she'd have to walk across the hall to Nick's office and face him while James Carmichael's cryptic comments drifted through her mind.

Enough. She wasn't the passive teenager Nick had once known, and she wasn't going to hide from this situation. If she couldn't get the truth about the merger from her father-in-law, she'd get it from Nick. If either one of them had a hidden agenda, she needed to know it, because her boys' futures were at stake.

She stood up, fired with determination, and pulled the door open. And there was Nick, fist raised to knock.

"Sorry." He opened his hand in a small gesture of apology. "I was just coming to see if you were in yet."

"I'm here." She opened the door a little wider, trying to ignore the way her heartbeat accelerated. "Is there something you need? I was about to come and ask."

He moved past her into the office, and once again she had that sense that he was taking over her space. He prowled across the room, seeming in no hurry to get to business. His gaze touched the photograph of Jimmy on the bookshelf, then lingered on the picture of her with the boys that stood at the corner of her desk.

She watched him, uncertain how to go after the reassurance she needed. Nick looked different today. His navy blazer and gray flannels were a far cry from the jeans and sweatshirt he'd worn playing soccer with the twins. In some obscure way the more formal clothing put her at ease, establishing this as a business meeting.

Then he turned toward her. The navy of the jacket deepened the deep blue of his eyes, reminding her of that moment across the restaurant table when something, she wasn't sure what, had sparked between them. Memories, she told herself sternly. Just memories.

"I hope the boys weren't too wound up after you got home last night."

So he'd noticed the effect he had on them.

"It only took two or three demands that they stop talking and get to sleep to settle them." She smiled. "Actually, that's normal. Part of raising twins is that they're always on the same schedule. There's never a time when you're dealing with just one of them."

He leaned against the corner of her desk, focusing on her. "That worries you, doesn't it?"

"Sometimes." She moved so that she could see the photo. How could Nick still read her so easily, after all these years? "I'd like to have more one-on-one time with them, but it never seems to happen. I don't think it bothers Trey, but David…." She let that trail off, not sure she wanted to discuss her boys with him.

"If Jimmy were here, it wouldn't be a problem."

"I guess not." She touched the silver frame of the picture, feeling the cool metal under her fingertips. "Sometimes I think it would be easier to be a single parent if they'd been girls." She smiled. "Not that I'd trade them for an instant."

He shifted, and the movement put him a little closer to her. "I'm not very good with kids, but I'd say you're doing a great job from what I can see."

"Not good with kids?" Her eyebrows lifted. "Then why can't my two stop talking about you?"

"Really?"

That was genuine pleasure in his eyes, and the expression warmed her. For an instant she smiled back, feeling as if the years had somehow slipped away and they were friends again. Then he reached toward the photo and his hand brushed hers.

Warmth traveled along her skin, and her breath caught. She took a step back. She and Nick had too much history between them to ignore, and this wasn't safe.

How had they gotten so far from what she intended to say? She'd better get back to business and keep the personal out of the conversation.

"So how did your first day go? Are you finding the information you need about the company?"

For a moment his gaze lingered on her face. Then he shrugged. "It's early days yet. How soon do you think your father-in-law will be back in town? I really need to discuss some things with him."

James Carmichael wouldn't have any problem lying in this situation, but she didn't intend to do that.

"I think he'll be in the office on Monday." Could he read the evasion in her face? "I'm sure he'll be ready to meet with you then."

"I'm looking forward to it." His jaw tightened, denying the conventional words.

Again she had a sense of intentions being hidden from her. She struggled to find the words that would make Nick open up.

"This merger with Ex Corp—my father-in-law feels it will mean a lot to us." At least that broached the subject.

"Financially?" His eyebrows lifted, sarcasm in his tone. "I should think the Carmichaels were already pretty well off."

If he could see her bank account he wouldn't think that. But he wasn't ever going to know. No one was. She'd go on pretending until the boys reached college age. Then their trust funds would kick in, and she wouldn't have to worry about their futures.

"I didn't mean that." She tried not to let her personal fears creep into her mind.

"So who are you worried about? This town?"

The raw edge of bitterness in his voice stung. Her heart jolted with the realization. If Nick felt that amount of anger toward the town, how much more anger did he feel toward her?

"This is a one-industry town," she said quietly. "Everyone depends on the mill in one way or another. I guess we'd all like to believe that the merger will bring good changes."

They stood only a few feet apart, but the coolness in his gaze put a gap the size of the Grand Canyon between them. Apprehension coiled inside her. This wasn't the Nick she'd known. This was a stranger.

"Mannington can be sure of that." He smiled, but his eyes were cold. "Things are about to change."

* * *

The reason he felt like a creep, Nick admitted to himself as he left the mill that afternoon, was because he'd acted like one. He yanked the car door open, letting the heat spill out. The weather had been more like July than late September the last few days.

No rain had come along to cancel that soccer game Emily's twins were in. Well, he didn't have to go. He slid into the car. He hadn't promised he'd be there. And Emily certainly would prefer it if he stayed away.

Unasked, the image of her face filled his mind, those golden-brown eyes hurt at his harsh words.

He shouldn't have said anything. No matter how much bitterness he felt toward Carmichael or toward this town, Emily didn't deserve to have it dumped on her. She wasn't the only one who'd let him down.

Now where had that thought come from? He'd better keep reminding himself that Emily didn't figure into this equation at all. All right, she'd dumped him, but he hadn't come back because of that. That had stopped hurting a long time ago. Hadn't it?

He could drive straight home. Tell the boys, the next time he saw them, that he'd been busy with work. That would be the best thing for all of them—to cut off any relationship before it got started.

But he couldn't do it that way. He couldn't just let them down, because he could remember only too well what it felt like.

He must have been ten or so, because it had been peewee football. They'd finally been in one town long enough for him to move up to first string, and his father had promised to come and watch him play.

It wasn't easy to concentrate on the game when half his time was spent scanning the sidelines, looking for the figure that wasn't there. Maybe that was why he hadn't seen the tackle twice his size bearing down on him.

A broken collarbone, that was all. But the assistant coach had to go with him to the emergency room, and they hadn't managed to track his dad down for a couple of hours. He'd been busy, probably with a union meeting or a political rally or a demonstration for one or another of his causes.

No, he wouldn't just ignore the soccer match. He'd stop by, speak to the twins, make his excuses and leave. But he wouldn't just ignore it.

The late-afternoon sun slanted through the oaks in the park, dazzling his eyes as he walked toward the soccer field. The oaks clung stubbornly to their color, but here and there a maple announced that it was fall, whether it felt like it or not.

It looked as if soccer didn't get quite the attention football did—the crowd consisted of a handful of parents in lawn chairs along the sidelines.

He saw Emily first, of course. She'd shed the jacket she'd worn at the office and sat talking with another woman. That mop of unruly red hair must belong to the girl who'd been her best friend in high school. What was her name? Lorna. That was it.

For an instant he contemplated a world in which you made friends as children and kept them. Emily's world, that was. Not a world he'd ever lived in, or would ever be likely to.

Lorna glanced up, recognized him and nudged Emily. He saw her stiffen and noted that she carefully didn't look his way.

He strolled toward her, nodding to anyone who happened to meet his eyes. They all knew who he was, obviously. If you lived in a town where everyone knew everyone else, a stranger stood out. Especially a stranger who came with the baggage Nick O'Neill did.

"Emily." He paused, then held out his hand to the woman with her. "This has to be Lorna. I'd know that red hair anywhere."

She grinned, not looking a day older than she had in high school.

"It's pretty identifiable, all right. Nice to see you again, Nick."

He thought he picked up a discontented murmur behind him. Someone who didn't agree with Lorna, obviously. He ignored it.

"You have somebody playing in this game?" His eyes searched the crowd of navy-clad players surrounding the coach, picking out Trey and David. Then he saw the one who had to belong to Lorna. "The redhead, of course."

"Poor kid never had a chance." Lorna shook her

head. "Redheads on both sides of the family tree. I married Ken Moore, you know."

He vaguely remembered Ken from football, a gangly carrottop whose father worked at the mill.

"So you and Ken stayed here."

She shrugged. "We went away to school, but then Ken got a good offer from the mill, so we came back home." She smiled. "Free baby-sitting, with both sets of parents in town."

He suspected Emily didn't enjoy that kind of free baby-sitting, not with the father-in-law she had. He frowned. Why was he thinking about Emily again? He needed to be making his excuses and getting out of here. Then the crowd around the coach broke up, and the twins and the little redhead ran toward them.

"You came!" Trey reached him first, with David close behind.

"Yes, well, I…" This was the moment to wish them luck and say he couldn't stay.

David leaned against him. "I'm glad you came."

The boy looked up, and Nick could read the apprehension in his eyes. That expression jolted something deep inside him.

"Listen." Nick squatted next to the boys. "You're going to do fine, you hear? Just keep your head in the game, the way we talked about. Think about what you're going to do, not about what might go wrong. Okay?"

Trey nodded, bouncing on the toes of his sneakers. "Okay."

"You'll stay, won't you?" David asked.

"You bet," he heard himself saying. "I wouldn't miss it."

He sank down on the grass near Emily as the whistle blew. The kids ran back to their coach.

"You don't have to stay."

Emily's voice was so soft that probably no one other than he and Lorna heard it. And Lorna was studiously watching the players line up on the field, pretending she wasn't listening.

He glanced up at Emily. The sunlight behind her turned her hair into a golden halo, dazzling him. The shock he'd experienced the first time he saw her after his return shot through him again.

Maybe first loves were harder to forget than he'd thought.

"They wanted me to stay. I don't like to let people down."

He thought she flinched at that—inside, where no one could see. No one, it seemed, but him.

Her mouth firmed, and she sent a warning glance toward the cluster of people behind him.

"It's very good of you. I'm sure the boys appreciate your interest."

The words were as formal as if she greeted him at an afternoon tea, and he had to suppress a smile. She'd had those manners even as a teenager. Maybe if you were the doctor's daughter in a town like Mannington, you were born with them.

The game started then, giving him an excuse to look away. Probably giving Emily the same excuse. Each time he stole a sideways glance at her, she seemed focused on the players.

David ran toward a loose ball, and her fingers tightened on the arm of the lawn chair until he thought she'd break it off.

"Kick it, David!" he shouted and held his breath.

To his surprise David actually connected with the ball. Emily's fingers relaxed, and he thought he heard a small sigh of relief.

"All right! Way to go, David!" The voice, right behind him, was accompanied by a sharp nudge. "Did you see that?"

He turned. The nudger was a girl, probably fifteen or sixteen, with blond hair in a ponytail and a spattering of freckles across her nose.

"I saw."

She grinned. "Sorry. Guess I got carried away."

"Hi, Mandy." Emily gestured toward him. "This is Mr. O'Neill. Mandy is our baby-sitter."

"Puh-leeze! The boys hate that word!" She leaned forward, elbows on blue-jeaned knees.

"So they tell me. Constantly." Emily talked across him as if he weren't there. "Are you still okay to stay with them tonight?"

The girl nodded, her ponytail bouncing. "Sure thing. I'll go home with you after the game."

Emily glanced at her watch. "I wish I didn't have

such an early meeting. It's really going to push me to run back to the house."

"Can I help?" The words came out of his mouth before he remembered that he wasn't going to become any more involved with Emily and her boys. Still, it seemed ridiculous not to offer when they both knew he was driving practically to her door. "I can give Mandy and the boys a ride home after the game."

Emily looked torn between relief and a strong desire to say no. Then someone in the group behind them gave an audible gasp, as if shocked by the very idea.

Emily's lips tightened. "Thank you, Nick. I appreciate it."

"We won!"

Trey bounced so hard that Nick had to take another look to be sure his seat belt was fastened.

"You sure did." Nick smiled at him in the rearview mirror. "And it was your goal that sealed the win."

Mandy leaned back over the seat to ruffle his hair. "You're a hero, Trey."

"And Coach is going to buy us candy apples at the fair." He leaned back, beaming, as if life could hold no more.

"I'm sure your dentist will appreciate that."

The boys didn't seem to catch that remark, but Mandy smiled at him.

"You've gotta have a candy apple at the fair," she

said. "It's practically a law. Did they have the fair when you lived here?"

Since the fair was, as he remembered, a century-old tradition, the innocent question made him grin.

"Believe it or not, they really had the fair and candy apples that long ago."

"Are you going to the fair, Nick?" David had been quiet all the way home, but now he reached forward to press his hands against the seat back. "Are you?"

"I have to work, David, remember?"

"But you could go on the weekend, couldn't you?" Those golden-brown eyes pleaded with him in the mirror. "You'd like it if you went."

"We'll see." He wasn't about to promise anything he couldn't deliver, not to a kid. "If I have time, I might go."

"I'm going on the big Ferris wheel this year," Trey announced.

David shot a look at him. "You're not."

"Yes, I am!"

"Mommy won't let you." David's voice went up.

"Last year she said next year, and now it's next year, so I'm going! If you're scared, you don't have to go. You can ride the little Ferris wheel or the merry-go-round."

The squabble had sprung up so quickly, it took Nick by surprise. Should he be doing something about it?

"I'm not going on baby rides!" David turned on his brother, fists clenched. "I'm not a baby!"

Nick took a breath, but it was Mandy who spoke.

"Knock it off, guys." She sounded bored. "You want Mr. O'Neill to think you don't know how to behave when somebody's giving you a ride home?"

They subsided, although he caught a couple of furious glances between them when they thought he wasn't looking. Mandy would probably earn her baby-sitting money tonight.

He pulled into his driveway and parked, and everyone scrambled out.

"Okay, guys, let's go get something to eat." Mandy waved to him. "Thanks, Mr. O'Neill."

"Anytime."

The boys, doing a little muttering at each other, started toward their house, with Mandy following. Then suddenly David was running back toward him.

Nick glanced toward the car. Had David forgotten something?

The boy skidded to a halt next to him. "Nick, can I talk to you for a minute? Mandy says it's okay."

"Sure, sport." He sat down on the porch steps. "What's up?"

David sat down next to him. He stared down at the toes of his sneakers, as if he didn't know where to start.

"Is it something about the game?" Nick prompted. "I thought you did a good job, you know."

David sighed. "I guess I did better than last time." He fidgeted, then took a deep breath. "Mandy said Trey was a hero. Coach said that, too."

"I heard that," Nick said gravely. This was obviously important to the kid, but he didn't know why.

"Well, I was wondering…" David swallowed. "Well, do you think I'll ever be a hero?"

The wistful question caught him like a fist to the stomach. A hero. An eight-year-old kid, wanting to be a hero, not sure if he dared dream that.

"I guess that depends on what you mean by a hero." He picked his words more carefully than he ever had in any negotiation. "Sometimes people call someone a hero when they really mean he's good at something. Or even just lucky. You know what I mean?"

David nodded slowly. "I guess." He fixed those brown eyes on Nick's face. "What do you think a hero is, Nick?"

Whoa, he was really getting in over his head. But the boy deserved a straight answer.

"I guess I'd say a hero is someone who does what he figures is right. No matter what other people say, or how big the obstacles are, or how afraid he is."

"Oh." David studied his toes some more. Then he looked up. "You mean, like David in the Bible?"

Nick thought about the boy who'd gone up against the giant armed with nothing more than a slingshot and his confidence in God. He put his hand on David's shoulder.

"I'd say that's a really good example, David."

The boy frowned. "I think I'd be scared to fight a giant."

"I think I would be, too," he admitted. "Maybe even David got scared, when he saw how big that giant was. It's not wrong to be afraid, as long as you still do what's right."

He held his breath, wondering if he was giving any of the right answers. Wondering if Emily would have his head for talking like this with her son.

Finally David nodded. "Okay." He got up. "Thanks, Nick. 'Night."

He held out his hand gravely, as if they were two men saying goodbye. Nick took it, a lump in his throat the size of a baseball.

"Good night, David."

He watched the small figure trudge back across the lawn and wondered how he'd gotten in so deeply in such a short period of time. And how he was ever going to get out again.

Chapter Seven

"Mommy, hurry up!" David and Trey charged through the turnstile at the fairgrounds' entrance, their excitement bubbling so much that Emily expected them to float over the barrier. "Hurry!"

She smiled at Gus Traynor, who'd been manning the admissions booth since she was Trey and David's age. "They can't wait."

He grinned back and slid her change across the wooden counter. "Lot of that going around. Have fun."

"We will." She scooped up the coins and followed the boys through the gate, their excitement spreading to her. She couldn't restrain them, because she remembered only too well what it was like. At their age, this had been like the moment in *The Wizard of Oz* when everything changed to color. What was, for the rest of the year, a few empty acres and a scattering of barns became transformed every September into something magical.

She took a deep breath, inhaling the mingled aromas of sweet cotton candy, pizza and sawdust, to say nothing of the odors wafting from the poultry barn.

Trey and David each grabbed a hand.

"Rides first, Mom. Please?" Trey wheedled, his eyes blazing with excitement.

"For goodness' sake, Trey, give me a chance to take a breath. Don't you want to look around first?"

He shook his head, hair falling in his eyes. "I told Brett I'd meet him at the Ferris wheel, soon as I got here."

Brett Wilbur, a year older than the twins, had a know-it-all attitude Emily didn't like. She looked at David, who studied the ground as if the sawdust might suddenly sprout candy bars. It didn't take a lot of mother's intuition to know something was going on.

"We'll walk toward the rides while we look around." She gave her older son a quelling glance. "No pestering, Trey. I want to enjoy the fair."

How could anyone help but enjoy it? A line of nursery school children wove by, holding hands, their eyes huge with excitement. County fair was like having a taste of Christmas in September.

"Winner gets choice," a barker called. "Everybody's a winner."

By the end of the day, of course, some of the smiles

would turn to tears as overtired children protested they couldn't walk another step. And more than one adult would wish he hadn't combined fried oysters and potato pancakes with butter crunch ice cream. But even that was part of the fair.

"Hey, guys! Hi, Emily."

Mandy leaned across the counter of the French fry stand to wave, and the boys rushed toward her.

"Hi, Mandy. Is Mr. Lane letting you run the fryer yet?"

Mandy's eyes sparkled. "I'm working on him. Before fair is over he will, you can count on it."

Fred Lane flicked a fryer basket into sizzling fat with a practiced hand and then gave Mandy a mock-fierce glare over his shoulder.

"That'll be the day. I didn't even let Emily do that, and she was a sight more responsible than you, missy."

Emily laughed. "Don't let him get you down. He always told me the same thing." She grabbed Trey, who was attempting to shinny up the counter. "We'll have some fries later."

"Just be sure you buy them from me," Mandy said.

That was another feeling she remembered—that eagerness to sell something and prove you were worth hiring. Every teenager in town who was willing to work prized a job at the fair. She'd spent three fairs working the French fry stand before graduating to one of the dinner stands. That was harder work, but she'd gotten tips.

A jangle of music sounded as they drew near the carnival attractions, and high-pitched squeals reminded her that she didn't like rides. They were swept briefly into a flood of excited children, then out again.

"When I get big enough, I want to work at the French fry stand," David said.

"Not me." Trey skipped ahead of her, then darted back, dodging an elderly couple holding hands. "I want to work at the basketball throw." He lofted an imaginary free throw. "That'd be fun."

She was about to tell him she didn't think the owner of the basketball toss would pay him to practice free throws when Brett Wilbur sauntered out of the crowd in front of the bigger Ferris wheel. He waved a fistful of ride tickets in Trey's face.

"About time you got here. So, you going or not?"

"Sure I am." Trey dug into his jeans pocket for the money he'd been hoarding the last month. "You coming, David?"

David stuffed his hands in his pockets. "I'd rather go on the bumper cars."

"Bumper cars are for babies," Trey snapped.

Before Emily could speak, someone grasped Trey's shoulder.

"You guys still having this argument?"

One part of her mind wondered how Nick knew what the twins were arguing about, while the other observed that the rumble of that masculine voice caused a regrettable weakness in her knees.

"I'm going on the big Ferris wheel," Trey said. "If David's not chicken, he can come, too."

That bravado surely was for Brett's benefit, but she still didn't like it. "If you can't be polite, Trey, you won't be going on any rides."

Trey opened his mouth, shot her a rebellious look, then closed it again.

"I don't see what all the fuss is about." There seemed to be a smile in Nick's voice. "Trey can go on the Ferris wheel with his friend, and David can go on the bumper cars with me."

"You like the bumper cars?" Trey's glance was filled with suspicion.

"Sure do." Nick steered an imaginary car. "I like rides where you get to do something, not just sit."

Emily hid a smile at Trey's expression. He'd been flaunting going on the Ferris wheel with Brett, and now he'd have to go through with it.

"That's settled then," she said briskly. "Brett and Trey will go on the Ferris wheel while Nick and David ride the bumper cars. And I'll wait on that bench."

Nick shot her a mischievous look. "Don't you want to join us?"

"Mom doesn't like rides," Trey explained. "She says they make her seasick."

"Really?" Nick lifted an eyebrow. "I know one ride she likes."

"What?" Trey and David spoke in unison.

"The merry-go-round."

Nick's blue eyes seemed to deepen as he looked at her. Without volition, memory spun her back to the one fair week Nick had spent in Mannington. Her treacherous mind put them on the merry-go-round, colored lights flashing, organ music playing. She'd protested that the carousel was for children, but Nick hadn't listened. He'd lifted her onto a painted palomino with a bright red bridle, his hands lingering at her waist for a moment before he swung onto the dapple gray next to it. The music, the lights, the motion, Nick's laughing face—it had all been part of falling in love.

"Do you like the merry-go-round, Mommy?" David tugged at her hand. "Do you?"

"Well, I…"

"After we have our rides, we'll take your mom on it," Nick said. "You'll see. She really loves it."

There was a challenge in those blue eyes as they met hers, a challenge she didn't know how to answer.

The gate to the bumper car ride opened and people swarmed through, intent on getting the cars of their choice. Nick grabbed the bright red one David had his eye on and held it while the boy hopped in. He snagged what looked like a replica of a '57 Chevy for himself.

With a grind, a crank and a jerk that snapped Nick's head back, the cars started to move. Grinning, David rammed into him, and the cars clanked as if someone had dropped a bucket of bolts.

"Good one, David." The acrid scent of ozone filled the air.

Exactly how, he wondered, spinning the wheel of the bumper car, his knees almost to his chin, had he gotten himself into this? Trouble was, he knew how. He'd seen the look in David's eyes when his twin challenged him to go on the Ferris wheel. He'd known what was coming and he couldn't stop himself from getting in another foot deeper with Emily's kids.

That conversation he'd had with David the night before flickered through his mind. He'd told the boy a hero was someone who did what was right, no matter the cost. How many times in his life could he say that about himself?

Keep your mind on the job, O'Neill, he chided. Don't get distracted from what you came here to do— not by a woman's soft glance or by the momentary admiration in a kid's eyes.

He swung the wheel to cut off an older kid intent on ramming David's car, sparks showering from the connections over their heads, and wondered how he was going to remain focused.

After the ride, they linked up with Emily and Trey. The boys hadn't forgotten the merry-go-round. They grabbed Emily's hands and dragged her, protesting, to the carousel.

He should walk away. Instead, he found himself climbing aboard the platform. And when he spotted a palomino with a red bridle, he couldn't keep himself from grabbing it.

"This one, guys." He looked a challenge at Emily as he spoke to her kids. "This is the one your mom likes."

Go on, Emily, deny it.

A flush rose in her cheeks, but she reached for the saddle horn, her hand brushing his. Before she could protest, he caught her by the waist and hoisted her onto the glossy painted steed.

He felt the quick catch of her breath and drew his hands away. This was dangerous, too dangerous. Too many memories crowded in on him—memories of that night at the fair, of walking Emily home, linked hands swinging between them, of kissing her in the moonlight just outside the reach of the street lamp.

Remember the other night, he told himself, climbing onto the horse next to hers as the twins swarmed onto the pair in front. When he started getting mushy about his first love, he'd better remind himself of the night it ended. Of the fact that Emily hadn't loved him enough to believe in him.

That was the antidote to the soft memories. He managed a smile for the boys as the music started and the carousel came to life. Hold on to the bitter memories and think about why he'd come back to Mannington.

After the ride the boys took it for granted he'd walk along with them.

Just for a while, he told himself. Then he'd make some excuse and get out. He didn't have any desire to participate in Mannington's annual fall ritual.

Every other person they passed, it seemed, had a word for Emily and her kids. And a sidelong look for him. He should be getting used to it by this time—the wary glances ranged from mildly curious to outright suspicious. Mannington didn't know what to make of the black sheep's return, that was clear.

"There's the grange stand, Mom." Trey tugged at Emily's sleeve. "Are we going to stop for supper? Please? I want a sausage sandwich."

"Alison's there," David pointed out, and Nick saw the little redhead who played on their soccer team. The boy hung on his hand. "You'll eat with us, won't you, Nick?"

Emily's eyes met his over her sons' heads, and she gave him a smile tinged with the same wariness he saw in everyone else.

"You're welcome to join us if you don't have to be somewhere."

Was that what she hoped he'd say? The old reck-lessness took hold of him.

"Sure, I'd like to have supper with you. The sausage smells great."

Emily looked away from him, staring at the grill as if entranced by the sizzling sausage or the steam rising from bright red and green pepper strips and paper-thin white onion slices.

"I don't usually let the boys eat like this." She wore

a faint frown between her brows. "But fair only comes once a year."

"One serving of sausage and peppers won't hurt them. You're a good mother, Emily."

Her startled, unguarded glance told him volumes.

"I try." A smile tugged at her mouth. "The Lord knows how often I pray for wisdom. And patience. Lots of patience."

Her words curled around his heart as he followed her to one of the long tables set up under a green-striped canopy. Emily's faith was a matter-of-fact, everyday facet of her life. How long had it been since he'd thought of God in those terms? Had he ever?

"Hi, guys!" Lorna lifted a glass of lemonade in a salute. "Come join us."

Emily slid onto the chair next to her with what he thought was a relieved look. Relieved not to be eating alone with him and the boys? He suspected that was the case.

"Hi, Nick. You remember my husband, don't you?" Lorna gestured.

Nick half rose to shake hands with Ken Moore. Ken had filled out some since high school, and his carroty hair had darkened. His greeting seemed friendly enough, but he eyed Nick with the same wary look most of the town seemed to wear.

"So, how are you enjoying the fair, Nick?" Lorna's gaze darted, bright and speculative, from Nick to Emily and back again.

"It's about like I remember." He'd certainly been naïve to think he could come back and not be overwhelmed with memories.

"We've got some new things." Ken's tone suggested he took offense at the idea that nothing had changed. "There's the tractor pull, the country-western show…"

"So, what'll it be?" A teenage boy loped up to the table, whipping out a pad and pencil.

"Sausage and peppers all around?" Nick raised his eyebrows and got nods from Emily and the twins.

"For drinks you can have lemonade or lemonade," the boy said. "We ran out of iced tea an hour ago. Sorry, Ms. Carmichael. I know that's what you like."

"Lemonade's fine, Ted." She smiled at the boy, who blushed and loped away again.

Nick cocked an eyebrow at Emily. "An admirer?"

"Goodness, no." She looked startled. "Ted is Mandy's boyfriend."

"That doesn't mean he can't admire an older woman," Lorna said. "You're just such an innocent, you never notice things like that."

"That's ridiculous." That peachy blush rose on Emily's cheeks.

Lorna had it right, he realized. Emily had been married, had two children, but she still possessed that air of innocence she'd had at fifteen.

As if deciding she'd teased Emily enough, Lorna steered the conversation in other channels. Her inexhaustible flow of chatter was aided by her daughter. He noted with some amusement that Alison was a carbon copy of her mother in personality as well as looks.

He caught Ken's eye. "Do they ever let you get a word in edgewise?"

Ken grinned, face relaxing, becoming again the kid he remembered. "Not often," he admitted. "It's okay. I always wanted a daughter just like her mother."

His face tightened again, as if he regretted letting his guard down with Nick. "I guess you think it was pretty small potatoes, settling down here in the old hometown."

"Not at all." Nick picked his words carefully. "I'd say it's probably a pretty decent place to raise a family."

Ken nodded. "That it is." His glance skipped from his wife to his daughter. "And I'd do anything for them."

Nick stared down at the sausage sandwich that had grown suddenly tasteless. Ken worked at the mill. He didn't know what was going to happen once the merger went through. He couldn't guess that the life he'd picked for his family was about to be disrupted.

His jaw clenched. If innocent people got hurt in all this, that was Carmichael's fault, not his. Besides, he could make sure Ken received a good offer to move south to the facility that would replace Carmichael Mills.

"Look at that." Trey nudged him and nodded toward the corner of the food stand. "There's Mandy and her boyfriend."

Mandy, apparently taking a break from her stint at the French fry stand, stood close to Ted, smiling up at him. The boy slipped a possessive arm around her waist and whispered something that made her laugh and lean against him.

"They're going steady," David announced. "Mandy told me."

Nick put down his sandwich and frowned at Emily. "Isn't she a little young for that?"

"Young?" Emily raised a startled gaze to his. "Mandy's almost sixteen. The same age—" She stopped as if she'd bitten the words off.

But he knew what she was thinking. Mandy was the same age Emily had been when they'd gone together. When he'd told her he loved her. When he'd urged her to go away with him.

The realization was like a kick in the stomach, and he looked again at Ted and Mandy. They're babies, he thought, incredulous. Babies. Like Emily was when I wanted her to go away with me. When I wanted her to marry me.

The truth stared him in the face, and he didn't like looking at it. He'd been blaming Emily, holding on to his anger and sense of betrayal even while he told himself he didn't feel anything for her. And all the while Emily had been absolutely right.

* * *

She could tell something was bothering Nick. Emily sent a searching glance at him as they followed the boys toward the rides again. He'd been preoccupied since they finished supper. Maybe he was trying to think of an excuse to leave. Not that he needed one, she assured herself hurriedly. They didn't owe each other anything.

"Can we go on the rides again, Mom?" Trey tugged at her hand. "It's not so late."

She glanced at her watch. "I don't…"

Nick's fingers encircled her wrist, obscuring the watch. "Please?" His eyebrows quirked, and there was an expression in his midnight blue eyes she didn't understand. "Just a little longer."

She hesitated a moment, then nodded. Nick's fingers tightened briefly before he let go.

She had to resist the urge to close her hand over the warm place on her wrist as she watched Nick catch up with the boys.

He leaned over, saying something softly to David. Her small son's gaze met Nick's, held for a long moment. Then he nodded. Nick squeezed his shoulder. Now what, exactly, was that all about?

"Ask your mom," Nick prompted.

"Nick and me are going on the big Ferris wheel." David's hands clenched, but his voice didn't wobble. "Okay, Mommy?"

A whole host of objections flooded Emily's mind.

David didn't have to do this; it was okay to be afraid; no one cared. She caught the warning look Nick flashed her and swallowed them.

"That's fine, David. If you really want to."

He nodded, mouth firming. "I want to."

Amazingly, Trey didn't argue that David was being singled out for something special. He stood beside Emily, watching as David and Nick moved up in the line. She realized he was holding his breath.

Nick and David reached the head of the line, and the next seat swung down toward them. The attendant steadied it. David seemed to hesitate, and Emily held her breath, too.

Then, with a glance at Nick, David scrambled in.

She watched the tall figure settle into the seat next to her son and let out the breath she'd been holding.

"He'll be okay, Mommy."

Trey so seldom called her "Mommy" any longer that she treasured it when it happened. She rested her fingers lightly on his shoulder. "He's scared."

"He'll be okay," Trey said again. "Nick's with him."

She wanted to object to his calm assurance that Nick would make things all right. But she couldn't, because that was exactly what she felt, too.

She saw Nick double-check David's seat belt, then give him a thumbs-up sign. David's answering smile was a bit uncertain, and then the Ferris wheel swung them up.

The first time they swept around, David wore a frozen smile that made her want to stop the ride and pull him off it. She saw Nick's lips moving. He was talking to David, his hand resting casually on her son's shoulder.

The second time around, David was talking to Nick.

The third time around, he actually let go of the bar long enough to wave at them.

She smiled at Trey. "He did it."

Trey nodded, then looked down and kicked at a clump of sawdust with the toe of his sneaker. "I'm sorry. About teasing him before."

She brushed a strand of hair out of his face, her heart swelling with love. "I know. Don't you think you'd better tell him?"

"I will. But he knows, anyway," Trey said matter-of-factly.

That unspoken bond between the twins had the capacity to surprise her at times. "He'd still like to hear it."

The last bad moment came when the Ferris wheel stopped to disgorge passengers, leaving David and Nick at the very top. The seat swayed gently, and she saw Nick's arm move, as if he gestured at the view.

A few minutes later they were getting off. David bounded toward her, a wide grin splitting his face. "It was so cool, Mom! It really was. You could see everything from on top—the mill, even our street."

Giving in to the need to touch him, she tousled his

hair. She didn't dare make too much of his conquering the fear, knowing it might hurt his tender pride.

"That's great, David. Did you thank Nick?"

"No thanks necessary," Nick said quickly. "I enjoyed it. Now I think Trey owes me a ride."

She wanted to thank him for helping David, but the words remained unspoken as Nick maneuvered the next few rides so that they were never out of earshot of the boys.

It wasn't until Nick walked them toward the parking lot that the moment finally came. The twins skipped ahead, leaving them alone together under the trees that surrounded the fairgrounds.

"Stop a minute, Nick." She put her hand on his arm to slow him, then couldn't seem to take it away as he swung toward her.

"What?" His voice was soft, questioning.

"I just… I—I wanted to thank you." She seemed to be stammering the words, and the night kept mixing itself with a long-ago evening when they'd stood under the trees and heard the music of the carousel wafting toward them on the night air.

"You don't owe me any thanks. That was between David and me."

A cloud moved across the nearly full moon, casting his face in shadow briefly, then illuminating it.

"You were kind to my son. Can't I say thanks?" The words came out too soft, too breathless, making her sound like the girl she'd once been.

"Still seeing the best in everyone?" The words should have sounded bitter, but they didn't.

"Isn't that better than looking for the worst?"

Nick's arm was still under her hand, and he stood only a breath away.

"Emily, you…"

That began on a note of exasperation, then died away as he caught her arms and drew her toward him.

"Emily," he said again gently, and then his lips found hers.

Warmth flooded her, and barely recognizable feelings tumbled through her. She should stop this— she wanted this to last forever—

Nick let her go abruptly, and the evening air was cold on her lips.

"Good night." It was a barely audible murmur, and then he turned and was gone.

Chapter Eight

Nick nursed a mug of coffee between his hands and stared out at a sunny Sunday morning in Mannington. If he'd been in the city apartment that he treated as little more than a hotel room between jobs for Ex Corp, he wouldn't even have known without a calendar that it was Sunday. He'd have been insulated from the life around him.

But nobody was insulated from his neighbors in a small town like Mannington, except possibly the likes of James Carmichael, in his mansion on the hill. The Sunday newspaper had thudded against Nick's door, followed by the sounds of his next-door neighbors, apparently headed for an early church service.

He glanced at the clock, then discovered he was at the kitchen window from where he could see Emily's house. Ridiculous, wasn't it? But he stood there, half-hidden behind the curtain, until he saw her and the boys start down the walk. The twins wore identical navy pants and white shirts, while Emily had on a flowered dress of some soft fabric that flirted around her legs as she walked.

They were off to Sunday school, obviously. He let the curtain fall. If Emily was bothered by what had passed between them the evening before, she wasn't letting it show.

A kiss, that's all. Just one insignificant kiss between two people who'd been close once upon a time. Nothing to make a fuss about.

So why was his heart thumping uncomfortably at the memory?

Because it shouldn't have happened. He was here with a job to do, and that didn't include getting involved with Emily again. Their childish infatuation had been over a long time ago.

That moment of realization he'd had when he looked at young Mandy and her boyfriend resurfaced, and he shoved it down again. He wouldn't go endlessly over his feelings, trying to figure out what had happened and why. He would ignore the whole thing.

The telephone rang, inadvertently aiding in that task. He picked up the receiver with a sense of relief. "O'Neill here."

"Hey, old buddy." Josh sounded cheerful for this early hour on a Sunday morning.

"Hey, yourself. Why aren't you sleeping in? Or on the golf course?" Nick leaned against the counter.

Josh made a disbelieving sound. "Are you kidding? Ex Corp doesn't recognize a day of rest, remember? Or is small-town life dulling your edge already?"

"Don't you believe it." The words came out with as much assurance as possible. Nick didn't have any illusions that Josh, despite his buddy/buddy attitude, was a friend. At least, he wasn't a friend in the sense that people like Emily and Lorna were friends. If Josh saw a way to push himself an inch higher at Nick's expense, he'd take it. "So, what's up?"

"That's what I called to ask you. Any scoop on the rumor I passed on to you about Carmichael?"

"Nada." Nick frowned. "He's been unavailable since I got here, supposedly away. I should be able to see him tomorrow."

"The sooner, the better. Donaldson would like this rapped up in a hurry."

Keith Donaldson, vice president in charge of acquisitions, always wanted everything wrapped up in a hurry. Before the target of his acquisition looked too closely at the sweet deal Ex Corp was offering and saw the flaws.

In this case Nick's views coincided with Donaldson's. "Don't worry, I'm moving on it. Carmichael will sign on the dotted line."

And soon after that, Ex Corp would announce that it was too cost-inefficient to keep the Mannington mill open. It would be closed, its operations moved south to another mill, and one more of Ex Corp's competitors would be gone.

"Be sure he does." Josh's voice contained a vague note of warning. "You know how Donaldson feels about losing."

Everyone who worked for him knew how Donaldson felt about losing. Make a misstep that cost the corporation, and you'd be gone.

"He doesn't need to worry." Nick made his words crisp. "This one is in the bag."

After he'd hung up he paced back to the window, frowning out at the sunshine. He'd forced himself to sound confident for Josh because that was how you played the game. If Donaldson suspected Nick was tied up in knots right now because of a brown-eyed girl from his past and a pair of cute kids, he'd be abruptly reassigned to another job.

So the thing to do was get on with things as quickly as possible. And that meant seeing Carmichael.

If Carmichael were back in town, he'd probably be at church this morning. Nick frowned. If, that is, the man had ever left. All of this delay could be just a game designed to remind Nick O'Neill that he wasn't worth the great man's time.

There was one way to find out. He turned toward the stairs. Get dressed, go to church and see if Carmichael was there.

Half an hour later he went up the stone steps to the double doors that stood invitingly open, trying to remember how long it had been since he'd gone to Sunday services. Obviously, if he couldn't remember, it had been a long time.

The organ was sounding as he stepped into the rear of the sanctuary, and for a brief instant the carousel music flashed into his mind. He shoved the thought aside, put on a confident smile and took the bulletin an usher held out to him.

He paused at the center aisle. It had been years, but he remembered where James Carmichael always sat—halfway down, on the right side of the aisle. There wasn't a nameplate on the pew, but no one else would claim it.

Carmichael wasn't in church this Sunday morning. There would have been no mistaking that head of pure white hair. But someone else occupied the Carmichael pew.

Emily sat next to the twins. Her golden-brown hair brushed the shoulder of her dress as she bent to whisper to Trey, and David smiled up at her.

Something settled into place in Nick's mind, bringing with it an absolute certainty. Whatever he'd been telling himself, he hadn't come to church this morning to see Carmichael. He'd come because he wanted to see Emily again. Because he needed to set things right with her, once and for all.

Emily heard the rustle of movement as someone slid into the pew behind her, and the briefest sidelong glance showed her who it was. Not that she'd needed to look. She'd have sensed Nick's presence if she'd been blindfolded.

She frowned at Trey, who was nearly bouncing off the pew in his eagerness to greet Nick. Then she turned, gave Nick the same polite smile she'd have given anyone else who sat behind her and turned her attention to the bulletin.

When she'd read the announcements three times without having them register, she knew she was in trouble. She seemed to feel Nick's gaze on the back of her neck, and his face, indistinct in the moonlight, kept intruding between her and the page.

How had that kiss happened? Was it her fault? All she'd wanted to do was thank him for his kindness to David, and somehow the situation had slid dangerously out of control.

Dangerous—yes, that was exactly the word for it. She shouldn't relive the moment when Nick's lips touched hers, shouldn't let herself remember the overwhelming emotion. Because if she did, she'd begin having ridiculous dreams of something that could never happen.

Nick probably regretted that moment just as much as she did. The last thing he'd want, in the middle of a business deal, would be an emotional complication.

No, it had been a momentary aberration, that was all. The best thing would be to pretend it never happened. She could only hope he wouldn't attempt to apologize or explain, because that would embarrass both of them.

Reverend Hayes entered the pulpit, and with a sense of relief Emily fixed her attention on him.

By the time the benediction had been spoken, Emily knew she owed Reverend Hayes an apology. She'd listened to his no-doubt excellent sermon on the ten lepers, of course she had. Unfortunately she couldn't seem to remember a word he'd said.

The organ postlude rang out, and people began chatting with their neighbors. The twins leaned over the pew back toward Nick as she turned and held out her hand.

"Good morning. Welcome to worship with us."

That was what she always said to a visitor in worship services. But her heart didn't usually pound this way, and a visitor's hand didn't generate this warmth.

Nick greeted the boys, but he didn't let go of her hand. Then his eyes met hers, and her heart gave a little lurch.

"Emily, we have to talk."

"We don't—I mean, we are talking." She was probably blushing for everyone in the sanctuary to see. She pulled her hand away quickly.

His mouth quirked a little at the corners, as if he knew what she was thinking. "Someplace more private."

She had the sense that he intended to do just what

she didn't want—bring up last night, apologize, pull the memory of that kiss out between them to look at and be embarrassed about all over again. At all costs, she had to keep him from doing that.

"I can't just now, Nick." She tried for a smile, but it felt stiff on her lips. "I'll see you at the mill tomorrow, I'm sure."

His lips tightened. "This doesn't have anything to do with the mill."

Donna Carter stopped at the edge of the pew just then, giving her a respite from Nick's intense gaze. She spun out the discussion about the fall rummage sale, hoping that when she turned back Nick would be gone.

He wasn't.

"Let's go somewhere and talk." He said it as if the interruption had never happened.

"I have to take the boys home and get them some lunch."

"I'll walk along with you."

Why couldn't he accept the fact that she just didn't want to discuss this? But that never had been Nick's style. He forged straight ahead at any target, no matter what was in his path.

"I don't think…"

"Hi, Emily. Nick." Lorna paused beside them, letting Alison hurry on back the aisle with the twins. "We're going to the Carriage House for brunch. Why don't you join us?" She smiled at Nick. "You, too, Nick."

Emily's fingers tightened on her handbag. The ten-dollar bill it contained wouldn't cover brunch at the Carriage House for her and the twins. Not that she'd go, anyway, if it meant another meal with Nick across the table, reminding her of emotions she didn't want to feel.

"Not today, Lorna. Thanks, but we have to get home."

She slid out of the pew and went quickly back the aisle, hoping Nick would be held up by whatever he had to say to Lorna's invitation.

Outside, she collared the twins, overcoming their protests that they weren't ready to go home and they wanted to go to lunch with Alison.

"Not this time." Her voice was sharp enough to get their attention. "Let's go home and get changed." She tried to think of something that would distract them from the denied treat. "Maybe we can take our sandwiches and go for a hike." That, at least, didn't cost anything.

Trey showed an inclination to continue pouting, but David brightened immediately. "Let's go all the way to the top of Pine Hill, okay, Mom?"

"Yeah, let's." Trey's pout vanished. "We can make peanut butter and banana sandwiches. Come on, David, I'll race you home."

The two of them bolted down the sidewalk. Emily followed, feet rustling through the fallen leaves. It looked as if…

"Peanut butter and banana sandwiches? Will they really take that over brunch at the Carriage House?" Nick fell into step beside her.

She should have known she wouldn't get rid of him that easily. "Isn't it a little silly for you to be walking home with us when you have your car here?"

"I wouldn't have to if you'd let me drive you." He smiled at her silence. "I thought not. Come on, Emily. Talking with me isn't that bad, is it?"

She swallowed. This appeared to be unavoidable. "If this is about last night…" There wasn't any good way to finish that sentence.

"About when we kissed, you mean?" His sleeve brushed hers as he kept pace with her.

She would not look at him, she wouldn't. But her gaze seemed to find his face without her permission.

He was smiling, a little ruefully. "It shouldn't have happened—is that what you're thinking?"

"Yes." Probably the women he usually dated would find this a laughable conversation. She decided she didn't want to think about the women Nick usually dated.

"That's not how you used to feel, Emily."

His tone was more serious than she expected. She focused on the boys, skipping through the fallen leaves halfway down the block.

"That was a long time ago. We both should know better by now."

"Maybe we should." He shook his head. "There

seem to be quite a lot of things I should know better than to do."

She brushed her hand over the wine-colored mums that made a brilliant display along a white picket fence. She wasn't going to ask him what those things were, but she suspected he was going to tell her anyway.

"I realized something last night."

She stole a glance at him and found he was frowning, staring absently down the street toward the boys.

Then he looked at her. "I owe you an apology."

"It was my fault, too."

He looked startled, then amused. "I wasn't apologizing for the kiss, Emily. Strange as it seems, I'm not the least bit sorry about that."

Color flooded her cheeks. "Then what are you apologizing for?"

"For…blaming you." He shook his head. "I finally got it last night, looking at that baby-sitter of yours and her boyfriend."

"Mandy and Ted?" What did they have to do with this?

"They're hardly more than babies."

She had to smile at the astonishment in his tone. "You know, that sounds awfully old-fashioned for Nick O'Neill."

He grinned. "It does, doesn't it? Maybe I'm finally growing up." He stopped and swung around to face her, sobering. "We were just that age when we went together."

She nodded, wishing she could walk away from this and knowing she couldn't. "Just about. You might have been a few months older than Ted."

He made a dismissive motion with one hand. "Not old enough for you to run away with me, Emily. I can't believe I asked you to do that. Or that I blamed you when you didn't."

"We both..." What? We both thought we were in love? She couldn't say that.

"I've held on to my resentment ever since and didn't even realize I was doing it. I'm sorry."

Her heart ached. "It's all right. We were just kids." She struggled to keep her voice steady.

"Luckily you weren't as immature as I was. If you'd gone with me that night, I don't want to think what a disaster that would have been."

Tears prickled, and she held them back by sheer force of will. "So it all turned out for the best, didn't it?"

"Yes, it did." He sounded relieved, she decided. "No regrets, right?"

"Right."

But if she didn't have any regrets, why did her heart feel as if it had just been trampled?

Okay, he'd told her what he wanted to say. Now he should just walk away. Trouble was, he didn't want to.

They'd almost reached Emily's house when the boys came rushing back to them.

"Nick, we have something to tell you." Trey looked as if he was trying to keep from grinning.

"What's that, guys?"

"You forgot your car at the church!"

The twins erupted into laughter, and he smiled with them.

"Yes, I guess I did. I'll have to walk back and get it, unless your mom wants to give me a ride."

"I can't, I'm afraid." Emily gave him the faint, distant smile she'd give a stranger. "My car's out of commission."

"The car broke down." Trey shoved the gate open by swinging on it. "Mom says we can't afford to get it fixed right now."

Emily went scarlet at his words. "Trey, I didn't…that's not what I meant. I just meant we can't get it fixed today. It's Sunday, so the garage isn't open."

From anyone else, he'd have accepted the words at face value. But something about the exchange set alarm bells off in his head. Emily's embarrassment was out of proportion to what had been said. Why was she looking so worried about something as simple as getting her car fixed?

He followed her up the porch steps to the house, wondering. "Do you need a ride to pick up a rental car until yours is fixed?"

"No." Her startled gaze met his, then slid away. "I don't need a rental car. Mannington's a small town. I can do without a car until it's fixed." She opened the door. "Now, if you'll excuse us, we have a date with some peanut butter and banana sandwiches."

He held the screen for her. "I'll wait while you get the boys started. There's something else I want to talk with you about."

He cut off the objections she was about to make by stepping through the door behind her, then giving her a bland smile.

"Fine." She tossed her bag on the sofa with something as close to a flare of temper as he'd seen from her. "Boys, you run up and change while I start your sandwiches."

"But maybe Nick…" David began, and received a firm look that silenced him.

"Go on now."

The twins, with a backward look at him, hurried up the stairs. Emily whisked toward the kitchen. He was alone and not sure why it seemed important to understand what troubled her.

Nick took a deep breath, looking around the large, square room that must be both living room and family room for Emily and the boys, judging by the unfinished puzzle on the drop-leaf table and the television in the corner.

The big old Victorian was in the right part of town—probably a wedding gift from Carmichael, if the truth be known. But it was comfortable, not elegant, with some chintz-covered pieces he remembered from Emily's home when she was a teenager.

It looked to Nick as if nothing had been spent on redecorating for some time. And that didn't fit the Emily he remembered.

Several things fell together in his mind. The way Emily had clutched her bag when Lorna asked them out to lunch. The way she'd reacted when Trey said she couldn't afford to have the car fixed. The troubled look in her eyes when he'd suggested the rental car.

He was standing there staring at her handbag when she walked back into the room.

"What's wrong?" Her eyes went instantly wary, as if she recognized the question in his mind before he'd even formed it himself.

"That's what I wanted to ask you." He felt his way to the question. "This business about getting your car fixed…Emily, what's wrong?"

"Nothing." Her denial was quick, maybe too quick. "Cars break down. It'll go in for service this week."

Was he making too much of this? Some instinct told him he wasn't, that she was hiding something.

"We're old friends, remember? Whatever's wrong, you can tell me."

She went very still. "I don't know what you mean."

"I think you do." The words came slowly as the thought shaped itself in his mind. "I've noticed things since I got back. Jimmy Carmichael's widow and kids should be set for life financially. Instead I find you worrying about spending the money to go out to lunch or get your car fixed."

"It's not that!" The words sounded defiant, but he could see that her hands gripped each other tightly. "I just didn't want to go, that's all."

"Save it for someone who doesn't know you as well as I do." Saying the words, he realized how true they were. He did know Emily, bone-deep. That hadn't changed, no matter what lay between them. "You're broke, aren't you?"

For an instant longer she glared at him. Then she turned away. "*Broke* is such an ugly word." She seemed to make an effort to say it lightly. "We're getting along on my salary, like everyone else does."

His mind whirled, trying to readjust his picture of Emily. "I don't understand. What happened to the money Jimmy left?"

"There was no money." She looked startled, as if she'd never intended to say the words and couldn't believe she'd done it. "Jimmy...Jimmy gambled."

His heart stopped suddenly at the thought of Emily struggling to provide for her boys alone. How could Jimmy have let her down like that? "But doesn't Carmichael help you?"

"No!" She swung toward him with something like panic in her eyes. "He doesn't know! I can't tell him—it would destroy him. He thought the world of Jimmy."

"But if you need help..."

"I get along fine." That momentary flash of panic seemed to have clarified things for her. She reached out, touching his arm lightly. "Nick, don't worry about it. We get along. I don't want Jimmy's father to know. And I don't want the boys to know. Eventually they'll inherit the mill, and everything will be okay. Things are just tight right now, that's all."

She stood looking up at him, and several things crystallized in Nick's mind. One was that he couldn't tell himself he didn't care about Emily and her kids. And the other was that the revenge he'd set in motion would hurt them in ways he'd never even considered.

Chapter Nine

The rain that spattered against his windshield as Nick arrived at the mill Monday morning accurately reflected his mood. His mind kept returning to one unpalatable fact. If he succeeded in what he'd set out to do, Emily and her children would be hurt.

He sat motionless behind the wheel, staring through gray droplets at the mill looming over him. They weren't his responsibility, some part of him insisted. Besides, Carmichael would provide for them, with or without the mill. He'd come here to see justice done, and if innocents were injured by that, it wasn't his fault.

A nice rationalization, he thought grimly as he stepped out into the cold rain. His father might have said something much like that. Trouble was, Emily and her kids weren't just some abstract, faceless names. They'd begun to trust him. And he was about to betray that trust for a principle they didn't know about and wouldn't understand.

He hurried into the lobby, shaking the moisture from his jacket. The receptionist looked up, eyes appraising as they rested on him.

"Mr. O'Neill, Mr. Carmichael is in his office now. He wants to see you as soon as you get in."

He nodded, appreciating the wording. James Carmichael was a master of the art of power. He'd set the terms and place of their meeting, and he probably intended to keep Nick cooling his heels in the outer office once he got there, just to remind him who was in charge here.

The implicit challenge quickened his pace as he headed for the elevator. He was about to see the man who'd ruined his father's life, and he was long past ready. By the time this meeting was over, they'd both know that Nick had the upper hand in this situation.

When Carmichael's secretary finally opened the door to the inner office, Nick clenched his fist to keep from adjusting his tie. Confidence, nothing but confidence, he told himself. There'd be no betraying little gestures to tell Carmichael he was nervous, and nothing about his expensively tailored suit or business school tie would suggest the boy he'd once been.

He stepped into the office, hearing the door close behind him. The first thing he saw was the bank of high windows overlooking the mill roofs and yard. The second was the man standing at the windows.

Was his memory playing tricks on him? He'd

pictured Carmichael as a giant of a man, of almost mythic proportions. Instead he saw an ordinary, elderly man.

Then Carmichael turned to look at him, and he realized the man wasn't ordinary at all. Age had only accentuated his aristocratic quality, and those piercing eyes still had the ability to cut any lesser man down to size.

Nick smiled, rising to the challenge he saw there, and moved forward, extending his hand.

"Mr. Carmichael. I'm relieved to find you back in the office again. I hope there was no problem?"

Carmichael took his hand for the briefest of contacts. "Problem?" His gaze was icy. "Of course not. One of the advantages to being the company president is the ability to take a day off whenever one chooses."

As opposed to lesser mortals like him, Nick supposed.

"I'm afraid Ex Corp doesn't offer that flexibility," he said smoothly. "And if our transactions can't be conducted quickly—" he shrugged "—we move on."

Carmichael gestured toward a chair, then seated himself behind the massive piece of mahogany that proclaimed his status. He smiled, apparently ignoring the implicit threat.

"I trust you're finding everything you need. Of course, you're already familiar with our operation."

"Ex Corp wouldn't send me in without the necessary groundwork."

Carmichael's silver brows lifted. "Actually, I was thinking of the fact that your father was once employed here. Before his unfortunate departure."

For just an instant Nick was blinded by pure rage. He took a breath, then another. Control. He couldn't let the man know how well that shot had found its mark.

He didn't speak until he was sure his voice wouldn't betray the slightest note of anger.

"Ex Corp isn't particularly interested in past history. We're more concerned about the current financial status. I haven't yet received the detailed tax records we requested. Perhaps you would turn them over to me now."

Carmichael made a dismissive motion with his hands, as if such tawdry details were beneath him. "I'll have Emily get them for you. I trust she's being helpful?"

"Yes." He discovered it was possible to talk between clenched teeth if he really tried.

"I thought she would be." Carmichael leaned back in his chair. "After all, you two were once such friends, weren't you?"

Ex Corp would definitely not approve of an executive who knocked over a desk in the middle of a business discussion. Nick managed a nod.

"How nice for both of you that you can combine business with pleasure on this trip."

Who did he think he'd been kidding? When it came to power, the old man knew all the buttons to push.

But it wasn't going to do him any good. He could win all the skirmishes, needle Nick as much as he wanted about Flynn O'Neill and about Emily. But when it came to the bottom line, he was going to lose the war.

Emily stopped inside the mill door, shaking raindrops from her umbrella. In a few minutes she'd see Nick again.

Something quaked inside her. How could she have done that? How could she possibly have revealed to him what she hadn't admitted to anyone in the four years since Jimmy's death?

She hadn't even told Lorna, who'd been her best friend since nursery school, although sometimes she thought Lorna guessed at least part of the truth.

But just like that, after all those years, Nick walked back into her life and saw things no one else did. Emily bit her lip, staring down at the droplets on the glossy tile floor. Was she that transparent where he was concerned?

Well, if so, she'd have to figure out some way of putting up a barrier. Letting Nick see her innermost feelings could only lead to heartache.

She had to talk to him, that was all. She had to assure herself he wouldn't tell, because otherwise she didn't know what she would do. *Please, Lord. Give me the words. I don't know how to handle this.*

Shoving her umbrella into the stand, Emily walked quickly to the receptionist's desk.

"Good morning, Betty. Is Mr. O'Neill in yet, do you know?"

Betty smiled with the air of one in the know. "He came in about half an hour ago and went straight up to Mr. Carmichael's office. They've been together ever since."

Emily could only hope her face didn't mirror her dismay. Nick might convince everyone else that his only concern with James Carmichael was to facilitate the merger. But just as he'd known her secret, she seemed to know his. And she could only pray that he wouldn't allow his feelings toward her father-in-law to lead him into using her as a weapon.

When she reached her office, she left the door standing open. She'd see Nick as soon as he came down from that meeting. As soon as she saw him, she'd…what? If he'd already told, it would be too late.

Please. She clenched her hands together on the desktop. *Please.*

She heard Nick first, his steps quick and angry on the tile floor. She moved to the door, to be met by what seemed waves of fury emanating from him.

"Nick. Do you have a moment?" She almost hated to speak, as if it might invite him to turn that anger against her.

He swung toward her, and for a moment it was as if he were so far away he didn't recognize her. Then he focused, frowning. "Can it wait?"

"No, I don't think it can." She held the door wide. This could only be made worse by waiting.

His frown deepened, but he stalked into her office. As soon as she'd closed the door, he spun around. "What's so important?"

She could try and lead up to what she wanted to say, but she didn't think that would work—not now. Not when he was obviously so angry.

"You've talked to James."

"Does it show?" He bit off the words, a tiny muscle at his temple twitching.

"Oh, Nick." Her concern for what he might have said was clouded for the moment by the bitterness she saw in his eyes. "Was it that painful to see him after all this time?"

"Painful? No, I wouldn't call it painful. I'd just call it instructive."

"I don't understand." She was feeling her way, trying to find the source of all that anger.

His lips tightened, as if to hold back the words, but then they burst out anyway.

"He actually had the nerve to bring up my father, after everything he did to him. As if…"

She took a step closer, wanting somehow to ease the pain she read in his eyes. *Please, Lord, guide my words. I don't know what to say, and he's hurting so much.*

"Tell me, Nick. Tell me about your father." She held her breath, waiting for an explosion.

It didn't come. Nick stared down at her, his blue

eyes dark with pain. Then he shrugged. "There's nothing to tell. You know what happened."

"I don't know what happened after you left Mannington." This wasn't the moment to tell him she'd waited and waited for a letter that had never come. She reached toward him, putting her hand lightly on his sleeve. "Please. Let me understand this."

He stared at her, his eyes unreadable, refusing to let her in. Then something seemed to ease in him, just for a moment. He shook his head. "Has anyone ever been able to say no when you look at them that way?"

She was encouraged enough to smile tentatively. "Plenty of people." *Including you.*

"Not so much to tell." He moved a step away, and her hand fell from his sleeve. "We tried another town. My dad thought he'd do better with the union somewhere else."

"Did he?" She thought she knew the answer from the way he looked.

"Funny thing about that." Nick's fists clenched. "No matter where he went, people seemed to know about him. Everything he tried went sour, until he couldn't get a job at all. And he knew who to blame."

She wanted to protest that her father-in-law wouldn't have pursued him that way, but what good would it do? Nick was too angry to listen, and she wasn't even sure she'd be right.

"What happened to him?" The words came out softly, as if they might hurt him.

"He died a year ago. Hit by a passing driver when he stumbled out into the road late at night. If I'd been able to get him to come and live with me, maybe it wouldn't have happened."

She reached toward him, compelled by the pain in his voice. "You don't know that."

"Maybe not. But I do know he never recovered from being branded a thief. And I know who to blame for that."

His angry gaze dared her to argue.

"Is that why you've come back? Because of what you think James did to your father?"

"I know what he did." He turned away from her, shutting her out. "But the answer to your question is that I'm here on a job. That's all."

She didn't believe it. That couldn't be all, not the way Nick felt.

"If you wanted to hurt my father-in-law…" She had to struggle to keep her voice steady. "If you wanted to hurt him, I gave you the perfect weapon, didn't I?"

He swung toward her, his face disbelieving. "You think I'd use what you told me against him?"

"I don't know." She had to keep reminding herself that he wasn't the boy she'd known. "Would you?"

His mouth twisted. "Strange as it seems, I'm kind of sensitive on the subject of a boy's relationship with his father." He stalked toward the door. "I wouldn't do anything to destroy your sons' belief in their father, Emily. But that's all I can promise you."

The door slammed behind him.

She sank into the desk chair, as sapped as if she'd just run several miles. All that anger… Didn't Nick realize what it was costing him? Obviously not, or he'd have found a way to deal with it by now. What harm must it be doing to his spiritual life, to be harboring so much bitterness?

Help me, Father. I don't know what to do.

She pressed her hands over her eyes, as if the momentary darkness might help her concentrate. Helping Nick, however much she might want to, could be beyond her ability. They no longer had the kind of relationship that would allow her to intrude so far into his life.

She put her hands down, stared at them clasped on the blotter. Her lack of ability to help Nick was failure enough. But she couldn't fail to protect her sons.

He'd said he'd never do anything to destroy their faith in their father. She wanted to believe that. But given the grudge he held against her father-in-law, how could she be sure he might not blindly strike out with the closest weapon at hand?

She shoved away from the desk. There was probably nothing else she could say to Nick just now that would help. But she could come at the problem from another direction. She could talk to her father-in-law.

She hesitated, staring at the photo of the twins.

She didn't want to do this. But if the battle between James and Nick blew up, her children could be the ones who'd suffer.

"Is this really so important you have to speak to me now?" James leaned back in his chair, looking pale. "I was about to leave."

Emily felt a pang of guilt. He wasn't well, and she shouldn't pressure him. But she had to know what was going on, for all their sakes.

"I really need to talk to you today. About the merger. I understand you met with Nick O'Neill this morning."

She watched him, but not the flicker of an eyelash betrayed anything.

"That's correct." His mouth looked suddenly as if he'd tasted something sour. "I could hardly expect to get through this merger without meeting him, so it seemed advisable to get it over with now."

"Did it accomplish what you hoped?" She so seldom questioned her father-in-law about anything that the very act of doing so gave her a queasy sensation in the pit of her stomach. For the boys, she reminded herself.

He shot her a faintly surprised look. "I would say so." He smiled thinly. "He may have a certain importance in Ex Corp's eyes, but in Mannington he's still the same person he once was."

"He's changed." The words came out before she had a chance to think they may be unwise.

Her father-in-law lifted an eyebrow. "You think so? Of course, you knew him far better than I. And you've seen much more of him since he's been back."

She stiffened. "That was your idea, you'll recall. You asked me to shepherd him through the merger process."

"I didn't ask you to have dinner with him at the fair." He leaned forward suddenly. "Or to walk home from church with him."

She was sure she flushed at the memory of what had followed that dinner at the fair. She wasn't going to think about that kiss, not at all, and certainly not when she was in the same room with her father-in-law. Besides, she and Nick had both agreed it was a mistake.

Not exactly, some part of her mind argued. Nick never agreed to that.

Well, he'd agreed that they were right to part, so it amounted to the same thing. And she would not let herself feel that pang around her heart at the thought.

Aware that her father-in-law was watching her, she tried to smile. "Since I'm working with him every day and he's living in the house next door, he's fairly difficult to ignore. I have to be polite when we meet."

"As long as that's all it is."

"Of course it is." She couldn't remember ever speaking to him so sharply. "I'm not fifteen any longer, and I'm well aware of my responsibilities. To the company and to my children."

He let the silence draw out for a moment, then steepled his fingers, frowning at them. "That reminds me of something I wanted to mention to you."

Not anything more about Nick, she hoped.

"Given the surgery my doctor insists upon, I've decided it's time to update my will."

"That can't be necessary. You're going to be fine."

He waved away the protest. "I believe so, but it's still as well to have everything in order. I haven't done anything about it since Jimmy's death." The skin around his eyes seemed to draw tighter.

She clasped her hands together in her lap. She'd never thought about her father-in-law's legacy other than to assume that someday his property would go to the boys. He didn't have any other relatives.

"I've given this a lot of thought, Emily." His gaze bored into her. "I'm sure that Jimmy left you and the boys quite comfortably situated, and of course there are the trusts for their educations."

"Of course," she murmured, wanting to ease away from the delicate subject of Jimmy's estate.

"I suppose some people would say I should divide everything among the three of you."

She looked up, startled. "That's not necessary."

"I'm glad you feel that way, because I don't intend to do that." His fingers pressed against each other. "I've weighed this carefully, and I dislike the idea of having my heritage split up. Therefore I've decided to leave my estate solely to my eldest grandson, Trey."

Chapter Ten

Weariness seeped through Emily as she turned into her street at the end of the day. Thank goodness the car had only needed a new battery, which hadn't been a great expense and was easily taken care of. Unfortunately she couldn't say the same for her latest assignment from her father-in-law. Apparently her father-in-law hadn't realized, when he'd casually said she'd pull together the final tax statements for Nick, just how time-consuming that would be. Finance wasn't her strong suit, and probably just about anyone would have done it more quickly.

It hadn't helped that she'd been still in a state of shock at James's unexpected announcement. She bit her lip, frowning absently at the tree-lined street. She'd always assumed, when she'd thought about it at all, that the twins would share equally in whatever their grandfather chose to leave them. This idea of his to leave everything to Trey had shaken her.

If Jimmy were here, maybe he'd have been able to make his father see how unfair that was. But if Jimmy were here, the problem wouldn't have arisen.

She'd tried to talk with James, but he wouldn't listen. It was his estate; he'd leave it as he decided. When she'd persisted, he'd pleaded fatigue, ushering her out of the office so he could rest.

She rubbed at the frown line between her brows. Somehow she had to make James see that this plan of his was as unfair to Trey as it was to David.

At least the boys would be at soccer practice for another half hour. She pulled into the driveway and cut the motor. She had time to change her clothes, start supper and somehow shake off the cloud that seemed to have hung over her since the moment she walked into the mill this morning.

But when she reached the front door, she realized her calculations had been off. The door was unlocked, the boys' backpacks lay on the sofa and the smell of something cooking emanated from the kitchen.

"Trey! David!" She hurried toward the odor. The twins shouldn't have been home this early, and certainly not home alone. And they knew better than to turn the stove on when she wasn't here. "What are you doing? You shouldn't…"

The words died in her throat. Nick, the sleeves of his dress shirt rolled to his elbows, stood at her stove, flipping something with a spatula. David was setting the table, while Trey rooted around in the refrigerator. They stared at her with looks ranging from wary to guilty.

"Well." She dropped her bag on the counter, giving her heartbeat time to return to normal. "What's going on here? Why aren't you boys at soccer practice?"

"Practice was canceled, Mommy." David's glance said he knew they'd taken a few liberties with her standard orders for what to do in that case. "Coach couldn't be there."

She focused on her sons. She'd deal with them first, before she took up the troubling question of what Nick was doing in her kitchen. "And what are you supposed to do if that happens?"

David studied the floral border of the plate he held. "Call you," he said in a small voice.

"But Brett's dad said he'd give us a ride home," Trey said, shutting the refrigerator door. "So we thought we should save you a trip," he added righteously.

"We thought you'd be home."

"But when you weren't we did just what you always told us to do." Trey looked as if he expected a commendation. "We went to a neighbor."

Nick definitely wasn't the neighbor she'd had in mind. She gave him a cautious smile. "I guess that explains why you're here." After the way they'd parted, this was the last thing she'd expected. Why, oh why, couldn't the boys have gone to elderly Mrs. Sanford's house instead?

"Guess it does." Nick's look didn't give anything away. Maybe he was remembering that bitter conversation, too.

"Thank you." She stared at the griddle, on which Nick was cooking French toast. "I appreciate your keeping an eye on the boys, but you certainly didn't need to cook for them. They could have just had a snack until I got home."

He shook his head, a smile finally creeping across his face. "You've forgotten how hungry boys get at that age. These two guys assured me they were starved."

Emily divided a glare between her sons. "You should have ignored them."

"I couldn't do that." He flipped a piece of French toast with an expert hand. "Besides, I knew you'd come home tired and hungry. It didn't seem fair you'd have to start cooking the minute you got in."

Some of her wariness dissolved in the face of his apparent good humor. If he could ignore what had happened earlier, so could she.

"That's what I do every day."

"Not today," he said. He sent her a sidelong glance, lips curving in a slight smile, black hair tumbling onto his forehead as he bent over the stove. "Unless you don't trust my cooking."

"I didn't know you could." Since there didn't seem

to be anything she could do about this situation, short of being rude, she'd have to accept it.

"Every man should know how to cook. That's what I was just telling these guys." He glanced at Trey. "Plate for the toast, please?"

"Right here." Trey held the plate carefully with both hands as Nick forked golden-brown slices onto it. The aroma filled the kitchen, teasingly reminding Emily that she hadn't had any appetite for lunch.

"Smells good." She started for the refrigerator. "I'll just…"

Nick stepped in front of her, blocking her path. His sudden closeness robbed her of breath.

"You'll just sit down and relax." He pulled out a chair. "We men are in charge tonight. You get to sit and be served."

The argument she was about to make slipped away at his teasing glance. "If you insist."

"We do," Trey said, grinning. "We're the chefs, Mom."

She slid into the chair, very aware of Nick's hands holding it, brushing her shoulders as he pushed it in. Stop it, she told herself firmly. Stop thinking about how good it feels to have Nick here.

Trey deposited the steaming plate of French toast on the table, then scurried to help David fill the water glasses. When an ice cube skittered across the floor she made an automatic movement, then subsided at Nick's warning glance. The guys were in charge.

"So every male should know how to cook, hmm? Where did you learn?"

"Here and there. I learned to cook Cajun in New Orleans and the best way to fix shrimp when I worked in South Carolina. The winter I did a job in New England, I mastered chowder."

"Wow!" Trey's eyes widened. "You've been lots of places. We've never been anywhere."

"We went to Washington on the Cub Scout trip," David corrected. "And Mom took us to the beach last summer and to Virginia to see our second cousins."

"Yes, but we never lived anywhere else," Trey said. "Not like Nick."

"There's nothing wrong with living in Manning ton." She made her voice firm and tried not to glance toward Nick. He undoubtedly had other ideas about that.

"Is this okay, Nick?" David gestured to the table, and then he and Trey looked up at him. They wore identical expressions that showed how eager they were to please him.

Something gripped her heart, tightening painfully. There again was the gap she could never fill, no matter how she tried. The twins needed a man to look up to, and right now that man was Nick.

It couldn't be. The bittersweet knowledge filled her. Nick, no matter how much the twins liked and admired him, could never fill that gap. Even if every-thing else that stood between them vanished overnight, she'd still know that sooner or later—probably sooner—he'd go away again.

Nick slid into a chair, telling himself he should go. Emily was home now, and there was really no excuse for him to hang around.

He reached for a piece of French toast, then paused when Trey, next to him, extended his hand.

"We always hold hands while we say the blessing," Trey said.

He took the small hand in his, then turned to his other side. Emily's smile seemed a little strained, but she put her hand in his. He closed his fingers around it in a firm clasp and bowed his head.

"It's your turn, Trey," Emily prompted.

"Thank you, God, for the food we have to eat. And bless Nick. He cooked it. Amen."

He discovered that there was a lump in his throat. Had he ever been mentioned in a boy's prayer before? It seemed doubtful.

When he'd realized Trey and David were at his door an hour ago, his first thought was to tell them to go home. With the black memories raised earlier by their grandfather still in his mind, he didn't want to be around them. But then Trey had explained that their mother wasn't home, and David had looked so bereft, that he'd promptly forgotten all about their grandfather. He'd experienced a protective urge so strong it should have come with a warning label.

So here he was, having supper with Emily and her twins, when it was probably the worst place in the world for him. He should have stayed away, but how could he when they needed him?

"Mmm, delicious." Trey smiled at him around a mouthful of French toast. "You make the best French toast in the world, Nick."

"Mommy's is good, too," David said loyally. He took a big bite.

Emily smiled. "That's all right. I don't mind giving the French toast crown to Nick."

He realized, suddenly, that the guarded look was gone from her eyes. She accepted him here, in her house, with her children.

Red lights ought to be flashing in front of his eyes. It would be way too easy to get used to this. He should leave.

He kept telling himself that while they ate the food he'd prepared. Then he reminded himself some more while they cleaned up.

When Emily insisted she'd do the dishes it was the perfect time to make his excuses and leave. And he would, just as soon as he finished kicking the soccer ball around with the boys.

They really were improving. He watched them jockey for position as they kicked the ball around an obstacle course he'd improvised. Now why on earth should that give him a greater sense of satisfaction than most of the high-powered business deals he'd been in on lately?

"You do it, Nick." Trey kicked the ball toward him, a challenge in his eyes.

"You think I can't?"

"I bet you can't get to the end without us stealing the ball."

With Emily's revelation about Jimmy's gambling fresh in his mind, his stomach roiled at the innocent phrase. He kicked the ball toward the lawn chair that was the first obstacle.

"I won't bet you, but I'll give it a try."

He almost made it. David nipped in at the last obstacle, neatly swiping the ball away before he could gain control.

"All right! Good one, David. Now you give it a try."

He collapsed on the grass, breathing harder than he ought to from this little bit of exercise. Trey flopped down beside him.

"You're doing a good job, Trey." He leaned back on his elbows. "I'll bet Coach plays you a lot the next game."

Trey nodded, watching his brother. David stumbled over the third lawn chair, lost the ball, then recovered it and tried again.

"David's better, too."

"He sure is."

"But he's not as good as I am at soccer." That could

have sounded like bragging, but it didn't. Instead, Trey sounded almost guilty.

"People are good at different things," he said cautiously, not sure what the boy was driving at.

Trey nodded vigorously. "That's what I told him. He's lots better than I am at math."

"What did he say when you told him that?"

Trey stared down at the grass. "He said nobody ever got to be on a team for math. And he'd rather be good at soccer."

He was tempted to say that math might serve them both better in the long run, but he had sense enough to know this conversation wasn't really about math or soccer. "What do you think about it?"

"See, Nick, it's like this." The boy looked up at him, intent, and Nick knew he was about to be entrusted with something important. "Me and David are twins. That's even better than just being brothers. We always did everything together."

Trey stopped, as if he'd just come to a hurdle that was too high to leap.

"So, now that you're getting older, sometimes you want to do different things?"

"I guess." Trey frowned, grappling with the words. "But sometimes maybe we want to do the same things, but one of us is better than the other one. And that makes the other one feel bad. And then the first one— the one that does better—well, he feels bad, too. So he thinks, well, maybe he should, you know, not try so hard."

Once again he was in way over his head with Emily's kids. He recognized a cowardly desire to duck the question, say he had to leave—anything. But the boy was looking at him as if he had all the answers.

"You know, Trey..." Where were the answers to questions like these? He didn't remember having talks like this with his father. He'd just have to wing it. "The way I figure it, everyone's born with some special talents that are just his. Even twins aren't exactly alike that way. I mean, it would be wrong if your mom gave one of you more allowance than the other one. But it's not wrong for one of you to have a talent the other one doesn't."

Trey's forehead wrinkled, but he nodded. "Mommy says God gives everybody special gifts."

He felt uncomfortable heading into theological territory, but he forged ahead. "That's true. So if somebody didn't try to do his best with his special gifts, that would be like saying God didn't know what He was doing."

He was considering each word as if it were part of a legal contract. No, as if it were far more important than a legal contract. How did parents ever figure out the answers to questions like these?

Trey nodded slowly. "So it's okay if one guy is, like, better at one thing than somebody else."

"As long as he doesn't make the mistake of thinking his special gift is more important than anyone else's."

Trey nodded. Then he looked up, and his serious expression dissolved in a smile. "Hey, there's Alison!" He jumped to his feet and ran toward the girl who had the same red hair as her mother, Lorna.

Nick leaned his elbows on his knees. Apparently the advice corner was closed. Had he said the right thing? Maybe he'd never know.

With Alison's arrival, he had a good excuse to stop. The three kids chased each other around the yard with an excess of energy he could only envy. Now it was time to leave.

But Emily had come out and was relaxing on the porch swing. As if drawn by a magnet, he climbed the steps and sat next to her.

"Don't they ever tire out?"

"If they do, they won't admit it while Alison's here." Emily smiled, shaking her head. "Alison is *very* competitive. She always wants to run fastest, climb the highest—you name it. The boys wouldn't want her to think they can't keep up."

At the moment, Alison was hanging upside down from the limb of the tall maple tree. Her long braids dangled. "Bet you can't do this!"

"Bet I can!" Trey scrambled onto the low branch. "See?"

In a moment the three of them hung there, with David looking a bit green.

"You look like three bats, hanging by your tails," Emily called. "Get down, you're making me dizzy."

Nick watched her lovely face as the children plopped down onto the grass. It was filled with love, pride and something else. Worry, he decided. Worry was planting an unaccustomed frown line between her brows.

"What's wrong, Emily?" The words came out abruptly. "You've been worried about something since you got home."

"No, I'm not." Her gaze met his, startled, then slipped away. She studied the bronze chrysanthemums the setting sun turned to flame. "I'm not worried about a thing."

He put his hand over hers where it lay between them on the slats of the swing. "You know, it's a good thing you didn't decide to become an actress. That was really not convincing."

Her eyes met his, half exasperated, half laughing. "I don't know how you do that."

"Old friends," he said, trying to keep it light. "You can never fool them." His fingers tightened. "Look, is it me? I guess I was pretty rough on you this morning. I didn't mean to be, but…"

"But he upset you." She didn't need to spell out who "he" was. "I'm afraid he upset me, too."

"What did he say to you?" He made an effort to keep the words from sounding harsh. If he came on too strongly, she'd never tell him what was bothering her.

She shrugged, frowning. "Nothing. I—I shouldn't have let it upset me so much. He's an old man. He has a right to be a little eccentric if he wants to be."

Something told him to proceed with care. "Just how eccentric is he being?"

"I shouldn't..."

"Anything you tell me won't go any farther, Emily. We're friends, remember?"

He could see the exact moment when the need to confide in someone overcame her.

"He started talking about revising his will." The words spilled out. "He said...he said he didn't want to split things up. He's decided he's going to leave everything just to Trey, because he's the eldest grandchild."

For an instant he couldn't say a word, because rage choked him. If that wasn't typical of that old tyrant, trying to manipulate a pair of children. And maybe it was a good thing he couldn't speak, because if he said what he really thought, Emily would never trust him with a secret again.

He didn't say anything until he was sure his voice was under control. "I wouldn't worry too much." He stroked the back of her hand soothingly as the porch swing creaked back and forth. "He's probably just talking. Anyway, he's a tough old bird. It'll be years before you have to deal with it. He'll change his will a dozen times over before he's done."

"Do you think so?"

There was so much relief in her eyes that he was glad he hadn't given in to the urge to tell her what he really thought.

"Sure." He patted her hand. "That's just what I think."

Actually, what he thought was that it might be a very good thing for Emily and her kids when the mill closed. That would end Carmichael's obsession, and in the long run it would set them all free of it. Trouble was, he didn't think Emily would see it that way.

"Hey, everybody!"

Mandy came around the corner of the house, closely followed by Ted. All three kids ran to greet them, the twins tackling Ted's legs like a couple of puppies.

Nick lifted an eyebrow. "Are you running an open house?"

"We do seem to be popular, don't we?" She smiled. "Hi, kids. Come and sit down."

"We can just stay a minute." Mandy plopped down on the porch step, while Ted wrestled on the grass with the twins. "I have to ask you a big favor."

"You want to get out of sitting with the twins?" Emily smiled, as if sure it couldn't be that.

"You know I love the guys." Mandy grinned. "Besides, I need the money. I'm saving up for a new dress for the Harvest Ball."

"I remember."

She was probably talking about the dress Mandy

wanted, but that wasn't what leaped into Nick's mind. The words released a flood of memories he hadn't known he had of the Harvest Ball they'd attended together. Emily had worn a pale peach dress, and she'd looked like an angel. He'd thought he was the luckiest guy in the world when she accepted his class ring that night.

"Well, anyway, the dance is Saturday, and we have a little bit of a problem." Mandy approached whatever it was carefully. "You see, some of our chaperons canceled out. So we thought—we hoped—maybe you'd be a chaperon. Please, Emily?"

He could feel Emily's reluctance as if it radiated from her skin. And he knew why. He knew she was remembering just what he was. Their dance, and its bitter aftermath.

He felt her take a breath. "Yes, of course I'll help, if you really need me."

"Oh, wow, that's great!" Mandy clasped her hands together. "Thank you so much."

Emily was carefully not looking at him. "It will be fun," she said without much conviction in her voice.

Mandy swung toward him. "What about you, Mr. O'Neill? We need another male chaperon, too. Will you do it?"

The swing stopped moving as Emily seemed to freeze. She wanted him to say no, he could sense it. She expected him to say no. He should say no.

"Sure, Mandy. Sounds great. Count me in."

Chapter Eleven

"Lorna, I do not need a new dress." Emily stopped on the sidewalk outside the Fashion Flair dress shop, trying to dig in her heels.

"It won't hurt to look." Lorna nudged her toward the door. "Come on, we'll just look."

Trying to stop Lorna from going into a dress shop was like trying to stop a bulldozer from ripping up the earth.

She shook her arm free from Lorna's grip. "All right, you win. I give up. I'll look just for a minute."

Lorna laughed, leading her into the lightly scented atmosphere. "Admit it. You want a new dress for the Harvest Ball."

"I'm not admitting any such thing. I told you, I don't need a new dress."

"Right." Lorna piloted her past the racks of casual clothes toward the rear of the store. "And what exactly are you planning to wear?"

"Why should I get dressed up at all? This dance is for the high school kids. Who cares what the chaperons wear?" An image flashed through her mind before she could stop it: herself, breathless with excitement at her first big dance, and Nick, handsome in a dark suit.

Lorna shot her a skeptical look. "You know perfectly well Mrs. Adams will be there. She's been wearing that lilac lace dress to every dance she's chaperoned for the last thirty years. You can't let her down by going in slacks."

"I didn't intend to wear slacks. I thought my navy suit…"

"Your navy suit is fine for church. It's not right for a dance." Lorna halted in front of a rack of dresses and smiled at the hovering salesclerk. "We're interested in something dressy."

"We're just looking," Emily said firmly. "All right, not my navy suit. What's wrong with my black dress, then?"

Lorna lifted a scornful eyebrow. "You look ready for a rest cure when you wear black—you know that. Something bright, that's what you need." She ruffled through the rack of dresses.

"I can't afford something new right now."

"Everything's on sale this week," the clerk pointed out helpfully. "Twenty percent off."

They were ganging up on her. She flipped through the dresses, trying to look as if she didn't like anything. That was the way her whole week had been going. First Mandy, with her insistence on involving her in this ridiculous chaperoning thing. And then Nick.

Why on earth had he said yes? She'd think chaperoning a high school dance would be the last thing he'd want to do on a Saturday night. Especially since...

She slammed the door of her mind on those memories. Maybe she couldn't keep them from coming back in her dreams, but she didn't have to let them in during the day.

Each time she'd mentioned the possibility of getting out of this commitment to Nick, he'd smiled and said he was looking forward to it.

"You've been staring at that black dress way too long, Emily." Lorna said, removing the hanger from her hand. "I told you, no black." She took a second look at Emily's face. "What's wrong?"

"Nothing." Emily glanced toward the clerk, but the woman had moved off to attend to another customer who actually planned on buying something. "Everything. If you think it's been fun, playing intermediary between Nick and my father-in-law while this merger goes through, you're crazy."

Lorna wrinkled her nose. "Guess that would be a problem. How's everything going, anyway?"

"Okay, I guess." She wished she had a better handle on the legal jargon Nick tossed around so easily. She'd had the feeling all week that the merger had taken on a life of its own, spinning out of control. "The preliminary papers have been signed. Now we have to get through the transition with the rest of Ex Corp's team next week. I just wish James would—"

She stopped, remembering that she wasn't free to confide in anyone, not even Lorna, about her father-in-law's illness.

"Would what?"

"Nothing." She pulled a lavender suit from the rack. "What do you think of this?"

"I think you'd look as if you were competing with Mrs. Adams." Lorna shoved the suit back. "Come on, get serious. You have to find a dress that will knock Nick's eyes out."

"I'm not interested in knocking Nick's eyes out." She tried for a dignified tone.

Lorna grinned. "Sure you are. The man is drop-dead gorgeous. You have to at least look like you belong together."

"We don't belong together." The denial came out quickly.

"You know what I mean." Lorna frowned at an aqua knit. "You can't be more casual than he is." Then she turned the frown on Emily. "Or are you really thinking that you do belong together?"

"Of course not!"

Lorna blinked at the vehemence in her voice. "You don't have to bite my head off. I mean, it wouldn't be such a bad thing, would it?"

"Bad?" Her voice rose, and she controlled it. "I can't get involved with Nick O'Neill!"

"Seems to me you already are sort of involved. I mean, you're certainly seeing a lot of him. And the kids adore him." She grinned. "Even Alison, and she's hard to please."

"That's just business." Emily tried not to think about Nick flipping French toast in her kitchen or kissing her under the trees at the fairgrounds.

"I always did think you two looked great together." Lorna's face lit with mischief.

She rolled her eyes. "Please. We're not in high school anymore."

"That doesn't mean you can't enjoy being with him. Or is this because of that old stuff about his father?"

Nick didn't consider it old stuff, and the insight she'd had into the depth of his bitterness still shook her. "It's not about that—not for me. But you know how people talk."

"Let them talk," Lorna said. "For crying out loud, Emily, you have to do what your heart tells you once in a while." She yanked a dress from the rack. "There!" Her voice filled with satisfaction. "This is the perfect dress."

Emily stared at the peach silk, then reached out to let it ripple through her fingers. If she did what her heart told her, she'd buy it, even if she had to go without lunches for a month. If she did what her heart told her about Nick, just where would that lead her?

* * *

Nick stared at himself in the mirror and adjusted his tie. He frowned at it. Too dark? Maybe so. He pulled it off with an abrupt motion and snatched another one from the tie rack.

Better, he thought, tying it, then smoothing it down. Now, just why did he care what tie he wore to this ridiculous dance? And how had he let himself get talked into it, anyway?

Not that Mandy had done much talking. One thought of the night he and Emily had danced at the Harvest Ball, and he'd signed himself up. He'd tell himself he regretted it, but the trouble was he didn't. Sooner or later all this would come crashing in on him, but at least he'd have had this one evening with Emily.

The telephone rang as he headed for the door, and he snatched it up with an impatient hand. "O'Neill."

"About time I caught up with you." Josh didn't sound quite as jovial as usual. "I thought you were going to call in today."

"Sorry." He bit off the word. "I've been busy."

"That's what Ex Corp expects, isn't it?" There was a slight warning in the words. "That you're busy and producing results."

It didn't take a genius to figure out the pressure was on. "Everything's moving about the way we expected. The preliminary papers are signed. Doesn't Donaldson trust me?"

Josh gave what might have been a laugh, but it didn't sound amused. "Donaldson doesn't trust anyone. You should know that by now. Somehow he's gotten the idea that you're dragging your feet on this one."

"That's ridiculous." His fingers tightened on the receiver. Was it? Or was Donaldson right for once? "This kind of job takes time. You can't rush people in a small town like this one, especially not in family-owned companies."

"Tell that to Donaldson."

"If necessary, I will."

"Okay, okay, you don't need to jump through the phone at me. Just thought I'd drop a little word of warning, that's all. The man's getting restless."

"He needn't. Everything is on track, and your team will be here next week to do the final transition. If Donaldson doubts it, tell him I said so."

"Sure, I will." Josh sounded placating. "Listen, I know the merger means as much to you as it does to us."

In a weak moment he'd confided in Josh about his father. He'd been regretting it ever since.

"This is business." He kept his voice crisp. "I'm keeping my personal life out of it."

He hung up, wondering if he could really say that about himself anymore. For years he'd driven straight toward success, straight toward a goal of proving that everyone who'd looked down on him was wrong. The goal had taken every ounce of energy, every minute of time. He'd kept his eyes fixed on it, and if life had something else to offer, he hadn't missed it.

Until he came back to Mannington. He adjusted his tie again, knowing full well it didn't need adjusting. Being here had churned up things inside him that were better ignored. This town had an effect on him. This town, and Emily.

"That town…" His father's voice seemed to echo in his mind, from somewhere in the past. *"That town, those people, they hated us."*

He could almost feel his father's heavy hand on his shoulder, could almost smell the scent of failure.

"People like that use people like us. Don't you forget, Nick. They use people like us and then they throw us away."

His mouth tightened. His father had been drinking at the time; he remembered that if he didn't remember anything else. But that didn't mean what he said wasn't true. And maybe he'd better concentrate on business and forget everything else.

His militant state of mind lasted while he drove around the block to the front of Emily's house, while he walked to the door and rang the bell.

Trey and David pulled the door open, four hands grasping the knob, both boys grinning. Mrs. Wilson, an elderly neighbor, stood in the kitchen doorway and gave Nick a wave. She was obviously there to baby-sit, and Nick reminded himself to find some diplomatic way to pay for her services.

"Hi, Nick. Mom's ready to go," the boys chorused.

He looked past the twins into the room. Emily was coming down the stairs. The overhead light shone on her golden-brown hair, and the dress she wore was the color of peaches.

It was as if he'd taken a surprise punch in the stomach. All of a sudden he was sixteen again, his breath taken away by the fact that he was going to the dance with the girl he loved.

Nick hadn't said a word since they left the house. Emily stole a sideways glance at him across the front seat of the car.

His hands rested easily on the steering wheel, as if he hadn't a care in the world. But he kept his gaze on the road as if he were alone in the car. Was he having regrets at agreeing to do this?

Well, she'd given him plenty of opportunities to cancel out, and he hadn't taken them. So it was his own fault, and if he didn't want to talk, neither did she.

Emily stared resolutely out at the dark street. Autumn fog settled into the valley. It drifted across the road and formed golden halos around the street lamps. Once on a night like this, they'd started for the Harvest Ball together, and she'd been the happiest she'd ever been in her life.

But she wasn't fifteen any longer, and she didn't have fanciful dreams of what her life would be. A dance was just a dance, nothing magical about it. They'd go; they'd watch the kids and drink fruit punch. Then Nick would drop her at her door and that would be the end of it.

That firm resolution lasted until the moment they walked into the high school gym, already crowded with teenagers. Being fashionably late had never caught on in Mannington. A local band played with more enthusiasm than expertise, but no one seemed to care.

"Hasn't changed much, has it?" Nick paused beside her, his hand clasping her elbow, and she had to remind herself what year it was.

"I guess there's not all that much you can do differently with a harvest theme." The predictable corn stalks were piled in the corners, and paper-cut autumn leaves dangled from the ceiling. "Do you remember the fuss over that glass ball?"

"Do I ever." Nick smiled, and for the first time she thought he looked relaxed. A harvest moon hung from the mirrored ball Nick's class had bought over the objections of the class advisor, who'd thought they should buy something educational. "I didn't think Mrs. Adams would ever forgive us."

"She hasn't." Emily smiled up at him. "She'll probably mention it when she sees you."

"You don't mean to say she's still chaperoning

dances—the woman must be a hundred and two by now."

A giggle escaped her. "That's probably what the kids think about us."

"They can't possibly." His eyes warmed as he smiled at her. "You don't look a day over fifteen."

She could feel the warmth in her cheeks. It was too much to hope Nick didn't see the effect. "Just wait. By the time this night is over we'll feel every year. Spending the evening with a crowd of teenagers does that."

"Here you are, sir." A gangly boy she didn't immediately recognize slid to a stop next to Nick and held out a yellow mum. "The chaperons all get flowers. There's punch on the table, and if you get tired, we've put some chairs over by the door to the boys' locker room."

She choked back a laugh at the expression on Nick's face.

"Thanks," he said evenly. "If we get tired, we'll take advantage of that. But I think we'll let the lady wear the flower."

The boy blushed. "That's what I meant… I mean, I thought you'd want to pin it on." He looked from Nick to Emily, and his blush deepened. "Have a good time." He made a fast escape.

"You're right. They do think we're a hundred and two." Nick held out the flower, looking at the neckline of her dress.

"I'll just carry it," she said quickly. "The pin might snag the silk."

He put it in her hand, his fingers brushing her wrist lightly. Warmth radiated from his touch, generating a flood of memories, and she drew back quickly, pulse pounding.

He stood looking down at her for a moment, eyes questioning under those dark brows. Then he held out his hand. "I know how to show them we're not as old as all that. Let's dance."

Sheer panic ricocheted through her at the thought of being in Nick's arms. That was the one thing she couldn't do, not if she wanted to keep the memories at bay.

"Chaperons don't dance," she said, trying to sound horrified at the thought. "Mrs. Adams would have us run out of town."

As soon as the words were out, she wanted them back. A muscle tightened infinitesimally in Nick's jaw, but his expression didn't change. "I've already done that, thanks." He took her arm. "Maybe we'd better find the other chaperons and check in."

Pain wrapped around her heart. This was an impossible situation. The whole evening was an emotional minefield, ready to explode at the slightest wrong word or touch. She should have gotten out of this if she'd had to sprain an ankle to do it.

Mrs. Adams presided at the punch table, casting an experienced gaze across the gym as she ladled bright pink liquid into paper cups. She turned a firm expression on Nick and Emily. Her square, ruddy face looked just the same as it had for the last twenty years.

"I expected you people here earlier to receive your assignments."

Emily felt as if she'd turned up late for class without her homework. "I'm sorry, Mrs. Adams. You remember Nick O'Neill, don't you?"

"I never forget a student." She turned a steady look on Nick. "Glad to hear you're succeeding in business. Does that mean you remember some of the calculus you learned from me?"

"Yes, ma'am." He held out his hand, giving her the smile that would charm a statue off its pedestal. "I had the best grounding of anyone in my college class."

While Mrs. Adams interrogated Nick on where he'd gone to college and when he'd received his M.B.A., Emily let her gaze wander across the crowded dance floor. There was Mandy, looking up at Ted with stars in her eyes.

The sight seemed to pierce Emily's heart. She'd looked like that once, danced like that under these same paper decorations and thought she was dancing on clouds.

Nick's hand brushed her arm as he gestured, and her heart lurched. It was probably a very good thing she'd made it clear to Nick she wouldn't be dancing tonight.

The band swung into a slow, romantic ballad, and she stiffened. If he asked her again…

Nick turned to Mrs. Adams and held out his hand in invitation. "Mrs. Adams, may I have this dance? For old times' sake?"

Mrs. Adams's face flushed the color of an old brick. Then she smiled, took his hand and walked onto the dance floor.

Emily discovered she was gaping and closed her mouth. Of all the sly maneuvers! Nick had just neatly cut the feet from under her every objection. Well, he wasn't going to find it that easy. She'd find some way to avoid dancing with him, because if she didn't... She realized she didn't want to finish that thought.

Mrs. Adams wore the softest smile Emily had ever seen on her when they returned from the dance floor.

"You mentioned our assignments?" Emily said quickly, before the situation could get even further beyond her control.

"Oh, yes." Mrs. Adams resumed her drill sergeant manner. "Keep circulating. Check the rest rooms every fifteen minutes. There's no smoking allowed. And you'd better walk out onto the breezeway a few times, just to make sure no one's out there. The rule is that once they leave the dance, they have to leave school grounds."

"I remember." Unfortunately she also remembered that Nick had stolen a kiss or two on that breezeway.

She raised her eyes for an unguarded moment to find him looking at her, that memory as vivid between them as if it had flashed onto a movie screen. Her heart thumped erratically, and she was fifteen again, feeling Nick's lips on hers.

Mrs. Adams went back to the punch table, and Nick held out his hand to her.

"I think I'd better check the girls' rest room," she said quickly.

Nick lifted an eyebrow, his gaze saying he knew exactly why she wanted to do it at this moment. "I'd ask you to dance, but duty comes first. I'll meet you back here."

She nodded and hurried through the crowd as if someone were chasing her.

The corridor outside the gym was empty. Heels clicking on the tile floor, she crossed to the rest room door and pulled it open.

No one was in the outer lounge, and Mrs. Adams would be relieved to know she didn't smell any smoke. She paused, seeing her own image staring back at her from the mirror.

Her cheeks were flushed, and she pressed both hands to them. She could always use the excuse that it was stuffy in here, but...

"And I told her I was going out with Tim, and you wouldn't believe what she said."

The girl's voice, drifting over the partition, caught off guard. She'd thought the room was empty.

"You can't go out with him." The other young voice sounded determined. "Just think what people will say."

Just think what people will say. She didn't hear the girl's answer, because the words kept vibrating in her mind. *Just think what people will say.* How many times had her father said that to her when she was growing up? He'd constantly impressed upon her the need to behave in a manner befitting his daughter and, good girl that she was, she'd obeyed. Even when it came to Nick.

The rest room walls seemed to be closing in on her. She hurried out, then along the hall to the glass doors leading onto the breezeway. She had to get outside, breathe some cool air, compose herself before she could think about going back inside and facing Nick again.

The cool night air fanned her as she stepped outside, and the closing door shut off the sound of music and laughter from the gym. No teenagers lingered in the shadows, waiting to be chased away.

She took a deep breath, then another. This was silly. Why had she let herself become so panic-stricken? No one cared anymore why she'd done or not done something when she was a teenager. Nick had said she'd been right when she refused to go away with him. Averted a disaster, that was what he'd said. It didn't matter at all that she'd done the right thing for the wrong reason.

She'd go back in and...

The door opened, letting a burst of music out on the cool air, then closed again. She knew, without turning around, that it was Nick.

He stopped behind her. "What are you doing out here?" He put his hands on her arms. "Besides freezing."

Her skin warmed at his touch, and she wanted to lean back against him.

"I just…" The words died as he gently turned her to face him.

"Running away?" His voice was softly mocking, but the glow of the streetlight showed her his face, and it wasn't mocking at all.

She shook her head, not finding any words.

Nick's hand lifted slowly. He touched her cheek, his fingertips gliding across the skin, warming it. Then, inevitably, his lips met hers.

Her arms went around him, drawing him even closer. Home. She'd come home from a long, lonely journey. She was safe in his arms, her heart so full it might burst, and she never wanted to be away from him again.

Nick pressed his cheek to hers. "Emily." Her name came out on a sigh. He drew back a little. "They say you never forget your first love. I guess they're right."

She tried to arrange her lips in a smile, but they didn't seem to cooperate. Was that all it was to him? A reminiscence? A trip down memory lane while he was back in the old hometown?

"We'd better go back inside." That didn't come out as cool and composed as she'd have liked, but he didn't seem to notice.

He nodded. "Mrs. Adams will be after us for setting a bad example."

He held the door open for her, and she went through it as the music surrounded them again. She might as well not have worried about whether or not she'd dance with Nick tonight, because it hadn't mattered in the least. It hadn't taken a dance to show her that she was falling in love with Nick O'Neill all over again. And Emily knew she was going to get hurt just as she had the last time.

Chapter Twelve

That wave of panic swept over her again as they went back into the crowded room. Love? She couldn't possibly be thinking that, not about Nick. Not when she knew, beyond any possibility of doubt, that it could never be.

Lord, why did You bring him back here again? What am I going to do?

If there was an answer, she didn't hear it.

She clenched her hands, pressing them against the silk of her skirt. If something couldn't be, then you didn't admit it. Not to herself, and certainly not to Nick. He must never know this was anything more to her than it was to him. So she'd keep smiling, keep it light and get through the rest of the evening as best she could.

"Is everything all right, Emily?" Mrs. Adams's wise old eyes seemed to see through her.

She managed a smile. "Of course." She watched Nick, who was working his way through the crowd toward the stage. His broad-shouldered figure made the high school boys look like children, and he cleaved a path with no effort at all.

"Seems to have turned out pretty well." Mrs. Adams apparently had no difficulty in following Emily's train of thought. "After a rocky start."

"Yes." She really didn't want to discuss Nick with Mrs. Adams or anyone else until she'd had a chance to get her own thinking straightened out.

"Funny, his coming back here now." Mrs. Adams wasn't discouraged by the monosyllable, it seemed. "I'd think this is the last place he'd want to be. Unless, of course, he has a special reason...." Her gaze probed Emily, making Emily feel like a worm being eyed by a hungry robin.

"I'd better make my rounds again," she said, and fled.

Nick caught up with her as she reached the edge of the dance floor.

"Just the person I was looking for." He took her hand. "I think this dance is mine, isn't it?"

The loud, fast song blared in her ears. "Not with this music. Maybe Mandy can dance to this stuff, but I can't."

Nick smiled as the number came to an abrupt end. "I predict they'll play something you like."

The band swung into a ballad, and Nick drew her

onto the dance floor. Her breath caught as his arm went around her waist.

Light, remember? Keep it light.

"Now why do I think you set this up?"

A smile tugged at Nick's lips. "It only cost me five bucks." He twirled her around, drawing her a bit closer. "I think it was worth it to dance with the prettiest woman in the room."

"That's not saying a lot, since every other female is either under seventeen or over sixty."

His arm tightened, and suddenly her temple was against his cheek. If he tried, he'd be able to feel her pulse pounding.

"It wouldn't matter if the room were filled with cover models." His voice was soft, and his breath stirred her hair. "You'd still be the prettiest."

Another couple bumped them, and Nick turned her, his movement as protective as if she were made of glass. Everything about the moment, from the smooth wool of his coat to the hard muscle underneath, from the paper leaves to the shimmering glass ball, engraved itself on her heart. She wanted to hold this little piece of time safe, forever.

The rest of the evening passed in the same way. They watched the kids; they talked to the other chaperons. They danced again, and she found she was smiling constantly.

She seemed to be moving in a dream, and yet it was

a dream where all the edges were sharp and clear. The sort of dream you never forgot.

When Nick drew the car up in front of the house, she knew it was time for the dream to end. She grasped the door handle.

"You don't have to see me in, Nick."

He didn't answer, just came around the car to open the door and help her out as ceremoniously as if she were a princess alighting from a coach. His fingers tightened on hers.

"I always escort the lady to her door."

"Well, I…" The rest of the objection vanished when he put his arm around her. She had a thoroughly demoralizing need to lean against his strong shoulder.

"Come on, Emily." His voice was low. "It's not as if I never walked you home before."

Keep it light, remember?

"Seems to me we were always about one second ahead of my curfew." She glanced up and saw his smile in the golden glow of the street lamp.

"Your sons don't give you a curfew, do they?"

"No, but the baby-sitter's meter is running."

Just a few more steps, and she could close the door behind her and drop the illusion that this was a casual, meaningless evening between two old friends.

"I'll pay for the extra minutes."

Nick stopped, drawing her to a stop, too. They stood in the shadow of the overgrown lilac bush, between the circle of light cast by the street lamp and that of her porch light.

"I'd better go in." The words came out on a breathless whisper.

"Not yet." Nick ran his fingers through her hair, then along the line of her jaw. Her skin warmed; her breath caught. "We used to stop under the willow tree in your front yard for a good-night kiss. Don't you remember?"

She ought to say no but she couldn't when Nick's touch set every nerve ending tingling. "I remember."

"I didn't want your father to see us kiss." His lips came closer to hers. "Now I don't want your sons to see it."

"Are we going to kiss?" She tried desperately to keep it light.

"Definitely." Amusement threaded Nick's voice.

Then his lips found hers, and everything else vanished in the warmth of his kiss. She nestled closer, feeling the strength of his arms around her as the sidewalk rocked beneath her feet.

An eternity later his lips moved to her cheek, and she felt his breath against her skin. "Emily." He leaned back a little, still holding her, and his gaze met hers. "Spend tomorrow with me. You and the boys."

"I—we have Sunday school and church, then in the evening we have to go to my father-in-law's for dinner…."

"I'll meet you at church, and afterwards we can have the whole afternoon together."

She should say no. She wanted to say yes. Her heart clenched. Nick would leave again soon; that was the way it would be. Surely she could have one lovely afternoon to remember.

She looked up at him and nodded.

"Tomorrow."

The fact that he saw the sun come up was a measure of how much that evening with Emily had disturbed him. Nick stared out the kitchen window at the back of her house. A vagrant breeze took a few more leaves from the maple, sending them groundward in a shower of gold.

Emily, smiling up at him while they danced. Emily, her lips soft under his when they kissed.

That had been a mistake, hadn't it? Trouble was, it didn't feel like a mistake. It felt right. It felt like something that had been delayed far too long, but now was set right at last.

He put down the mug of coffee he'd been nursing. Time to face facts. By the end of this week, his business in Mannington would be finished, and he'd be leaving. He wouldn't see Emily or her kids again.

That was all the more reason to have one last time with them. One day when they could enjoy each other's company without either the past or the future shadowing it.

How much would Emily enjoy his company once the future of Carmichael Mills was known? Probably not much at all. He could tell himself that it would be best for Emily and her kids in the long run to no longer have the mill hanging around their necks like an albatross. He didn't think she was going to see it that way.

One last day, that was all he'd have. So it might as well start as soon as possible. With a spurt of energy he headed for the door. If Emily wasn't awake yet, it was time she got up.

Wet grass soaked his sneakers, and small leaves clung to them as he crossed the lawns.

Nobody on Emily's street was up this early on a Sunday morning, that was clear. A dog barked once, somewhere in the distance, and then it was quiet again. The sun lifted over the treetops, gilding everything it touched with gold.

No lights showed in her windows, and he didn't see any stirring behind the curtains. If he rang the bell, he'd rouse the whole house.

He searched in the flower bed for a handful of pebbles, feeling like the kid who'd thrown gravel at his love's window for one last good-night. He fingered the pebbles, told himself he was an idiot, and tossed one toward the window of what he guessed was Emily's bedroom.

Nothing. Either she didn't hear, or she wasn't in there. He threw another one.

This time he got results. The curtain ruffled and she

stared down at him, eyes startled. She turned away, then reappeared, fastening a bathrobe at her throat.

He motioned raising the window. She shook her head at him, half smiling, then pushed up the sash.

"What are you doing?" Her whisper floated down to him.

He grinned. "Saying good morning."

"Good morning." She glanced from side to side, as if expecting an irate neighbor to demand they be quiet.

"No good." He shook his head. "I can't say a proper good morning from this distance. Come on out."

"I can't do that." She clutched the robe tighter. "The boys are still asleep, and I'm not even dressed."

"So come out in your robe. No one's going to see you."

"I can't!" She looked shocked at the thought. "For goodness' sake, I can't run around outside in my robe."

"Why not?" He lifted an eyebrow. He suspected he already knew the answer to that one. "Still afraid of what people will think, Emily?"

"I..." Something, maybe a noise behind her, made her turn. Then she turned back toward him, putting her hands on the window frame. "The boys are awake. I have to get them ready for Sunday school." She smiled. "I'll see you at church. You can say good morning there."

That was Emily, too worried about what everyone else thought to think about what she wanted for herself. He shouldn't blame her for that. Maybe it was part of what she needed to survive in a small town.

Later, seated beside Emily and the boys in the sanctuary, it occurred to him that once again Carmichael wasn't in church. That was odd enough to be noteworthy. In fact, he'd only seen the man two or three times in the last week, even though they were finalizing something of crucial importance.

Maybe Carmichael's absence was for the best, given how he felt about the man. As well as how Carmichael felt about him, for that matter. He'd had the distinct impression James could barely stand to be in the same room with him.

It was a good thing the rest of the family didn't feel the same way. David leaned against his arm as the pastor mounted the pulpit, and Trey smiled at him. There was a certain softness to Emily's smile, too, that hadn't been there before. It was as if she'd come to some conclusion about him, or about their relationship.

He fixed his gaze on Reverend Hayes, trying to concentrate. That was safer than thinking about a relationship with Emily that wasn't going to be.

Not that the minister's text was particularly restful, at least not for him. *Bear with each other and forgive whatever grievance you may have against one another.*

His mouth tightened. He'd much rather hear a sermon today about justice, because justice was about to be done. James Carmichael might benefit from hearing that, too.

He listened, mind half on the sermon, half on Emily. No, he had to be honest, his attention was far more on Emily. What would they do today? She'd promised him the afternoon, but it had to be something the boys would enjoy, too.

He broached the subject as soon as they reached her front porch. "Where would you like to go today? You name it."

There was a quick exchange of glances between Emily and the boys, and he could see they'd discussed it already.

"How would you feel about a picnic? It's a gorgeous day, and this nice weather isn't going to last forever."

"We could go to the state park," Trey said.

"And go hiking," David added. "You like to hike, don't you, Nick?"

He hadn't pictured anything quite so energetic as tramping through the woods. "Is that really what you want? We could drive into the city, if you'd rather."

"A picnic sounds great." Emily gave him the smile that would melt a heart of stone. "If that's okay with you."

He touched her hand. "Your choice."

"A picnic, then. We'll change and get the food ready, and meet you back here in about an hour."

"Not quite. You work all week and do the cooking,

too. Today you get a rest. I'll take care of the food." He headed for the car before she could protest. "Back in half an hour."

Actually it took a little longer than that to change his clothes and then stock up on fried chicken and the fixings, but he was soon back at Emily's. The twins were hanging on the porch rail and came running to the car at the sight of him.

"Mom, come on!" Trey shouted. "Nick's here."

He opened the car door for the boys to pile into the back. If Emily hoped to keep their little excursion from the neighbors, it wasn't going to work.

She came hurrying out the door, a red thermos jug swinging from one hand. At his look, she gave an apologetic smile.

"I thought you might not remember drinks, and the refreshment stand at the park is so expensive."

Emily shouldn't have to worry about the cost of soft drinks for her kids. An irrational anger toward Jimmy filled him. Jimmy shouldn't have left her in this position, dependent on his father and unable to tell him what she needed. He'd like to tell the old man that himself.

But he couldn't. He held the door for Emily, then slipped behind the wheel. She'd made her feelings clear, and he respected that. He checked the twins in the rearview mirror, making sure they both had seat belts fastened. And what he'd said to Emily was true. He'd never want to be the one to destroy the boys' image of their father.

"Ready?" He glanced at Emily, and she nodded. "We're off, then."

Off on their last time together, a little voice in his head insisted. He had to savor every moment and put all thoughts of business aside. Once Emily and the twins knew what was going to happen to the mill, they wouldn't want to be within twenty yards of him. This time when he went away, he wouldn't be coming back.

"Thank you, Mrs. Carson, that will be all."

Emily watched as her father-in-law's housekeeper slipped through the swinging door to the kitchen. James Carmichael had to be the last person in town to have a full-time housekeeper. She couldn't imagine what he'd do without Mrs. Carson to keep him in order and produce meals like the one they'd just finished.

Trey caught her eye and grinned at the remains of the coq au vin on his plate. She suppressed a return smile, knowing exactly what he was thinking. He'd enjoyed that cold fried chicken at the park with Nick far more than the elaborate meal at his grandfather's table.

At least, thank goodness, they'd gotten through this with no spills. Something about the mahogany table and lace tablecloth usually brought on such nervousness that they seldom got through Sunday night dinner without one or the other twin knocking over the milk.

James cleared his throat, as if about to start a board meeting. She glanced at him, registering his pallor and the way he leaned on the table.

"Would you like us to leave early?" she said impulsively. "I'm sure you're tired, and with the surgery coming up on Tuesday, you need your rest."

He stiffened. "I am not in the least tired. And I particularly want to speak with you and my grandsons about something."

Trey and David immediately looked apprehensive, as if examining their consciences for some misdeed. She discovered she was clenching her fists on the arms of the ornate mahogany chair and deliberately relaxed them. Sunday night dinner was often uncomfortable, but it wasn't an ordeal. She should be happy James wanted his family around him tonight. He'd already told her he didn't want her to come to the hospital once he'd been admitted.

"Is something wrong, Grandfather?" Trey, of course, was the one to muster up the courage to ask.

"Not at all." Her father-in-law looked at him with as much softness as he produced for anyone. He turned his gaze to Emily. "Do they know I'm going into the hospital?"

She nodded. "I thought it best they know ahead of time."

"I see. Well, perhaps that makes it easier." He divided a gaze between the boys, and they seemed to move a little closer together.

"As I told your mother a few days ago, I've been revising my will." His look sharpened. "You do know what a will is, don't you?"

Her heart sank. She'd hoped he'd forgotten this nonsense.

"Sure we do," Trey said, but his expression said he wasn't sure.

"It's a piece of paper where you write down who you want to have what if you die," David explained.

"Maybe we should write one down." Trey wiggled on his seat. "I could say that you get my bike and my soccer ball. But you have to promise—"

"It's highly unlikely that you need a will just now," his grandfather interrupted. "On the other hand… well, let's say that at my age it's important to have your business affairs in order."

She couldn't let this go on. "I really don't think either of the boys need to know this. Why don't we drop the subject?"

James gave her a frosty look. "I have a responsibility to them. I want them to hear my decision from me."

Trey propped his elbows on the table, apparently forgetting tonight's lecture on table manners, delivered in the car on the way over. "What decision, Grandfather?"

"I've decided that I don't want to split up my share of the mill or the other property I own." He frowned. "I don't suppose you'll understand, but I've always believed it's safer to keep property together."

The twins' foreheads wrinkled, as if they were trying their best to follow his statement.

"Well, now." Even James seemed a little uncomfortable under those unblinking stares. "I've made a decision to leave everything to Trey, since he's the elder of the two of you. Do you understand? This doesn't mean I don't care about you, David. But I feel—"

"No."

James stopped, staring at Trey. "What did you say?"

Trey slid off his chair and stood very straight. "No, thank you, sir."

A flush of color came into James's waxen face. "Trey, you don't understand. This is a complex business matter."

"I understand. You want to give me more than you give David. That's not fair. So I don't want it."

She thought her heart might burst with pride in her son. Pride, and something else. Shame, maybe, that Trey had more courage than she did. "Thank you, Trey. I'm proud of you."

"Emily, I don't think—"

For the first time in their relationship she willingly interrupted her father-in-law. "I think Trey has put it very clearly, James. He's old enough to know what's right. And he speaks for all of us."

She stood up. "Now, I'm sure you should be resting." She went briskly around the table and bent to kiss his cheek. "Good night."

Chapter Thirteen

By the time she got the boys into bed, Emily felt as if she'd run twenty miles. Maybe that wasn't surprising, given the emotional content of the weekend. She paced around the downstairs, unable to relax, still feeling the amazing rightness of Trey's standing up to his grandfather.

Jimmy had never done that. For an instant the thought seemed disloyal, but she forced herself to confront it. All his life, Jimmy had lived in fear of disappointing his father, so much so that it practically guaranteed he would.

How surprising it was that Trey would not only oppose his formidable grandfather, but that he would be willing to give up his inheritance rather than treat his brother unfairly. She touched the photo that stood on the phone table, the two boys smiling up at her. Maybe this defined the boundaries of the competition she'd sensed between them lately.

When she'd questioned Trey about it on the way home in the car, he'd been nonchalant. But then, he didn't realize exactly what it was he risked giving up.

And then he'd quoted something Nick had told him—something he'd probably garbled a bit about treating people fairly even while you competed with them. When she'd pushed him on it, he'd just shrugged.

"It was guy stuff, Mom," he'd said.

Guy stuff. A hand seemed to clench her heart at that. Her sons needed a man's guidance. They needed a man to look up to, to talk to about the things they didn't want to bring to her. Somehow, in such a short space of time, Nick had stepped into that role.

She'd seen it when they were together at the park. The boys looked to Nick in a way she hadn't expected—a way that actually gave her a momentary vision of the four of them as a family.

She shouldn't let herself think that way. But she couldn't help it. Hope blossomed in spite of her common sense.

She put her hand on the phone. Nick would like to hear what Trey had done. Even more, she'd like to share it with him. Quickly, before she could think about it too much, she dialed his number.

The phone rang six times, seven. Finally she hung up, then walked to the kitchen window. Nick's house was dark. She felt disappointed out of all proportion to the cause that he wasn't there.

Tomorrow. She'd see him at the mill tomorrow, and she'd tell him then.

There was a different atmosphere at the mill. She could sense it the moment she walked through the door the next day. The heightened tension wafted from Betty, behind the receptionist's desk, who looked unusually efficient and busier than she had in years.

Emily stopped at the counter, lifting her eyebrows. "What's going on?"

Betty put her palm over the receiver of the phone. "They're here," she whispered. "A whole team of people from Ex Corp."

"I see." Well, she'd known the transition team would be arriving this week, but she hadn't expected it so early. They must have come into town last night, and that was why Nick had been out. "Is Mr. O'Neill in his office?"

Betty shrugged. "He went up, but he had a couple of people with him. I don't know where they are right now."

This was a place of business, and she had work to do. She went quickly down the hall toward her office. She definitely shouldn't be thinking about how much she was looking forward to seeing Nick again. Or about how special their afternoon with the boys had been.

She paused outside the office they'd assigned to Nick, but the lights were off. Presumably he was somewhere in the building with the people from Ex Corp.

She turned the knob and went in. She scribbled a quick note, saying she'd like to speak with him, and left it folded on his desk. That certainly wasn't compromising or unprofessional, was it? The only unprofessional thing was the way her hand lingered for a moment on the back of his chair.

Back in her office she switched on the computer and brought up on screen the brochure she'd been working on, but her mind refused to concentrate. She spun her chair, looking out at the mill yard. Probably everyone in the building felt the same distraction right now. Change was in the air.

She picked up the phone. Perhaps Betty knew something by now.

"I understand they've all gone up to Mr. Carmichael's office. I don't know why." Betty sounded disappointed that that particular piece of news had escaped her. "Do you want me to ring there?"

"No, thanks, Betty. I'll just go up myself."

She had every right to go up to her father-in-law's office, after all. And if she happened to catch Nick on his way out...well, that would be a coincidence.

But when she entered the secretary's office, it was clear she'd missed him again. The door to James's office stood open, and it was empty.

"Martha, is my father-in-law around?"

Martha Rand didn't turn from the filing cabinet that seemed to be occupying her attention. "He left a few minutes ago, on his way home."

With his surgery scheduled for the next day, that made sense.

"What about Mr. O'Neill? Has he been here?"

Martha slammed the file drawer, the sound shocking in the quiet office. "He was here." She turned around, and Emily realized that her eyes were red-rimmed from crying.

"Martha!" She took a step toward the woman. "What is it? What's wrong?"

"Don't you know?" Martha looked at her strangely. "Do you really not know?"

A shiver of panic swept down her spine. "Know what? What's going on? Is it James?"

Martha shook her head slowly. "It's the mill. Those people from Ex Corp just announced it. They're closing the mill. Carmichael Mills isn't going to exist any longer."

"I don't like being taken by surprise, that's all." Nick glared across his desk at Josh, still dapper and bright-eyed after the trip from New York last night and an early meeting this morning. "You should have told me you were going to drop the bomb today."

Josh shrugged, leaning back in the padded armchair and inspecting his manicured nails. "Listen, old buddy, what difference does it make when we told them? We both knew it would come out soon."

Nick's hands, pressed against the desktop, clenched into fists. "The difference is that you didn't tell me first, *old buddy*. You made it look as if I'd planned it that way, when I didn't know a thing about it."

"Wake up and smell the coffee." Josh abandoned the casual pose and leaned forward, narrow face intent. "We both knew what was going to happen to Carmichael Mills when the merger went through. It was what you wanted, too, remember?"

"I wanted—" He stopped, knowing what it was he wanted. He wanted to talk to Emily, to explain, to tell her this wasn't about her.

Josh stood. "You wanted what? Revenge? Well, you got it. Be happy."

For an instant he just stared at Josh. The man was right. He'd gotten what he wanted, what he'd come to Mannington to do. So why wasn't it enough?

Emily's face, bright-eyed with laughter over something the twins had done, flashed in his mind. Emily. Emily was the reason the vengeance he'd longed for had turned to ashes in his mouth. He loved her.

The idea was as astonishing as it was true. The truth of it settled into his heart. He loved her. Maybe he'd never stopped loving her. And he had to see her, had to explain...

The door burst open. Emily stood there, her amber eyes blazing, her face white.

Josh looked from Emily to him, then waved his hand in an awkward gesture. "Maybe I'd better…"

"Yes, maybe you had better." He had to talk to Emily, and he certainly couldn't do it with Josh there.

Josh sidled past Emily and closed the door. They were alone.

"Is it true?" Her gaze struck him like a blow.

"Emily, please." He went around the desk toward her, mind racing. How could he make her understand? "Come and sit down."

"I don't want to sit down. Is it true?"

All the softness was gone. This was an Emily he hadn't seen before. He wouldn't be able to escape or evade those questions. Nothing but the truth would do.

"I don't know what you've heard, but it's not as bad as you think."

"I've heard that the mill is closing." That soft chin had never looked so uncompromising. "Is it true?"

"Yes." There wasn't any other answer.

For an instant her eyes seemed to blank him out, as if she couldn't bear to look at him. When she did look at him again, those warm amber eyes were stone cold. "That's really why you came here, isn't it? To close the mill."

"Ex Corp is closing the mill, not me." That was a cop-out, and he knew it. "Look, this is a business decision. We can fill the orders more economically from our plant in Tennessee, that's all. It would take more to modernize this place than it's worth."

"So that's it?" Her anger blazed at him. "You throw two hundred people out of work because it's more economical?"

"We're not throwing them onto the street. We'll offer jobs at our other plants to as many as we can."

She rejected that with a sharp cut of her hand. "What if people don't want to leave? Mannington is their home."

Why was she so obsessed with this place? "Mannington's not the only town in the world. Maybe some of them will be better off elsewhere."

"It will kill this town." Her eyes clouded with pain. "It will kill James."

"Carmichael." He crossed the space between them and glared down at her. "Is that all you can think about? Let me tell you something about James Carmichael."

Her face softened slightly. "Nick, I know you dislike him because of his dispute with your father. But that's no reason…"

"Dispute? Is that what you call it?"

A flush rose in her pale cheeks. "All right, your father was fired. After the theft was discovered, James thought he had good reason."

"My father was framed. There never was a theft." He threw the words at her. "That was the threat Carmichael used to force him to leave, just because he tried to unionize the place, to force almighty James Carmichael to give his employees decent wages and health benefits. And not content with framing my father and running him out of town, Carmichael kept him from ever getting a decent job again." Anger burned along his veins. "That's your precious father-in-law for you."

She went pale again. "I don't believe you."

"No, I don't suppose you would, any more than the rest of this town would. But now the scales are balanced."

"Vengeance, Nick?"

"Justice."

She shook her head. "I don't see any justice in throwing two hundred people out of work to right a wrong you think was done to you."

Something hardened in him at that. She was never going to understand. "It's my father he destroyed, not me."

"No." Her voice was soft. "You're doing a good job of that all by yourself."

"Most people would say I'm pretty successful."

"Most people wouldn't look inside you and see the pain. Or the damage you're doing to yourself with this…this vendetta."

For a moment he couldn't speak. At a time like this only Emily would care about the damage she imagined he was doing to his soul.

"Emily." He caught her hand, and his voice roughened. "I'm sorry I couldn't warn you what was coming. But you've got to look past the moment. I know change is difficult, but this was inevitable. If it hadn't been Ex Corp today, it would have been somebody else next year."

"You don't know that." Pain etched itself between her brows. "And anybody would have been better than you."

"If I hadn't come, we wouldn't have seen each other again." He tried to warm her cold hand in his. "If I hadn't come, I might never have known I love you."

"Love?" She winced, as if the word had been a blow.

"Try and understand. This is going to be better for everybody in the long run. You and the boys don't have to stay in Mannington any longer. You don't have to be dependent on Carmichael. We can build a life for ourselves somewhere else."

She pulled her hand away. "On the ashes of other people's lives?"

He was losing her; he could see it in her eyes. But he couldn't lose what he'd never had. "Do you love me, Emily?"

She flinched. "I thought I did. But I guess I didn't even know you."

She walked out, closing the door quietly behind her.

Emily managed to preserve that deadly calm across the hall to her own office. Safely inside, she closed the door and leaned back against it. Then she pressed both hands against her chest.

Funny, that the pain really could feel as if her heart were broken. As if, if she could look at it, she'd see the tiny separate pieces of what had been her love for Nick.

The phone was ringing. She crossed to the desk, took the receiver off the hook, put it on the blotter. Then she sank into the chair and buried her face in her hands.

How could this happen, Lord? How could Nick do this?

The trouble was, she knew the answer. He could do it because of what he believed had happened to his father. He could do it because his heart was so eaten up with revenge that there wasn't room for anything else.

Like love. She winced at the word. She loved him. She couldn't turn it off and pretend it hadn't happened. Maybe she'd always loved him, in that special place in her heart that was reserved for her first love. Then he'd come back, and she'd thought, she'd hoped....

And now he'd betrayed them all. She tried not to think of how she'd talk to the boys about this. The man they'd begun to see as a hero had turned on them.

Lord, he doesn't know what he's doing to himself. He's destroying himself, and he doesn't even realize it. Even if what he believes about James is true, Nick is hurting himself far more than he'll ever hurt James.

She straightened, massaging her temples. All the lights on her phone were blinking now. Clearly the word was out. People were calling her, expecting her to have answers, and she didn't.

She felt a brief spurt of annoyance at James, who'd gone home and left her to deal with this. At least he might have talked with her so that she'd have some idea what to say to people.

She shoved back away from the desk. She had to see him. She had to find out how he expected her to handle this. The whole town depended on the mill, and they'd expect answers.

And she had to find out the truth about Nick's father. She put her hand lightly on the photo of the twins. If their grandfather really had done such a terrible thing... Her mind reeled at the consequences.

She had to know the truth. Whatever it was, she'd find a way to deal with it, for the boys' sakes. But first, she had to know.

More than an hour later she argued her way past the nurse and reached the door of James's room. She'd gone to the house first, only to find that he'd headed directly for the hospital to check in for his surgery. She'd driven there, seeming to feel the accusing gazes of people on the streets as the news spread up one side of Main Street and down the other.

She took a deep breath, sent up a silent prayer for guidance and opened the door.

James was tucked up on the high hospital bed, his maroon silk robe contrasting with the white bedclothes. His gaze stabbed accusingly at her.

"I told you I didn't want you to come to the hospital."

"I had to come." She approached him, some of her determination ebbing as she saw how white and strained he looked. "The mill—did you know this was going to happen?"

Anger tightened his pale lips. "Know? Of course I didn't know. Do you think I'd have agreed to any deal if I'd realized what they had in mind? This was all O'Neill's doing." Two bright spots of color showed on his cheeks. "I should have suspected the moment I heard he was their representative. He's wanted to get back at us for years. Just like his father."

"That's why he did it." Somehow she had to get to the truth. It was the only thing that would help any of them. "Because of his father. Because of what he believes you did to his father."

James stared at her, blue eyes frosty. "I don't know what you mean. The man was a thief. What would you expect me to do?"

"Nick says he wasn't—that it was all a lie."

"What would you expect him to say? It's all nonsense."

That came out with his usual assurance, but his gaze slid away from hers, focusing instead on the tile floor. A cold hand seemed to clasp her heart.

"He's right, isn't he?" Her breath caught, threatening to choke her. "He's right. His father wasn't a thief."

"That's nonsense, sheer…nonsense." His voice faltered on the last word, and he leaned back against the pillow. His eyes closed, then opened again. His hand moved, restlessly smoothing the sheet that covered him.

"James." She took his hand, holding it firmly. "Tell me the truth. I have a right to know."

She thought he wouldn't answer. Then his head moved slowly from side to side, and she seemed to feel the defiance seep out of him.

"Tell me," she said again, more softly. "At a time like this, be honest with me."

"I just wanted to be rid of him." His voice came out in a whisper. "That's all. He was causing trouble, making demands we couldn't meet. He was trying to unionize the place, but a union back then would have ruined us."

She waited, dreading to hear the rest of it. *Oh, Lord…* She wasn't even sure what to pray.

His hand moved feebly in hers. "Donovan handled it. I didn't tell him what to do. Mack Donovan, the foreman, you remember him."

Her memory produced an image of the wiry, graying foreman who'd retired years ago and left Mannington. "I remember. What does he have to do with it?"

"He said he'd take care of it." His hand trembled slightly, and the sign of weakness hurt her. "When O'Neill was caught, I wondered. But I didn't do anything. I should have, but I didn't. He left, and my people were safe from him. I told myself that was all that mattered."

"After he left, what did you do about him?" The rest of Nick's accusation couldn't be left unanswered.

"Do?" His gaze focused on her, and a little strength seemed to come back into his voice. "I didn't do anything."

"You didn't try to keep him from getting other jobs?"

"Of course not. I don't even know where he went. I just thought I'd heard the last of him." His mouth twisted in an attempt at a smile. "I should have known better. Your sins always find you out, one way or another."

She couldn't think of anything to say to that. It was true, and unfortunately a lot of other people were going to pay for this particular misdeed.

"What are we going to do?" Her fingers tightened on his cold ones.

"Nothing." His voice failed on the word, and he struggled to repeat it. "Nothing to do. Tell them—tell them I'm sorry."

She started to move away, but he held her. "Wait. Emily, tell my attorney to come in. Right away, before the surgery."

"Can't it wait? You should be resting." He seemed too weak to face an operation.

"No. I've decided." A ghost of a smile crossed his face. "Trey was right. I'm going to sign everything over to you now. I know you'll do what's right for the boys and for the mill."

It was a burden she didn't want, but she didn't have a choice. There wasn't anyone else. "I'll do my best."

"One more thing," he whispered. "If I come through tomorrow, I'll give O'Neill my apology. I don't suppose he'll forgive me, but I'll try."

She nodded, turning to the door. Too late, that was all she could think. It was too little, too late, for all of them.

Chapter Fourteen

The rest of her day passed in a haze of misery. She went back to the office, because someone from the family had to be there. The phone never stopped ringing. Everyone wanted to know if it was true, wanted details, wanted someone to blame, wanted to be comforted.

Ironically, the people suffering the most seemed to be those who were receiving the offers at Ex Corp's other plants. They were torn between staying and facing an uncertain future and going, giving up homes and familiar surroundings for the unknown. She choked down her own pain and tried to listen, knowing she didn't have answers.

Nick, how could you do this? How could you hurt so many people?

There didn't seem to be an answer to that, either.

The phone rang yet again, and Emily reached for it, trying to compose her heart to listen. But this person didn't want sympathy. It was one of the Ex Corp people.

"Josh Trent here, Ms. Carmichael. I wanted to inform you that Mr. Donaldson, our vice president for acquisitions, will be here tomorrow. He'd like to make arrangements for the final disposition of the plant and its fittings."

The words had a funereal sound. "I see."

"He'd like to meet with you…well, let's see. Not tomorrow, he'll be too busy. The next day at ten, if that's convenient, in Mr. Carmichael's former office."

It was less a question than a command.

"At ten, then."

Somehow, between now and then, she'd have to figure out if there was anything she could use to push Ex Corp into doing better by the workers. She didn't think an appeal to their better nature would help. Before she could stop it, her mind flew to Nick. Since he'd come back, she'd begun, without even realizing it, to count on him. Now she knew she couldn't, but some small part of her heart still wanted to.

By the time she went home, she was emotionally and physically exhausted. It didn't help to hear the twins coming up the walk from school in the midst of a full-blown quarrel.

"You're a dummy, that's all," Trey yelled.

"I don't believe it." David dropped his backpack on the floor, his mouth set in a firm line as he frowned at his brother. "Nick wouldn't."

Her heart sank. There wouldn't be any respite from what was going on here, either. The only way to handle it was to face it—her sons deserved honesty. She sat down, feeling as if her legs wouldn't hold her up any longer.

Please, Lord. Give me the right words. They've begun to care for him, too.

"Come here, guys." She held out her hands, drawing them to either side of her on the couch. "Okay, now tell me what's going on."

"We heard the mill's going to close." David looked up at her, small face troubled. "It's not, is it, Mommy?"

"I'm afraid so." She put her arm around him.

Trey kicked his heels against the sofa. "Some of the kids said it's Nick's fault. That he did it."

She could sense the pleading under his words. He wanted her to say that it wasn't true, that the person he looked up to wouldn't do that.

"He didn't, did he?" David's eyes filled with tears. "He wouldn't do that."

Where were the right words to help them deal with the fact that their hero was tarnished?

"Nick works for the company that bought part of the mill, and they've decided to close it. It's not just his decision. It's his boss's decision, too."

"But couldn't Grandfather keep our part of the mill open?" Trey offered the idea as if it would solve everything.

"I'm afraid it doesn't work that way, Trey." She

smoothed silky hair out of his eyes. "You see, the person who has the biggest share gets to decide for everyone. And that's Ex Corp."

"Nick could have stopped them if he wanted to." Trey's mouth set in a stubborn line. "I hate him."

David leaned against her. "I thought he was our friend." A tear trickled down his cheek.

She drew them both close. "I know." Her arms couldn't shield them from this kind of pain. "I thought so, too."

It seemed much later than nine o'clock by the time the boys were finally settled for the night. Emily walked slowly into her bedroom. Maybe she ought to go to bed herself and let sleep block out the terrible events of the day. Or maybe she'd just dream about it, over and over.

Nick's class ring still lay in her dresser drawer. She took it out, trying to remember how she'd felt about the boy who'd given it to her.

She'd loved him, at least as much as a fifteen-year-old could understand the word. Her heart had, she'd been sure, broken when he'd gone away.

She held the ring against her cheek, feeling the cool, hard metal.

And then he'd come back, and she'd loved him again. She hadn't intended to, hadn't even known it was happening until it was too late. She loved him, and he'd betrayed them all, including himself.

He wasn't the same person. That was what she had

to face. The fact that she loved him didn't change that. She'd probably continue loving him for a long time, but she couldn't be with the person he was now. He'd let his bitterness and anger turn him into a man who didn't even recognize the wrong he was doing.

The tears threatened to overflow, and she sank down on her knees beside her bed, burying her face in her hands.

Lord, show me how to deal with this. Show me what to do, because I just don't know.

She took a deep breath, then another, feeling the panic dissolve slowly.

Forgiveness. That was what was wrong with Nick—he hadn't been able to forgive. If she didn't want to confront the same bitterness he lived with, somehow she had to forgive.

I don't think I can forgive him in my own strength, Lord. But I know Your strength is sufficient. So I'll forgive him and trust in You to make it so.

Comfort seeped through her, erasing the tension and easing the pain. She should have learned by now that relying on her own strength was a recipe for disaster. But there was always One she could lean on.

She prayed for the boys and for James and for all those who would be affected by the mill's closing. Then, finally feeling at peace, she prayed for Nick.

On Tuesday afternoon Nick paused outside the door to what had been Carmichael's office. Donaldson had taken it over when he arrived that morning, brisk and full of determination to clean things up and move on.

Mrs. Rand still sat at the secretary's desk, talking on the telephone. When she caught Nick's gaze on her she cut the conversation short, then looked up at him, eyes icy.

"I trust you don't object to a brief personal call. I wanted to check with the hospital."

"Hospital?" For some reason his mind leaped to Emily and the boys. "Who's in the hospital?"

She sniffed. "Mr. Carmichael, of course."

He could only stare at her for a moment. "I didn't know. What happened?"

"His surgery was this morning." Then, apparently recognizing the blank look he gave her, she went on. "I thought you knew. He had to have heart surgery."

"No, I didn't know." Emily hadn't told him. But then, she wouldn't. He was the enemy. "How is he?"

Mrs. Rand contrived to look a bit stiffer. "I understand he came through the surgery fairly well." She paused. "That was Mrs. Carmichael."

He pictured Emily waiting at the hospital, waiting for word, worrying about Carmichael, about the mill, about the people who were going to be unemployed. She'd probably been worrying about Carmichael's health for days, in addition to everything else. In addition to the burdens he'd put on her.

He didn't particularly like this train of thought. He

ought to…what? His mind jeered at him. Send flowers? Neither Carmichael nor Emily would appreciate that. He ought to leave well enough alone. He'd done what he came to Mannington to do, and the only favor he could do Emily right now was to stay away from her.

But he couldn't. He didn't want to. He wanted to try, one more time, to explain.

He glanced at his watch. He had a couple more hours of work to do before he could leave. Maybe by that time Emily would be home from the hospital. He could stop by the house and tell her… His mind ran up against a blank wall at that point. Tell her what?

He still hadn't decided by the time he left the office. He just knew he wasn't going to leave Mannington without trying to see her again.

He was so occupied with his thoughts that he didn't notice the group of men gathered in the parking lot until he was close to them.

"O'Neill." Ken Moore, Lorna's husband, looked considerably more threatening than he had that night at the fairgrounds. "We need to talk."

"Oh?" Nick sized up the distance to his car, the distance back to the building. "Looks like you brought some friends along to help you talk."

Ken's large fists clenched. "I don't need any help. I just want to know one thing. Why? What did we do to you?"

For a moment he was tempted to be honest. You branded my father a thief—you and the rest of this town.

But he wouldn't give them the satisfaction. "It's business. Ex Corp decided this plant wasn't worth the money to modernize."

"Ex Corp decided? Or you decided?"

He bit back a sharp retort. Nobody would thank him for starting a brawl in the company parking lot.

"It was a corporate decision."

"Corporate." Ken took a step closer, close enough so that Nick could see the pain as well as anger in the man's eyes. "What kind of corporation takes a man's livelihood away from him?"

"Look, we're trying to offer jobs to as many people as possible." He knew Ken was one of those who'd received the offer; he'd made sure of that. Unfortunately he'd also heard what his answer had been.

"We don't want your jobs!" Ken's voice rose. "We want our jobs. We want our town back the way it was before you came along."

Nick's fists tightened. He didn't want to fight the man, but he'd protect himself if it came to that.

Ken seemed to see the movement. For a long moment he stared at Nick, then his hands opened, gesturing as if to push something away.

"Forget it," he said. "We're not going to take you on, O'Neill. We have wives and kids to take care of, and you're not worth the trouble." The contempt in his voice stung. He turned away, and the group of men sidled back with him.

Nick let out a breath he didn't realize he'd been holding.

Ken looked back over his shoulder. "Too bad Emily and her kids didn't have someone to take care of them."

The verbal blow stung as much as a punch would have. Emily and her boys. Obviously people had been talking. For the first time he understood why that bothered her so much.

The men moved away, not looking at him. So he was back to being a pariah in this town. Well, he'd been there before. He could deal with it.

Trouble was, now that he had his revenge on Carmichael, he didn't seem to feel the satisfaction he'd expected. He didn't seem to feel anything at all.

"Thank you, Doctor. I'll be in again sometime tomorrow." Emily hung up the phone and looked at the twins, bookends on either side of Alison, who'd come to play. "Good news." She tried to look cheerful. "The doctor says your grandfather is doing much better now."

They didn't look convinced.

"Are you sure?" Trey said. "Somebody said at school Grandfather might be going to die."

She ruffled his hair. "Who are you going to believe, his doctor or somebody at school?"

Trey grinned. "Okay. I guess Brett didn't know what he was talking about. Sometimes he doesn't."

"Right." She set three glasses of juice in front of them. "Maybe in a few days he'll feel well enough that you can go to see him. In the meantime…"

The doorbell rang. Her heart pumped into overdrive at the sound. Silly. Maybe it was a measure of how much stress she'd been under that the least noise should set her nerves on edge.

The twins stampeded toward the door.

"I'll get it!" Trey yelled.

"No, me."

That brought a smile as she followed them. It sounded as if things were getting back to normal, at least a little.

The smile faded when she saw who was stepping into her living room. Nick.

The boys just stood, staring at him.

She didn't have anything to say to him. And whatever she did say, she didn't want the twins to hear.

"Trey and David, you and Alison take your juice out to the back porch, please."

Trey's small chin jutted out. "We want to talk to Nick."

David nodded.

"No." That came out sharply, but it couldn't be helped. Maybe she hadn't protected anyone else from Nick's revenge, but she was going to shield her children. "Do what I say, now."

Their faces wore identically startled expressions, but they went. She didn't turn back to Nick until she heard the slam of the back door.

"You were a little hard on them, weren't you?" His voice was mild, his deep blue eyes questioning.

"I don't think that's your concern. Why are you here?" She longed for a protection from his intent gaze. If he looked too hard, he just might see how much she was hurting.

"I…" His hand moved in a small, almost pleading, motion. For once he seemed to be at a loss for words. "I wanted to talk to you."

Please make him go away before I let him know how much I care.

"I think we've said everything there is to say."

He shook his head in a characteristically impatient gesture, a lock of black hair falling over his forehead. "Emily, look, first of all, I'm sorry about your father-in-law's health problems. I didn't know. How is he doing?"

A welcome spurt of anger went through her at that. "Do you care?"

"Oddly enough, I do." He shrugged. "I don't know why. Maybe it's your influence, Emily. You care about everybody."

She pushed away a fresh spasm of pain. It would be tempting to believe she could change him, but she didn't. "He's come through the surgery all right. He's very weak, but if there are no complications, the doctor is hopeful."

"If I'd known you were carrying that burden, along with everything else…" He stopped, as if he didn't know what to say.

She shook her head. "It wouldn't have made a difference, Nick. Admit it. You were so bent on revenge that nothing would make a difference." There was something else, something he had a right to hear, whether she wanted to say it or not. "Maybe you were right."

"Why do you say that?" His gaze sharpened.

She took a deep breath and forced herself to look at him. "I talked to James before his surgery. Asked him about what you told me."

"Did he admit it?"

"He said he wanted to be rid of your father—to protect the mill and his workers. He believed the union would cost too much, put them out of business. He suspected the foreman rigged the charges against your father, but he didn't do anything about it. He knows that makes him guilty. He's sorry."

Bitterness twisted Nick's mouth. "A little late now. Isn't it?"

"Nick, don't." His emotion seemed to spark her own pain. Didn't he see what he was doing to himself? "You have what you wanted. You've gotten your revenge. Is it enough? Does it make you happy?"

The door banged, as if emphasizing the question. Trey raced into the room.

One look at his white face told her something was very wrong.

"Mommy, come quick! Alison fell out of the tree." He grabbed her hand. "She won't wake up!"

Chapter Fifteen

Nick raced after Emily and Trey, through the kitchen, across the porch, across the lawn. Emily got to the still figure first, reaching for the child, with him right behind her.

"Don't!" He caught her hand in his. "Careful. Better not move her."

Some of the panic left Emily's eyes at his tone, and she nodded. She reached out carefully to put her fingers on Alison's neck.

"Her pulse is strong." Her voice seemed to catch a little. She leaned closer and listened to her breathing. "She's breathing all right, too," she added.

"Looks as if she hit her head when she fell." He'd already seen the rapidly darkening lump on her temple. "Better call for an ambulance. I don't think we should risk moving her without a backboard."

She nodded again. "Stay with her. I'll be right back." She ran toward the house.

His mind went through the little first aid he knew. It wasn't much, but he was sure they were right not to move her. He could understand Emily's first instinct to gather the child into her arms, though. It seemed all wrong for a live wire like Alison to lie so still.

David edged a little closer, his knee bumping Alison's arm.

"Don't touch her," Nick cautioned.

The boy looked stricken at his words.

"She'll be all right, son." He touched David's shoulder lightly. "We just don't want to move her until the ambulance comes and they can do it right."

David's eyes were huge. "Can't I do something?"

"Why don't you run and get a blanket to keep her warm. Can you do that?"

"Sure." David scrambled to his feet, carefully avoiding Alison. "Right away."

Trey knelt next to Nick. His small body shook with a choked sob, and his hand crept forward until he was just touching Alison's sleeve. "It's my fault."

"Why do you say that?" He kept his voice carefully neutral.

"I dared her. Mommy always says not to dare people, but I dared her to stand on the limb. It's my fault she got hurt." His face crumpled, another sob escaping.

"Trey…" Careful, careful. Don't say the wrong thing. "You didn't mean for your friend to get hurt. It was an accident."

He clasped the boy's shoulder in a reassuring grip. Trey jerked away as if he'd struck him.

"What do you know about it?" Trey's grief changed suddenly to anger. "You hurt your friends, and you didn't even care!"

It was like being kicked in the heart. The expression on Trey's face weighed him, judged him and found him guilty. And there wasn't a thing Nick could say that would make this all right.

Emily hurried back, closely followed by David, arms filled with a blanket he'd probably ripped from his bed.

"The ambulance will be here in a few minutes. I sent a friend to try and find Lorna. She's gone shopping." Her voice trembled a little, but she tucked the blanket over the child with competent hands.

"What about Ken?"

"I don't know where to look for him." She bit her lip. "Maybe Lorna will know."

The wail of the ambulance sent her to her feet. She hurried to the side of the house, waving them in.

Nick drew the boys out of the way as the paramedics examined Alison and slid a backboard under her. Her eyelids fluttered when they moved her, and she tried to say something.

"Mommy?" she whispered.

"It's okay, Alison." Emily moved beside her. "Mommy will be here soon, and I'll stay with you until she comes."

She glanced at Nick, and he nodded.

"You ride in the ambulance with her. I'll bring the boys and meet you at the emergency room."

She was shaking her head before he got the words out. "I'd rather they stay here. The hospital's no place for them."

"Trust me on this one." He looked meaningfully at Trey. "They need to be there. I'll take good care of them."

She didn't look as if she agreed, but the paramedics were already lifting Alison. "I'll see you there, then." She hurried after them.

The two boys stared at him with identically doubting expressions. Funny, that that look should hurt more than almost anything had since he came back to town.

"Come on." He tried to make it sound routine, tried not to think about how badly hurt the child might be. "My car's in the driveway. We'll be at the hospital before you know it."

Emily backed out of the emergency room cubicle, giving the medical people more room to work. She'd been in this same spot several times with the boys, and it never failed to give her that weak-in-the-knees feeling. Maybe you could only go on being strong as long as you were needed.

She could hear a doctor ordering a CAT scan, and her stomach seemed to turn over. How badly hurt was

Alison? She'd been unconscious for several minutes—that couldn't be good.

Father, be with her. Guide the doctor's every move.

Where was Lorna? Judith Wells had promised to keep looking until she found her, no matter what it took, and Judith was a woman of her word. She'd track Lorna down and bring her here, to face…what?

She knew only too well the guilt that Lorna would feel over not being there when Alison was hurt. It might be totally irrational, but there wasn't a mother on earth who wouldn't understand.

She pushed away from the wall and took a few steps into the lobby. The door swished open and Lorna charged into the room, heading first for the desk and then veering when she saw Emily.

"How bad is it?" She clutched Emily's arm. "Where is she?"

Emily embraced her, feeling her friend tremble in her arms. "The doctors are with her now. They haven't told me anything yet. She fell from the tree and hit her head." Her own guilt kicked in. "Lorna, I'm sorry. I should have been watching them more closely."

Lorna shook her head, tears spilling over to be dashed quickly away. "It's not your fault. She wanted to go shopping with me, but I thought…"

"It's not your fault, either." She gave Lorna a little shake. "Make sense. She didn't fall just because you didn't want to take her shopping this afternoon."

"No, of course not." Lorna brushed away an errant

tear and took a deep breath. "Okay. Do I look calm enough to go in now?"

"You're fine." She nodded toward the waiting room. "I'll be out here when you need me."

She watched the white curtain close behind Lorna, heard a soft "Mommy" and wiped away a tear of her own. *Please, Father. Hold this child safe.*

When she turned back to the waiting room, she saw that Nick and the twins had come in. She stood for a moment, watching as they found seats, Nick sitting between the two boys.

She'd depended on him. In that moment of crisis, when life turned upside down all in an instant, she'd counted on Nick in spite of everything he'd done.

And it had felt right. That was the scary thing—how good it had been to rely on his strength, to have another person helping with the responsibility.

Not just another person. She'd thought that often enough in the years since Jimmy died, but she didn't need just any other person. It was Nick she'd leaned on. Nick, with all his flaws, that she'd known instinctively she could trust.

She watched him lean toward David, saying something softly that eased the tension in his small face.

Oh, Nick.

Her throat went tight with anguish. There was so much good in him, so much strength and fortitude. But it was all being eaten away by bitterness, and he didn't even know it.

She swallowed hard, then crossed the waiting room toward them.

"Mommy!" Trey bolted from his seat to meet her halfway. "Is she all right? Did she wake up?"

Emily stroked his hair as she led him back to the others. She sat down, pulling the chair around so that she could face both boys on their level.

"She's waking up a little bit. I heard her say something to her mommy. So that's good."

"Is she all right? Can she go home now?" David wiggled forward on his chair, as if ready to run into the other room and take Alison by the hand.

"Not yet. The doctors are still checking her. They have to do some tests to see how much her head is hurt. Remember the X-ray you had when you fell off your bike, Trey?"

He nodded. "It didn't hurt."

"No, and Alison's tests won't hurt, either. We just have to wait and see what the doctors say."

"Isn't there anything we can do?" Trey grabbed her hand, and she felt his urgency. "I want to do something."

She managed a smile. "I think we'd better pray for her. That's the best thing we can do right now." She held out her hands to the boys.

Trey clasped her hand like a lifeline, but when Nick extended his, Trey drew back in a quick, angry movement. She saw the flicker of pain in Nick's face, immediately masked.

"Trey." At the moment, she cared more what Trey's

anger did to him than to what it did to Nick. "Take Nick's hand, please."

"Don't…" Nick began, but she silenced him with a look.

"I don't want to. He's not our friend anymore."

"Listen to me, Trey. This is important. You can't go to God with a prayer for one person when you're holding a grudge against someone else. Do you understand that? And you have to forgive other people when they do something wrong just as you want God to forgive you."

She watched his face. This was a big spiritual lesson for one so young, but it was one he had to start learning now. He'd probably keep on learning it all his life, just as she had.

Trey stared down at the floor. She thought he was fighting tears, but she didn't move. This one he had to battle out himself.

Finally he looked up. He nodded. Then he held his hand out to Nick.

She closed her eyes. "Dear Father, we bring Alison to You now. We ask that You be with her and heal her. We ask You to guide her doctors and give them wisdom. We ask You to comfort her parents and be with each of us. In Jesus' precious name, Amen."

Nick discovered that the lump in his throat was too big to swallow. If he tried to say anything at all, he might choke or give way to tears. Emily's soft-voiced prayer, the grip of the boys' small hands on his, the thought of little Alison, lying pale and motionless on the ground—it all rolled over him, threatening to knock him flat.

The sound of rushing feet came from the entrance. Ken raced in, his face distraught. Emily moved toward him, and he grasped her outstretched hands.

"Alison?" The naked fear in his voice ripped into Nick's heart.

Nick was probably the last person Ken wanted to see right now.

"Come on, guys." It took an effort to sound normal. "Let's find a soda machine and get everyone something to drink."

He spent as much time as he could on the simple task. When they got back to the waiting room, Ken had vanished, probably into the examining room. Emily stood in the doorway, and he thought she looked a little more relaxed.

"Thank you, Trey." She took the soda can the boy held out to her. "I was with Ken when he spoke to the doctor. Alison has a concussion." She glanced from Trey to David. "That's what happens when you hit your head really hard. They're going to keep her in the hospital for a bit just to watch her, but it looks as if she'll be all right."

"Can we see her?" Trey's tone was pleading. "Please, can we see her? I have to tell her something."

"I don't think they'll want her to have visitors today. Maybe you can make a card for her."

He shook his head, and Nick knew exactly what put that stubborn expression in his eyes. The kid was still blaming himself, and he wouldn't be able to rest until he'd told Alison he was sorry.

"I have to see her. Please, Mom."

He had to think of something that would ease the boy's pain. "Maybe if we wait until they're ready to move her to a room, you can say something to her on the way up." He looked at Emily. "It's important," he said quietly.

He expected her to argue, but she didn't. She just nodded.

"All right. We'll wait."

The boys scurried back to their chairs, as if afraid she might change her mind.

"Is Ken okay?" He seemed to hear the man's voice echoing in his head. *We have wives and kids to take care of.*

Emily's eyes held a question she didn't ask. "He was better as soon as he saw Alison. Not knowing is scary."

"I'd like to…" He let that trail off. Ken wouldn't appreciate hearing anything from him.

"What?" Emily's direct gaze didn't allow equivocation.

He shrugged, suspecting he looked like one of the kids when he'd done something wrong. "I'd like to express my concern, that's all. But under the circumstances, it might be kind of awkward."

She looked at him steadily. "Does that matter, if it's something you should say?"

He didn't doubt she'd apply those same standards to herself. "Maybe not."

"He's gone to the admissions desk to fill out some forms. You can catch up with him there." She nodded down the hallway.

Looked as if Emily wouldn't let him get out of this one. Maybe she was right, and he needed to do this. Maybe it would still the churning that had been going on inside him.

He walked down the green-walled hallway quickly, automatically checking off the signs. When he came to the admissions desk, he saw Ken frowning down at a sheaf of papers. The young woman across the desk looked bored.

She reached across to tap a line on the form with a red-tipped nail. "Right there. You have to put your insurance information on the sheet before we can process the admission."

Nick stopped in his tracks, knowing what Ken was going to say. What he'd have to say.

"Look, I work...worked at the mill. Our insurance has been terminated." Nick recoiled in shock. Had he overheard correctly? Had Ex Corp already terminated the insurance plan? That wasn't supposed to happen so quickly. "But I'll pay." He heard Ken continue. "The doctor says Alison has to be admitted."

"No insurance." She took the paper back, looking less bored. "Does that mean you're unemployed?"

"Yes." Ken sounded as if the word had a bad taste.

"Unemployed. No insurance." She scribbled something on the form. "Are you on welfare?"

"No!"

He could see the vein pulsing in Ken's temple. The man was an inch from exploding.

"Then I'm afraid we'll have to have the money up front. You can't expect the hospital to treat your daughter for free, can you?"

"You…"

He stepped forward before Ken could bring his fist down on the counter.

"You do accept cash, don't you?" Nick pulled out his wallet. "What are the charges going to be?"

Ken whirled, glaring when he saw who was there. "Stay out of this, O'Neill. If it weren't for you, we wouldn't be in this fix."

"Look, I just want to help."

"Help?" His fists clenched. "Get out of my sight before I do something I'll regret. I'd rather panhandle on the street than accept money from you."

Ken spun back to the desk, saying something about writing a check. Nick took a step back, an image blossoming in his mind. His father, ranting about the wrong done to him by Carmichael. Raving that the man was responsible for all their troubles. That he'd rather beg on the street than accept help from the likes of him.

The piercing moment washed away all the excuses, all the rationalizations. He was left facing the stark, hard truth. He'd let his bitterness turn him into the very image of the man he'd hated all these years.

Chapter Sixteen

By the time she walked into the meeting with Donaldson the next morning, Emily felt as if she'd been steamrollered. The events of the past few days, coming so quickly one on top of the other, had left no time to take a breath between them.

At least the news from the hospital was good. Alison's condition had improved, and she'd probably be home tomorrow at the latest. And James was stronger—strong enough, in fact, for him to meet again with his attorney. His shares of the mill had been signed over to her, to manage as she wished for the twins.

Not that she'd be able to do much managing. She glanced at Jefferson Wade, the attorney, as he moved into the office behind her. He hadn't held out much hope that they'd be able to wring any concessions from Donaldson. They didn't, he'd said, have anything left to bargain with.

She sent a quick glance around the office, trying to adjust to the sight of a stranger behind James's desk. Or maybe she was really looking for Nick.

She'd expected he'd try to talk with her again after that trip to the hospital, but he hadn't. He'd simply disappeared.

Not that there'd have been any use in talking again. They didn't have anything to say to each other, and if that left her feeling as if there were a hole in her heart—well, she'd have to get over it. Someday.

Donaldson was tall and balding, with cold, shrewd eyes behind gold-rimmed glasses. He shook hands, gesturing her to a seat with a proprietary air that raised her hackles.

Jefferson Wade gave her a warning glance as he held the chair for her. She knew what he was saying. *Don't offend him. We're not negotiating from a position of power.*

"Now, Ms. Carmichael." Donaldson ruffled a sheaf of papers on the desk in front of him. "I called you here to discuss the final disposition of the mill's equipment before we put the building up for sale."

She had to swallow before she could speak. "I can't imagine that you'll find a buyer very easily."

He shrugged. "That really doesn't concern us. About the equipment…"

"I'd rather talk about the workers." The strength of her voice surprised her. "How many of our people have been offered new jobs?"

Donaldson's eyes looked like two black marbles. "We've found places for about twenty."

"Twenty out of two hundred?"

"We're not running a charity, Ms. Carmichael."

"But you can't—"

The door swung open, and Donaldson's expression changed, hardening even more, if that were possible.

"O'Neill, you're not needed at this meeting." His voice seemed to carry a warning.

Nick apparently intended to ignore it, if it was a warning. His gaze brushed her coolly, impersonally, and he nodded to her. "Ms. Carmichael. Wade."

A sliver of ice seemed to chip from her heart. This well-dressed, businesslike stranger bore no resemblance to the Nick she'd fallen in love with.

Nick turned to Donaldson. "I have something to say."

"We've already had this conversation." The man's tone dripped icicles. "The answer is no."

She wasn't imagining it. The tension in the room was palpable.

Nick's smile wasn't pleasant. "Perhaps you'd better look at this before you give me a final answer." He dropped a folder on the desk in front of Donaldson and took a step back. "I'll wait."

Emily exchanged confused looks with Jefferson Wade. The attorney seemed as much at a loss as she was. If Nick had some unfinished business with his boss, couldn't it wait until they'd made their plea?

The contents of the folder had an odd effect on Donaldson. He went first pale, then red. He glared at Nick.

"You can't be serious."

Nick's smile didn't change. "Can't I?"

"What do you intend to do with this pack of nonsense?"

"I think there are several regulatory agencies which might find something of interest there. The newspapers certainly would, to say nothing of the stockholders."

Donaldson's eyes narrowed. "You're committing professional suicide, you know that. Nobody will hire you after this."

Nick's eyebrows lifted and his lips curved in what seemed a more genuine smile. "You won't believe it, but that doesn't matter in the least." His face hardened. "You know what I want."

Emily had a sudden urge to say something, anything, that would break the tension in the room. Wade put his hand on her arm, giving a warning shake of his head.

Donaldson glared at Nick for another long moment. Then he folded the papers together and shoveled them into a briefcase. He turned to Emily.

"Ms. Carmichael, in accordance with Clause 52B of our contract, I am rescinding the agreement to merge Carmichael Mills with Ex Corp. Your attorney will have the pertinent papers by this afternoon."

He stalked out of the room, and Nick followed him without a backward glance.

Emily stared blankly at the door that had closed behind them. "I don't understand. What just happened here?"

"You heard him." Wade seemed as astonished as she was, but attempting to hide it under a professional manner. "Ex Corp had the option to back out of the deal, and they've done it." A totally unprofessional grin burst through his solemn façade. "They've backed down. Carmichael Mills is back in business."

"But…" She was too stunned to celebrate. "But why? What did Nick do?"

He shrugged. "I don't pretend to know what was in those papers he showed Donaldson, but at a guess, I'd say Ex Corp has sailed pretty close to the wind in some of their business dealings. Probably nothing outright illegal, but questionable enough to raise eyebrows and start an investigation if someone in the know started talking."

"Someone like Nick." She was still trying to absorb it all.

He gave her a shrewd look. "I'd say we owe quite a debt to that young man. Ex Corp isn't likely to forgive and forget, and they won't hesitate to make it hard for anyone else to hire him. Looks as if he's sacrificed his career for this town." Wade lifted the telephone. "Do you mind if I let a few people know?"

She shook her head, still trying to process it. Nick had saved them. First he'd betrayed them, and now he'd saved them. How did she make any sense of that?

* * *

Nick glanced around the study of the rented house. Funny that it had started to feel so much like home in the brief time he'd been there. Well, no longer. He dumped a few magazines in the trash can, then pulled one out and put it in his briefcase. Might as well have something to read on the plane.

The telephone rang, and he eyed it warily. When he'd come in he'd found several messages on the machine from Emily. Her voice had sounded wary, as if she didn't quite know what to say to him.

He'd already made up his mind that the best thing he could do for Emily and the boys was to leave. He shouldn't even speak to her again. He shouldn't. But he picked up the phone and said, "Hello."

"Hey, buddy." Josh sounded muted, and Nick had a wry image of him glancing over his shoulder and shielding the receiver so no one from Ex Corp would know whom he'd called.

"Hey, yourself. You sure you want to talk to me?"

Josh cleared his throat. "Just wanted to say—well, did you know what you were doing today?"

"I knew." And he knew the cost, too. But somehow, losing his career didn't stack up against the pain of losing Emily again. "How's Donaldson taking it?"

"He doesn't like to lose. I wouldn't count on getting a job anywhere in the industry for a while."

"Don't worry. I'm not." He didn't know what he

was going to do, but he knew it wouldn't be something where getting ahead meant trampling on other people.

"Well…" Josh seemed at a loss for words. Nick suspected his actions didn't fit into any frame of reference Josh knew. "I wish you luck, anyway."

He hung up, smiling a little. Josh didn't understand. Maybe he didn't understand all that well himself, but he knew he felt better than he had in a long time.

Thank you, Lord, for showing me what I was. Give me an idea of what I can be.

In the silence, voices floated through the open window.

"Maybe he's not there."

"He must be. The light's on. Go look."

"I'm not going. You go look."

Shaking his head, he went to the window. He should have known they'd come.

"Hi, guys."

They stood side by side in the pool of light from the window, looking up at him. They were so like Emily that his heart ached.

"Hi, Nick." As usual, Trey was the first to speak.

"We wanted to see you. Do you want to come out?" David sounded hopeful.

"I don't think so." He leaned on the windowsill. "I'm pretty busy with stuff."

"About the mill?" Trey asked.

"What do you know about the mill?" What would Emily have told them after that meeting?

"We know you saved the mill."

"Mommy said so."

Something that had been very tight inside him eased at that. "How is your mom?"

Trey wrinkled his nose. "She's been really busy. Lots of people keep calling about the mill, I guess."

David nudged him. "Ask him."

"You ask him."

David lifted his chin. "Okay, I will." He looked at Nick. "Will you stay, Nick? Please? We'd really like it if you would."

Something seemed to have his throat in a vise. He swallowed. "Afraid I can't, guys."

They exchanged glances, communicating in that wordless manner they had.

"Will you talk to Mom before you go?" Trey leaned forward, reaching up to put his hands on the sill. "Will you?"

Nick covered the small hands with his, then leaned down to tousle David's hair. "We'll see."

"That's what Mom said, too." Trey looked as if he were trying to hold on to some hope.

He cleared his throat. "Speaking of your mom, she's probably wondering where you are. Maybe you'd better get on home."

They exchanged glances again. Then they turned and darted off across the darkened lawn.

* * *

Emily came slowly awake and blinked at the clock. It was barely 6:00 a.m. What had wakened her so early?

The door to her bedroom burst open and the pajama-clad twins raced into the room.

"Mommy, you have to get up." David tugged at her.

Trey thrust her robe at her. "Hurry, Mom. You have to talk to Nick."

She swung her feet to the floor and took the robe. "Boys, calm down. I told you I'd talk to Nick today." She had to express her thanks, even though the fact that Nick hadn't returned her calls made it clear he didn't have anything to say to her.

"You don't understand!" David's face crinkled as if he were about to burst into tears. "You have to go *now*."

"I can't…"

"He's going, Mom. We saw him from our window. He's packed the car and he's leaving. You have to stop him."

"Hurry!"

David grabbed one hand and Trey the other. They tugged her toward the door.

"Wait…I have to get dressed."

"You can't wait." David's voice shook with urgency. "He's going right this minute."

"I can't go outside like this! What will people…"

She stopped, hearing her own words ringing in her

ears. Knowing she'd said them before, to Nick. Knowing what his response would be. *Still afraid of what people will think, Emily?*

No. She wasn't going to live her life any longer afraid of what people might think about her. She wasn't going to let Nick leave, not until she'd said what she had to say to him.

"All right, hurry!" She grabbed the boys' hands. "Let's go!"

Down the stairs, out the kitchen door, the wet grass soaking the hem of her robe. It didn't matter. It didn't matter how wet she got; it didn't matter if all of Mannington saw her. All that mattered was that she got to Nick before he drove out of her life.

"Nick!" The boys bolted ahead of her. They reached Nick just as he started to back out the driveway.

"Wait!" Trey pounded on the driver's side window. "You have to wait."

Face startled, Nick switched off the ignition. He got out, looking from one twin to the other. "What are you doing...?" Then he looked up and saw her.

She stopped, acutely aware of her tousled hair, wet robe and bare feet. "We were trying to stop you."

"So I see."

There wasn't any expression in his face at all, and her heart sank. He didn't want to see them.

"We want to talk to you." She had to go through with it.

"Look, if you're trying to thank me, you don't need to."

"I think so." She tried to smile. "You saved us."

Pain flickered in his face. "I was the one who put you in jeopardy."

Somehow that instant of pain gave her hope...hope that he wasn't gone from them entirely.

"And then you got us out again. Why, Nick? Why did you sacrifice your career for us?"

He looked at her soberly. "Because I had a look into my soul, and I didn't like what I saw. You were right about me. I was letting revenge turn me into someone not even I could like."

Tears welled in her eyes, and she blinked them back. "And now?"

His gaze slid away from hers. "And now I'd better leave. Before I cause any more damage."

Trey, apparently unable to be still any longer, nudged her. "Ask him, Mommy."

"Ask him," David echoed.

Ask him.

She held out her hand. "Please, Nick. We want you to stay."

For a long moment he didn't move. Then he took a step toward her, blue eyes blazing with hope. "Do you mean it?"

"We mean it."

She moved into his arms, feeling them close around her, strong and sure. She lifted her face to his kiss. If the entire town of Mannington chose to watch Emily Carmichael in her bathrobe being kissed by Nick O'Neill, she didn't care in the least. God had given them both a second chance at love, and she wouldn't let that love get away ever again.

Epilogue

"Kick it, David!" Emily shouted as the soccer players surged down the field. Maybe he heard her. He kicked, then grinned as the ball sailed into the net.

Trey was the first one to reach him, closely followed by Alison, red hair gleaming in the sun. They pounded him on the back. Next to Emily, baby Lisa lurched forward in her stroller, pounding the tray with her rattle.

Emily dropped a kiss on her daughter's soft black curls. The baby looked more like Nick every day, with those deep blue eyes and blue-black hair. "Your brother made a goal. You cheer."

Lisa gave her a grin that showed her two teeth and pounded the rattle again.

Surely Nick couldn't hear that, but he caught her eye from across the field, and her heart warmed at his look. He turned to exchange high fives with Ken. The two of them had taken over coaching the soccer team this year, and they were even more excited than the kids over every victory.

"Looks like we'll be buying everyone ice cream again tonight," Lorna said. "The traditional victory celebration is getting expensive."

"We can handle it," Emily said, smiling.

Truth to tell, there'd been some difficult times at the mill in the last two years, times when they'd all had to pinch their pennies. But thanks to Nick's wise management, the mill was thriving. His idea to offer a profit-sharing plan to the employees had been pure genius.

Even James had radiated approval from his retirement home in Arizona. Now everyone in Mannington, it seemed, had a stake in how the mill did. It belonged to all of them in a way it never had before, and that had made them a stronger community.

The whistle blew, and Emily watched her three guys come toward them across the field. Her heart filled with love so intense that she had to blink back tears.

Thank you, Lord. Thank you for giving all of us a second chance to do things right.

* * * * *

Dear Reader,

Thank you for reading my Love Inspired novel
Since You've Been Gone. I hope you enjoyed the
story of Emily's reunion with her first love, Nick, and
their triumph over the barriers that kept them apart. I
had fun creating the twins, Trey and David, and hope
they made you smile.

Forgiveness is one of those lessons I've had to learn
over and over in my life, but God keeps giving me
another chance to get it right. Perhaps that's true for
you, too.

Best Wishes,

Marta Perry

THE DOCTOR NEXT DOOR

For we are God's workmanship,
created in Christ Jesus to do good works,
which God prepared in advance for us to do.

—*Ephesians* 2:10

This book is dedicated to the dear writing friends and critique partners who kept me going all these years: Barbara, Andi, Laurie, Dave and Pam. And, as always, to Brian.

Chapter One

"**Y**ou've come back."

The young woman's golden-brown eyes filled with a mix of shock and some other emotion Brett couldn't identify.

She grabbed his arm, pulling him out of the flow of people coming through the front door of the gracious Victorian home. "It's about time, don't you think?"

"About time?" Dr. Brett Elliot hadn't expected his hometown to stage a welcome parade to celebrate his return. But he also hadn't expected to be accosted at his best friend's engagement party by a beautiful woman he'd never seen before.

There'd been no mistaking the sarcasm in her voice. "The party started at eight, didn't it?" He detached his arm from her grip. People clustered in the adjoining rooms, leaving the wide center hallway quiet.

"The party? Yes." She glanced toward the crowded living room of the rambling old house, where the party obviously centered. Auburn hair curled around her shoulders; creamy skin glowed against the soft coral of her dress.

No, if he'd known this woman before, he'd certainly remember.

"Well, then, I'm right on time." He probably wouldn't have ventured out at all on his first night back in Bedford Creek if he weren't one of Mitch's groomsmen. He could hardly avoid the party given for Mitch and Anne, especially since it was at the Forrester place, right next door to his parents' empty house. Apparently one of the Forrester sisters was a member of the wedding party.

He couldn't pretend he hadn't gotten home for it. Someone would notice his car or the light in the window. That was one of the drawbacks he remembered of life in a small town. Someone noticed everything.

So he had decided to make a brief appearance, smile at everyone and beat a quick retreat before too many questions were asked.

Nothing in that scenario included having a stranger look at him with such disapproval. He pushed down his annoyance and tried a smile. "You think I should have come early, Ms.—"

Her eyebrows went up in astonishment. "You don't know who I am?"

He riffled quickly through his mental file of high school friends. Trouble was, he hadn't come back to Pennsylvania often during college and medical school on the West Coast. He was much closer since he'd taken the residency at a Philadelphia hospital, but also much busier. And with his parents spending most of the year in Florida, there'd been little to bring him back. People had a way of changing when you didn't see them for years at a time.

"Well, let's see. You must be someone I went to school with, right?"

A dimple showed at the corner of her mouth, dissipating her frown. "In a way."

The smile encouraged him. She couldn't be that annoyed with him, even if he'd gotten the time wrong. Something about her made him think of Angela Forrester, his high school sweetheart. One of Angela's friends, maybe?

"Were you a cheerleader, like Angela?"

"No." Her amber eyes seemed to enjoy a secret laugh at his expense.

"You're not…"

Something about her eyes triggered recognition. He brushed the auburn curls back from her cheek, exposing the hairline-thin white scar.

She'd fallen from the willow tree in the backyard when she was five. He'd been the first person there, and he'd held the hem of his T-shirt over the cut, convinced that at ten he was grown up enough to take care of her. That might have been the moment he'd decided to become a doctor.

"Rebecca." Now that he realized, of course, it could be no one else. "Little Rebecca, all grown up."

She drew back casually from his touch. "People do, you know."

He shook his head. "It's impossible. You used to look like Orphan Annie, all frizzy red hair and big eyes."

Now she was beautiful. The idea stunned him. How could Angela's pesky kid sister look like this?

"Gee, thanks. I think."

"I didn't mean…" He was thrown ridiculously off balance. Of course Rebecca had grown up. She couldn't stay little forever.

"You expected me to look like a kid. Did you think nothing in Bedford Creek would change while you were gone, that we were all just waiting for your return? It's not Brigadoon, you know."

"Isn't it?" They'd done "Brigadoon" for their senior class play. Angela had been gorgeous in a tartan skirt. Somehow Bedford Creek had always had that Brigadoon aura—isolated, hidden by its mountains, remote from his busy urban life.

"Things do change. I grew up. Angela got engaged. You can't just walk back in and find everything the way you left it."

The edge in her voice startled him. Rebecca had been a quiet little tomboy, all skinny legs and sharp elbows. She'd tagged after him and Angela, always wanting to be just like them, until it nearly drove Angela crazy.

"I guess things *have* changed." He lifted an eyebrow. "Way I remember it, you'd no more have argued with anyone than you'd have flown off the roof."

She smiled, the flicker of antagonism disappearing, at least for the moment. "I think I did try to fly off the porch once, using Mom's tablecloth for a cape."

"So you did. Are you still a tomboy?" Teasing Rebecca felt like old times, and the tension he'd been carrying around for weeks seemed to slide away. "Still falling out of willow trees?"

"Not anymore." Her chin lifted, perhaps with pride. "I'm a physician's assistant now. I work with Dr. Overton at the clinic."

The mention of his old mentor's name jolted something inside him. He had to see Clifford Overton soon, but he already dreaded the encounter. Doc would have to be told what had happened to Brett's fellowship. And Doc would have expectations of his own about Brett's future.

"How is Doc?"

A troubled look crossed her face, dimming the sparkle of her eyes. "Getting old." She shook her head, as if shaking away something she didn't want to think about. "He'll be excited to see you. You haven't been in touch enough." She pinned him down with a straightforward look he remembered from the little girl she'd been. "You are here to stay, aren't you?"

Something tightened painfully inside him. Stay? Was that the only choice left to him? He rejected that quickly. With the end of his residency he'd lost his student apartment, so coming to Bedford Creek was the logical thing to do. But as soon as he found a new fellowship, he'd be gone.

When he didn't answer, Rebecca's intent gaze seemed to bore into his very soul. "That is why you've come back, isn't it? To take over the clinic from Doc, the way he's always planned?"

"Not exactly."

Coming to the Forresters had been a mistake. He should have waited to read about the party on the social page of *The Chronicle*. What gave Rebecca the right to put him on the spot?

"Then why are you in town?" The edge was back in her voice.

For an instant he wanted to spill the whole story and get it off his chest. The thought horrified him. Nobody needed to know Brett Elliot, M.D., once the pride of Bedford Creek High School, had sacrificed the prestigious fellowship his mother had probably bragged about in every letter to her friends.

"Just on a break." He took a step back. It was time little Rebecca stopped interrogating him—time he congratulated Mitch and Anne and then got out of here.

"A break?" She stared at him in disbelief. "What do you mean, 'a break'? Doc's been waiting for you to come back."

He fought down a wave of anger. "That's between Doc and me."

She didn't seem to agree. "You have an obligation here, remember? A debt to pay."

Her challenge stung, reminding him of too much he wasn't ready to face yet. "My debts don't concern you, Rebecca."

"Everything about the clinic concerns me." She shot the words back at him. They were suddenly on opposite sides of a chasm, glaring at each other.

"Look, if you think…" The rest of that sentence vanished when someone bolted through the archway from the living room and flung herself into his arms.

Memories flooded him. The same perfume, the same clinging hands, the same soft voice chattering a mile a minute. *Angela.*

"Brett! I thought I heard your voice, but I didn't believe it. I'm so glad to see you, I just can't believe you're here." She threw her arms around his neck, half choking him.

He tried to disentangle himself, but Angela's words had pierced the din in the living room. In a moment he was surrounded.

He wasn't going to escape the party in the foreseeable future. And over Angela's head he saw Rebecca waiting, apparently ready to demand the answers he didn't intend to give.

Tension tightened Rebecca's nerves as she took a step back from the flurry of greetings. The quarrel that had flared up between her and Brett had taken her completely by surprise, and she needed a moment to think.

A cold hand clutched her heart. Brett couldn't be backing out of his agreement. He couldn't. She longed to push her sister out of the way, grab Brett's arm and demand that he explain himself.

Lord, what's happening here? We've waited so long for Brett to come back. You know how much Doc needs him, how much this town needs him. Doesn't he know that?

The middle of Mitch and Anne's party was no place for a confrontation. Still, she felt the rush of unasked questions pressing on her lips as if determined to get out.

She took a deep breath and pasted a smile on her face. She'd known the instant Brett walked in that his presence meant trouble. She'd seen him and felt as if someone had punched her right in the heart.

She pushed the thought away. Her long-ago feelings for Brett had been childish adoration, that was all. Not love. She'd been a kid. She hadn't known what love was.

Mitch Donovan had reached Brett, grabbing his

hand to shake it, and Brett's face lit with pleasure at the sight of his old friend. Rebecca took the opportunity to get a good look at Brett, one uncolored by shock at seeing him after all these years.

Some things hadn't changed. His hair, the color of antique gold, still fell, unruly, over his broad forehead. Green-as-glass eyes warmed as he hugged Anne Morden, Mitch's fiancée. He was taller and broader than she remembered—his shoulders filled out the dark wool blazer he wore—and his skin was still tanned, even though it was fall.

He still had that cleft chin, of course, and his smile was the one that had devastated the girls of Bedford Creek High. It had probably devastated quite a few women since, too.

Everyone wanted to talk to Brett, the local boy who'd made good. People were proud tiny Bedford Creek High had produced a graduate who'd gone to one of the best medical schools in the country, and Brett's mother had never let an opportunity pass to tell people how well he'd been doing.

Rebecca could slip away, unnoticed, out of the range of that smile and the memories it evoked.

She crossed the center hall to the dining room, trying to concentrate on the buffet. The cherry table had all its leaves in to accommodate the food her mother had insisted on. The moment she'd learned Rebecca was going to be Anne's bridesmaid, she'd begun planning the party, maybe considering it a trial run for the parties that would accompany Angela's wedding next spring.

Rebecca checked the platters, listening to the buzz of conversation, and frowned a little. Was she the only one who noticed a faint shadow in Brett's eyes when the subject of his Philadelphia residency came up? Maybe so. Or maybe she was imagining things in the flow of chatter and good humor and congratulations.

She'd thought at the time he took the residency that he should have come home instead. After all, Doc had helped Brett's family pay for his medical-school education when they'd had a struggle to meet tuition payments. He'd helped other young people, too, but Brett was different. He'd always expected that one day Brett would take over his practice. They'd planned it together, and the only reason Rebecca knew was because she worked so closely with Doc.

But the years had slipped away. Whenever she brought it up, Doc was philosophical. Let Brett take the residency, he'd said. It would make him a better doctor when he did come back.

Well, now he was home, but apparently not to stay. Her throat tightened. She hadn't realized how much she'd been counting on his return until she saw him. How much longer could they continue at the clinic if he didn't take over? The secret Doc insisted she keep weighed on her heart. If only she could share it with Brett— "There you are." Brett touched her arm, and the cake platter tilted in her grasp. He grabbed it, setting it down. "Anne sent me over to tell you to relax and enjoy the party. There's plenty of food here. More fat and calories than this bunch should have in a month."

She managed a smile. *Keep it light. You can't confront him here, so keep it light.* "You're back in Bedford Creek, remember? A party isn't a success unless the hostess stuffs everyone."

"Nobody serves crudités and yogurt dip?"

"Not unless they're serving fudge and cookies with it."

This was better, joking back and forth with Brett as if it were the old days, burying her worries about the clinic, about Doc, about the future. And ignoring the tingle of awareness his closeness brought. She had to keep things on this level for the moment.

She tried unobtrusively to move a step farther away. Ignoring his warmth and strength would be easier if he weren't quite so close to her, close enough to smell a faint trace of spicy aftershave, close enough to see the gold flecks in his green eyes.

"Anne tells me you're a bridesmaid in the wedding next month."

She nodded. It was safe to talk about Anne. "We've gotten to be good friends since she moved here. She's really someone special." The secret of Emilie's birth parents had brought Anne to Bedford Creek, but it was the love she'd found with Mitch that made her stay.

She looked at Anne, bending to disentangle Emilie's tiny fingers from the bow of a present. She admired Anne's cool urban elegance without wanting to be like her.

He followed the direction of her gaze. "They are happy, aren't they?" He almost sounded as if he needed assurance.

"Of course." Her surprise showed in her voice. "They're perfect for each other. Don't you think so?"

He glanced down at her. "Guess I never thought Mitch would settle down. But once he met the right woman, it was all over for him."

She couldn't help but smile. "You make it sound like a prison sentence. Is that how you see marriage?"

"It is meant to be permanent."

He looked back toward the other room, and she realized he was watching Alex Caine, the third member of the trio of friends. Alex, his lean face serious as always, stood back a little, leaning on the cane he sometimes had to use.

"Alex is doing better." She answered the question he didn't ask. Alex had barely survived a plane crash the year before, suffering a head injury that eventually healed and a shattered knee that still pained him. It was small wonder his friends worried about him.

Brett nodded. "Alex is tough—nobody knows that better than I do. He'll be fine." He focused on her. "So how come I haven't heard about an engagement party for you? Guys must be standing in line."

"In Bedford Creek?" She lifted her brows. "There aren't enough eligible single guys to form a line."

"Don't give me that. You ought to be wearing a ring, too."

She shook her head. "Always a bridesmaid, never a bride. That's the way I like it, although I'll never convince my mother. She's eternally hopeful of getting both her daughters married off."

"She must—" Brett interrupted himself to look down. "Did you know there was someone under the table?"

She bent, lifting the hem of the linen tablecloth. "Come out, Kristie. Come on, right now."

A small, sticky hand closed around hers, and her niece slid out from under the table. Chocolate smeared Kristie's hands and mouth.

"Who's this?" Brett knelt beside the pajama-clad figure. "I haven't met you before, have I?"

Finger in her mouth, five-year-old Kristie had an attack of shyness. She leaned against Rebecca's skirt, shaking her head.

Brett looked up, a question in his eyes.

"Kristie is Quinn's daughter." It was useless to hope he wouldn't ask more questions. He and Quinn were the same age, and they'd been childhood friends. "Honey, this is Brett. He's an old friend."

"I don't think I knew your brother had come back home." Brett stood. "My mother's intelligence-gathering skills must be getting rusty."

"He's not. Home, that is." Her heart ached at the thought of her brother's battle with grief over his wife's death six months earlier. "He's finishing up a job. Kristie is staying with us until he comes back."

Brett seemed to process very quickly all the things she didn't say. He smiled down at Kristie. "Sounds like you're a lucky girl, staying with your grandma and aunts. Is there still a tree house in the willow out back?"

Kristie nodded. "Aunt Rebecca and me painted it. It's yellow now."

"I'd like to see that sometime. Do you let boys in?"

That earned a shy smile. "You're not a boy."

"I'm not?" He gave her a shocked look.

"You're a man!" She erupted in giggles, and he joined her.

Brett had made another conquest, not surprisingly. He always had been able to charm the birds from the trees. And there was genuine kindness behind his smile. Small wonder even shy Kristie responded to it, just as Rebecca had.

She must have been about her niece's age when she'd solemnly asked Brett if he'd marry her when she grew up. They'd been in the tree house, and she could still smell the lilacs that had been blooming in the garden.

Brett had been kind; he was always kind. He'd taken both her hands in his and assured her she'd meet someone she'd love lots more than him. He was going to be a doctor, he'd told her. He promised he'd come back and take care of all of them.

She'd tried to blink tears away, knowing a rejection when she heard it, even at five. She'd nodded, as if accepting his words, but her heart had known she loved him.

Now, she could only hope Brett had forgotten that embarrassing incident.

"Come on." She took Kristie's hand. "Time we got you back to bed."

At least that would get her out of Brett's company for a few minutes. She wouldn't have to pretend nothing was wrong, and she wouldn't have to pretend she wasn't affected by seeing him again.

Kristie's curly red head burrowed against her skirt. "I'm tired, Auntie Rebecca. Carry me."

Brett scooped her up before Rebecca could move. "I'll take her."

"Wait, let me wipe off the chocolate." She snatched a napkin. "You don't need to do that. You should stay here and visit with people."

She hoped there wasn't a desperate edge in her voice. The last thing she wanted right now was to be alone with him.

He ignored her. "Here we go." He hoisted Kristie, hands now clean, to his shoulder. "Hold on tight." He started for the archway, bouncing her so that she giggled and clutched his hair.

Managing a meaningless smile for anyone who might be watching, Rebecca followed.

They trooped up the wide staircase. At the top,

she nodded toward the door next to hers. "This is Kristie's room."

"Duck your head, Kristie." He stooped under the door frame, earning another giggle, and plopped Kristie on the white single bed with its bright quilt. "Ready for bed."

"Wound up, you mean." Rebecca pulled back the quilt. "In you go, and say your prayers. It's way past bedtime, and you have school tomorrow, remember?"

Kristie pouted. "Don't want to go to bed. Don't want to go to school." She bounced. "I want to stay at the party."

Rebecca could read the warning signs of a disturbed night. "Kristie…"

Brett sat down on the edge of the bed. "You're not going to tell me this girl goes to school, are you? What are you…fifth grade? Sixth?"

Kristie giggled, not seeming to notice that he was putting her down on the pillow, tucking the quilt around her. "I'm in kindergarten."

"Wow!" He managed a suitable look of surprise as he clicked off the bedside lamp, leaving the room bathed in the soft glow of the night-light. "So how do you like kindergarten?"

"Okay, I guess." She looked down. "Sometimes Jeffy takes my crayons. And he says I'm a…a carrot-top." She said the word as if it were monstrous.

Rebecca's throat tightened. She'd known something was wrong at school, but Kristie had been stubbornly uncommunicative about it. Now she'd blurted it out to Brett on the basis of a five-minute acquaintanceship.

"Do you know what a carrottop is?" Brett smoothed her red curls.

She nodded solemnly. "Grandma had some carrots in her garden."

Brett lifted a springy strand of red. "I'll bet she did, but Jeffy was talking about your hair. Because he thinks it's the color of a carrot." He glanced up at Rebecca, smiling. "Aunt Rebecca had hair this color when she was your age, and I always thought it was the prettiest hair color in the world. Maybe Jeffy thinks so, too."

Rebecca's heart gave a ridiculous *thump*. He was talking nonsense to soothe Kristie, of course. She couldn't let it affect her. Couldn't let it bring back sharp, evocative images of a much younger Brett. He wasn't that person anymore. And she wasn't that little girl.

"But he teases me."

"I'll tell you a secret." Brett leaned close to the child and lowered his voice to a whisper. "Boys only tease girls they like." He looked up at her again, eyes laughing. "Isn't that right, Aunt Rebecca?"

She kept smiling by sheer effort of will, heart thumping. "That's right."

She wasn't the child who'd idolized him any longer. But she'd have to do something about the ridiculous way her heart turned over every time he smiled at her.

Chapter Two

Memories assailed Brett as he poured a mug of coffee in the sunny kitchen of his parents' house the next morning. Memories of himself and Angela, back when she'd been the most important person in his world. He had to smile now at that infatuation. Angela didn't seem to have grown up at all since then. It was Rebecca whose maturity astounded him.

Mitch and Alex hadn't changed, though.

He smiled, thinking of them, but a shadow tinged his mind. He could keep his problems a secret from most people, but he couldn't withhold them from Alex and Mitch.

Still, their support was one thing he knew he could always count on, no matter what. The three of them had faced death together, once upon a time. That had created a bond nothing could break.

His mind drifted back to the party the night before.

Rebecca had been right—Mitch and Anne really were meant for each other. The fact that they'd be starting married life with a ready-made family of her adopted baby and his foster son just seemed to add to their glow.

Alex was another story. Brett frowned down at his cup. Alex might be able to hide his pain from other people, but not from him. He'd give anything for a look at Alex's medical charts. He owed Alex—owed him a lot. If there was a way he could make up for the past, he'd like to find it.

He put down the coffee. Somehow everything— every concern, every conversation, even every thought, led him straight to the clinic. Rebecca was probably wondering why he wasn't there already, and she wouldn't hesitate to tell him so. If he'd known pesky little Rebecca would turn into such a beautiful, determined young woman, maybe he'd have stayed in touch.

Or maybe he'd have avoided her like the plague.

He didn't owe Rebecca an explanation, regardless of whether she agreed. But he certainly owed one to Doc, easy or not—and it was time he paid him a visit.

He drove out to the corner, then turned uphill. In Bedford Creek you were always going either up the mountain or down toward the river. There wasn't anything between. The town was wedged tightly into the narrow valley, with mountain ridges hemming it in.

The new tourist brochures his mother had sent him described Bedford Creek and its mountains as the Switzerland of Pennsylvania. People had obviously tried to live up to that billing, decking houses with colorful shutters and window boxes. Now, the boxes overflowed with marigolds and mums.

Apparently the publicity campaign was working. Strangers slinging cameras dotted the sidewalks, and a line waited to board the old-fashioned steam train for a jaunt through the mountains to see the autumn foliage. In another week or two the woods would be in full color, and the place jammed.

Doc Overton's clinic sat at the top of the hill, its faded red brick looking just the same as it always had. Brett's first glimpse of the familiar white clapboard sign swamped him in a wave of nostalgia. He pulled into the gravel lot and got out of the car slowly.

What had led to that promise he'd once made Rebecca about becoming a doctor? One of those early visits, when Doc thumped him and patted his head and told him he was fine? Or when Doc had responded to the interest he'd shown in some procedure, taking the time to explain it to him? Whenever it had been, Doc Overton had certainly been part of it.

It had been too long since he'd been back, too long since he'd let Doc know how much he appreciated his mentoring. That had to be a part of the talk they needed to have. He took the two steps to the porch and opened the door.

New wallpaper decked a waiting room that was far more crowded than he ever remembered it being. It looked as if he'd have to postpone their conversation. Clearly Doc wouldn't have time for a talk this morning—not with all these patients waiting.

He didn't intend to rush this conversation. Telling Doc the changes he wanted to make to the future they had once planned wouldn't be easy.

Maybe the best course was to see Doc and arrange a time when they could be alone, uninterrupted. He exchanged greetings with people he knew as he edged his way to the desk.

He nodded to the receptionist, wondering if she was someone he should remember. "I'm Dr. Elliot. I'd like a word with Dr. Overton when he has a moment."

"Brett." Rebecca appeared from behind the rows of files, looking startled. "I didn't expect to see you so soon."

He lifted an eyebrow. "Funny. I got the impression I'd better show my face around here pretty quickly or someone might get after me. Can't imagine why I thought that."

A warm flush brightened her peaches-and-cream complexion. "I can't either." She gestured toward the hallway. "Come on back."

The treatment area had changed even more than the waiting room. Cream paint unified it, and a modern counter had replaced the old rolltop desk where Doc had once kept a jumble of papers. Charts were neatly filed, and an up-to-date computer system ruled the countertop.

He stopped, assessing the changes, then turned to Rebecca. She'd changed, too. Her bronze hair was tied back from her face, and a matching bronze name pin adorned her neat uniform. Everything about her spoke of efficiency and professionalism. How strange to see little Rebecca so grown-up and businesslike.

"Were you responsible for all this?" He gestured toward the changes, knowing old Doc wouldn't have modernized a thing if someone hadn't pushed him into it.

She looked startled. "I guess I did suggest we were due for some up-to-date touches."

"You mean you nagged him until it was easier to say yes." He smiled at her. "Don't fib to me, Rebecca. I know both of you too well."

"Something like that." She smiled back, but there was a shadow behind it. She was probably still thinking about their unfinished conversation the night before—   "There you are."

The familiar voice sounded behind Brett, and he swung around.

"About time you were getting back here to see us."

"Hasn't been that long, has it?" He gripped Doc's hand, emotion flooding him. It *had* been too long. Rebecca had been right. Doc Overton was getting old.

The hair he remembered as iron gray was white

now, and Doc's shoulders stooped, as if he'd spent too many years carrying all the medical burdens of the town. The lines in his face formed a road map of wisdom and caring.

"Come here, boy." Not content with a handshake, Doc pulled him close for a quick hug, then pounded his shoulder. "Good to see you. How are they treating you at that big city hospital?"

There was the question he didn't want to answer, and it was the first one out of Doc's mouth, of course.

"Things are going okay." He managed a smile. "It was tough getting used to Philly after all those years in California."

"Not enough beaches, huh?" Those wise old eyes surveyed him. "If you want to succeed in this business, you have to make some sacrifices."

"Like having any time for yourself," Rebecca said. She held out a chart. "I'm sorry to interrupt the reunion, but you're running about an hour behind already."

"Doc always runs an hour behind," Brett said. That was probably because Doc had never heard the notion that the physician should spend only ten of his precious minutes with any single patient. And if he heard it, he'd dismiss it. He knew his patients too well to rush anyone out of the office. When you were closeted with Doc Overton, you felt as if you were the most important person in the world to him. "Don't people still set their clocks by him?"

Rebecca smiled, but it was more an automatic response than an agreement. "I'm afraid people are a bit more impatient than they used to be."

Doc shrugged, lifting his hands. "What can I do? This young woman runs the place, and she runs me, too. We'll have to get together later."

"How about supper tonight? We can catch up." And talk about the future.

Doc nodded. "Sounds good, if I get out of here at a decent hour. I'll call you."

"I'll see you later, then." He should be ashamed at the relief he felt over putting off the difficult conversation.

"Why don't you stay and help out?" Rebecca's voice stopped him before he took a step toward the door. "You're licensed in Pennsylvania, aren't you? You could see some of Doc's overflow and let him get through by lunchtime for once."

"You think people really want to consult a doctor they knew when he was a kid?" His reluctance surprised him. Maybe it was the thought of treating people he knew so well—people who'd watched him grow up.

"Don't worry about it." Rebecca gave him a challenging look. "They accept me as a professional, believe it or not. They'll listen to you."

His gaze clashed with hers. She'd made her attitude clear last night, even though they hadn't had a chance to talk about it again. She thought it was time he took over for Doc, and she probably couldn't imagine there might be something better than a one-doctor practice, either for the town or for him.

"Good idea." Doc nodded. "Let folks see a real city doctor for once."

Brett forced a smile. He wasn't about to let little Rebecca push him into saying anything to Doc about his plans in front of her, if that was in her mind. But he could hardly walk away with Doc looking at him so expectantly.

"Sure. I'll be glad to see some patients."

He caught the satisfied look on Rebecca's face, and his jaw tightened. Rebecca might have won this round, but if she thought she could manipulate him into doing what she wanted, she'd better think again.

Was her plan going to work? The question kept revolving in Rebecca's mind while she found a lab coat for Brett, showed him the examining rooms, led him through her system.

She hadn't been able to sleep after the party, her mind constantly returning to Brett. What had he meant when he'd said he was just home on a break? Didn't he realize how much Doc needed him? How much all of Bedford Creek needed him?

It had taken her longer than it should have to realize she needed to pray about it. Even then, she'd found herself wrestling with the situation, trying fruitlessly to see an immediate solution.

Finally, exhausted, she'd left it in the Lord's hands

and gone to sleep. And when she woke, the answer seemed so clear.

Brett wouldn't listen to her, and he certainly wouldn't let her tell him what to do. But if she showed him how desperately Doc needed him, he'd do the right thing, wouldn't he?

Doubt gripped her. The idealistic boy she'd known would have. She wasn't so sure about the sophisticated stranger he'd become.

Well, doing something was better than doing nothing. The opportunity to show Brett how much he was needed had come. She had to take advantage of it.

"If you're all set, I'll just see which of the patients would be willing to switch to you."

Brett raised an eyebrow. "Don't you mean, would agree to be fobbed off on the new guy?"

It was going to be tough to keep a professional distance, she thought, if he persisted in looking at her with that devastating smile. "I'm sure there won't be a problem. I'll just try to keep everyone happy." She shuffled rapidly through the charts.

"Is that your main objective in life?"

The question caught her by surprise. "What do you mean?"

He leaned against the counter next to her. "Keeping everyone happy. You seem to do a lot of that." He gestured at the renovated office. "You're certainly keeping Doc happy. And making a difference here. Is that why you chose a medical career?"

"I..." She bit back the response that sprang to her lips, shocked at her impulse to tell him he was responsible for that decision. That was something Brett didn't need to know about her. "I guess, in a way. Doc needs help, and it's not easy to find qualified medical personnel who want to come to a small town and work in a one-doctor clinic."

"So you felt it was your duty?"

He really seemed to want to understand. "It wasn't just that. My family's here, and after Dad died, they needed me."

The familiar picture formed in her mind. Her father, his face lined and tired, grasping her hand in his. *You're the responsible one, Rebecca. You'll have to take care of them.*

Brett nodded, but she could see the question still in his eyes.

"There are plenty of opportunities for physician's assistants these days," he said. "You could go almost anywhere."

"I'm happy here." Why did he assume that just because *he* couldn't wait to leave Bedford Creek, other people felt that way? "Not everyone's destined for the medical fast track."

He gave her a wary look. "Is that aimed at me, by any chance?"

She wouldn't get anywhere by antagonizing him. "No, of course not." She picked up a chart. "Are you ready for the first patient?"

His gaze probed for a moment, as if he tried to see into her thoughts.

Finally he nodded. "Bring them on. I'm ready."

She put Minna Dawson's chart in Brett's stack and showed him to an exam room. Chronic indigestion— and Minna was anxious to get back to the shop. She'd agree to see Brett if that meant moving her appointment up.

Doc fell further behind with every patient; everyone knew that. But everyone didn't know how tired he was. They didn't see the little lapses she'd been vigilant at catching and correcting.

Tension knotted her stomach. Doc had to have help, and soon. If only Doc would be honest about how much he needed Brett.

As she took histories for the other patients, did preliminary work-ups, and moved smoothly through the morning's routine, her brief conversation with Brett played over in her mind.

She'd have to be careful. Brett wouldn't respond to her trying to make him feel guilty. She knew that instinctively. Just as he seemed to know too much about *her* instinctively.

If he saw through her so easily, he'd figure out what she intended before she'd even started. She couldn't let that happen.

Somehow Rebecca had to see to it he realized this was where he belonged.

Please, God. Please let this work.

Repeating her prayer silently, she went to see how Brett was doing with Minna.

"I don't believe it, that's all." Minna sat on the edge of the table, clutching the paper gown around her with both hands, a mix of anger and fear on her face. "You're just making a big mistake!"

The woman's words rang in Brett's ears. *You're making a big mistake.* Those had actually been the supervising physician's words when he found Brett following his ethics instead of the hospital rules. Brett had known in that instant that he would have to sacrifice his fellowship for his principles.

Now he was hearing those words again, and by the look on the woman's face, she didn't have much trust in her new doctor.

His jaw clenched. Whether she trusted him or not, he had to make her listen.

"Now, Minna, you don't mean that." Rebecca's calm voice cut through the tension in the small room. Just her presence seemed to take the level down miraculously.

"Dr. Brett is a fine doctor," she went on, "but if you'd rather see Dr. Overton, we can arrange that. I'm afraid there will be a wait, though. He's so booked up today. It might delay your getting back to the shop."

The woman's death grip on her gown relaxed a little. "I can't have that." She scowled. "What a mess that girl will make of things if I'm not there, and there are plenty of visitors in town today."

Obviously Rebecca knew just what tack to take with the woman. Of course she knew the patients well. The Bedford Creek Clinic wasn't like a city hospital emergency room, where you treated someone and never saw him again.

"Now, Mrs. Dawson, I just want to run a simple test," he said. "It'll take no time at all." He met Rebecca's gaze over the woman's head. "EKG, okay?"

He saw the flicker of doubt in her eyes, and it nettled him. Who was the doctor here?

"Right away," she said, calmly professional whether she doubted his judgment or not.

"Don't see why I have to do that." Mrs. Dawson's lips pressed together. "It's worse than usual, but it must be my indigestion, see? Doc always gives me a prescription, and that fixes me right up. I don't need any test."

"This is like the one we did on your husband last year," Rebecca soothed. "You remember. It's just a precaution."

He seized on the word. "Just a precaution. It'll only take a few minutes, and then you'll be out of here. And if you want, we'll have Dr. Overton take a look at the results, too."

She nodded slowly. "Guess if Doc looks at it, it'll be all right."

He suspected he knew what Rebecca was thinking. That he was being presumptuous, that he was over-riding Doc's opinions. He nodded toward the hall, and Rebecca followed him out.

"You're thinking it's her heart?" Her golden-brown eyes were troubled.

He shrugged. "I don't like the pain she's having, or the rapid pulse." He tried a smile. "Could be because I was holding her hand, but I don't think so."

She didn't argue, but he could sense the reservation was still there.

"Well, we'll know soon enough."

He stayed out of the way while Rebecca went to get the EKG machine then returned to the exam room. The last thing the patient needed was any white-coat anxiety at the sight of a new doctor. Especially a new doctor she didn't particularly trust.

He frowned. He was more concerned about Doc's reaction. The first patient he saw, and she'd put him in the position of contradicting his old mentor. Doc had been treating her for indigestion, not angina.

He shook his head. At least Doc would probably be more forgiving than Dr. Barrett had been when Brett disagreed with him.

"The woman should have been sent to the county hospital." Dr. Barrett's tone had been icy. "They handle the indigent cases."

Brett could have protested that she needed care immediately, but Barrett would have disagreed. He could have said that for the first time in a long while he was doing what God called him to do, but that argument wouldn't have impressed Barrett. As far as Barrett was concerned, *he* was God in his little medical world, and no hapless resident should try to challenge him.

So Brett had put himself on the line, insisting the woman be admitted and going over Barrett's head when he had to. Barrett had given in, but the payback had come soon enough. The surgical fellowship he'd been a shoo-in for had disappeared.

"Here it is." Rebecca came out into the hall with the strip, just as Doc appeared. Obviously she had alerted him, and Brett felt another spurt of annoyance.

Doc reached for the strip. "Let's have a look."

His tone was neutral, but Brett's jaw tightened. He didn't like being in opposition to Doc, even though he was sure he was doing the only thing possible.

Doc frowned.

Brett's tension edged up. "How's it look?"

"The EKG is definitely out of normal range." Doc pushed his glasses into place on his nose, his hand fumbling with them. "I should have suspected it was more than indigestion before this. If I'd done an EKG last month, it might have shown something then." He handed Brett the strip. "Mind if I talk to her? It might come better from me. She'll have to go to the hospital for more tests on her heart."

He shook his head. "Of course not. She's your patient. She'll want to hear it from you."

He should feel good. He'd been right. But he couldn't erase the stricken look from Doc's eyes.

He stayed out of the way while Doc soothed the

woman and talked to the husband called in from the waiting room, and Rebecca made efficient arrangements for her transport to the nearest hospital.

"Forty miles away." He stood next to her as she hung up the phone.

"Forty miles by mountain road." She grimaced. "It's okay for Minna, but sometimes…"

She let that thought trail off, but he knew what she meant. Forty miles might as well be four hundred, in some cases. Bedford Creek should have a better choice than one overworked doctor or a forty-mile drive.

"Now, you're going to be fine." Doc went to the door with Minna and her husband. "They'll take good care of you, and I'll be by to see you tonight."

The fear seeped from the woman's face at the words. "All right, Doc. If you say so." She looked at him with absolute confidence.

The door closed behind them. Doc came back, rubbing his head wearily.

"You shouldn't drive clear over there tonight." The words were out before it occurred to Brett that Doc might take offense at his meddling.

Doc just shrugged. "Got to. She wouldn't rest easy if I didn't stop in. She trusts me." He straightened, looking at Brett. "That was a good call, Brett. I'm glad you were here today."

Funny. He'd forgotten, in all those years away, how much Doc's praise meant to him.

Chapter Three

Rebecca took a step back from Brett's smile, her heart thumping. He looked so… She wasn't sure what it was—but then suddenly she knew. He looked as if he belonged here once again, just as she'd hoped.

She tried not to jump to conclusions. It was a long way from treating one patient to deciding to stay. But she had to find out what he felt.

"I guess you get more exciting cases in Philadelphia, don't you?"

"Some." He shrugged. "But you're involved with people's whole lives here. That's worth a lot."

"It's satisfying."

So maybe Brett wasn't as happy in his big hospital career as he'd thought. Maybe, if she could talk him into helping at the clinic for a while, he'd realize this was where he belonged.

She eyed him cautiously as he consulted with Doc

over a chart. He glanced up, gave her a quick smile and turned back to their consultation.

Her heart clenched. A quick smile—that's all it had been, but it had transported her back in time. She saw herself, an awkward thirteen-year-old, watching as the boy she loved pinned an orchid to her sister's prom gown. He'd looked up for an instant, noticed her and smiled. Then all his love and attention had veered back to Angela, leaving Rebecca alone and bereft.

She swallowed. "I'll order sandwiches from the café for lunch. Brett, what would you like?" She tried to sound like the cool professional she was.

He turned toward her, his arm brushing hers. Her breath caught in her throat.

If he stayed—as he must—they'd be working together every day. She had to find a way to handle that. She couldn't let Brett turn her into a lovesick adolescent again.

She wouldn't, that was all. He obviously still regarded her as his almost-kid sister. He'd never look at her any other way, and she didn't want him to. He wasn't the boy she'd fallen in love with, and she wasn't sure she even liked the man he'd become.

When lunch arrived from the Bluebird Café, they sat around the table in Doc's office with their sandwiches. Rebecca let the conversation flow between the two men, watching them. Doc was so tired, and yet so happy Brett was here. Didn't Brett see that?

Finally Doc pushed the empty sack away and stretched. "Good sandwich." He said that every day about the turkey club Cassie sent for him. "Do I have enough time to rest my eyes?"

She consulted her watch. "Plenty of time. You take a quick nap, and I'll call you five minutes before your first appointment."

"I don't nap," he said with dignity as he got up. "I just rest my eyes."

"Right." She smiled at Brett as the door closed behind him. "And he snores while he rests his eyes."

Brett smiled back, but then he sobered. "He's getting old. I know you said that, but I didn't believe it until I saw him. I always thought he'd go on forever."

"He thinks so, too." She tossed the lunch remains in the trash. "That's part of the problem. He won't take it easy. He can't. I'm afraid one day he'll lie down for his rest and not get up again." *Please understand.*

Brett frowned. "Is he all right? Has he had a thorough work-up?"

"As thorough as he'll let me do." She spread her hands flat on the table. This was the first time she'd felt able to talk to someone about this. If only she could tell him everything…but she couldn't. She'd promised Doc.

Still, it was good to share the worry. Good because it was Brett, whom Doc loved like a son and took pride in.

"He claims he's just tired out, that's all. He works a schedule that would exhaust a younger man, and he never takes a break."

Brett's green eyes darkened. "There has to be something we can do."

You can take over the practice, the way he planned. She closed her lips on that. It would only lead to another argument.

"Maybe he'd let you check him out." She hesitated, half afraid to say anything else. If Doc knew she'd suggested a checkup, he'd be furious. But she had to. No one else would. "Look, I know you said you were just here on a break." The word tasted bitter, but she pushed on. "But you could help out while you're here."

His frown deepened, creating three furrows between his eyes. "That's not a solution."

Her resolve slipped. "The best solution would be for you to stay."

He shoved back his chair, stalked to the window, and stared out at the aspen tree, tinged now with gold. "You really think that's what these people need? Horse-and-buggy medicine? A one-doctor town?"

She shot to her feet. "Doc's a good physician. He gives people everything he has."

He lifted his hand as if to stave off her attack. "I know that. But I also know it's worn him out."

She fought down her anger. Anger wouldn't help. She had to get him to make a commitment—just a small one.

"He needs a rest. He'd get that if you helped out for even a week before you go back to Philadelphia."

"I'm not going back to Philadelphia." He swung around, but she couldn't see his face clearly with the light behind him.

"What do you mean? Your residency—"

"I completed my residency. I thought I'd be starting a surgical fellowship, but the one I expected to have isn't going to be there."

His voice sounded flat, denying any emotion, but she knew better. She rose, moving toward him until she could see his expression clearly. It didn't tell her much. He was hiding something; she knew that without analyzing how or why she did.

"Then you're free to stay in Bedford Creek, aren't you?"

His mouth tightened at her persistence. "You'd better understand, Rebecca. I'm not prepared to settle down in this town for the rest of my life. There are other fellowships out there."

The anger she'd been trying to suppress spurted out. "So you're just home while you look for a new fellowship. You're going to ignore the debt you owe to Doc."

"I'm not ignoring anything." His green eyes sparked with anger. "This is between me and Doc."

"You haven't even told him yet!" She wanted to shake him. Didn't he understand what was at stake?

His face hardened, becoming the face of a stranger.

"I'll tell him when we have supper together tonight. Until then, I'd suggest you stay out of it."

Brett found he was still fuming at the memory of that conversation as he drove up Main Street toward the café to meet Doc. Who did Rebecca think she was? She didn't have the right to interfere.

Didn't she? The reasonable question slid into his mind, deflating some of the righteous indignation he'd been fueling. She was obviously a big part of what kept the clinic going, so she had a stake in its future, if not in his.

Maybe part of his problem was the whole idea of little Rebecca, the tag-along kid sister, lecturing him about his responsibilities. A rueful smile touched his lips. He'd better admit it—he still hadn't gotten used to the grown-up Rebecca she'd become while his back was turned.

Who'd have guessed the gawky kid would blossom into a beautiful young woman? He'd found himself wanting to touch her cheek, just to see if it was as soft as it looked. Wanting to tangle his fingers in that silky hair…

Whoa, back off. This was little Rebecca he was thinking about—the Rebecca he'd always thought of as a kid sister. She undoubtedly still considered him a big brother. That was why she felt free to lecture him, just the way she would lecture Quinn. She'd never think of him any other way.

He couldn't possibly be attracted to her. He saw again those golden-brown eyes, warming with a smile for him, and felt a jolt that had nothing brotherly about it. Okay, maybe he could be attracted to her, but he wasn't going to do anything about it.

Nothing about a relationship with Rebecca could be at all casual, and he knew it, so there wasn't going to be anything. The future he had mapped out for himself didn't include the possibility of marriage for a long time. He travels fastest who travels alone—and he intended to keep moving.

So he'd ignore the surge of attraction he felt every time he saw Rebecca. Given the way she felt about him right now, that shouldn't be difficult. She'd be only too happy to ignore him.

He pulled into a parking space in front of the Bluebird Café, switched off the ignition and took a deep breath. Telling Rebecca he wasn't staying had been difficult enough. Telling Doc seemed almost impossible.

He got out and stood for a moment. The setting sun edged behind the mountain, sending streaks of orange along the horizon, softening slowly to purple. He'd forgotten how quickly twilight came in the narrow valley, closing in as the sun disappeared.

It had been a long time since he'd stood still and watched the sun go down. Peaceful. He could use some of that peace right now, as he prepared to break the news to Doc. He turned, pushed open the door, and saw Doc waiting at a table in the back.

The opportunity he needed didn't come immediately. Doc had already consulted the cardiologist who'd seen Minna at the hospital, and he clearly wanted to talk about his diagnosis and treatment plan. It wasn't until Doc had scooped the last bit of chicken gravy onto his roll and popped it in his mouth that he began to run out of shoptalk.

Finally Doc pushed his plate aside and propped his elbows on the red-and-white checked tablecloth. He peered at Brett over the top of the glasses that constantly slid down his nose, his faded blue eyes intent.

"Okay, out with it."

Brett discovered he was clutching the checked napkin like a lifeline. "What do you mean?"

Doc lifted his eyebrows. "You think I'm so old I can't tell when something's wrong with you?"

"No, I guess not." Some of his tension slipped away. "I've been working up my nerve to tell you something."

"Wouldn't have anything to do with a difference of opinion you got into with a supervising physician, would it?"

He hoped his mouth wasn't hanging open. "How did you know that?"

Doc shrugged. "I still have my sources. You want to talk about it?"

The café was empty except for them, and Cassie James, the owner, after checking at least three times to be sure they had everything, had retired to the kitchen.

"There's not much to tell." Brett frowned, studying the bluebird on the heavy white coffee mug. He didn't want it to sound as if he were making excuses for himself. "I was doing an ER rotation, and the paramedics brought in a street person in pretty bad shape. Standard procedure was to send them to county, but I felt she wouldn't stand the trip. I scheduled her for surgery." He took a breath, remembering. "Dr. Barrett didn't agree, and I had to go over his head."

"Were you right?"

He reached inside himself for the answer. Was he right? "Yes."

Doc nodded sharply. "Then that's what matters. Forget Barrett. He's not as important as he thinks he is."

"Unfortunately he's important enough to control who gets the surgical fellowship. And it's not going to be me."

He met Doc's gaze, and saw instant sympathy reflected there, followed by a sudden spark of hope. He had to get the rest of it out before Doc could build too much on his words.

"Doc, I know we used to say I'd come back here after my training and take over the clinic so you could retire." He found his throat closing. How could he say that the life Doc loved wasn't the one he wanted?

Doc looked away, seeming to stare out the window that overlooked Main Street. When he looked back at Brett, there was no condemnation in his face—just understanding. "Your dreams have changed."

He nodded. "Yes, I guess they have." His voice

sounded husky, even to himself, and his throat felt tight. "I didn't realize then what possibilities there are in medicine. Now…"

"Now you want something more." Doc rearranged his cup and saucer, his hand trembling slightly. "Can't say I'm surprised. I guess I always figured you might discover talents you didn't know you had."

"I don't want to let you down." The strength of that feeling surprised him. "I'd never want to disappoint you. I'll repay every cent you loaned me. But I'd like to try for another surgical fellowship."

There, it was out.

Doc didn't say anything for a long moment. Then he smiled. "Any program head who doesn't take you is a fool." He reached out to clasp Brett's hand. "You're going to make us all proud, son."

"But you—"

"I'm not ready to retire yet," Doc said quickly. "The right person will come along to take over the clinic long before I'm ready to hang it up. Shoot, what would I do if I quit? Chase a little white ball around a golf course? Not for me."

"You might get to like it."

"I like what I'm doing now just fine." Doc shoved his sleeve back to glance at his watch. "Speaking of which, I'd better get on the road to the hospital. Minna's expecting to see me."

"I'll pay you back, you know. I mean it."

Doc shook his head. "Help someone else instead."

He put his hand on Brett's shoulder. "It's all right, Brett. You're not letting me down."

It was one thing to hear Doc say the words. It was quite another to believe them. Brett watched Doc make his way to the door, stop to exchange some joking words with Cassie, then go out. His shoulders were stooped, his walk almost a shuffle.

Pain gripped Brett's heart. It wasn't all right. Even if he didn't intend to settle down in Bedford Creek for the rest of his life, he couldn't just walk away. Somehow, he had to do something.

Rebecca sat on the front porch swing, watching the stars come out one by one in the sliver of sky that wasn't blocked by the maple trees lining the street. She should go in. She shivered, pulling her sweater more closely around her shoulders. Nights got cool in the mountains in September.

She glanced across the lawn to the house next door. She might as well admit it. She was waiting for Brett to come home from his meeting with Doc.

She'd really messed up her fine plan. She bit her lip. The plan wasn't at fault, her temper was. She'd let it get control of her tongue, and she'd antagonized Brett so thoroughly that now he'd never listen to her.

Lord, please help Doc do a better job of this than I did. I'm sorry I spoke hastily and messed things up.

The Lord must get tired of hearing her confess the same sin over and over again, she thought. She pushed the swing with her foot, listening to the comforting *creak*. Each time, she promised to try harder, but trying harder didn't seem to be the answer.

She tried to picture Doc and Brett talking together over their meal. She'd like to believe Doc was insisting Brett follow through on his promise. She'd like to, but she couldn't. Doc would never admit how desperately he needed help.

Headlights pierced the darkness, illuminating the trunks of the maples. Brett parked at the curb, got out, and stood for a moment, looking in her direction. Then he walked toward her, and suddenly her heart seemed to be beating way too fast.

Enough, she lectured. *Brett doesn't mean anything to you anymore, remember?*

His footsteps crunched through the fallen leaves on the walk. "Mind if I join you?"

She shrugged, moving over to make room on the swing. It creaked as he sat. He leaned back, and she tried to ignore the warmth that emanated from him. Tried, and failed.

"This has to be the same swing." He pushed gently with his foot. "I remember the creak."

"You should. You and Angela spent enough time out here."

She remembered, too. Remembered sitting at her bedroom window in the dark, listening to their soft, private laughter and the creak of the swing. Wishing *she* were sitting beside him.

"The good old days." He leaned back, staring up at the stars as she had done. "Seems like a lifetime ago."

"It probably seems longer to you because you've been so many different places since then." She bit back the words that wanted to spill out about where he'd been and where he was going in the future.

"I guess." He pushed again, the swing moving back and forth with a little more energy, as if it picked up on some agitation he didn't show.

She couldn't pretend she didn't know where he'd gone tonight, and she couldn't act as if it didn't matter. She'd just have to choose her words carefully, that was all. Brett seemed willing to forget their earlier quarrel, and she had no desire to remind him.

"Did you and Doc have a nice supper?" That was neutral enough, surely.

A faint smile flickered on his lips. "We ate at the Bluebird Café. Hasn't anyone in this town heard of healthy cuisine?"

"Only the newcomers. Let me guess. Doc had chicken and gravy."

He nodded. "Got it in one. And rolls with butter, and mashed potatoes."

"Nobody can resist Cassie's homemade rolls." This didn't seem to be getting them any closer to the subject she needed to discuss, but at least they weren't sniping at each other.

"Doc should at least cut down on the butter, and

he knows it. That's what he'd tell a patient." He frowned, turning to face her. The swing stopped abruptly as he planted both feet on the porch. "He needs to retire."

"Did he say so?"

"No." He gave an exasperated sigh. "Of course he didn't say so." He shook his head. "Go on, ask. You know you want to."

He sounded frustrated, but not angry, so maybe it was safe to broach the sore subject.

"Did you tell him?" She held her breath, waiting for an explosion.

His jaw tightened. "Yes. I told him. I think he'd already guessed most of it."

"What did he say?"

"About what you'd expect."

She swallowed hard. "That's it, then." She hated saying the words. "He's given you his blessing. You can go away and forget about the clinic." *About us.*

"You know I can't."

She looked up at him. He was very close to her, but it was hard to make out his expression in the dark.

"What do you mean?" She held her breath. Maybe he was about to say—

"I mean you were right. I can't ignore this. I owe Doc too much for that."

Hope surged through her. "You'll stay?"

He shook his head, and the hope died as quickly as it had come. "I can't. Try and understand that, Rebecca. Doc does."

"I don't." If that was incitement to a quarrel, it would have to be. "You admit you owe Doc. Is that how you intend to repay him? By leaving?"

"I'll help out at the clinic for the time being." He sounded grimly determined. "And while I'm doing that I'll figure out a way Doc can retire with an easy mind. But as for the future…" He shrugged. "I don't think it's going to be the way you wanted."

She already knew that. Dreams didn't come true, not in real life. Prince Charming didn't come back for Cinderella.

"I guess not."

The swing creaked as he moved. Then he touched her chin lightly, the way he'd tease a smile from a child. The warmth of his hand flowed through her, and her heart stuttered.

"Don't think too badly of me, okay? Maybe none of us should be held to promises we make when we are kids. After all, you promised to marry me if I'd just wait until you were grown up."

He must feel the warmth that flooded her cheeks. "That was a long time ago."

"Now you're all grown up, and everything's changed." His hand still lingered against her cheek. "I've changed, too. But I'm going to do my best to help Doc, so I guess we'll be seeing a lot of each other."

A faint hope flickered. He'd be helping out at the clinic every day. Maybe being there would make him realize this was where he belonged. Maybe God was giving her another chance to convince him to stay.

The trouble was, she'd have to find a way to do it without having her heart broken by the man she'd given it to when she was five.

Chapter Four

The good thing about going to the café for breakfast, Brett decided, was that no one bothered you unless you wanted to talk. When he'd walked in the door, the early morning regulars had greeted him as if he'd been there yesterday morning, instead of years ago. Then they'd gone back to their newspapers or conversations about the weather and the state of tourism.

Nostalgia had prompted him into the third booth from the back, the one that had belonged to him, Alex and Mitch when they were in high school. The blue-padded seats looked like the same ones. With a mug of Cassie's coffee steaming in front of him, he shook out the newspaper and prepared to get up-to-date on Bedford Creek news.

Halfway through the front page, someone slid onto the bench across from him. He looked up to find Mitch flagging Cassie and the coffeepot.

She got there before he could gesture again. "Like old times, the two of you sitting here together." She set the heavy white mug on the table and filled it in a swift, efficient movement. "You just need to get Alex here with you."

"We'll work on it." Mitch waved away a menu. "Just coffee, thanks."

Brett raised an eyebrow. "Does Anne have you on a diet?"

"I had breakfast two hours ago. Cops get an earlier start than doctors."

Mitch might have been up for hours, but his blue uniform was as sharply pressed as if it had just come off the rack. That was the lingering effect of years in the military, Brett had always supposed.

"When I was interning, I don't think I ever went to bed. Come on, Mitch, admit it. You've got it soft these days. Cushy job in a small town, beautiful wife-to-be…"

Mitch grinned. "Plus a couple thousand tourists, no staff to speak of and two kids."

"And you love it," Brett pointed out.

"And I love it." Mitch's smile softened, as if he were thinking of Anne. "I'm one lucky guy." Then his gaze focused on Brett. "What about you?"

The mixture of relief and guilt he'd felt the night before flooded back. "I told Doc last night."

"And?"

Brett shrugged. "Great, fine, I have his blessing.

You know Doc. He wouldn't say anything else."
Maybe that was what bothered him most—that Doc
would be so unfailingly supportive, even when Brett
was disappointing him.

"Look, you have to do what you're called to do."
Mitch spread big hands flat on the table. That was
what he'd said when Brett told him the day before.
"We both know that. Doc knows it, too."

"I wish it were as clear-cut as that. If Doc were ten
years younger, it might be. But I've seen him at the
end of the kind of day he's putting in at the clinic. He's
exhausted. It's time he took it easier—even thought
about retirement."

Mitch shook his head. "Doc won't retire. Face it.
He'd rather die in harness."

"I'm not going to let it come to that."

"So what are you going to do? You can't force him
to take it easy. He's the only doctor in town, remember?"

The decision he'd made the night before still
seemed right. "That just means I have to act fast. I
have to find someone else to work at the clinic, eventually take over for him. That's the only way."

Mitch's skeptical look spoke volumes. "Easier said
than done. The clinic board tried that a couple of
years ago. The world isn't filled with doctors who
want to settle down in a town of five thousand, miles
from anywhere. And anyone who was interested, Doc
didn't think was good enough."

"There has to be someone." Stubborn determination filled him. "And I'm going to find him. Or her. I've already talked to Rebecca about it."

Mitch frowned. "I guess we both know what Rebecca thinks you should do."

"She's made that abundantly clear," Brett said. His mouth twisted wryly. "She looked about ready to have me horsewhipped when I said I wasn't back to stay."

"I can imagine. She feels pretty strongly about Doc."

"I know." Brett turned the bluebird-patterned mug in slow circles on the tabletop. "I don't quite know why she's here, though. She could have gone anywhere when she finished her training."

"That's about when her father was diagnosed with cancer," Mitch said. "You know how close they were. Rebecca came home to see him, and just stayed. Doc was in and out of the house all the time. John Forrester was a friend as well as a patient."

"He was a good man." John Forrester—quiet, unassuming, honest—had been part of Brett's life for as long as he could remember. "I can understand why she came back then, but not why she stayed."

"I guess she felt her mother needed her," Mitch said. "Face it, Angela's got a good heart, but she doesn't have a whole lot of common sense. And when Quinn's wife died, his little girl moved in with them. Rebecca's got her hands full, I'd say."

"Yes, I guess she has." And probably a big debt she felt she owed Doc.

"One thing's sure." Mitch smiled, but his eyes were serious. "If Rebecca thinks anything you do will hurt Doc, she really will horsewhip you. I guarantee it."

Rebecca couldn't let it go. She paused in the parking lot outside the clinic, lifting her face to the September sunshine. That conversation with Brett ran through her mind over and over again.

He would leave. That was the bottom line. He'd try to solve Doc's problems before then, but she knew the reality of the situation, even if he didn't. He wouldn't find a solution—not in a few short weeks, not even in a few months, probably.

That panicked sense of time running out gripped her again. What was she going to do?

She closed her eyes. *Help me, Father. Please. You'll have to guide me, because I don't know what to do.*

When she opened her eyes, the autumn colors seemed a little more golden. She took a deep breath, some of the tension in her shoulders ebbing. Now if she could just remember to leave the burden in God's hands, instead of picking it up again, she'd be better off. She took another deep breath and walked into the clinic.

Brett was already there. He stood at the cabinet, looking over some files, and her heart thudded at the sight of him. He glanced up, sea-green eyes frowning, and waved a chart at her.

"Where are Alex's medical records?"

She frowned right back. "Are you seeing him today?"

"No." He eased away from the drawer, looking surprised that she'd question him. "But I'd still like to see them."

She hesitated. What would Doc say to that? Brett didn't really have any official standing, but…

"You're the one who wanted me here," he reminded her, seeming to finish the thought for her. "If I'm practicing medicine and treating Doc's patients, I have a right to see the records."

And he expected her to jump to do his bidding. She stiffened. It was easy to forget that kind of attitude existed when you worked for Doc, who always asked, never ordered.

"Yes, Doctor," she said with careful formality. She marched to the cabinet and pulled the files he wanted. "The records are on the computer, as well."

He reached out, but instead of taking the folder he closed his hand over hers. Her pulse ricocheted against his grip.

"Sorry." He gave her a rueful smile. "I didn't mean to snap. I was preoccupied. Thank you." He released her hand, took the files.

She had to resist the urge to put her fingers over the warm spot where his touch had been.

"You're welcome." Her gaze met his and lingered. Then she cleared her throat and stepped back, heart pounding. "Is Doc in yet?"

"I'm here."

She spun at the sound of his voice. Doc stood inside the back door, eyeing them with an expression she couldn't interpret. She felt her cheeks grow warm. How long had he been watching?

"Brett." Doc walked toward them and dropped his bag on the countertop. "I didn't expect to see you today."

Brett shrugged. "I thought you might be able to use a little help while I'm in Bedford Creek. You're not going to kick me out, are you?"

"Course not." Doc's gravelly voice roughened a little. He turned toward his office, then looked back over his shoulder. "Rebecca, will you come in when you have a minute?"

She followed him into the office. Once the door was closed he looked at her, frowning a little. "Why is Brett here?"

She felt instantly guilty, as if Doc had heard her discussing him with Brett. "I...well, you heard him. He wants to help out while he's home."

"You suggest that to him?"

She couldn't lie to Doc, of all people. "I told him I thought you ought to take it easy for a bit. But coming in today is his idea. He wants to be here."

Doc's frown deepened. "You didn't tell him about my little problem."

"That series of dizzy spells you're having isn't a 'little' problem."

"Two isn't a series. Did you tell him?"

If only she could believe there had just been two. "No, of course not. But I think you should."

"Out of the question."

"But, Doc, he cares about you."

"That's why," he said gruffly. "Bad enough having you hovering over me, telling me to rest, wanting me to see a specialist. I don't want to hear it from him, too."

"I haven't given you advice you wouldn't give any other patient." Her mind raced through the possibilities suggested by Doc's dizzy spells, his forgetfulness. None of them was good.

"I'm fine." He dodged that truth, as she knew he would. "If Brett wants to help out, all right. But I'm holding you to your promise. He's not to know."

"He won't hear it from me."

But if Brett was the physician Doc thought he was, he'd figure it out for himself, sooner or later. What would his reaction be? Apprehension prickled her skin. She might have predicted the reaction of the idealistic young Brett he used to be. But not of the man he was now. And she wasn't sure she could trust what he might do with the knowledge.

The day's routine started to roll, carrying her with it and wiping out the time for worrying. Rebecca quickly discovered that handling the system for two physicians was considerably more difficult than handling it for one. By afternoon she sensed that she, like Doc, was falling behind.

She was on the phone, trying to set up a series of tests Doc had ordered, when Brett appeared in the hallway and dropped a chart in front of her.

"I've finished with the maternity case. Did you do the preliminaries on the next patient?"

She put her hand over the receiver. The lab had put her on hold, anyway. "Not yet. I'm setting up some tests for Doc." And how could he possibly be done with his last patient already?

"Can't someone else do that?" He frowned, looking around the office as if expecting to see a complete staff suddenly appear.

"There isn't anyone else, except the receptionist. And she doesn't have a firm enough touch to deal with the lab. They'd be scheduling Doc's patients for the middle of next year if she did it."

His fingers drummed on the countertop. "This isn't a good use of your time or mine."

Her temper flared. "You've been here less than twenty-four hours. Do you think you know your way around the clinic better than—" The lab came back on the line just then, interrupting her before she could say anything more. "No, that won't do," she said firmly. "Tomorrow at the latest." The lab prepared to argue.

Brett, frowning, picked up the next chart and went to call the patient himself. The expression on his face annoyed her so much that she snapped at the lab, with the surprising result that Doc's patient was scheduled for that very afternoon.

She hung up, feeling guilty. She shouldn't have snapped, either at Brett or the lab.

My temper, again, Lord. I'm sorry.

Brett was relentlessly formal the rest of the day. By the late afternoon lull, she knew she had to do something to make amends. She fixed a mug of coffee and carried it into the office, where Brett was catching up on some of the endless paperwork.

At least, that's what she'd thought he was doing. She found him on the phone.

"…must know someone." He paused at the sight of her, then gestured her in. "Sure, that's okay. It's a town-owned clinic—currently one doctor and a physician's assistant."

He reached for the mug. She was so stunned that it took her a moment to react. She handed it to him.

"Tell anyone who's interested to contact me here. Thanks a million, Tom. I won't forget it."

He hung up.

"You're already looking for someone else."

He turned a surprised look on her. "Of course. Isn't that the whole point?"

"I just didn't think you'd be working on it already."

"You mean you hoped I wouldn't be working on it at all."

Maybe that was what she'd hoped, but she didn't

intend to admit it to him. "You're not wasting any time."

The words came out more bitterly than she thought they would. She'd known he'd do this, but she hadn't expected it so quickly. She'd thought he'd take the time to get used to the clinic's needs, involving himself while he did. She'd thought she'd have more time to convince him to stay.

Brett pushed himself away from the desk, standing to lean on it with both fists. "That's right. I said I didn't intend to let Doc struggle on his own, and I don't. If I can get a couple of viable candidates, I'll present them to the board."

"Doc will have something to say about whether they're viable or not."

"Let me handle Doc." He seemed to withdraw, becoming again the stranger she didn't know. "Just don't interfere, Rebecca. I'm doing what's best for all of us."

She bit back the words that would lead to an open breach between them. She couldn't afford that, not when there was the slightest chance he'd decide to stay. He might think he could talk Doc into something else, but she knew better. But her hope was becoming dimmer by the moment.

Rebecca walked into the house with a sense of relief. Home. The welcoming atmosphere surrounded her as soon as she closed the door. She could relax and give herself a brief respite from worrying about Doc or thinking about the clinic. Best of all, she could stop fretting about Brett Elliot.

"Aunt Rebecca!" A small tornado hurtled down the steps. Kristie threw herself at Rebecca, trusting she'd be caught.

"Hi, sweetie." Rebecca hugged her, enjoying the feel of small arms around her neck and silky hair against her cheek. "How was school today?"

"Come see." Kristie tugged her toward the living room. "See all my papers." She pointed to the array spread atop the coffee table.

The kindergarten class had obviously been painting. Bright colors splashed across large sheets of construction paper and ran exuberantly into each other.

"Wow. Did you do all those?"

Kristie nodded proudly. "I wore my painting shirt, and I didn't get any paint on me. See?" She stretched out her knit top for inspection.

"That's great, Kristie." She leaned over the table, hoping she'd be able to recognize something. "What a lot of nice colors you used."

"See, there's Grandma's house." Kristie put a small forefinger on a gray blob.

With that lead, Rebecca was able to identify the rest of the picture. "You painted the tree house. Neat."

"And there's Daddy." Kristie's voice wavered a little on that, and Rebecca's heart cramped.

"Who's this?" She pointed to two stick-like figures under a tree.

"That's me and Jeffy on the playground."

This was something new. "Are you and Jeffy getting along better now?"

She nodded. "I told him what Dr. Brett said about my hair. Dr. Brett knows lots more than Jeffy does, doesn't he?"

"I guess so." And why she should be so annoyed at having to admit that, she didn't know. She was glad Kristie had resolved her differences with Jeffy, even if Brett had been the catalyst.

"I like Dr. Brett." Kristie leaned against her confidingly. "Don't you, Aunt Rebecca?"

"Sure she does." Angela stood in the archway, looking at Rebecca with a mischievous smile.

"Angela…"

Her sister ignored the warning note. "She's always liked Dr. Brett. A lot."

"I was five at the time," Rebecca said shortly. "I grew out of it."

"I don't think so." Angela scooped Kristie up and danced with her across the room. "When Brett took me to the prom, you were green with envy—admit it."

Her cheeks got ridiculously hot. "I won't admit any such thing. When are you going to grow up? You're the one who was madly in love with Brett, remember?"

Kristie's eyes got huge. "Are you in love with Dr. Brett, Aunt Angela?"

"Course not, silly. I'm in love with Ron. We're going to get married, and you're going to be the prettiest flower girl there ever was."

"But Aunt Rebecca said—"

"She was just teasing, sweetie." She set her niece down. "You scoot into the kitchen. Grandma wants your help with supper."

Kristie darted through the swinging door to the kitchen.

Rebecca frowned. "I wish you wouldn't say things like that in front of Kristie. What if she repeats it?"

Angela's blue eyes sparkled with mischief. "So what? And that's a great idea, don't you think?"

"What's a great idea?"

"You. Brett."

"What about me and Brett?"

"You've always been crazy about him."

"Stop saying that." Rebecca glared at her. "It's not true."

Angela's eyebrows arched in disbelief. "He's back. You're here. You have a lot in common. Maybe this is your chance to get together with him."

"Get together? Angela, that is the most ridiculous thing I've ever heard."

"Why? It's not like you're seeing anybody else. Neither is he, as far as I can tell. I think you'd be great together."

"I think you're overdosed on wedding plans. Brett

doesn't see me that way, and I am certainly not interested in him."

"I don't know. I saw the way he looked at you at the party. He couldn't take his eyes off you."

Her heart gave a silly little *thump*. "That's just because he expected me to look like a kid."

"You could—"

"Forget it!" Rebecca glared at her. "No matchmaking, understand? Just because you're engaged doesn't mean you can go around putting everyone else in pairs."

The doorbell rang, cutting off whatever retort Angela might have made. Rebecca went quickly toward the welcome interruption, pausing for one last word over her shoulder to her sister. "And I absolutely do not want to hear another thing about Brett Elliot."

She yanked the door open. Brett stood on the porch.

After a frozen moment, he raised his eyebrows. "Am I too early?"

It was an echo of the first conversation they'd had when he came back. "Too early?"

"For supper."

When she didn't answer, a smile quirked his lips. "Let me guess. You didn't know your mother invited me for supper tonight. And you're not delighted at the news."

Chapter Five

Brett had been pleasantly surprised at the call from Mrs. Forrester inviting him to supper. Judging by the expression on Rebecca's face, she was equally surprised, but not pleasantly.

Maybe she'd just have to get used to the idea. Mrs. F had always had a soft spot for him, and he'd like her to go on thinking well of him. This dinner invitation was his chance to… What? Justify? Explain? That suddenly seemed kind of petty.

Rebecca, apparently becoming aware that she was blocking the door, stepped back with what should have been a welcoming gesture.

"I'm sorry. Mom didn't mention it to me. I was just surprised."

Soft peach color bloomed on her cheeks, reminding him again of the longing to touch. That feeling was better ignored.

"Maybe she thought you'd object if she told you." He moved inside, unable to resist the urge to tease her, just a little.

Her color deepened. "Of course not. After all, it's not as if it's the first meal you've had here."

"I did mooch quite a bit back in the old days, didn't I?" When he and Angela dated, and even earlier when he and Quinn had played ball together, he'd probably had as many meals here as at home.

"You were always welcome."

Rebecca's stiff reply amused him, but before he could tease her again, a small figure bounded into the hallway, closely followed by Angela.

"Dr. Brett!"

"Hi, Kristie. How's everything? Anyone called you carrottop lately?"

"I told Jeffy what you said," she announced. "So he doesn't call me carrottop anymore." She held out her hand. "Want to see my pictures?"

Angela linked her arm through his, smiling at him. "Let him relax, Kristie. He doesn't want to look at pictures now."

He didn't need the sharp glance from Rebecca to tell him what to say to that. He freed himself and took Kristie's hand. "Sure, I'd love to see them. What about Aunt Rebecca? Did she see them yet?"

Kristie nodded. "She said they're really colorful." She turned to Rebecca. "But you can look at them again, Aunt Rebecca, if you want to."

"I need to change my clothes first." Rebecca edged toward the staircase. "You show Brett, all right? Especially the nice one with you and Jeffy."

Since he didn't think Rebecca was anxious to get away from her niece, he suspected he was the cause of her sudden need to disappear. He smiled at her. "I'll see you at supper."

She nodded, then turned and hurried up the steps.

With a proprietary air that amused him, Kristie led him to the living room and proudly displayed her artwork. He made admiring noises, conscious that he was relaxing in an atmosphere that didn't seem to have changed in the last fourteen years. The same comfortable, overstuffed chairs, what looked like the same framed photos on the piano... Mrs. F must find reassurance in the familiar.

He could feel Angela growing impatient next to him as Kristie's art show continued. When the little girl pulled out the papers she proudly called her homework, Angela shook her head.

"Not now, Kristie. Brett and I want to visit. You go help Grandma in the kitchen."

Kristie pouted. "But I have to do my homework. Somebody has to help me."

"You know Aunt Rebecca will help you later. She always does. Go on, now, scoot."

So Aunt Rebecca was the one who helped Kristie with her homework, as well as tucking her into bed and painting the tree house with her. Rebecca seemed to be taking on most of the parenting duties with her brother's child.

He'd expected to enjoy catching up with Angela. But after listening to endless details about Angela's engagement, her wedding plans and her fiancé Ron's apparently brilliant career at the bank, he found he longed for Rebecca's return. Even when Rebecca was arguing with him, she was never boring.

But Rebecca didn't reappear until they gathered around the oval dining table. There her mother seemed to take it for granted that Rebecca would ask the blessing and supervise Kristie's meal.

Mrs. F handed him the platter of pot roast. "I fixed your favorite, Brett. You see, I haven't forgotten how you boys used to eat."

If he ate like this on a regular basis, he'd be a walking blimp. "Looks wonderful." He forked off the leanest piece he could see, and found Rebecca watching him with suppressed amusement in her amber eyes. She obviously knew just what he was thinking. "It's too bad Quinn can't be here to enjoy it."

"Poor Quinn." Mrs. F's soft brown eyes filled with quick tears. "You know about his loss."

"He knows." Rebecca sent a warning look toward Kristie.

Again he was surprised by the sense Rebecca was the responsible one. Why should Rebecca, the baby of the family, be the one who took charge? Because she wanted to? Or because no one else would?

It occurred to him that John Forrester, for all his quiet, unassuming air, had been the glue to hold the family together. Apparently Rebecca had taken over where her father had left off.

Angela handed him a steaming bowl of mashed potatoes. "Brett, we're just dying to hear about your plans. I know they're lots more exciting than anything we're doing in Bedford Creek."

"Oh, I don't know. Things seem pretty…controversial around here to me."

He watched Rebecca flush again at his use of the word. They both knew most of the controversy was between the two of them.

Rebecca's smile had an edge to it. "Do tell us about your plans. We all want to hear."

His gaze clashed with hers. He wasn't about to let little Rebecca make him uncomfortable, so he responded with a brief résumé of his completed residency.

Rebecca lifted her eyebrows. "And what comes next?" Her unspoken criticism came through loud and clear.

"I hope to do a surgical fellowship next. I have a couple of applications out, so I'll see where that leads."

"Where would you go?" Angela seemed more interested in the locale than the position.

"One's in San Francisco, one's in Chicago." He shrugged. "It's just wait and see, right now. Wish me luck."

If he'd been hoping for encouragement and support, he got it from Angela and her mother. But in the midst of their enthusiasm, he found he was watching Rebecca. Funny, suddenly her opinion was the one that mattered.

And he already knew what that opinion was.

Rebecca clenched her water glass until her fingers whitened. Why on earth had her mother invited Brett tonight of all nights? Things were happening too fast. She hadn't yet had an opportunity to process everything that had been said between them during the day, and now here he was, sitting across the table from her, perfectly at ease.

Or was he? She watched his strong fingers grip his knife as he cut the meat deftly. Maybe he was holding on a bit too tightly, just as she was. Maybe this evening wasn't any easier for him than it was for her. Oddly enough, the idea made her feel a bit better.

She turned to encourage Kristie to eat her peas, then snatched another quick look at Brett. His tanned skin glowed against the forest-green shirt he wore, echoing the green of his eyes. The strong line of his jaw, perhaps a little tense, accented the cleft in his chin. Fine lines crinkled around his eyes as he responded to some laughing remark of Angela's, and her heart suddenly hurt.

She'd felt this way before—the awkward, tongue-tied little sister—watching the two of them laughing together. They'd always seemed charmed, as if nothing could dent their perfect lives.

She gave herself a mental shake. Brett and Angela weren't a couple anymore. They'd broken up their senior year over Brett's determination to go away to college. And she wasn't a kid. She had to stop slipping back into childish ways of looking at Brett Elliot, and figure out how to deal with him.

"…why, I almost thought he didn't remember that I'd been in just the week before with bronchitis."

Her mother's voice penetrated her thoughts, and she realized with alarm that they were talking about Doc. How long had that been going on, while she'd sat there mooning about Brett?

"I suppose he'd just been busy. After all, he sees a lot of patients in the course of a week," Brett said. But he sent her a questioning glance, and her tension level cranked upward.

"Well, I know Rebecca mentioned that he—"

"More potatoes, Brett?" Rebecca thrust the bowl toward him, interrupting whatever heedless words her mother was about to utter. Not that she could blame Mom. She shouldn't have voiced her worries about Doc—not to anyone.

"No, thanks." The words were casual, but his sharp glance wasn't.

"Rebecca, you can see we're finished. Why don't you clear while I bring in the dessert and coffee." Her mother turned to Brett, distracted for the moment from the subject of Doc. "I made apple crumb pie, just for you."

He'd better have a big piece and eat every crumb, or Mom's feelings would be hurt, she thought as she headed for the kitchen. But she didn't need to worry about that. Brett always managed to say the right things. Maybe that was why he'd gone through school in his perfect charmed circle, while she'd stumbled around, saying the wrong things and then being embarrassed and regretful.

She rinsed the dishes and stacked them quickly in the sink, then hurried back. What indiscreet things might her family say if she weren't there to head them off?

"Hasn't the clinic board done anything to help Doc out?" Brett was saying when she returned. "After all, running the clinic is their responsibility."

He gestured with his fork, as if pointing it toward the five-member board charged by the town to oversee the clinic. Her heart clenched. This was dangerous territory.

Angela shrugged. "You know they've never had to work very hard at that job. They always just take Doc's word for everything. I don't think they even checked Rebecca's references when they hired her on his say-so."

"My references were perfectly fine." Rebecca reminded herself not to get distracted from the real point. "The board does their best. They're devoted to Doc."

"I'm sure they are." Brett frowned.

Was he thinking the board should be devoted to the welfare of the town, not to Doc? Brett's words about horse-and-buggy medicine rang in her mind.

Her mother broke in with a comment about the difficulty of getting good people to serve on the town's boards, and the conversation became more general. But Rebecca couldn't relax, her mind twisting and turning with a new worry.

The clinic board was devoted to Doc, yes. But how might they react if they knew he wasn't well? They'd want, as she wanted, the best for him. Would they see the quandary, as she did?

How could you do the right thing for Doc if he didn't want it? How could you do it without hurting him terribly in the process?

By the time her mother pushed her chair back from the table, Rebecca could feel only relief that this interminable meal was over. Kristie slipped from her seat and darted around the table to clasp Brett's hand.

"You wanted to see my tree house," she reminded him. "Let's go now, okay? Aunt Rebecca, will you come with us? Please?"

She picked up the dessert plates. "You go ahead. It's my turn to wash the dishes." The excuse would do as well as any to get her out of Brett's disturbing presence for a little while.

Angela snatched the plates from her hands. "It's not your turn, it's mine."

Rebecca looked at her sister blankly. "No, it's not." This sounded ridiculously like the arguments they'd had as kids. But it wasn't Angela's turn, it was hers. And Angela never took an extra turn—not unless forced into it.

"Yes, it is." Angela nudged her. "Go on, Brett's waiting. You and Kristie show him the tree house."

Angela's blue eyes sparkled with mischief, and Rebecca suddenly realized what was going on. That teasing earlier had had a point. Angela was matchmaking, with her and Brett, of all people.

"Go on, dear," her mother prompted. "Brett is waiting."

She was outmaneuvered. If she went on arguing, it would only call attention to the fact that she didn't want to be in Brett's company.

She managed a smile and a nod as she took Kristie's hand. It looked as if she'd end up back in that tree house with Brett, whether she wanted to or not.

Now what, exactly, was bothering Rebecca about showing him the tree house? It had been perfectly clear to Brett that something unspoken was going on between the Forrester sisters in that little exchange. But what?

He followed Rebecca and Kristie through the kitchen and out the back door, into the tree-shaded yard. Again, he had the sense that nothing had changed.

"Still looks the same. I see your mother's thumb is as green as ever." A vegetable garden flourished in a sunny spot. Pumpkins, beginning to shade from green to gold, sprawled among still-laden tomato plants.

Rebecca smiled, some of the tension seeming to go out of her. "She grows enough to feed the whole neighborhood. People run and hide when they see her coming during zucchini season."

"The lilacs are higher." He nodded toward the hedge that separated the Forrester backyard from his parents'. "I used to be able to see over it."

"You mean you used to spy over it on Angela and her girlfriends, don't you?" Teasing him, Rebecca became the friend of his childhood instead of an adversary he had to battle. "Of course, they'd have been disappointed if you hadn't."

"I remember." It seemed an eternity ago, and yet in some ways as fresh as yesterday. "Where would you have been? Hiding in the tree house so you could listen to them?"

"Probably," she admitted, her smile reluctant. "I was always trying to figure out the secret."

Kristie ran to the tree and swarmed up the ladder.

"Secret?" He stepped under the trailing branches of the weeping willow, holding them back for Rebecca. She stepped inside. He let them fall, and the leafy green barrier enclosed them in a private world.

"You know. The secret. What made them so

popular." Rebecca's nose wrinkled, as if she still tried to figure it out. "I wanted to be like them, but I guess I always knew I never would be."

His heart caught at the image of the child she'd been, hiding in the tree house, wishing she were the beautiful, popular older sister. "Then you grew up and had your turn."

She shook her head, laughing a little. "Trust me, I never caught up with Angela in the popularity department." She gestured toward the ladder nailed to the trunk. "After you."

He grabbed a rung and shook it. "You sure this thing will hold me?"

"If it doesn't, there's expert medical attention right at hand."

Above him, Kristie peered over the edge of the platform, wiry red hair falling around her face. "Come up, Dr. Brett. I won't let you get hurt."

"I'll hold you to that, Kristie." Aware of Rebecca watching him, he started to climb.

Actually, the ladder was perfectly solid. He should have known Rebecca would make sure of that before she'd let her little niece play in the tree house. *Responsibility* seemed to be Rebecca's middle name.

He reached out a hand to Rebecca as she scrambled up after him, suddenly longing to understand what made her the person she was. That was logical enough, he told himself. If he understood her better, maybe he'd see a way to get her on his side.

He clasped her hand, pulling her up, and as she scrambled over the edge she leaned against him for an instant. Her warmth and softness sent a jolt right through him, and he knew perfectly well that he had more than one reason for wanting to understand Rebecca Forrester.

Kristie gave him an escorted tour of the tree house, complicated by the fact that it really wasn't large enough for three.

The second time Rebecca brushed against him, she abruptly sat down, her back against the trunk. "Maybe I'd just better stay in one place. After all, I've seen the tree house."

"Is the tire swing new?" Brett asked. "I don't remember it."

Kristie nodded, her curls bouncing. "Aunt Rebecca put it up, just for me."

Of course it would be Rebecca who'd done it. "It's great. Doesn't it make you dizzy, though?"

She shook her head violently. "I can spin and spin and not get dizzy. I'll show you."

Before he could stop her, she scrambled back down the ladder and hopped on the swing. He turned, groaning a little, and sat down beside Rebecca. "Where does she get that energy? After that meal, I just want a nice nap."

Rebecca's smile was tinged with sadness. "I didn't realize how much she misses her daddy until I saw how she reacted to you. I think she's just showing off for you."

"How is Quinn?" He lowered his voice so Kristie couldn't hear from the swing. "I'm sorry I mentioned his name at the table. I didn't mean to start anything awkward."

"It wasn't your fault. We need to be able to talk naturally about Quinn in front of Kristie, without bringing up Julie's death."

"I was so sorry to hear about it." He didn't want to imagine how Quinn felt, losing his wife, in an instant, to a drunk driver.

She nodded. "It's pretty difficult and lonely for him. We're trying to do our best with Kristie, and he talks to her every day."

He studied her serious, intent face. "Don't you mean *you* are?"

Her golden-brown eyes met his, startled. "Well, we all are."

"Yes, but mostly Aunt Rebecca. You're supposed to be the baby of the family, remember? Who made you the responsible one?"

He said it teasingly, but in the sudden darkening of her eyes he saw that he'd hit a nerve. He clasped her hand in an instinctive gesture. "I'm sorry, Rebecca. What did I say?"

She shook her head, but not before he'd caught the sheen of tears in her eyes. "Nothing. It's all right."

"It's not nothing." He lifted her hand, holding it warmly between both of his. "Something upset you. Come on, if you can't tell an old friend, who can you tell? This tree house has seen plenty of secrets in its time."

He felt her hold out against him for another moment, then the need to talk seemed to overcome the need to keep her secret.

"It's just…that's what my father said to me. About being the responsible one. He said every family has someone who's the responsible one, and it's not always the one people think it should be."

It didn't take a genius to read between the lines. "When he was ill, you mean."

"When he was dying," she corrected softly. "I was working in Boston when he got sick, and he wouldn't let Mom tell me or Angela how serious it was. Finally Doc called and broke it to me. I came home right away so I could take care of him."

Remembered pain tightened her face, making her look older than her years. He longed to take the pain away, but that was another one of the things he couldn't do.

"You were here when he needed you most. That's what counts."

"I hope so." She shook her head. "Sometimes I think I should have seen something earlier. If I had been here, maybe—"

"Don't." He gripped her hand more tightly. "People always think that, and medical personnel are the worst about it. You know Doc did everything that could possibly be done."

She nodded. "I know." She gave him a watery smile that almost broke his heart. "In my mind I know, but in my heart—" She broke off, then started again. "How we'd have gotten along without Doc I can't imagine. He and Pastor Richie were here every day toward the end. Doc sat up with Dad at night so I could get some sleep. Mom and Angela tried, but they got too upset."

He felt as if something had a stranglehold on his heart. "Doc's that kind of person. He's always there for you."

"Yes." Her gaze met his, forthright and honest. "I owe him everything."

They both knew what she was saying. He'd wanted to understand what made her tick, and now he did. Rebecca had every reason in the world to protect Doc, and no reason at all to see things Brett's way.

Chapter Six

"Let us pray."

Rebecca bowed her head obediently as Simon Richie began the pastoral prayer, but her mind persisted in straying to her own concerns.

She yanked her wandering thoughts back to the prayers of the church. *Lord, why can't I stop worrying about this situation and leave it in your hands?*

Next to her, Kristie wiggled, then settled when Angela frowned at her. Rebecca handed her the crayons she'd put in her bag as she did every Sunday, and Kristie began coloring the bulletin.

The past few days at the clinic had left her increasingly unsettled. It had been bad enough to be constantly in Brett's company before the night he'd come to dinner. It was worse afterward.

Each time she was near him, she relived those moments in the tree house when they'd been so close.

She'd confided in him the way she had at five, when her worst worry had been learning to ride a two-wheeler.

At least, it had seemed that way, right up until the moment he took her hand in both of his. The resulting tingle had moved from her hand straight to her heart. Now, each time she was with him, she seemed to feel that again.

Her discomfort would be worth it if her plan was working, but she didn't see any sign of that happening. Brett showed up at the clinic every day promptly, he saw patients, he consulted with Doc. In Doc's eyes, it was probably just as he'd dreamed it would be. And he must be hoping it wouldn't end, even though he knew it would.

But Rebecca knew about the calls Brett made to what seemed a wide network of medical acquaintances, putting out feelers for a replacement. Next he'd probably be putting ads in the journals.

Well, no, he wouldn't do that without talking to the clinic board. But that could be next on his agenda, and she didn't know what to do.

Please show me, Lord. I don't know what else I can do to get him to stay.

She tried to concentrate on the rest of the service. And when she couldn't, when her restless mind refused to cooperate, she focused on the Emmaus window behind the pulpit. Morning sunlight streamed through it, illuminating the figures of Jesus and the two disciples on the Emmaus road that first Easter. It had never failed to comfort her in the past, and it didn't fail now.

She lingered for a few minutes after the benediction instead of following her family, listening to Ellie Wayne play the postlude on the organ. Ellie's long, dark hair fell like a curtain hiding her face, but the arc of her body over the keyboard expressed the devotion that flowed through her fingers.

Somehow the sight, the music, and the light streaming through the window combined to bring the peace that had eluded her for days. She got up, breathing a silent prayer of thanks. God would give her the answer in His own time, not hers.

She emerged from the sanctuary to find the hospitality committee serving lemonade on the lawn. People clustered around white-draped tables laden with platters of cookies and fruit. She could see a number of tourists mingling with the regulars.

She was helping herself to a cup of lemonade when Anne Morden came up beside her. "Have one of the oatmeal squares," Anne said. "Emilie thinks they're wonderful." She bounced the toddler on her hip, and Emilie waved a sticky cookie at Rebecca.

"You keep that one, sweetheart. I'll get one of my own." Rebecca blew a kiss to Anne's adopted daughter.

"Did you try on your dress yet?" Anne smiled and shook her head. "Listen to me. I sound like every other bride-to-be, totally preoccupied with my wedding. I'm sorry, Rebecca. How are things going at the clinic?"

"Yes, I tried on the dress." The simple street-length dresses Anne had chosen for her attendants suited Rebecca. "The alterations will be done next week. And things are fine at the clinic."

She thought she'd sounded perfectly normal, but Anne shot her an inquiring look. Maybe, being an attorney, Anne had learned to listen to what lay behind the words.

"What's going on? I thought Brett was helping out."

"He is." She followed Anne's glance across the lawn, to where Brett stood with Alex and Mitch—who were talking about football, to judge from the gestures. Davey, Mitch's foster son, hung on every word.

"Then what's wrong? I know you've been worried about Doc's workload." Anne grasped her daughter's hand just before the sticky cookie landed on her dress.

"Here, let me." Rebecca took the baby wipe and mopped Emilie's hands and face, to be rewarded with a smile. Emilie had to be one of the happiest babies she'd ever seen.

Anne put her daughter on the grass, then turned her determined look on Rebecca. "Don't evade the subject. Isn't it helpful to have Brett there?"

"Yes, of course. It's just…" She couldn't tell Anne the worst of it—the battle that was going on in her heart every time she was near him. "It just makes me realize how bad it will be when he leaves."

"Maybe he'll stay." Anne watched her husband-to-be laugh at something Brett said. "I mean, look at the three of them together. Their friendship really means a lot to them. Maybe Brett will realize he'd be happier here, with people who care about him."

Anne's words dropped into Rebecca's mind and settled. Why hadn't that occurred to her, in all her struggling? Anne was right. Brett's lasting friendship with Alex and Mitch could be a strong motive for staying in Bedford Creek, if he'd let it.

Was there a way she could remind him of how much that friendship meant to him? She looked at Anne, wondering.

"Are you and Mitch going to the festival kickoff on Wednesday?" The Fall Foliage Festival was a four-day extravaganza designed to lure tourist dollars, but it generally ended up being even more fun for the townspeople.

"I gather it's not something we can miss," Anne said. "Mitch has been complaining all week about the extra work it causes the police department, but I think he's looking forward to it."

"Maybe Brett would like to join you." She hoped the suggestion didn't seem pushy. "I mean, since his parents aren't around."

Anne gave her a speculative look. "That sounds like a good idea."

"What sounds like a good idea?" Mitch appeared at Anne's side. Alex and Brett were right behind him.

Rebecca's heart gave that familiar, annoying little lurch at the sight of Brett. She ought to be getting used to it by now.

Brett knelt and held out his hands to Emilie. "How's my pretty girl? Come see Uncle Brett."

Emilie launched herself into his arms, and he stood up, smiling.

"We were just talking about the Fall Festival kickoff," Anne said.

Mitch groaned. "Don't remind me. I've been recruiting every available volunteer to direct traffic." Even in a suit instead of his uniform, Mitch looked every inch the police chief he was. "It's a massive headache."

"You love it," Alex said. His dark, often somber face creased in a smile. "Admit it. You wouldn't miss it for anything." He turned to Brett. "You are coming Wednesday night, aren't you?"

"Why don't you join us?" Anne said quickly. "Both of you, and your little boy, of course, Alex. It'll be fun. Rebecca's coming, too."

Faces turned toward her, and she had to hide her consternation. That wasn't what she'd intended when she'd mentioned inviting Brett to the festival.

Brett looked at her, arching an eyebrow. "Are you, Rebecca? You'd better. I need protection from all these kids." He bounced Emilie, and she squealed.

Rebecca pasted a smile on her face. An evening in Brett's company was a small price to pay if it helped convince him Bedford Creek was where he belonged.

"Of course. I wouldn't miss it."

Rebecca had managed to get through most of Monday morning at the clinic without being alone with Brett. She'd consider that a major accomplishment, except that it didn't seem to be solving the problem of her reaction to him. She didn't need to be alone with him to feel a wave of warmth every time his gaze drifted to her, or to flush whenever he smiled at her.

Professional—that was the attitude she had to maintain. She straightened her lab coat, running her hand over the bronze nameplate. She had to stay professional in her dealings with him, in spite of her mother asking him to dinner, in spite of Angela's matchmaking, in spite of the prospect of spending Wednesday evening in his company. Her heart gave a little *thump* at the thought. And that was another thing that had to stop.

Militantly erect, she marched into the office where he'd holed up after seeing his last patient of the morning. She'd find out what he wanted for lunch, and she wouldn't let herself be distracted by the cleft in his chin or the way his eyes crinkled when he smiled.

Brett looked up from the computer. "Lunchtime already?"

"Just about." She couldn't help glancing at the screen to see if he were perusing the physician-wanted ads. But the display seemed to be an article from a medical journal. "Doing some research?"

"In a way." He swung the screen to face her. "Take a look at this."

She leaned across the desk to read it, uncomfortably aware of the spicy scent of his aftershave. The piece seemed to be a report on a new technique in complex knee surgery.

She glanced at him, finding his face very close to hers, his eyes intent. She straightened, breathing a little quickly. "You're thinking this technique might be a solution for Alex?"

He frowned. "I don't know. I certainly don't want to second-guess Doc, but I'd like to see Alex making more progress than he is."

His affection for Alex came through clearly in his voice.

"I know." The words came out impulsively. She didn't want to second-guess Doc, either, but he would always put the patient first. "You know Doc would welcome any suggestions. Why don't you take this to him?"

"There's not enough here." He looked frustrated. "This cross-references another article, but I can't get it to come up." He gave her a half smile. "Maybe the machine is just out to get me."

"Let me give it a try." She leaned across again,

trying to ignore his nearness. "There are a couple other ways it might be listed."

He tossed his pen onto the desk. "If I'd started my surgical fellowship by now, I'd be in a lot better shape to give advice."

Rebecca clicked, frowned, and started another search. "You never did tell me what happened." She shot a questioning glance at him, realizing she might be treading too close to a painful subject. "I'm sorry. If you don't want…"

He leaned back in the desk chair. "It's nothing that complicated, although I have to say it seemed pretty traumatic to me at the time." He shook his head. "I was working the ER when paramedics brought in a street person. Standard procedure was to send them to the county hospital, but I was afraid she'd lose her leg if we did that. So I sent her up to surgery. The chief of service didn't approve."

She wasn't fooled by his dry tone. "It must have been a bad scene."

His mouth twisted. "The worst. I'd dared to defy him, and even went over his head to get her admitted. That was something he didn't take from any resident. He didn't file any charges against me, but the next day I found out the surgical fellowship I had counted on had evaporated. I guess I'd known that from the look on his face, anyway."

"Why did you do it?" He might not answer, but she really wanted to know. She'd have guessed he was too intent on his career to make waves with someone who had that kind of power.

He shrugged. "Because I trusted my judgment. Because…" He frowned. "For the first time in a long while I really felt God was calling me to do this." He glanced up at her. "Dr. Barrett would have thought that deluded, at best."

"I wouldn't," she said softly. Her heart clenched. She hadn't had to make any difficult faith choices like that. She only hoped that if she did, she'd be strong enough to do the right thing.

His green gaze met hers—met and held. The moment stretched out, motionless in time. She felt as if she were seeing all the way to his soul in those emerald depths. Her breath caught.

Brett shook his head suddenly, glancing away from her, breaking the bond. "What—" He cleared his throat and nodded toward the computer. "Are you finding anything?"

That was it, then. He didn't want to share that kind of moment with her. Well, she didn't either, did she? Where had her resolution to stay professional gone?

"I don't think so. Wait, yes, here it is. Do you want me to print it out?"

"Print out a couple of copies, so you can go over it, too. I'd like your opinion."

That didn't mean anything, she told herself. He just wanted her professional opinion, nothing else. And that was good, because that was all she had to give him.

She handed him the first copy off the printer, then took the second one for herself. She leaned against the desk and tried to concentrate on the article.

When she looked up, Brett's green eyes were shining. "What do you think? On paper, Alex sounds like a good candidate for the surgery, don't you think?"

She saw the enthusiasm in his face. "Maybe. But there might be things we don't know about it, things that would eliminate him from consideration."

"At least we have something." He grabbed her hands in both of his and squeezed them. "You don't know how much it means to me to find something that might help. Thank you, Rebecca."

Any notion she'd had that she was in control of her feelings vanished with the warmth that flooded through her at his grasp. "I…I'm glad I could help." She realized she was stammering and took a deep breath. "I know your friendship means a lot to you. Maybe, a few months from now, you'll be able to see Alex throw his cane away for good."

A shutter seemed to come down over those clear green eyes. "Maybe." He muttered the word, and she knew in an instant what he was thinking. He was thinking that in a few months, he wouldn't be in Bedford Creek to see anything.

Brett was still thinking of Rebecca as he drove home that evening. He wondered if her reluctance to attend the festival with him stemmed from their continuing disagreement over the clinic. They were as far apart as ever on that subject. Or was it that she felt the same surge of attraction he did and was determined to deny it?

He pulled into the driveway. The bed of chrysanthemums by the garage was putting on a brilliant display of bronze, in spite of being ignored. He probably ought to spend some time on yardwork while he was here.

And thinking of things he ought to do, he really ought to forget the feelings Rebecca stirred in him. It would be far better for both of them if he could go on treating her like a little sister. Because the bottom line was that eventually he'd be leaving, so anything between them could only lead to disappointment.

He'd reached the porch when he heard a step behind him on the walk. He turned.

"Dr. Elliot?" The man—middle-aged, middle height, middle everything—had the indefinable air of someone who didn't belong in Bedford Creek.

"I'm Brett Elliot. What can I do for you?"

"Matthew Arends." He held out his hand. "I'm an administrator at Lincoln Medical Center."

Brett did a quick mental review of the cases he'd seen in the last few days as he shook hands. None of them, other than Minna, had been sent the forty miles to the large regional hospital.

"What can I do for you, Mr. Arends? If this is

about one of our clinic patients, you really should talk to Dr. Overton."

"No, it's nothing like that." Matthew Arends looked rather pointedly toward the house. "Mind if we go inside to talk?"

Brett shrugged, then opened the door and led the way into the living room.

Arends glanced around as he took the armchair Brett indicated. "Lovely room. This is your parents' home, I understand?"

Now how and why did Arends have that information about him? Brett nodded. "I'm in Bedford Creek briefly. What is this about?"

"You prefer to come to the point, I see." Arends leaned forward. "Excellent. So do I. This is about the Bedford Creek clinic. Or rather, it's about the future of the clinic."

Brett hoped his expression didn't change. "Again, any questions about the clinic should be directed to the doctor in charge. I'm just helping out for a few weeks."

Arends's face remained expressionless. "We've had several discussions over the years with Dr. Overton about the clinic. Right now, what we'd like to do is enlist your aid."

Dealing with bureaucrats was a skill he'd never really mastered. "My aid to do what? Exactly what do you want?"

"We're prepared to make the Bedford Creek clinic

a part of Lincoln Medical Center's satellite clinic network. Prepared, that is, if we can come to a reasonable agreement."

Brett hoped he didn't look as dumbfounded as he felt. What on earth was going on? If the regional hospital actually wanted to take over the clinic, why hadn't Doc mentioned it to him? And why was Rebecca so worried about what the future held?

"I can see you're surprised." Arends folded his hands neatly. "But it's not such an unusual development. You might even call it the wave of the future in medicine. These small one-doctor clinics are a thing of the past."

"Horse-and-buggy medicine." The words were out before Brett had a chance to think about it.

"Exactly." Arends beamed. "I can see we think alike about this subject."

Brett shook his head. "You're still talking to the wrong person. Dr. Overton is in charge of the clinic."

"As I mentioned, we've talked to Dr. Overton a number of times. He doesn't seem interested in our offer, and the clinic board has always been guided by his wishes. Of course, he's nearly retirement age. The question arises as to what will happen to the clinic when he's no longer able to carry on."

"And you'd like to take over." He suppressed a wave of optimism. On the surface it sounded like the perfect solution for everyone, but there were bound to be drawbacks. "Frankly, Mr. Arends, I'm surprised.

I wouldn't think the practice here in Bedford Creek would be large enough to interest you."

"Well, the clinic wouldn't stay in Bedford Creek, of course," Arends said, as if it were a given. "That wouldn't be practicable. We'd combine the Bedford Creek clinic with the one in Townsend."

That had to be the main reason Doc wasn't interested in the center's proposal. He wouldn't want his patients to drive nearly twenty miles every time they needed to see a doctor.

"I still don't see what you want from me."

"Your influence," Arends said promptly. "From what we understand, you're the one person who might persuade Dr. Overton that this is best for everyone. I'm sure you see the advantages."

"I suppose." It was the kind of medicine he was used to—the big hospital, with its expensive technology and its ranks of specialists, staffing the small local clinic. "Much as I appreciate what your facility has to offer, I don't know that I feel comfortable trying to influence Dr. Overton if he's not interested."

"Well, now, we both know how reluctant these elderly physicians can be to accept changes." Arends rose. "Just let me send you some information on what we have to offer. You can look it over and make a decision. That's all I ask."

Brett got up slowly. "I can't make any promises."

"Fair enough." Arends held out his hand. "We aren't asking for anything more than that you consider it."

Consider it. Brett stood at the doorway and watched Arends drive away. He'd be hard put to think of anything else, now that the man had dropped a possible solution to everyone's problems right in his lap. Not just everyone—Rebecca. If this went through, Rebecca would be free to leave Bedford Creek. He didn't want to picture a future in which he wouldn't be seeing her.

Chapter Seven

"Doc?" Rebecca rushed across the examining room the next morning. Doc leaned against the table, hand to his head. "What is it? What's wrong?"

He straightened instantly. "Nothing. I'm fine." But his face was pale, his eyes tired.

"Don't fib to me. I can see you don't feel well." Her fingers sought his pulse.

"Just tired."

"I'm getting Brett." Ignoring his objections, she hurried to the door.

Doc was firmly in control of himself by the time she got Brett to the room. He allowed Brett to do a quick exam, insisting the whole time he was fine.

Brett's gaze met hers over Doc's head, and he shrugged. "You're taking the day off, Doc. Like it or not. Rebecca and I won't take no for an answer."

"That's right," she echoed.

Doc glared at them for a long moment. At least she had Brett to share the intensity of that look. She wouldn't have been able to stand up to it alone.

Finally Doc nodded. "All right. Just today, mind."

She could breathe again. "I'll drive you home." Doc would have walked the four blocks as always, but she wouldn't let him walk home.

When she got back to the clinic, after leaving Doc in his housekeeper's capable hands, Brett was dealing with an office full of patients. He greeted her with a lifted eyebrow as he grabbed a chart.

"Everything okay?"

"As okay as possible, I guess."

The urge to pour out her worries about Doc's health nearly overpowered her, but she'd promised Doc. She wouldn't break her word—not unless... well, not unless it was a life or death situation, she supposed.

It wasn't, not yet—but at some point it might be. She was stuck between two bitter alternatives, and there didn't seem any way out.

Brett, apparently taking her words at face value, went on to the next patient. Giving herself a mental shake, she took the patient log from the receptionist. Dealing with the day's problems was all she could do. At least Brett was there to share the load. For the moment, anyway.

At some point in the hectic rush, she realized that one of the patients Brett had finished with hadn't yet come out of the exam room. Frowning, she glanced at the chart. Wanda Peterson, pregnant with her first child. She tapped on the door, then opened it.

"Wanda? Do you need some help?"

Wanda slumped in the chair, tears welling over. Rebecca knelt beside her.

"Wanda, why are you crying? Are you in pain?"

"N-no." She rubbed her eyes with the back of her hand. "I'm okay."

Rebecca pulled the other chair close, taking both of Wanda's hands in hers. "You're not okay, or you wouldn't be crying." She gave a regretful thought to whatever patients were still waiting. Some delays couldn't be helped. "Tell me about it."

"I guess I'm being silly." Her lips trembled. "But Dr. Brett said it wouldn't be long now, and I started thinking about how I never did this before, and what if it hurts as much as people say, and what if something's wrong with the baby…" She ran out of steam and choked back a sob.

"Did you say any of this to Dr. Brett?"

Wanda shook her head. "I was going to ask him, but he seemed like he was in such a hurry, I didn't want to bother him. And now I'm bothering you." The tears threatened to overflow again. "I'm sorry."

"It's not a bother," Rebecca said firmly. She put her arm around the young woman's shoulders, mentally reading the riot act to Brett. Why hadn't he seen how apprehensive the patient was? "I'm sure the baby's as fine as can be. You haven't noticed any difference in his activity, have you? Or in the way you feel?"

"No. Except that some days I really want to go and get it over with, and other days I don't want it ever to happen." Wanda's face screwed up with anxiety. "Is something wrong with me?"

"You're just like every other woman who ever had a first baby," Rebecca assured her. "Everyone feels that way."

"They do?" Sunlight began to break through Wanda's tears.

"They do."

It took another five minutes of reassurance, but when Wanda left the office she was smiling. Rebecca held her smile until the woman was out of sight, and then stormed off to find Brett.

Luckily he was alone, making notes on a chart. He looked up when she pushed through the door, eyebrows raised.

"Something wrong?"

"You bet something's wrong." She tossed Wanda's file at him. "You just saw Wanda Peterson."

"The maternity case. So? She's fine."

"She's not a case." She said the words distinctly. "She's a twenty-two-year-old having her first baby, with no family in town for support. She's not fine. She's scared. And you certainly didn't help any."

His face tightened. "She didn't say anything to me about being frightened. If she had—"

"She didn't say anything because you were in too much of a hurry. She didn't want to bother you."

"I'm not a mind reader, Rebecca." Anger flashed in his green eyes. "And I don't need you to tell me how to handle patients."

"No, you know how to handle them, don't you?" She was too angry to think of being tactful. "Is that what they taught you at the big city hospitals? Treat your patients like numbers and get through with them as quickly as possible? That's not how Doc runs this clinic."

He strode toward the door. "Doc's not here, remember? You're the one who wanted me to stay. So don't complain now that you've gotten what you wanted."

If the swinging door could have slammed, he'd probably have slammed it. As it was, he gave it such a push that it swung wildly back and forth for several minutes.

She'd lost her temper again. She'd said too much, and already regretted it. Oh, not that she'd spoken up. She'd had to do that. She didn't regret the content, just the way she'd delivered it.

Brett had changed. The idealistic boy she'd known had vanished, and he was probably gone for good.

Brett wasn't done fuming yet when the receptionist announced Alex Caine was there to see him. The reverence in her voice suggested that special treatment was due the local aristocrat who happened to be the richest man in town.

Brett managed a smile at her attitude. He'd known Alex too long to be awed by the Caine name. Alex was just his friend, a friend he wanted badly to help.

Pushing away his irritation with Rebecca, he rose to shake hands as Alex came in. It must be one of Alex's bad days, since the cane he sometimes used was in evidence.

"Doc says he'd like you to have a talk with me." Alex's intelligent dark eyes said he knew who to blame for that. "What's up? Some new medicine for which you'd like a guinea pig?"

"Not exactly." Brett spread his hands flat atop the file on the desk. "You know I wouldn't experiment on you, don't you?"

Alex cocked an eyebrow. "What about when you fixed me up with that cousin of yours? If that wasn't an experiment, I don't know what was."

"Amanda?" He grinned, relaxing. "Actually she turned out pretty well. But back in high school…"

"You told me she was a cheerleader at her school. You didn't mention it was an all-girls school and she was captain of the basketball team and five eleven."

Brett shook his head. "You shouldn't let yourself be so influenced by a girl's looks."

"I was fifteen," Alex reminded him. "I was just as dumb as most fifteen-year-old boys. You owe me, pal."

The casual words pierced Brett's heart. He did owe Alex, although not in that way. Maybe this was finally his chance to repay him.

"How's this for evening things up?" He made an effort to keep the words light. "I think I can help you get rid of that cane for good. And the pain that goes with it."

Alex's expression didn't change, but something flickered briefly in his dark eyes. "I'm listening."

He'd given a lot of thought to how he'd present this to Alex. He didn't want to give the impression this was in any way a sure thing. The surgical technique was new, but it had worked in a number of difficult cases.

Brett watched Alex's face as he worked his way through what Brett had to say. He leveled with Alex, giving him a careful presentation of the technique, the pros and cons, the successes the surgeons had experienced.

He might not give all the details to some patients, but he knew Alex would demand to know everything. He knew, too, that Alex was intelligent enough to understand.

You see, Rebecca, he addressed her silently, *I have a perfectly good manner with patients, even if it's not exactly like Doc's.*

But Rebecca wasn't there to argue with him. He felt a faint twinge as he tried to concentrate on Alex's questions. Maybe Rebecca had a point, but she'd managed to hit a sore spot with her criticism.

He took back the article he'd given Alex to read. "So, any more questions?" He tried to keep his voice casual. He didn't want to pressure Alex. He might need more time to see the advantages to the surgery.

"No, you've made it perfectly clear." Alex frowned down at the cane. "I appreciate the time and study you've put into this, Brett."

He hadn't expected Alex to jump up and down with excitement, but he had anticipated more enthusiasm than that. "This could be the answer for you."

Alex nodded slowly. "I can see the advantages you describe. But it's not for me."

He couldn't be hearing correctly. He'd expected some hesitancy, but not a flat turndown. "I don't think you understand. This could get rid of your pain entirely if it works."

"If it works," Alex repeated, then smiled slightly. "I understand what you're saying, Brett. You're looking at possibilities. But I have to look at what's right for me— for my family and my business. I'm afraid this isn't it."

He stood before Brett could marshal an argument. "Thanks, pal. I appreciate it." He held out his hand. "See you at the festival, right?"

All Brett could do was nod. "Maybe we could talk about this more later."

"I don't think so." Alex limped toward the door. "But thanks."

Brett stared at the closed door for a long moment. Didn't Alex understand what Brett was offering him?

He wanted to go after Alex, make him listen, but it seemed fairly clear that doing so wouldn't help.

He'd just hit the downside of a medical practice back in the old hometown. It hurt too much when you couldn't help someone you cared about.

He'd probably felt more useless than this sometime in his life, but he couldn't think when. Maybe he'd been in Bedford Creek too long. Maybe it was time he got back to the kind of impersonal medicine he was really cut out to do.

He thought again about Arends's proposal for the clinic. If it worked, it could solve everyone's problems. He ought to sound Doc out about it, but first he had to be better prepared.

The information Arends had sent painted a rosy picture. He needed to know the downsides and try to find solutions to them before he could hope to convince Doc that this was the answer.

The photo album was on the bookshelf next to the piano. Rebecca pulled it out that evening and sat down on the piano bench. She leafed slowly through the pages, not sure what she was looking for.

There were tons of pictures of Quinn, the oldest. Her parents had used up plenty of film on him. Quinn and Brett playing basketball in the driveway, Quinn and Brett in their peewee baseball uniforms.

And Angela, of course. Angela in her dancing class tutu, Angela in her scout uniform, Angela with the flute she'd attempted to play. And finally, Angela with Brett when they started dating.

She bit her lip. Was this what she was looking for—this boy with the smile that would charm the birds from the trees? This was the Brett she remembered—kind, handsome, patient with the obnoxious kid she'd no doubt been. This was the boy who'd told her he was going to be a doctor and come back to Bedford Creek and take care of all of them.

He'd changed in so many ways she couldn't begin to count them. He was certainly still handsome; that hadn't changed. His face, green eyes lit with laughter, formed in her mind, and her heart seemed to skip a beat. Actually that *had* changed. He was far more dangerously devastating now than he'd been at sixteen.

Was he still kind? Maybe, when he took the time to be, but unfortunately he didn't seem to be taking that time. And all that lovely idealism had vanished as if it had never been. The only glimpse she'd seen of it had been when he'd talked about why he risked his fellowship by defying the senior physician.

He'd said he was doing what he felt God called him to do. She frowned down at the photo album.

Aren't You calling him to stay here and honor his promise, Lord? And if You are, why isn't he listening?

She closed the book on all those bright, innocent young faces. Maybe she was being naive to think promises made then meant anything now. Life changed people.

Certainly her brother had never anticipated the grief that was in store for him. And Angela, who'd talked for years about when she'd be old enough to leave Bedford Creek for the big city, was settling down perfectly happily in her hometown.

Brett had changed, too. That was what Rebecca had to remember. In one sense, maybe, that change was just as well. It certainly ought to make it easier for her to ignore the feelings she had for him.

She shoved the album back on the shelf and glanced at the mantel clock. Nearly seven-thirty. Time to round Kristie up and get her ready for bed.

Her niece didn't seem to be in the house. Rebecca glanced out the front window, then went to the back door. Kristie was probably out on the swing. That had become a favorite spot lately.

She glanced around the yard, rubbing her arms in the evening chill. No Kristie. She had opened her mouth to call when she heard the voice above her.

Kristie was in the tree house again. And she wasn't alone. That was the rumble of a masculine voice answering her. *Brett.*

She walked closer, reluctant to call and disturb what seemed to be a serious conversation. Just outside the veil of willow branches, she paused.

"…wish my daddy was here." Kristie's voice was soft and sad, like the coo of the mourning dove that came to the bird feeder.

"I bet you do. I'd like to see him, too. We were

friends a long time ago, when we were about your age."

"Did you know my mommy?"

Rebecca's breath caught. That was the first time Kristie had voluntarily spoken of her mother since Julie's death. Rebecca was conscious of an edge of resentment. Kristie's confiding should have been in her, not Brett.

"No, I'm sorry I never met her." Brett was gently matter-of-fact, probably not wanting to overreact. "I've seen her picture, though. She was very beautiful."

The night was so still that Rebecca could hear Kristie sigh. "I wish I could be beautiful like her. But Grandma says I look just like my daddy did when I was his age."

"You know what? I think your Grandma's wrong about that. You look a lot like that picture of your mommy. And I bet when you grow up you'll be just as beautiful. And you know what else? I'd say every time your daddy looks at you, you remind him of her."

"You think so?" Kristie sounded as if she wanted to believe him, but couldn't quite manage it.

"I do. I really, really do."

That was the confident Brett charm that had convinced Rebecca of far more improbable things when she was Kristie's age. Tears stung her eyes. She could only hope it convinced her niece, too. She brushed the dangling branches aside and reached the ladder.

"Hey, up there."

Brett leaned over the edge. "Come on up."

If he didn't remember the bitter words with which they'd parted earlier, she did. "I think it's time for Kristie to get ready for bed."

Kristie's small face appeared next to Brett. "Just a little bit longer, Aunt Rebecca," she wheedled. "Please."

"Please, Aunt Rebecca," Brett echoed. He smiled down at her, his earlier anger apparently forgotten, or at least put aside for the moment.

"Just for a little bit," she agreed.

She climbed the ladder, pretending she didn't see the hand Brett held out to help her. But as she reached the top, he grasped her arm, pulling her over the edge with apparently effortless strength. She landed between him and Kristie, a little breathless.

It would be too much to hope he didn't notice.

He raised an eyebrow. "Getting out of shape, Aunt Rebecca?"

She started to deny it heatedly, then realized that would raise the uncomfortable question of why, then, she was out of breath. She settled for a smile and put her arm around Kristie.

"Aren't you getting chilly, honey?"

Kristie shook her head, snuggling closer. "I'm warm enough."

On Rebecca's other side, Brett seemed to radiate heat. She tried to keep from touching him, but that wasn't easy in the confines of the tree house.

She glanced at him, lifting her eyebrows. "Giving some good advice?" she said softly.

He shrugged, looking at Kristie with a tenderness she hadn't seen in his eyes for a while. "Just listening, mostly."

"Tree houses are good for confidences." She stroked Kristie's wiry red hair. With a gentle sigh, Kristie leaned over, pillowing her head in Rebecca's lap.

"Yes, they are." Brett brushed her arm as he reached across to pat Kristie.

Warmth tingled along her skin.

He'd changed from his slacks, dress shirt and lab coat to jeans and a flannel shirt, the sleeves rolled back to the elbows. She tried not to think how ruggedly handsome he looked that way.

"Thank you." She murmured the words, trusting that Kristie, already half asleep, wouldn't understand what she meant.

Brett's smile was gentle. "Any time. I seem to remember a few conversations with you up here."

She nodded. She should be glad he seemed willing to forget their quarrel, but the unexpected intimacy of the moment disturbed her. An owl called somewhere in the woods; something, a cat or a rabbit, perhaps, rustled in the lilac hedge. Otherwise, they seem to be alone in the quiet universe.

Brett glanced up through the overhanging branches. "Look, the first star." He pointed toward a pinprick of light. "Remember we used to call out when we saw the first star."

"And first to see the streetlights come on," she added, smiling at the memory. "Kids still do that. I've heard them on summer nights, playing hide-and-seek in the hedges."

He leaned a little closer, so close that the scent of him touched her. "I'm glad that didn't change… glad some things are the same here."

"Kids still play the same games we did." She stroked Kristie's hair gently. "With the addition of some computer ones, of course. People still go to church, raise their kids, join the PTA. Bedford Creek docsn't changc all that much."

"Really is like Brigadoon." His words gently teased, reminding her of their conversation that first night.

"It's good to have a place where you can rely on things." She hoped she didn't sound defensive. "And people." She shivered a little, thinking suddenly of Doc. None of them would be able to rely on Doc much longer. He'd seemed fine when she'd checked on him this afternoon, but she knew the truth.

"You're cold." He put his arm around her, tugging her and Kristie close to his side.

She felt the soft nap of his flannel shirt, the warm smoothness of his skin. She tried not to lean against him, but she couldn't seem to help herself. "Brett—" She looked up at him, not sure what she wanted to say.

The moonlight filtered through the branches of the willow tree, touching his face. It made his hair look almost silver and cast shadows along the strong line of his jaw. Her breath caught, and words vanished.

Brett went very still, his gaze intent and searching on her face. He was so close that she could feel his breath against her cheek.

"No." She pulled back from him, heart pounding. "I mean, it's getting late. Kristie's almost asleep. I'd better get her inside."

He held her for another moment, then eased away, nodding. "I'll climb down first, and you can hand her to me."

His voice sounded perfectly natural, as if he hadn't been affected at all by that moment of closeness. She couldn't say the same for herself.

Her conviction that the changes in him made it easier for her to ignore her feelings seemed laughable now. There was no possibility at all of ignoring the way Brett made her feel, no matter what he did.

Chapter Eight

"Aren't you ready yet, Aunt Rebecca?" Kristie popped into Rebecca's bedroom with the question for the fourth or fifth time.

Rebecca smiled at Kristie's reflection in the mirror. "Just about."

"That's what you said the last time." Her niece bounced with excitement. "Dr. Brett just came out his front door. You have to be ready."

Her pulse insisted on racing at that bit of news. "You go talk to him," she said. "I'll be right down."

Kristie vanished, and her footsteps thumped down the stairs. Rebecca stared at herself in the glass.

It was ridiculous to be taking this much trouble over what she wore to the festival. Everyone would be in jeans, anyway. Nobody would be interested in whether her turtleneck matched her eyes, or whether she took the navy sweatshirt or the green windbreaker for later. And nobody would notice how her cheeks flushed at the thought of a whole evening in Brett's company.

At least, she hoped nobody would. She snatched up the green jacket, smoothed the patchwork quilt that had covered her four-poster since she was three and hurried toward the stairs.

In the hall below she heard Brett's deep voice, saying something laughingly to Kristie. The teasing note seemed to touch something deep inside her, something she couldn't shrug off.

Well, she'd have to hide it, that was all. Thank goodness they'd decided to take Kristie to the festival; thank goodness they'd be with a group of people. She could only hope that would keep her from betraying her silly susceptibility to Brett Elliot. She took a deep breath and started down the stairs.

Seen from above with the hall light shining on him, Brett's hair lightened from gold to flax. She wasn't going to notice how broad his shoulders looked in the forest-green sweater. She wasn't—

He looked up and saw her. His clear-as-glass green eyes darkened. He smiled slowly, the lines around his eyes crinkling in the way that made her heart turn over.

She gripped the railing, then forced herself to return his smile and walk steadily down to meet him.

"Rebecca." Brett looked from her to Kristie. "I don't know how I got so lucky. I get to escort the two prettiest girls there tonight."

"Aunt Rebecca's not a girl," Kristie protested. "She's a grown-up woman."

"I noticed." Brett's gaze lingered on Rebecca's face long enough to raise a flush. "Believe me, I noticed." He reached out to adjust the collar of her turtleneck. "Matches your eyes," he said softly.

She had to put a stop to the way Brett's touch made her feel. "We'd better get going. We don't want to keep the others waiting." And she certainly didn't want to be alone with Brett with only Kristie as a buffer between them.

The secret amusement in Brett's eyes suggested he knew just what she was thinking. He took Kristie's hand and gestured toward the door.

"Ladies, your carriage awaits."

The festival centered on the park that ran beside the river at the valley floor. Brett wove carefully through the crowds of people who meandered, apparently confident no one would hit them, across the narrow street. He backed expertly into the last available spot.

"I'm glad to see this is still a park." He held the door as Rebecca slid out. "Nobody's tried to put up condos or pave it for extra tourist parking."

Rebecca helped Kristie put on her jacket. It was already a little chilly so close to the river. "You've forgotten the flooding we get sometimes. Nobody's foolish enough to want to build in the flood plain, even if the town would let them."

She glanced across the smooth green swath that stretched from the railroad tracks to the water. It was crowded now with booths and people, and lights winked in the gathering dusk.

"Nice, isn't it?" Brett's voice softened as he followed the direction of her gaze. "I'm glad we decided to come." His hand closed over hers, and her pulse beat so fast that she was sure he must be able to feel it.

She saw Mitch beckoning them. "Look, there they are." Relief flooded her as they started across the lawn to join the others.

Mitch and Anne had toddler Emilie in a stroller, while Alex's son, Jason, trailed along with Davey. Alex had apparently left his cane behind for the evening, but Rebecca easily read the pain lines in his face.

What had happened between Brett and Alex when Alex came to the clinic? Brett had been terse and irritable the rest of the day, suggesting things hadn't gone as well as he'd hoped. She thought she saw some reservation now in the greetings he and Brett exchanged.

A moment later she told herself she'd been imagining things, as the three men began swapping stories, each one beginning *Remember when...*

She and Anne exchanged amused glances, then fell into step with each other. This was what she'd hoped for from this evening. So why did she feel abandoned?

They wandered easily through the park, stopping each time one of the kids wanted to try a game or buy a hot dog.

"Let me get that." Brett's hand closed over hers as she reached for her bag when Kristie stopped at the candy apple stand. "She's going to break the bank tonight."

"It's for a good cause." It took an effort to ignore the warmth of his grip. "Everything raised is going toward the new fire truck for the volunteer firemen. We ought to be nearly there by the end of the week."

He smiled, lifting one finger toward the boy behind the counter. "Are we milking the tourist dollars to pay for the truck?"

"The festival did start out that way. But I think we enjoy it more than the tourists."

He handed the sticky candy apple to Kristie and glanced inquiringly at Rebecca. "Sure I can't get one for you?"

"I'm holding out for homemade ice cream at the church stand. I heard they have teaberry this year."

"That's for me, then." He wiped his fingers on a napkin. "I don't think the rest of the world has even heard of teaberry ice cream."

Kristie stopped so abruptly that Rebecca almost bumped into her. "Look, Aunt Rebecca." She pointed to the lawn under the maples, where the school boosters had set up games. At the moment a spirited egg-and-spoon race was ending.

"Do you want to be in some of the races?" she asked. "I'll bet they have some just for your age."

Kristie, attacked by shyness, leaned against her, shaking her head.

Brett exchanged a glance with her and then knelt next to the child. "Come on, it'll be fun. I'll hold your candy apple for you."

She looked longingly at the fun, then shook her head again.

"Tell you what. Aunt Rebecca and I will do it first. Then you can give it a try. Okay?"

Kristie's smile appeared. "Okay."

Brett stood, holding out his hand to Rebecca. "Looks like there's a three-legged race starting with our name on it."

It wasn't that she minded joining in the games, especially not if it got Kristie involved. But did it have to be the three-legged race?

Brett bent to tie the strip of cloth around their ankles, binding them so close that it was impossible to keep any distance between them.

"Does it have to be that tight?"

"Unless you want to trip over it, it does." Brett put his arm around her waist. She stiffened, and he raised an eyebrow. "I don't think we can win this if we don't work together."

"Do you always play to win?" She tried, without success, to still the tingle that danced along her nerve endings everywhere they touched.

His gaze met hers. "Always."

She looked away first. "Maybe we'd better practice."

"Right." Brett hitched his arm more firmly around her. "We have to stay together. Outside step, inside step. Outside, inside."

"Just try it." *And let's get it over with before I start getting used to being so close.*

They'd barely managed to get in a few awkward steps before the starter waved them into position.

Brett's hand tightened at her waist. "This is it. Ready?" He was as eager as if they were launching into the Olympics.

"As ready as I'm going to be," she said, resigned.

The whistle blew, and they started forward.

Outside, inside, outside, inside…she counted the steps as they raced forward, Brett's long strides eating up the ground. He was so intent on the finish line that he almost carried her along.

A rebellious spark ignited. Maybe, for once in his life, it would do Brett good to let someone else win, like the high school kid behind them who was probably trying hard to impress his girlfriend.

It didn't take much, just one mischievous step out of rhythm. Brett stumbled and clutched her for balance. And then they both toppled to the soft grass.

She hadn't anticipated the effect of tumbling to the ground so close to him. His arms went around her protectively, and he twisted so that he hit first. She landed against him, in his arms.

Her breath seemed to stop entirely. For just a moment everything disappeared—the crowds, the music, the laughter. There was nothing on earth but Brett, holding her.

He tightened his grasp. "Rebecca? Are you all right?"

"I will be when you stop squeezing the life out of me." She rolled away from him, tried to get up and was brought back down by the cloth tying their ankles together.

"You can't get away from me no matter how you try." He grinned, reaching down to untie them.

He was right, she thought, trying to get her breathing under control before she had to say anything else. She couldn't get away from him or the way he made her feel, and it didn't matter how many people were around.

Brett balanced the paper bowls of ice cream and worked his way through the crowd to the picnic table under the trees. Rebecca had already settled on a bench next to Kristie. He watched her laugh at something Mitch said, and an uncomfortable jolt of longing swept through him.

How had this happened? When had he started feeling this way about Rebecca? He'd probably been trying to deny it for days, but it wasn't until he'd held her in his arms that he'd actually recognized how desirable she was, and how strongly he was attracted.

This was Rebecca, remember? Little Rebecca. Somehow the reminder didn't do any good. She wasn't "little Rebecca" any longer.

That didn't matter. She was still out of bounds to him. His plans for the future didn't include a serious relationship for a long time. He'd seen too many marriages that didn't survive the pressures of big hospital residencies. That meant he had to get back to thinking of Rebecca as a kid sister, and fast.

He slid a bowl of ice cream in front of her and another in front of Kristie, then found a place on the bench opposite. "I predict a stomachache coming on if she eats all that." He nodded toward Kristie's dish.

"Don't worry, she won't eat much after everything else she's had." Rebecca lifted a spoonful to her lips, then closed her eyes in enjoyment. "Mmm, wonderful."

He took a spoonful of his own, savoring the tart sweetness.

Alex paused, looking at his half-empty bowl. "Do you think we like it so much because it really is that good, or because we only get it once a year?"

Mitch, smiling, threw a balled-up napkin at him. "Quit analyzing, will you? Just enjoy it."

"He can't enjoy it without analyzing it," Brett said. "Never could, never will."

He kept the words light, but he caught the inquiring glance Rebecca threw his way. *Careful.* She already guessed too much about him for comfort.

The conversation bounced around the table, reflecting the easiness of people who knew each other well. He tried to relax and join in, but found he was watching Rebecca, noticing the gentle curve of her cheek, the love in her eyes when she looked at her niece, the way her dimple showed when she laughed. No, it wasn't going to be easy to go back to thinking of Rebecca as a skinny little kid.

Obviously, no one else thought of her that way. The others treated her as a professional, someone worthy of their respect. She was, of course. He'd learned that about her in his time at the clinic. She was good, she was efficient, and most of all she cared. No one came in the clinic door that didn't get one hundred percent from Rebecca.

Kristie pushed her barely touched ice cream away and leaned against her aunt. Her eyelids drooped.

Rebecca put her arm around the child. "What's wrong, sweetie? Are you tired?"

"I can stay up longer." Kristie made a valiant effort to sit up straight. "I'm not tired."

"Maybe you're not, but I am." Brett took a last bite of his ice cream. "And you're my date, so you have to leave when I do."

That made her giggle, erasing the frown from her face. She slid from the bench and took the hand he held out to her.

"Come on, Aunt Rebecca," he said lightly. "Time we called it quits."

"If you want to stay longer…" she began, but he shook his head.

"She's drooping and so am I." He swung Kristie's hand. "We're ready to go."

They said their good-nights and started toward the car. They'd made their way through most of the crowd when a familiar figure stopped in front of them.

"Dr. Elliot." Minna Dawson looked considerably better than she had the last time he'd seen her.

"How are you doing, Mrs. Dawson?" Judging by the way her husband clung to her arm, he must not think she should be wandering around the festival.

"'Bout a hundred times better than I was." She held out her hand. "I've been wanting to stop by and say thank you." A brick-red flush mounted her cheeks. "I wasn't very nice to you, and that's a fact. But seems like you probably saved my life."

He found he was unaccountably touched. "Just doing my job. I'm glad you're better. Did you get started on cardiac rehab?"

She nodded.

"You keep it up, then." Kristie began to drag on his hand, so he picked her up. Her arms looped around his neck. "Have a good time at the festival, but watch what you eat."

"No fear I'll cheat. George won't let me do that." She pressed his hand again. "We'll never forget what you did, Doc. Never."

Rebecca looked at him curiously as they headed on

toward the car. "What is it? You look a little stunned. Didn't a patient ever say thank you before?"

He considered the question. "Well, not that many of them. And I certainly never ran into a patient at a social event."

She shrugged. "It happens all the time in a small town. You get used to it."

He wouldn't be around long enough to get used to it. And the thought somehow wasn't pleasant. "She called me 'Doc.'"

"So?" Rebecca lifted an inquiring brow.

He shrugged. "Doc Overton is 'Doc.' I'm just Brett around here."

"Not anymore, you're not." She smiled. "I told you they'd accept you as their doctor."

He thought about that as he drove them home. Bedford Creek accepted him as a doctor, instead of as the class clown he'd once been. It accepted Rebecca, too, as the medical professional she was. Things had changed. Was he the only one who couldn't accept that?

Rebecca had been sure Brett would drop them at the door and be on his way, maybe back to the festival to rejoin his friends. That would certainly be for the best.

But he showed no inclination to do any such thing. Instead he helped tuck Kristie in, then followed Rebecca into the living room and accepted the offer of coffee she felt constrained to make.

She carried the tray in and set it on the coffee table,

making up excuses in her mind. It was late; they both had to get up early.

But it wasn't late, and Brett knew perfectly well what time they had to be at the clinic. And he'd settled back on the chintz-covered couch as if he intended to be there for a long time. She sat down at the opposite end and poured the coffee.

"It was good to get together with Mitch and Alex, wasn't it?" She might as well try to find out if her aim for the evening had been successful.

"They're the best." He frowned a little. "I wish…" He stopped.

Something to do with Alex, she was sure. "What is it? I know something's wrong. It's been wrong ever since you saw Alex at the clinic."

She waited for him to tell her it was none of her business, but he just shook his head.

"I talked to Alex about the surgery." His frown deepened, sending harsh vertical lines between his brows. "He's not interested."

"I see." She thought she did see, in a way. "Because of the time he'd have to be away from Bedford Creek, I suppose."

"Why do you say that?" Brett stiffened. "Did he say something to you?"

"No, of course not." She struggled to account for the assumption that had come so easily. "I just thought it might be a problem. He'd have to be away for over a month, probably."

"Isn't that a small price to pay for getting rid of the pain he's having?" Brett demanded.

"I guess it might be to most people. But Alex Caine isn't most people."

"You don't need to tell me that. I'm one of his oldest friends. I know him as well as anyone."

She tried to say what she needed to without hurting him. "Of course you're one of his oldest friends. But you haven't seen him all that much in the last few years."

"I haven't forgotten what he's like, if that's what you're implying."

"He's changed since the accident." She frowned, choosing her words carefully. "Since his wife left. I'm not sure you realize how much."

Brett seemed to bite back his impatience. He probably longed to tell her she didn't know what she was talking about.

"If you know something I don't, I wish you'd tell me. Granted, he took it hard when his wife ran off, but I don't see what that has to do with his recovery from the accident."

"Look, I'm going on my own instincts here, and maybe I'm wrong." But she didn't think so. "He's carrying a big load of responsibility. He's a single parent, and he's trying hard to be everything to Jason. And he's got the responsibility of the business. Apparently his father left things in a mess when he died shortly after Alex was hurt."

Brett was still frowning, but now it was a thoughtful frown. "He always did take it seriously, owning the business that employs half the town. I can see him deciding to sacrifice his own welfare for everyone else. That's like him." He made a fist. "I want so much to help him."

"Why?" The word was out before she had time to think about it. "I mean, why does it hurt you so much? I know he's your friend, but it seems more than that."

Now he really would tell her to mind her own business. What was she thinking to probe so deeply into his affairs?

Brett leaned forward, hands clenched in front of him. She held her breath, waiting for an explosion, but it didn't come.

"Do you remember anything about the camping-trip accident our senior year?" he asked abruptly. "Or were you too young?"

"Of course I wasn't too young. How do you think I'd forget something the whole town talked about for weeks? You and Mitch and Alex were lucky you weren't killed."

A shiver ran down her spine at the memory. The stories she'd heard had given her nightmare images of the three of them, caught in the abandoned quarry, nearly drowning when the water rose.

"Alex came close." His hands were locked so tight the veins stood out. "If Mitch hadn't pulled him out, he would have died." He looked at her, his eyes very dark. "It was my fault."

"Your fault…" She looked at him blankly. He was serious. "What do you mean, your fault? It was an accident. No one expected the flooding to hit so fast and so hard. That wasn't your fault."

"It was my fault we didn't get back when we were supposed to." He looked past her as if she weren't even there, as if he looked into another time. "I was in charge of the map. I'm the one who lost it. I'm the one who thought it would be great to explore the quarry."

He reeled off his transgressions like an indictment. She didn't know what to say.

Please, Lord, give me the right words. He's really hurting, and I never knew it. I thought I knew him so well, but I didn't know this.

"What do Mitch and Alex think?"

That seemed to break through his abstraction, and he focused on her. "They've never blamed me, if that's what you mean. But I'm still responsible." He shrugged. "For the longest time I couldn't hear the rain without seeing Alex's face when he slipped into the water. If Mitch hadn't grabbed him…"

"Brett." She covered his hand with hers. "You were being a seventeen-year-old kid. You thought you were indestructible. All three of you. But you found out differently. That doesn't make you guilty. It just made you a kid."

"Maybe so. But however you look at it, I owe Alex." He gave her a crooked smile. "I owe the richest man in town, and I thought I'd finally found a way to repay him. But he won't take it."

Her fingers tightened around his. "You have to let him make that decision for himself, Brett. He's the one who knows what's best for him. You wouldn't really want the responsibility of making the decision for him."

For a moment he looked as if he'd argue the point. And then he smiled a genuine smile. "Not even if I think I'm right?"

"Not even if you're the best doctor Bedford Creek has ever produced."

The tension ebbed from his face. "I'm the only doctor Bedford Creek has ever produced, as you well know." He reached out to tug lightly at a strand of her hair. "How did little Rebecca turn out to be so wise?"

He was so close that she could see the fine gold flecks in his eyes, so close she could feel his warm breath on her cheek. All in an instant the air between them had changed, becoming charged with something that made her breath catch.

He seemed to feel it, too. His eyes darkened, and his hand moved to her cheek. He stroked the line of her jaw, and her skin warmed at his touch. She'd stopped breathing entirely, and surely her heart was too full to beat.

His mouth, sure and warm, found hers. For a

fraction of a second she hesitated, held back. Then her arms went around him, drawing him even closer, so close she could feel his heart beat.

Then, abruptly, he pulled away.

She stiffened at the shock on his face.

"I…" He stopped, shook his head. "Good night, Rebecca." He got up and was gone before she could gather her wits to say anything.

She sat for a long time, hand on lips that were still warm from his kiss. Could he have guessed what was in her heart? Was that what had made him long for escape?

She had to hope not. Because she'd fallen in love with Brett Elliot all over again, and sooner or later, she knew he'd leave and break her heart.

Chapter Nine

How much did Brett regret that kiss? That question occupied Rebecca's mind when she arrived at the clinic the next morning. Was *regret* even the right word? Maybe to him it was nothing but a casual kiss between colleagues. Maybe he wouldn't think twice about it.

The trouble was, she really didn't know him any longer. She'd thought she did when he came back, but she'd been wrong. He kept her constantly off balance, far from her usual conviction that she knew exactly where she belonged and what her duty was.

Well, she couldn't sit in the car, staring blankly at nothing. She had to go into the clinic, face him and try to preserve whatever dignity she had left. Because one thing was certain—she didn't want Brett to know what that one kiss had done to her.

She let herself in the back door. The offices slept in

early morning silence. Usually she loved this time—
loved the chance to get caught up on paperwork,
consult with Doc, plan the day's work in peace. Today
peaceful was the last word to describe her state of
mind.

"Rebecca, that you?" Doc poked his head out of
his office. "Thought it was. Any coffee?"

She smiled at the familiar greeting. "I'll get it on
right away, Doc," she said, as she did every morning.
She hesitated, hoping she could sound casual enough.
"Brett in yet?"

"Not coming today."

Luckily Doc had disappeared back into his office.
His wise old eyes would have seen the surprise she
couldn't hide. If Brett wasn't here, where was he? His
car had been gone when she left the house this
morning. Was this somehow related to what had
happened between them the night before?

Nonsense. Brett wouldn't be upset by a little kiss.
She started the coffee, then went back to Doc's office.
She'd ask, that's all. Surely it was normal for her to
want to know why he hadn't come in today.

"Doc? Are you all right?"

He was leaning back in his chair, eyes closed, but
he sat up when she said his name. "Fine. Or will be,
when I get some coffee."

"You drink too much coffee," she said, as always.
"It'll be ready in a minute. Why didn't Brett come in
today?"

Doc shrugged. "Just said he had to be out of town for the day. I didn't pry." His tone suggested she shouldn't, either.

So she wouldn't. But that didn't mean she didn't wonder. Brett had left early and apparently expected to be gone the whole day. If it had been an emergency, Doc would have said. So that meant it was something planned, something he had chosen not to mention to her.

The fellowships he'd applied for... The thought gripped her and refused to let go. Her active imagination bolted forward, picturing Brett accepting a fellowship, packing his bags, leaving forever.

It doesn't necessarily mean that. There had to be plenty of other things that would take him out of Bedford Creek for the day. Trouble was, once she started thinking about the fellowship, she couldn't think about anything else.

The day, starting badly, continued to go downhill. The waiting room bubbled with a steady stream of patients. She hadn't realized how much she'd come to depend on Brett until he wasn't there. How had they ever gotten along without him?

Panic gripped her for an instant. How would they get along when he'd gone?

By late afternoon, when Doc had written the wrong prescription for Dean Wagner's insulin and forgotten to suggest an ultrasound for Louise O'Neill, Rebecca felt like a juggler with too many plates in the air. If she hadn't caught Doc's mistakes...

Neither of them was critical, she reminded herself. She had caught them, and no one else needed to know. But she drove home determined to wait on Brett's front porch as long as necessary, until he came back and she could demand to know what he was doing.

As it turned out, no such measure was necessary. When she pulled into the driveway under a canopy of red maples, Brett was just pulling into his drive on the other side of the hedge. They got out of their cars simultaneously.

Without stopping to think about it, Rebecca pushed through the gap in the hedge she'd been using since she was old enough to walk.

"Rebecca. Hi."

Brett looked... She wasn't sure how to describe his expression. Pleased about something, maybe that was it.

She thought of the fellowship, and panic gripped her again. He wouldn't look that happy unless they'd offered it to him.

"Where have you been?" Fear made her abrupt.

He raised his eyebrows at her tone. "No polite greeting? No asking how my day went?"

"I know how your day went. You look like the cat that swallowed the canary. Where were you?"

Brett pulled a briefcase from the back seat and slammed the door. He nodded toward the house. "Come on in, and I'll tell you."

Being alone with Brett was probably the last thing

she ought to do. But it was the only way she'd find out the truth. She followed him into the house.

Brett led the way to the living room. He put his briefcase on the cherry coffee table and opened it, taking out a sheaf of papers clipped together. "Take a look at this." He shoved them into her hands.

"What is it?"

He threw himself into the armchair across from her, loosening his tie. "I don't know how people manage to wear these things all day. Felt like I was choking." He nodded toward the papers in her hand. "Go on, read through that. I want your opinion."

If he wanted her opinion on a fellowship offer, he wouldn't like what he got. She sank down on the couch and started to read. After a moment she looked at Brett.

"This is a physical-therapy plan."

He nodded. "For Alex." He seemed to register her surprise. "Why? What did you think it was?"

"Nothing. It doesn't matter," she said quickly. She shuffled through the papers. "This is very comprehensive. Where did you get it?"

"Philadelphia." He leaned back, yawning. "A buddy of mine from med school runs an orthopedic clinic that's got a state-of-the-art therapy program. I took him Alex's records and asked him to design a treatment plan. What do you think?"

She took her time, leafing through the papers, checking out the detailed charts. Finally she looked up again.

"I think it looks excellent. Unfortunately, I also think you won't get Alex to go to Philadelphia for treatment."

He gestured impatiently. "I don't intend to. That's the whole point. He won't take the time a decent therapy program would require, so I'm going to bring the program to him."

"Bring it to him," she echoed. She had to admit, he had a point. She'd tried without success to get Alex to attend sessions even twice weekly at the regional hospital. He'd gone once or twice, then dropped it, saying he couldn't afford the time to drive forty miles each way.

"That's right." Brett's eyes danced with contagious enthusiasm. "Believe me, I'm going to make it impossible for him to say no."

"But how? If he won't go to a clinic—" She gestured with the papers. "Bedford Creek doesn't even have a health club. No one in town has this kind of equipment."

"Leave it to me. I've got a plan that can't fail." He raised an eyebrow. "You in to help?"

He obviously wanted to keep his scheme a secret. "Yes, of course I'll help." She stood, holding the papers out to him. "I'll make a couple of copies of that at the office tomorrow, if you want, so I can study it more closely."

He got up, looking at her with a quizzical expression as he took the papers. "You seem to be in a hurry."

She took a step toward the door. "I have things to do."

And staying here, thinking about how devastating Brett looked when he was excited about something, was definitely not a good idea. He apparently intended to ignore what had happened between them the night before, so she would, too.

He closed the gap between them. "You seem a little stiff. You're not mad at me for taking the day off, are you? It was for a good cause."

"No, of course not." If only he wouldn't stand so close to her, she'd find it easier to keep her tone light and unflustered.

"Then it has to be last night. Am I in the doghouse for stealing a kiss from an old friend?"

The light words cut her to the heart. That's all she was to Brett. All she'd ever be. *An old friend.*

Her only choice was to play along and pretend it meant as little to her as it obviously did to him. The trouble was, she wasn't sure she could succeed—not with his intent gaze fixed on her face.

"When did anyone ever manage to keep you in the doghouse?" She managed a smile. "You always charmed your way out." She spun, holding on to the smile with an effort. "I really have to go. I'll see you tomorrow."

"I'm telling you, Mitch, it's never going to fit." Brett looked from the beat-up chest to the attic stairway late the following afternoon. "We'll break our necks trying to get it up those narrow steps."

"Wimp," Mitch teased, grinning. "Come on, let's see what you're made of. I promised Anne I'd have that room cleaned out and ready for Emilie, and that's what I'm going to do."

"If it kills me," Brett grumbled, but he hefted one end of the chest. "Okay, let's give it a try."

At least moving furniture was a change from his current worry. No, make that plural—worries. Rebecca and Doc.

The chest made it halfway through the narrow doorway, then stuck. He looked at Mitch over its top. "I told you so."

"Put your back into it," Mitch advised. He gave a shove, and the chest popped through, nearly flattening Brett in the process.

He rubbed his shoulder. "If you disable me, what's Bedford Creek going to do for medical care?"

"Same as it always has," Mitch said. They hoisted the chest the rest of the way to the dusty attic. "Depend on Doc."

"How long do you think that can last?" It was on the tip of his tongue to mention the hospital's proposal to Mitch, but he bit it back. He shouldn't talk to anyone else about it until he'd talked to Doc.

Mitch shoved the chest against a wall, wiped his forehead and looked at Brett, eyes narrowing. "Why? What's wrong?"

Rebecca was the one he should talk to about this particular problem, but talking to Rebecca had become difficult. They'd worked together with patients and on the therapy plan for Alex, but she'd been consistently evasive, slipping away every time there was a chance they might be alone.

He had to talk to someone, and he could trust Mitch's discretion. "I'm worried about Doc."

Mitch leaned against the chest, looking ready to stay there all day, if necessary. "What's wrong with Doc, other than being overworked?"

"I'm not sure." He frowned. "Maybe it's nothing. People do make mistakes. Even doctors."

"No, really?" Mitch mimicked astonishment. "I thought you guys took lessons from Superman."

Brett punched his arm, as he'd have done back in high school. It was like hitting a brick wall.

"Guess that's how I think about Doc. That he shouldn't make mistakes."

Mitch sobered. "And he has?"

"Nothing big. Nothing either Rebecca or I didn't catch." He wondered how many other errors Rebecca had caught and corrected without saying anything. "I just…it worries me," he admitted.

"You're sure they were errors? I mean, not just something you might have done differently?"

"No." He thought of the blank look on Doc's face when he'd mentioned Mrs. Clancy's blood pressure. "These were mistakes a raw intern wouldn't make."

Mitch didn't respond for a minute, his face impassive. Brett knew that guarded look. It meant Mitch was struggling with something unpalatable.

"You think it's just that he's worn out?" he said finally. "Or you think it's something more serious?"

A fly buzzed lazily in a patch of sunlight from the attic window, and Brett took out his frustration by swatting at it. "Wish I knew. I've been trying to get Doc to let me do a thorough physical exam, but he always has an excuse."

"What does Rebecca say?"

The other part of his problem loomed. "I haven't talked to Rebecca about it."

Mitch looked astonished. "Why not? If anyone knows what's going on with Doc, it's Rebecca."

"Rebecca and I haven't been doing a lot of talking lately." *Not since I kissed her.* No, he couldn't say that to Mitch. Back when they were in high school, maybe—but not now.

"Why not?" Mitch's eyes narrowed. "You haven't hurt her feelings, have you? Treated her like she's still a little kid?"

That was the least of his problems. "Not at all. It's just that Rebecca thinks it's my duty to stay, so she suspects everything I say about Doc. You know Rebecca—she's a great one for doing your duty."

"Nothing wrong with that." Mitch, with his background in the military, set a high value on duty, Brett knew.

Brett lifted an eyebrow. "Does that mean you think I should stay, too?"

"I think it's between you and Doc," Mitch said firmly. "And nobody else's business."

Except God's. He suspected that was what Mitch was thinking, but wouldn't say. Mitch didn't believe in preaching to his friends, but the way he lived his life made his own beliefs clear.

Mitch clapped him on the shoulder. "Come on, let's get back to work. If you take my advice, you'll talk to Rebecca about it." He nodded toward the stairwell. "You'll have a chance soon. That's her with Anne now."

"I've got the border, but we need a pail of water." Rebecca looked back at Anne, who carried brushes and a plastic drop cloth.

"I'll get it." Anne dropped her load in the second-floor hall of Mitch's house. She glanced over Rebecca's shoulder. "Or better yet, Brett can get it."

"Brett." She swung around, nearly losing the rolls of wallpaper border she carried. Brett and Mitch had evidently just come through the attic door. Brett had a smudge of dust on his cheek, and she resisted the urge to wipe it away. "I didn't expect to see you here."

And didn't want to. She'd spent the last couple of days avoiding him, at least as much as it was possible to in a small office. Now here he was, and she'd committed herself to working on the baby's room with Anne.

"Just helping Mitch move some things."

He seemed ill at ease, which surprised her. Cool, confident Brett was never ill at ease.

"We'd better get it finished," Mitch pointed out. "The women want to work in there."

Anne smiled up at him. "We wouldn't object to some help."

Yes, we would, Rebecca thought, but there was no use saying it. Mitch would be delighted to help Anne do absolutely anything, and neither Brett nor she could back out gracefully now. It looked as if they were destined to spend the next several hours together.

Brett waved toward the door. "After you."

She tried to imagine a clear glass wall between herself and Brett—a nice barrier to let her stay detached. It didn't work. Even her imagination wasn't good enough to achieve that.

She dropped the rolls of border on a stack of newspaper and glanced around the small room. "This is going to be perfect for Emilie." She knelt on the padded window seat, looking out at the apple tree in the backyard. "What did you use it for, Mitch?"

"Officially, a guest room." Mitch picked up a box and shoved it into Brett's arms. "Actually, it turned into a catch-all. But don't worry. Brett and I will have the rest of this out of the way in no time."

"No time, he says." Brett staggered toward the door. "I'll just run right up the attic steps with this thing. What do you have in here, rocks?"

Mitch grinned. "And after we get this cleared, we'll bring up the baby's furniture from the garage." He hoisted another box and followed the sound of Brett's groan.

Anne's deep blue eyes clouded with worry. "I told Mitch I thought we should use movers instead of imposing on his friends."

"Don't be silly. Brett wants to help. Besides, it will do him good to do some manual labor for once."

"A little hard on him, aren't you?" Anne looked at her questioningly. "Or is that a smoke screen for what you really feel?"

Rebecca felt her cheeks warm, and she bent to pick up the tape measure. "I don't know what you mean. Are you thinking of new curtains in here?"

The conversation returned to decorating, and she tried not to think about how she must be giving her feelings away. Even Anne, who'd known her for months instead of years, could tell. She had to get a grip, or Brett might start suspecting something.

At least Mitch's and Anne's presence would preclude any private conversations with Brett. She could handle this. They were a work party, not a double date.

And she did handle it, keeping the conversation light and general while they put up the fanciful animal border. Everything went fine, right up until the moment when both Anne and Mitch vanished downstairs on separate errands, leaving her alone with Brett.

She concentrated on the last bit of border, smoothing out an invisible wrinkle from a smiling bunny. She felt, rather than saw, Brett's approach.

"Looks nice." He stopped inches from her step stool. "I didn't know you were a paper-hanger, too. Is there anything you can't do?"

"Plenty." She hopped down from the stool, putting a few additional inches between herself and Brett. "Too many to list. Maybe I'd better see if Anne needs any help."

Brett stood between her and the door. "Just a second. I want to talk to you."

"Can it wait? I want—"

"No, it can't wait." He frowned. "I've been trying to have a serious conversation with you, but you always manage to slip away."

That was true enough, but she hadn't known he noticed. Tension shivered along her nerves. If Brett wanted a serious conversation, it couldn't be about anything good. Had his fellowship come through? Or was it something more personal?

"I'm here now." She crossed her arms protectively. "What is it?"

His frown deepened. "What's wrong with Doc?"

The attack came out of the blue, and she wasn't prepared for it. "What do you mean?"

"Don't pretend you don't know what I'm talking about." He transferred the frown to her. "You know as well as I do that something's wrong with him."

"I don't…" She let the words die. Denying it wouldn't help. "All right, he forgets things now and then. He's working too hard."

"How long have you been covering up his mistakes?"

So Brett had noticed. "That's why I'm there, to pick up on those little things."

"Not so little, Rebecca." His tone was somber. "The things I've noticed weren't minor, by any means. And I'm wondering how many other things I *didn't* see." He leaned closer to her, face intent. "Come on, level with me."

She was caught again, between what she wanted to do and her promise to Doc. She took a deep breath. She'd have to trust Brett with some of the truth and hope he used it wisely.

"It's been about a year." She turned away, staring out the window so she wouldn't have to look at Brett. "I've noticed him failing for about the last year."

"A year?" he echoed. "And you haven't done anything about it?"

She was too upset to be angry at his tone. "At first it really was forgetting just little things. But it's gotten worse lately." Her throat tightened. "I don't know what to do."

She felt his hands on her shoulders, warm and strong.

"Well, the first thing you have to do is not try to carry everything yourself. It's not just your problem, you know."

"In a way, it is. There's no other medical professional I can turn to. I thought, when you came back…" She stopped, unable to go on.

"You thought I'd take over." His hands dropped from her shoulders. "I've already told you that's not going to happen. But that doesn't mean I don't care about Doc. Has he seen another doctor?"

She managed a smile. "You know the answer to that one. Of course not, no matter what I say. I even made an appointment for him, but he cancelled it."

"Stubborn old coot." Affection filled the words, so that she couldn't take offense. "What do you think is wrong? You must have an opinion."

This was where it got difficult. She could only hope he'd understand. "All I know is what I've observed, because he hasn't let me run any tests." She turned so that she could see his face. "And Doc made me promise not to discuss his health with anyone. Including you."

"Are you saying you won't tell me what you've seen?" He sounded as if he doubted her sanity.

"Brett, please understand. I promised Doc. How can I break my word?"

His eyes flashed. "That's plain stupid. How am I going to help him if you won't tell me what's wrong?"

"You've seen the same things I have." Her anger sparked in return.

"I haven't been here as long as you have, Rebecca. I don't like working in the dark."

"Then why don't you insist on giving him a physical?"

"I'll do that, but it would help to know what you think." He glared at her, baffled and angry.

It *was* stupid, that was all she could think, echoing Brett's word. Stupid that the two of them, who loved Doc, were incapable of helping him.

Her anger ebbed, replaced by worry. She reached toward him tentatively, willing him to understand. "Think about it, Brett. You know if he'd made you promise, you'd feel the same way."

"That's different." His response was quick.

"Why? Because you're the doctor?"

His face was tight, holding his anger against her. For a long moment, he didn't say anything, and then he shook his head.

"All right. I guess I can understand why you don't want to betray his confidence. I'll try and get him to let me do a thorough work-up. But if he won't…"

He paused, and her heart seemed to stop.

"If he won't, I'll have no choice but to talk to the clinic board. I don't want to, but I will."

Chapter Ten

Was there anything else she could have said to Brett? Rebecca still worried about it the following morning as she puttered around the house doing her usual Saturday morning chores. They both wanted what was best for Doc, didn't they?

Unfortunately, they probably wouldn't ever agree on what that was. If Brett pushed Doc too hard about a checkup; if Doc got his back up and wouldn't let Brett examine him; if Brett made good on his threat to go to the clinic board…

Her thoughts went round and round. What could she do? There had to be a way to resolve this that wouldn't hurt Doc.

Maybe if she talked to him seriously, told him how worried Brett was, how worried they both were—maybe then he'd see that he couldn't just keep stonewalling everyone about the state of his health.

She paused, arms full of a load of laundry. Doc usually went to the office on Saturday morning, even though he didn't see patients then, to catch up on paperwork. This might be the perfect opportunity to talk with him in an unhurried way before Brett tackled him about a checkup. It could be her only chance to smooth the way, so she'd better take it.

Half an hour later she'd changed clothes and started for the clinic. But she'd forgotten, in her worry, that the festival was still going on. The streets were crowded with people determined to enjoy themselves.

It took her extra time to get to the clinic, but when she arrived, Doc's battered station wagon was the only vehicle in the parking lot. She unlocked the back door and went quietly in.

Doc sat at his desk, a file open in front of him, but he didn't seem to be reading it. He leaned back, eyes closed, and tears slipped down his cheeks.

She felt a stab of pain in her heart. "Doc, what is it?" She hurried to his side. "Are you all right?"

He jerked upright, startled, and then wiped at the tears with the back of his hand. He fumbled for the glasses he'd pushed to the top of his head, sliding them into place like a barricade.

"All right? Why wouldn't I be all right? What are you doing here?"

Her heart started beating again when she heard his usual testy tone. "I came in to see you." She took his hand, conscious of the fragility of the hands that had once been so strong. "What is it, Doc? Please tell me what's wrong. You were crying."

He shook his head irritably, then snatched up a tissue and mopped his face. "Allergies, that's all."

"You've never had an allergic reaction in your life."

Somehow she had to make him level with her. They just couldn't go on this way. She leaned across to look at the file, realizing with a sense of shock that it was her father's.

He must have seen the expression in her eyes. He fumbled with the folder, sliding it into the desk drawer.

"Why did you have that out, Doc?" She tried to keep emotion from her voice. "That's been over with a long time."

For a moment she thought he'd try to dismiss it.

Then he shook his head. "Just thinking. Wondering."

"Wondering what?"

He fidgeted with the drawer pull. "If I'd missed something. If I should have caught it sooner. Maybe…"

Panic clutched her. That was what she'd been feeling for two years, but she'd never realized Doc was going through the same thing. Brett's words came back to her. Every medical professional does that— blame himself.

"Oh, Doc." Her voice was thick. "You know everyone thinks that when they've lost someone they love. Especially medical personnel. We think we should have been able to save them." She put her arms around him, resting her cheek against his head. "But we can't save everyone. We're not God."

I'm sorry, Daddy. I'm sorry. The pain she hadn't realized was still hiding in her own heart flared for an instant, then seemed to ease.

For a long moment Doc held her as if she were his lifeline. Then he pulled back, clearing his throat, probably embarrassed by the unusual show of emotion.

Unusual. The word reverberated in her mind. It was unusual, yet another piece of the puzzle she and Brett had to unravel somehow.

"I need to get back to work," Doc said gruffly. "And you've got better things to do with your Saturday than hang around here."

She leaned against the desk. "I'm not leaving until I have your promise. Doc, you've got to let Brett give you a thorough going over. You've got to. And you might as well give in, because I won't."

"That's good advice, Doc."

She spun to find Brett standing in the doorway. He came toward them, face determined.

How long had he been standing there? Had he heard her repeating his own words?

Doc looked from Brett to her. "You two ganging up on me?"

"We didn't plan to," Brett said. "But we're both

worried about you, Doc, so you might as well make up your mind to go along with us."

She touched Doc's shoulder. "We love you, you know. It's not right to shut us out like this. Give us a chance to help you."

Doc's eyes closed, as if he had to withdraw from the two of them a bit. Was he remembering his grief over not healing her father? Did he realize how much they needed the chance to help him?

Please, Lord. Please.

She glanced at Brett, willing him to give Doc the time to decide, and had the quick impression he was praying, too.

Doc looked up at them finally, weary but somehow resigned. "I guess if I've got to trust my health to someone, it might as well be the two of you." He stood, shrugging off his jacket. "Let's get on with it."

Brett was as coolly professional as if Doc were a patient he'd just met for the first time. She stayed in the background, helping as unobtrusively as possible, but she couldn't stop her busy mind.

What was Brett thinking? Of the same possibilities that had haunted her in recent weeks—Parkinson's, impending stroke? Or something she hadn't even thought of?

When he'd finished, Brett stood looking down at the chart, frowning. He transferred the frown to Doc. "You know what I'm going to say is the next step. It's the same thing you'd say to a patient with your symptoms."

Doc's face tightened. "You want me to see a neurologist for a complete work-up. But I don't—"

"That's what you'd recommend, isn't it?" Brett interrupted firmly.

Stubborn silence ensued. Finally Doc nodded.

Rebecca discovered she could breathe again. "I'll call and make the appointment."

"Maybe next month, when we're not so busy," Doc began.

"As soon as I can get you in," she said. "And you're going, if we have to tie you down and take you there."

Doc divided a glare between the two of them, but it lacked his usual fierceness. "Guess you two think you're pretty smart, don't you?"

Brett put his arm across Doc's shoulder. "If we are, we both know who to blame it on." He glanced at Rebecca, as if reminding her they were in this together. "We went into medicine because of you, both of us."

"Now, you just keep turning that," Pastor Richie said, his blue eyes twinkling, "and we'll have the best batch of homemade ice cream at the festival."

Brett couldn't help but smile back at the man who'd been his pastor since he was a kid. Cranking ice cream wasn't how he'd planned to spend the last night of the festival, but it was tough to say no to Pastor Richie. At least he didn't have to serve the dishes and cones. Rebecca had been drafted to do that.

He glanced at her as she handed a top-heavy cone to a small boy. So far he'd managed to evade her questions about Doc, but that couldn't last forever. Now that the whole thing was in the open, sooner or later they'd have to discuss the possibilities. But he had a respite as long as the steady stream of customers kept her busy.

Unfortunately, turning a crank on the ice-cream maker left his mind free to worry about Doc. He frowned. Had he done all the right things?

He had, of course he had. But he was discovering it wasn't so easy to be satisfied with your actions when the patient was someone you cared about.

He pictured Doc the way he'd seen him at the office, agonizing about the care he'd given Rebecca's father. Two years later, and still he worried over whether he'd done the right thing. Would that be him, two years from now, berating himself because he imagined he'd missed something with Doc?

The ice cream must be stiffening, because the handle grew suddenly harder to turn. He put his muscles into it, expending the energy he didn't want to spend worrying.

This was what it was like, being a general practitioner in your own hometown. Knowing people too well, worrying about them, fearing that maybe you hadn't done your best. It added an emotional layer to medicine that he didn't like. Far better to be detached, able to turn off the thoughts when the shift was over.

"Brett's doing a batch of chocolate now," he heard Rebecca tell someone.

She glanced toward him. "Is that almost done? I'm getting requests from the chocoholics."

"Getting there." He shoved the handle, muscles straining. "How do you tell when it's ready?"

"By the feel of it." Rebecca knelt beside him, putting her hands next to his on the crank and giving it an experimental turn. "I'd say another minute or two will do."

Easy for her to say. She wasn't the one who had to finish it.

He let his gaze rest on Rebecca as she returned to the counter to try and convince three teenage girls they really wanted peach. He could sense the mixture of relief and worry she tried to hide. Relief that they were finally getting help for Doc; worry at what that help would entail.

At least there was a well-known neurologist at the regional hospital. He'd rather have taken Doc to Philadelphia, but Doc had vetoed that suggestion out of hand.

Well, maybe it was for the best. Maybe being at Lincoln Medical Center as a patient would alleviate some of the antagonism Doc had toward the hospital and the clinics it ran. He'd assumed Doc wouldn't want to go there, wouldn't want the medical center having any additional ammunition for use in taking over the clinic. But Doc seemed resigned to it.

He glanced toward Rebecca again. He should take the opportunity to sound her out about those clinics. She undoubtedly had an opinion very similar to Doc's. And he could hardly badger Doc about it while he was waiting out his appointment with the specialist.

"Okay, Rebecca, I think this is ready." He hefted the ice-cream maker to the table. "I'm making no guarantees, though."

She lifted the lid.

"Maybe we'd better make you taste it first, just to be sure it's safe." She scooped up a plastic spoonful and held it to his lips. "What do you think?"

He held it on his tongue for a moment, savoring the sweet coldness. "Best ice cream I ever tasted."

She lifted an eyebrow. "You might be prejudiced."

"Try it yourself." He dipped a spoon in and held it out to her.

Smiling, she took the spoonful. He managed to get a dab of it on her chin, and wiped it off with his finger. Her skin was warm and smooth, and he suddenly realized how close they stood in the small booth.

Apparently she did, too, because she backed up, bumping against the counter. "That's…that's very good." She turned away. "Let's get the chocolate lovers served."

But the chocolate lovers seemed to have vanished. Pastor Richie popped back into the booth.

"Everyone's finding a spot to watch the fireworks." He picked up the container of chocolate, sliding it into the freezer. "We won't have any customers until the show is over, so you two might as well go watch."

"I don't need—" Rebecca began, but the pastor made shooing motions with his hands.

"Go, go on now, both of you." He shepherded them out of the booth. "Take her on the bridge, Brett. You'll get the best view from there."

Brett smiled at Rebecca's expression. "You might as well give up and watch the fireworks. You know what he's like once he gets an idea. We'll never hear the end of it if we don't go out on the bridge."

Rebecca nodded, falling into step with him.

Plenty of other people had the same idea, but the bridge across the river was long enough for them to spread out. He found a spot about halfway down and leaned his elbows on the rail. In the distance, the high school band tuned up.

Rebecca hesitated a moment, then leaned against the rail next to him. "It's beautiful, isn't it?" She lifted her face to the breeze that swept along the river, letting it ruffle the bronze curls around her face.

"Beautiful," he agreed. Then he turned to look at the view. Well, it was beautiful, too.

The river stretched like a sheet of pewter, glistening in the dusk. Along its edges, the shadows of the trees made a black border that rustled and moved, wavering on the surface of the water.

"First star," Rebecca said softly.

He glanced up. One pale star flickered in a gray-blue sky. The western ridge was purple, the more distant mountains shading away until he wasn't sure whether he could see them or not.

His throat went tight. Rebecca was right. It was beautiful. He'd just been too preoccupied most of the time to notice.

"They're going to play 'Yankee Doodle' first," she predicted, nodding toward the band that was arranging itself on a makeshift stage by the riverbank.

"How do you know?" He leaned a little closer, his elbow brushing hers.

She smiled. "Because they always do. If there's one thing you can be sure of, it's that the band will start with 'Yankee Doodle' and end with the '1812 Overture.'"

The strains of 'Yankee Doodle' floated across the water. "You win," he said, clasping her hand.

She didn't pull away. Somehow the events of the morning had made them…friends? Colleagues? Allies? He wasn't sure what, but he knew they were closer now than they'd ever been.

She glanced up at him. "Thinking about Doc?"

"In a way, I guess." He stared out at the water, watching a bat swoop low over the shining surface. "It's hard not to."

Her hand tensed under his. "I know you don't want to guess. But what do you think they're going to find?"

She was right. He didn't want to guess. "If I knew that, I wouldn't have to send him to a neurologist."

"You must have an idea."

"You can fill in the blanks as well as I can, Rebecca." His fingers tightened on hers. "Now that it's out in the open, you can level with me. Is there anything you've noticed that Doc didn't tell me?"

She shook her head, giving a little sigh. "Nothing. Brett, you don't know how relieved I am. I wanted all along to talk to you about it, but how could I? I'd promised."

Stubborn, responsible Rebecca, with her loving heart and her strict sense of honor. He wouldn't want her to be any different.

"I know," he said. "It's okay. Now…" He tried to find something reassuring to say. "We just have to hope for the best. I've heard good things about this Dr. Morrisey he's seeing."

"I have, too." She frowned. "I know you wanted him to go to Philadelphia, but Morrisey has an excellent reputation."

This might be his chance to sound her out about the medical center. "We're lucky there's a tertiary care hospital only forty miles away. Plenty of people have to go farther than that."

"I guess so." She stared out at the water, her voice noncommittal.

"I heard the hospital took over a practice in Henderson and set up a clinic there." *Maybe they'll do that here.* No, he wasn't ready to say that yet. Not until he'd talked to Doc about it.

She swung to face him. "You know what they did there?" she demanded, her tone already telling him she hadn't approved, whatever it was.

"Something you didn't like, obviously."

She ignored that. "They retired the two doctors who were in practice there originally. Then they staffed the clinic with residents, who rotated in and out every few months. Imagine! Every time you go in, you have a different doctor."

It didn't seem strange to him, but Rebecca was used to care from the doctor who'd delivered her. "That's not really so unusual," he ventured.

"It is around here." She frowned at him. "I suppose that's an example of big-city medicine."

"Family-medicine residents have to gain experience somewhere." He didn't think she'd be convinced.

"Well, not here," she said tartly. "I'm glad Bedford Creek is too small to interest the medical center. They've been buying up practices all over the area, but they wouldn't want to set up in a town this size. I suppose it wouldn't pay."

Not unless the Bedford Creek clinic were folded into a larger one. Then it would pay very well. He considered telling her about the hospital's plan…considered it and rejected it.

He had to talk to Doc first, that was clear. And since Doc apparently hadn't confided in Rebecca about the offers he'd already turned down, the situation was doubly difficult.

A preliminary *crack* sounded from the fireworks staging area. "They're starting." Rebecca swung back toward the view, her voice as eager as a child's.

A rocket whooshed into the night sky, sending out a shower of red and blue flares. Rebecca grasped his hand, and he heard her gasp.

"Oh, how beautiful." She looked up at him, eyes shining. "I just love fireworks, don't you?"

Actually, he'd never thought all that much about fireworks. But anything that could wipe the worry from Rebecca's eyes had his vote.

"Love them," he said firmly.

Another one shot across the darkening sky, this time arcing so low that the sparks actually fell into the water.

"Now you see why they do it over the river," Rebecca said. She leaned closer to him, shivering a little as the breeze freshened.

He put his arm around her, feeling the gentle curve of her shoulders. She leaned against him, relaxed and trusting for perhaps the first time since he'd come back.

Trusting. The word echoed in his thoughts. He might as well enjoy this moment, because it wouldn't last long. Sooner or later they'd clash again, about Doc, about the clinic, about what the future was meant to be. And when they did, the fireworks weren't going to be nearly as pretty as these.

Chapter Eleven

Too many things had been conspiring to keep him focused on Bedford Creek. Brett picked up the telephone on Monday morning with a fresh sense of purpose. He hadn't followed through with a phone call about the Chicago fellowship because he'd been so preoccupied with Doc, the clinic, his patients, and everything else that was going on.

With Rebecca, a little voice whispered in his mind. *You've been thinking about Rebecca.*

It was time he stopped that particular useless line of thought. He and Rebecca weren't destined to be anything other than friends. In fact, when he left Bedford Creek she'd probably no longer consider him even a friend.

There was definitely no future in thinking about how her incredible amber eyes mirrored her every thought—sparkling when she laughed, flashing when she was angry with him, warm with concern when she looked at patients, filled with love at the sight of Kristie. He didn't think he'd ever known a woman who could say so much with a single look, and the funny thing was that she didn't even realize it.

When she'd leaned against his shoulder while they watched the fireworks from the bridge, he'd experienced a mix of emotions that alarmed him. He didn't think he'd ever felt quite that way before—a jumble of protectiveness, tenderness, desire, longing…

Enough. He was shaken all over again just remembering it. A good antidote to his pointless feelings for Rebecca was to call the Chicago program and find out the status of his fellowship. That would remind him of where his priorities ought to be. He couldn't achieve the future he dreamed of without intense, single-minded focus on his objectives. And that meant no wandering off to remember how soft Rebecca's lips had been against his.

Fifteen minutes later he hung up the phone, somewhat startled at how quickly his mission had been accomplished. Not only was his application still in the running, but they wanted him for an interview, as soon as possible. He'd had trouble putting them off until the following week.

Predictable, he thought, unable to suppress a grin. They hadn't bothered to call him, but they wanted him to drop everything and rush to Chicago at a moment's notice.

But he couldn't. All those responsibilities he'd been thinking about interfered. Doc's tests were this week, and he wouldn't leave without knowing the results. And Mitch's wedding was coming up on Saturday. The earliest he could possibly be there was Monday, so that would have to do.

He'd sensed the promise in the voice of the program head. If the interview went well, there was every chance the fellowship would be his.

He should be happy. He was happy. But still... He frowned out the front window at his mother's flower bed. He'd changed since he'd returned to Bedford Creek. Maybe the change had started earlier, back in Philadelphia, the moment he faced the decision to treat that homeless patient. He'd suddenly felt a need to make a decision because it was God's plan, not just because it was best for him.

So was this fellowship God's plan for him? It was a difficult question to ask, because he had to take the answer seriously.

Most of his colleagues back in Philly wouldn't even consider the question. They'd make a decision based on career advantage, and that was it. Rebecca, of course, probably asked that question first. Just thinking about her made him think about how seldom he'd consciously taken God's will into account.

How did anyone know what God's will was in a particular situation? Too bad Pastor Richie hadn't covered the topic in Sunday's sermon.

His medical talent was a gift from God—that he was sure of. That was one belief that had been bedrock all his life. He'd known instinctively that whatever gifts he had, God was the source. Wouldn't God expect him to use those gifts to the fullest?

The fellowship in Chicago would certainly do that. He'd be working with some of the best surgeons in the country. His excitement grew at the thought. He might actually be the one chosen. Surely that meant it was the path he should follow.

Rebecca wouldn't agree. The thought slipped into his mind, and he had to make a conscious effort to eject it.

It didn't matter what Rebecca thought. She wasn't a determining factor in his future.

Rebecca looked doubtfully at the load of equipment Brett proposed unloading at the Caine mansion. It had taken a rented van to get it all here. Now she, Brett and Mitch were going to set up Alex's very own treatment facility.

"Does Alex know all this is coming?" She stepped back out of the way as Mitch opened the van door.

Brett grinned, taking one end of the heavy carton Mitch was pulling out. "He hasn't a clue," he said. "I didn't know what he'd say if I told him, so I didn't tell him."

She stared at him, not knowing whether to laugh or not. "What if he tells us to turn right around and take it away again?"

"He won't do that." He nodded toward a smaller box. "You bring that one."

She picked it up with an effort. It was heavier than it looked. "How do you know he won't kick us out?"

"Because he's not here." He flashed her that self-confident grin. "I talked Maida Hansen into cooperating with us. She'll let us in, and she cleared out a room for us to use."

Everyone knew that Maida, the Caine family's longtime housekeeper, was devoted to Alex. If Maida thought standing on her head would help Alex get better, that's what she'd do. She probably hadn't even questioned Brett.

Well, it wasn't Rebecca's job to question, either. She followed the two men up the three steps to the portico that swept around the mansion. Surely, in a house this size, it hadn't been a problem to find an empty room to put the equipment. Whether Alex would agree to the program was another question.

Maida held open the double doors whose frosted glass panels bore an etched *C.* Old Mr. Caine had been proud of his name, so people said.

"This way." Maida ushered them in and glanced back down the sweep of the circular drive, her angular face lined with worry. "Mr. Alex shouldn't be back for an hour, but I don't know."

"Now, Maida." Brett let Mitch support the weight of the box while he patted Maida's shoulder. "You know we're doing the right thing. Even if Alex complains, this is for his own good."

Her mouth set in firm lines. "It's high time he did something for his own good, that's for sure. You just tell me what to do to make him better. I'll do it."

"That's the spirit." Brett took the end of the carton again. "Okay, let's get rolling. We're going to have a fitness center set up for Alex by the time he walks through the door."

"I'm going to need a massage by then," Mitch said. "Can I put this down yet?"

"In here." Maida hurried to push open another door. "Will this room be all right?"

"Perfect," Brett said.

Rebecca nodded, glancing around. Maida had picked the old conservatory, empty of plants now that there was apparently no one with the time or interest to look after them. Even empty, the room was charming, with its bank of windows and French doors opening onto the patio at the rear of the house. Given the size of the Caine estate, Alex would have perfect privacy for his workouts, in spite of all the windows.

Mitch ripped open the first carton. "You want to set this up before we bring in the next?"

Brett nodded. "At least that way we'll have something to show Alex, in case he comes back before we're done."

She looked at him sharply. Maybe Mitch didn't hear it, but she did. There was an undertone of tension in Brett's voice that told her clearly what he was thinking and feeling.

This was his way of paying Alex back. In some obscure, masculine way of keeping accounts, he felt he'd been left owing Alex a debt for his part, however innocent, in the camping accident. He wouldn't be happy until he'd figured out a way to repay that debt.

Men, she decided as she opened the box she'd brought in, were strange creatures. She glanced again at the two of them, engrossed in putting together the fitness machine.

They both wore jeans and T-shirts, but it wouldn't matter what Mitch wore. He always looked like a cop. She'd never figured out exactly what it was that conveyed that, but she knew it was true. As for Brett…

Her heart gave its usual *thump* when she looked at him. The man was dangerous to her self-control, unfortunately. Jeans and a white T-shirt emblazoned with a Run for Your Heart logo didn't do a thing to detract from his appeal. His skin glowed with good health, and the muscles that rippled as he wrestled the machine into place declared that he took fitness seriously.

He glanced across at her. His gaze held hers for a long moment, during which her heart forgot to beat. Then he smiled, slowly. Devastatingly. She forced herself to frown intently down at the contents of her box, as if engrossed in putting whatever it was together. In fact, she hadn't a clue what it was—and if Brett didn't stop looking at her she felt as if she'd self-destruct.

"What do you think, Rebecca?" Mitch's question came out of the blue. She looked up, startled, sure she was flushing.

"Think?" she echoed. She must have missed their conversation while she daydreamed about Brett.

"About this thing." Mitch had swung himself into the saddle of the machine, and he did an experimental leg raise. "Looks pretty good, doesn't it?"

"Yes, of course." She could feel her cheeks burning. Nonsense. Neither of them could possibly guess what she'd been thinking. Nobody knew that her feelings for Brett were anything but friendship for a childhood neighbor. "It'll work fine, if we can get Alex to use it."

"He will." Brett sounded sure, but again she heard the worry—almost fear—beneath the confident words.

Her heart hurt for him. He wanted so much to help Alex. If he could do this for his friend, it would mean the world to him. His happiness mattered to her almost as much as the possibility of Alex regaining his health.

Please, Lord. Please let this work, for both of them.

The three of them kept at it, and at the end of an hour the room had turned into a reasonable facsimile of a therapy room, complete with mats, weights and workout machines.

"Pretty good," Mitch said, mopping his forehead as he looked around.

"Pretty good?" Brett grinned, clapping him on the back. "It's great. We did it."

Before Rebecca had time to feel left out, he'd flung his other arm across her shoulders. "Trust me—Alex isn't going to be able to resist this."

Maida Hansen thrust her head in the doorway, looking agitated. "He's coming! Oh, Dr. Brett, he's coming. Are you ready?"

"We're all set. Send him in the minute he gets here."

Brett's smile was confident. Nevertheless, she seemed to hear his unspoken prayer. *Please, Lord. Please.*

The three of them stood frozen in place when Maida had gone. Rebecca heard the housekeeper's footsteps on the tile floor as she went to the door, heard Alex greet her.

"Dr. Brett is waiting for you in the conservatory," she said, just the smallest quaver in her voice.

"The conservatory?" Alex sounded startled. "What on earth is he doing there?"

His uneven footsteps came toward them, echoing on the tile. Rebecca held her breath.

Please, Father. This means so much to him.

She should be ashamed of herself, thinking of Brett when it was Alex they were trying to help. But she couldn't seem to help herself. She cared too much.

She just cared too much about Brett, and there was no going back.

"Brett?" Alex shoved the door open. "What in the world—"

He stood in the doorway, staring at them in amazement.

Rebecca didn't know about the other two, but her smile felt petrified.

"Surprise," Brett said quietly.

"What's going on here?" Alex moved forward slowly, eyes focused on Brett. "What are you up to?"

Brett gestured around the room. "You didn't have time for therapy. So we brought therapy to you. Now you don't have any excuses. You're going to get rid of that stick, once and for all."

"Pretty decent setup," Mitch said. "Maybe you'll let me come over and work out with you once in a while. It sure beats the barbells I've got in the cellar."

Alex shook his head slowly, his serious expression not changing. Then, just when Rebecca's heart began to sink, the smallest smile curved the edge of his lips.

"You guys…" He shook his head. "I suppose I don't stand a chance, not since you've all ganged up on me, do I?"

His words were so similar to Doc's that her heart skipped a beat. She glanced at Brett. His gaze met hers in a moment of shared understanding before he turned back to Alex.

"Not a chance, buddy," he said. "We've got a whole

treatment plan worked out for you, and one of us will be here every night for a while to walk you through it. The only way you're getting rid of us is to throw us out, if you think you can."

Alex's smile grew. "I might manage to toss Rebecca out, but I don't stand a chance against you two. I guess I never did." He sounded perfectly happy about that state of affairs.

Rebecca's tense muscles relaxed. *Thank you, Lord. Thank you.*

Of course they had to try out all the equipment, and then walk Alex through the first level of the program Brett had devised for him. The whole process turned into a lot of joking, reminiscing, and snatches of high school memories.

Not having been part of their high school years, Rebecca could only listen, smiling. A dozen times she thought she should leave the three of them alone together, but she'd come with Brett in the van, so she couldn't just go home.

Brett grinned at her, as if he knew what she was thinking. "Rebecca will be here tomorrow night to give you a hand, then I'll be here the next night. So you're not going to have any excuses for blowing it off."

"You don't need to do that," Alex protested. "I can keep at it myself."

"No chance," Brett said.

"You need someone to spot for you at first,"

Rebecca put in, before Alex's male pride could be offended at the idea that he couldn't do it alone. "We may need to adjust some of the exercises for the best effect, and we won't know that unless we're here."

Alex's expression said he knew what she was doing, but he nodded. "All right. Thanks."

Mitch glanced at his watch. "Good grief, look at the time. I'd better get moving."

"Expecting a crime wave?" Brett asked.

Mitch punched him lightly. "I'm getting married on Saturday, in case you'd forgotten. I want to spend a little time with my bride-to-be."

"How could we forget?" Alex protested. "Because of you, we've both got to wear monkey suits for the day. I'll look great, of course, but I won't answer for Brett."

That earned him a punch.

Rebecca smiled at their horseplay, but her heart was touched. It wasn't everyone who'd have this close a relationship years after high school. Maybe there was something special about these three. Maybe it was the effect of facing death together and coming out of it in one piece.

The joking continued as they walked to the door. But at the portico, Alex put his hand on Brett's arm.

"Listen, Brett…"

His voice was so intent, so filled with emotion, that Rebecca knew his words weren't intended for her to hear. She quickened her steps, catching up to Mitch with some laughing remark about the wedding.

But her heart seemed to constrict, then expand. It was all right. She didn't know how she knew, but she did. This was in God's hands, and he was working Alex's healing out for his own purposes.

"Don't you have to take the van back?" she asked when Brett pulled into the driveway at his house.

"Not until tomorrow." He slid out, then came around the front.

She opened the door, but wasn't in time to jump out by herself. He caught her hand and helped her down, his fingers warm and firm on hers. He led her to the gap in the hedge.

"After you." He held the overhanging branch back with a sweeping gesture.

"I can find my own way home from here," she protested, ducking through the opening. "I have been for years."

"Yes, but tonight I have to spend a little time thanking you." He followed her across the lawn. "That could take a while."

"That's not necessary." She turned on the step, then discovered too late that the movement brought her face level with his and far too close. Her pulse beat the by-now-familiar tattoo. *Retreat,* her cautious mind cried. But he'd taken both her hands in his, and retreat was out of the question.

"Maybe not, but it's desirable." His voice caressed the word, as if he talked about something other than thanking her. His green eyes darkened suddenly, and her heart thumped so loudly that she thought he must be able to hear it. He shook his head, his eyes never leaving hers. "Rebecca, you…"

"Aunt Rebecca! Dr. Brett!" Kristie whirled out the door in her pajamas. "I've been waiting and waiting for you to come home and tell me good-night."

"Well, here we are." Brett gave Rebecca a slow smile that disintegrated all her defenses. Then he turned to Kristie. "You look like you're all set for bed."

Kristie nodded, holding on to his hand. "Grandma said I should go to bed early, on account of going to the orchard tomorrow, but I couldn't sleep." Her slipper-clad feet danced a bit on the porch floor. "I'm too excited about the apples."

Brett raised his eyebrows and turned an inquiring glance on Rebecca. "Apples? What's exciting about apples?"

"Kristie and I are going out to Baylor's Orchard tomorrow after the clinic closes to pick apples. Kristie's never done that before, so she thinks it's pretty exciting."

"And Grandma's going to make applesauce, and apple pie and apple butter, all with the apples we pick."

"Wow." Brett looked suitably impressed. "You must plan to pick a lot of apples."

Kristie nodded, red curls bobbing. "Lots and lots."

She looked up at him, head cocked to one side. "You could come and help us, Dr. Brett. Then we could pick even more. I'll bet Grandma would make you a pie."

Rebecca's heart did a little somersault. "I don't think Dr. Brett has time for apple picking. He has lots of things to do."

Brett knelt beside Kristie. "You really want me to come?"

She nodded vigorously. "Sure I do. Aunt Rebecca does, too, don't you, Aunt Rebecca?"

Brett looked up at her. His eyes danced with mischief, and her heart seemed to flip again. "Do you, Aunt Rebecca?"

Do I? I'd walk a mile just for that smile. "Of course," she said primly. "If you're sure you want to come."

"That's settled, then." He stood, swinging Kristie's hand back and forth. "We'll all go pick apples tomorrow."

She was crazy, Rebecca told herself as she said good-night to him and bundled Kristie upstairs to bed. She was just plain crazy. Given what he did to her heart, she should run the other direction, make any excuse to avoid being with him.

What's the point? an honest little voice inquired of her heart. She loved him, there was no getting away from that. That love wasn't going anywhere, because he didn't return it. But she couldn't change how she felt.

And sooner or later—maybe sooner—he'd go away. When that happened she'd be devastated, no matter what she did or didn't do now. So she might as well enjoy whatever time she had with him. It would be over with before she knew it. At least this way, she'd have thoughts of one afternoon at the apple orchard to add to her collection of Brett memories.

Chapter Twelve

Brett could hear Rebecca's voice in the hallway the next afternoon, saying goodbye to Donna Wright, the receptionist. In a moment she'd be ready to leave for their expedition to the apple orchard. But was he?

It had been instinctive, saying yes to Kristie, anticipating the time together. Now that he'd thought about it, he questioned that automatic response. What was he thinking, letting himself be made happy by something as simple as picking apples with a woman and a child?

Bedford Creek was doing something to him, and it didn't have anything to do with his outside life and his career goals. Maybe it really was like Brigadoon.

Actually, he'd thought Rebecca would be the one to make some excuse when Kristie came out with that spontaneous invitation. For a moment her face had frozen, and he'd been sure she'd find a reason, however feeble, to exclude him.

Then something had changed. He wasn't sure what. He just knew that she'd looked at him with something that might have been resignation in those clear eyes before she'd agreed that yes, it would be lovely if Brett came along to the orchard.

What had she been feeling? He didn't know, and that fact nettled him. He'd told himself he could read everything she thought, but on this occasion he couldn't. And he didn't like it.

He heard her footsteps in the hall, and in an instant she'd swept into the room.

"All right, we're free. The last patient is gone. Let's get out quickly before the phone rings again."

There was so much happiness shining in her face that he couldn't possibly say he'd decided not to go. Besides, he didn't *want* to say that. No matter how much wiser it might be to keep his distance, he wanted this time with Rebecca.

"I'm ready." He closed the patient folder and shoved his chair back.

The phone rang. Making a face, Rebecca leaned across to pick it up. "Bedford Creek Clinic." She listened, then frowned. "One moment, please."

She held the receiver out to him, a question in her face. "It's for you."

He took it, to hear Matthew Arends's smooth voice in his ear. Instinctively he covered the receiver and turned to Rebecca.

"This won't take long. Why don't you go on

home and change, and I'll meet you and Kristie there."

"Okay." She seemed to file the question away. "Don't be long."

"I won't." He waited until the door closed to return to the call.

"Mr. Arends. I didn't expect to hear from you today."

"Just thought I'd check in and see if you'd thought any further about my suggestion. You did receive the material I sent?"

"Yes, I did."

"What did you think?"

He hesitated. But there was no reason not to tell Arends what he thought of the proposal. "It seems very comprehensive. I can certainly see it would be a far more efficient way of providing medical care to the community."

"And have you found an opportunity to tell Dr. Overton your opinion?" Arends's voice was smooth as silk, but there was an undertone of something… knowledge, maybe.

"Not yet. Dr. Overton hasn't been well."

"I understand he's seeing one of our neurologists this week," Arends said.

So he had known. Somehow Brett thought that little fact wouldn't escape him. "I'd prefer to wait until he doesn't have this on his mind."

"Of course." Arends had begun to sound very confident. "Perhaps Dr. Overton's health problems will precipitate a change sooner than anyone expected."

In other words, Doc's health might make him no longer a factor in the equation. If Doc couldn't carry on, the hospital would get its way by default.

"That may be true." His voice was stiff. "In any event, I can't imagine discussing it with him until next week, at the earliest."

"That's fine." Arends's good humor was unimpaired. "I'll look forward to speaking with you."

After he'd hung up, Brett sat for a few minutes, frowning. Arends was perfectly right in his assumption. Brett thought so himself. The plain truth was that Doc's health problems could force the Bedford Creek clinic into the twenty-first century, ready or not.

In the long run, the community would get more efficient care, care in keeping with modern medical practices. Medicine wasn't a calling or an art anymore, or at least not solely. It was big business, and it had to be handled that way.

That was what he'd been trained to believe. Ninety percent of his colleagues in the residency program would say that. Why did he feel so miserable about the prospect?

One way or another, his time in Bedford Creek was coming to an end. That made it doubly important that he not do anything to create an emotional involvement with Rebecca. He could hardly back out of the orchard trip now, but he'd have to keep reminding himself they were friends, that was all. Just friends.

"We're here, we're here!" Kristie bounced out of the car, hauling with her the small basket her grandmother had provided. "I want to pick an apple. Which apple can I pick, Aunt Rebecca?"

"Just a second, sweetie. Let us get organized, and then I'll show you." She took the basket Brett unloaded from the trunk.

He smiled. "How long will all that enthusiasm last, do you think?"

"About a dozen apples' worth, I should say." She tried to steel her heart against that smile. "I hope you're ready to do some serious picking. Mom will be disappointed if we don't bring at least two bushels home."

"I'll do my best." He slammed the trunk lid. "Lead me to them."

"You're just like Kristie. Do you want me to show you which ones to pick?"

"I'm guessing the ripe ones." He put his hand on her shoulder with an easy gesture he might have used with Kristie. "Didn't we used to earn a few bucks doing this when we were in middle school?"

Memorize the feeling of warmth spreading out from his hand. She was going to enjoy this day to the fullest, but without letting Brett know what she felt. That would be disaster, to let him know she loved him.

Create a memory, she told herself as she led the way to the red-laden trees. Then she'd have something to take out and look at in the lonely days after he'd gone away. She wouldn't rail at God, asking why he'd let her love someone who didn't love her back. She'd just take it and go on. That was what responsible people did.

"Okay." She dropped the basket underneath a tree and caught Kristie before the child could scamper off. "We only pick the ones that are ripe or almost ripe." She lifted the child to inspect the nearest branch. "See? This one is just right. This one is too ripe—it's already getting soft. Get it?"

Kristie nodded solemnly, and Rebecca set her in the *V* of a low branch.

"There. You pick just what you can reach from there, okay? Tell me when you're ready to get down, and I'll help you."

She turned, to find Brett flipping open the small step stool the owner had left in the orchard. "I'll go up and do the higher ones. You get the ones you can pick from the ground, okay?"

"Afraid I'll fall?"

He grinned. "You've been known to do that."

For a few minutes they picked in silence, broken only by the *plop* of apples dropping into the basket. It wasn't an uncomfortable silence; it was the silence that develops between people who know each other so well they don't need to fill up the spaces with chatter.

She leaned back, stretching, and took a deep breath. Any memory she created had to include the smells: the mingled scents of ripe apples, crushed grass, and the faint, persistent aroma of wild mint growing in the ditch by the road.

"Beautiful, isn't it?" Brett inhaled, looking up. "Have you ever seen the sky so blue?"

She glanced up, catching sight of the sky through a tracery of green leaves, brightened here and there by red apples. "Perfect," she agreed. "Clear as crystal."

"Autumn days," Brett said. "I'd forgotten how clear and crisp they are here. As crisp as the taste of an apple." He polished one on his T-shirt and then bit into it.

"You're supposed to be picking, not eating." Her gaze traced the trickle of apple juice on his chin.

He wiped it with the back of his hand and grinned, then held it out to her invitingly. "Have a bite. That's the reward for picking."

She crunched into the apple, feeling the tart juices explode in her mouth. "Mmm. Wonderful." She wasn't sure whether she was talking about the apple or about the way he brushed the excess juice from her chin.

"Aunt Rebecca! I'm ready to get down."

She turned away and lifted her niece to the ground. "You can run around if you want. I think there's a swing in the old tree at the end of this row. Just stay where you can see me, okay?"

Kristie nodded. "Okay. I'll stay where I can see you." She scampered off.

Brett watched Kristie run. "Until I came back, I'd forgotten how much freedom we had as kids. And how much time just to run around and do whatever we wanted. All my friends' kids seem too busy with organized stuff ever to just play."

"It's good for kids to amuse themselves, I think." She dropped a couple of apples in the basket. "We did, and we didn't turn out too badly. I have to admit, though, I'm really feeling my way with this parenting thing."

"Looks to me like you're doing a pretty good job." Brett reached over to toss a handful into her basket. "Kristie's a lucky girl to have an aunt like you to take over for her daddy for a while. Why isn't Angela doing more?"

She found she was blinking away sudden tears at the praise. "I try. Angela tries, too, but she's spending so much time with Ron, planning the wedding. We all felt Kristie would do better here, in familiar surroundings. Everyone here knows and cares about her."

He nodded, stepping down from the stool and moving it. "Bedford Creek has a way of doing that. Guess that was another thing I'd forgotten."

She moved the basket closer to him. "In a way, I'm glad the tourist season is over. It's fun having extra people around, but it's good to get back to just us." She sniffed an apple, inhaling the spicy scent. "Getting ready for winter. That's a good feeling."

"Sleet, icy roads, snow down the back of your neck, being cut off from the outside world," Brett teased.

"Skiing, sledding, hot chocolate in front of the fire, being cut off from the outside world," she countered.

He grinned. "You might have a point there."

His smile touched something deep inside her, setting up a warmth that radiated through her. If he were around all the time, she wouldn't need a winter jacket.

"I think if I got up on that branch, I could reach a lot of ripe ones," she said, testing the lowest branch of the tree.

"You're not still climbing trees, are you?"

"You think I can't get up there?"

His green eyes crinkled with laughter. "Let's say you'd better wait until I'm in position to catch you."

She hoisted herself to the lowest branch. "I don't need any catching, Brett Elliot. I can do it myself." She reached for the next branch, found a foothold, and swarmed up, surprising herself when she landed on the branch she'd pointed out. She looked down at him, a little breathless. "See?"

His face was tilted up, looking at her, all angles seen from above. "I see you're still a tomboy."

"I'll have you know I haven't fallen out of a tree in years," she said tartly.

"I'm surprised you fell at all," he said. "You always did climb like a little monkey."

She remembered that day so clearly. "I went too high. Then I got scared." She remembered looking down, seeing how far away the ground was, panicking.

"What were you trying to do? See how far you could get?"

"Actually, I was trying to figure out what you were doing. You were over by the garage working on something, and I couldn't see you from my usual perch."

He shook his head. "It probably wasn't anything that exciting. We were always building something, and usually it didn't work, whatever it was."

"I'm glad you were there that day."

He shrugged. "Maybe if I hadn't been, you wouldn't have fallen." He leaned against the trunk. "Anyway, I hope you don't do a lot of tree-climbing when I'm not around. Come on down, now. You've made your point."

She reached for the nearest ripe apple. "I'll drop them down to you."

"Rebecca." He frowned. "Come down. I'm getting a stiff neck looking up at you."

It really did bother him, having her perched on the branch above his head. The feeling gave her a heady sense of power.

"I'm fine." She reached for an apple, wobbled a bit and grabbed the branch. "Or maybe I'm not." The ground suddenly looked awfully far away.

Brett held his hand up to her. "Come on. I'll help you down."

"I can make it." She turned, clutching the branch,

and lowered herself slowly down to the next limb. "I'm fine. I—"

Her sneaker slipped, and in an instant she was dangling from her hands. The breath caught in her throat.

"I've got you." Brett's hands were strong on her legs. "Come on, just drop down. I've got you."

He had her. She let go, dropping into his arms.

"You need your head examined, you know that?" But he was laughing as he turned her to face him. "What if I hadn't been here?"

"Then I wouldn't have climbed up there to begin with," she pointed out.

She looked up at him, and their faces were very close. Her breath caught, and her heart seemed to stop beating, then to accelerate so it was about to jump out of her chest. Her lips parted, but she couldn't think of anything to say.

Brett's eyes darkened, his smile stilled. He searched her face as if looking for something. Then he kissed her.

The instant his lips touched hers, she knew this was what she'd waited for all day. Maybe all her life. Her arms went around him, feeling the strong flat muscles of his back. He held her just as closely, and the world spiraled away until no one else existed but the two of them.

This was what she wanted, she thought. Just to be allowed to love him with an overflowing heart. And then she didn't think at all.

* * *

What was he doing? The little voice at the back of Brett's mind whispered with outraged caution. Whatever was he doing? He'd promised himself he wouldn't let this happen. It wasn't wise; it didn't fit in with his plans for his life.

And he didn't care. He trailed kisses across Rebecca's cheek, and it had to be the softest thing he'd ever touched. She felt like velvet, and when he inhaled he caught a hint of lilacs. There had been lilacs in bloom that day so long ago when she'd told him she loved him.

He leaned back a little, looking at her. Her golden-brown eyes shone with sunlight, and her lips, slightly parted, looked pink and very kissable. So he kissed her again.

This time she was the one to lean back, looking up at him with a question in her eyes. "Brett? Do we know what we're doing?"

"We're sure not doing what I intended." He lifted a bronze curl back from her cheek, then slowly traced the delicate curve of her face. "I planned not to let this happen."

Her expression grew solemn. "Why? Because I'm still a little sister to you?" She pulled away from him, and he thought that was a spark of anger in her eyes.

"No." He drew her back into his arms. "Because you're not." He gave up trying to resist and kissed her again.

This wasn't smart; it wasn't what he should be doing. But he couldn't seem to help it.

Something hurtled into his legs, and he looked down at Kristie. "Dr. Brett! Are you done picking apples already?"

Rebecca laughed softly, her eyes shining with love as she looked down at the child. "No, sweetheart, we aren't done." Her eyes met his, still laughing. "We were just taking a little break."

"That's right." He picked up the basket, trying to cover his embarrassment with action. "We'd better get busy and pick the rest of these apples, or your grandmother will be unhappy with us."

He was ridiculously embarrassed. What did it matter that little Kristie had seen him kissing Rebecca? She probably didn't even realize what she'd seen. Or was he embarrassed that it had happened, regardless of whether anyone had seen?

He glanced at Rebecca. She calmly showed Kristie a branch low enough to pick from, and there wasn't the faintest trace of embarrassment in her voice. In fact, she seemed to radiate a peace and maturity that confused him.

He'd always been the big brother, the mature one who showed little Rebecca what to do. Now, suddenly, he felt gauche and uncertain, while she acted as if nothing at all had happened.

The world had turned upside down, and he didn't know what to do about it.

Chapter Thirteen

"Now hand the ring to the bride," Pastor Richie instructed, and Anne's friend from Philadelphia, Helen Wells, produced a gaudy plastic toy ring to stand in for the real thing.

The small group that was gathered in the sanctuary for rehearsal broke up, relaxing the tension of taking part in something both joyful and solemn. Rebecca looked across the aisle at Brett, and it seemed her heart would burst with happiness at the sight of his face. If she'd ever been happier in her life, she couldn't remember it.

"With this ring, I thee wed," the pastor intoned, and Anne repeated the words. Her expression as she looked up at Mitch spoke of so much love that Rebecca's eyes stung.

That was what she wanted. To stand in this sanctuary, hearing Pastor Richie say those words, and to be looking up at Brett with that sort of love in her eyes. The forever kind of love, the kind of love that promised home and children and being together no matter what happened.

She looked again at Brett. Did she dare to hope he was thinking the same thing? During the last few days, they'd been closer than they'd ever been. They'd laughed together, worried together about Doc, worked together.

He didn't look at her as a kid sister now; she knew that. He saw her as a woman—a woman who attracted him. But he hadn't mentioned love.

"What God has joined together," Pastor Richie said, "let no one put asunder." His hands were lifted over Mitch's and Anne's heads, and his cherubic face creased in a broad smile. "And that's it. Do you feel comfortable with who does what when, or do you want to run through it again?"

He glanced from face to face, questioning.

"I'm okay with my part," Brett said. "All I do is stand."

Pastor Richie gave him a reproving look. "The groomsmen support the groom," he pointed out. "You won't know how much your presence means to Mitch until you're the one standing here."

"I guess you're right, Pastor." Brett didn't look at Rebecca, but she was sure a faint flush touched his cheeks.

"Well, that's it, then." Pastor Richie stepped back, rubbing his hands over a job well done. "Ellie will play the recessional, and off you go. Let's practice walking out, so we do it smoothly."

Ellie Wayne, at the organ, swung into the recessional. Mitch, his arm linked with Anne's, started back up the aisle. Then Alex took Helen, the maid of honor. Rebecca stepped toward Brett.

"Shall we?" He held out his arm, his eyes crinkling as he smiled.

"Of course," she said gravely, and took his arm. They started back up the aisle in step, and a smile she couldn't suppress curved her lips.

It was going to be all right. Of course it was. Even if Brett hadn't mentioned love, she knew he had feelings for her. Surely they had a future together.

Don't be so optimistic, a little voice warned in her mind. *Things don't always work out the way you want, no matter how right it seems.*

It would. She quashed the soft warning. This time it would all work out.

They stopped at the back of the sanctuary, and Mitch glanced at his watch. "We're right on time. Rehearsal dinner coming up next, don't forget." He turned to Rebecca. "I didn't get a chance to ask you before. How was Doc's checkup?"

Probably the whole town knew by now that Doc had spent the last two days undergoing a battery of tests at the medical center. It was impossible to keep something like that quiet in a small town, especially when it was Doc, whom everyone loved and depended upon.

"It went pretty well, I think." Rebecca could hear the relief in her voice. She hadn't realized how tense she'd been until Doc got back that afternoon, safe and sound. "He's been working too hard, that's all. He's under strict orders to take it easier, and we intend to make sure he does just that."

"Glad to hear it." Mitch spoke for everyone, apparently, judging by their expressions. "He's a good man. We don't want anything to happen to Doc."

"He's going to be fine," she said firmly.

He was, of course he was. He'd assured them the specialist couldn't find a thing wrong with him other than that he worked too hard for someone who was seventy-two.

She glanced at Brett. Somehow he didn't look as happy as she thought he should.

In the hubbub, as people found their jackets and bags to leave for the restaurant, she caught his hand. "Is something wrong?" She searched his face. "You don't look very happy about Doc."

"I'm fine." He gave her a quick smile. "I guess I just wish Doc had been a little more forthcoming about exactly what the neurologist said."

The concern in his voice penetrated the haze of happiness in which she'd spent the last few days. She moved a step away from the door, letting the others leave.

"But…he said he was all right. Don't you believe him?"

"Sure." He patted her hand. "Sure I believe him. I wanted more details, that's all."

Doc *had* been a little sparing with the information he'd given them. He'd let her drive him back and forth to the hospital, but he'd flat-out refused to allow either her or Brett to accompany him inside.

"He just needs a little rest, that's all." She looked up at Brett, repeating Doc's words as if they were a talisman. "That's what he said. And we can manage that. There's no reason why he should come in at all next week, with both of us there."

Brett's gaze slid away from hers. "Actually, that might be a bit of a problem."

"What do you mean?" She stared at him blankly. "What kind of a problem?"

It wasn't her imagination. There was something Brett didn't want to tell her. Something he had to tell her but didn't want to.

"I won't be in the office on Monday, I'm afraid. Maybe not Tuesday, either."

Something cold seemed to close around her heart. "Why won't you?"

"I have to be in Chicago on Monday for an interview." His gaze met hers, determined and a little defiant. "I heard from that fellowship program. They're definitely interested in me."

For a moment she couldn't say anything. She could only stand there, staring at him stupidly.

"It's not as if it was unexpected." He apparently

didn't like the silence. "After all, it's what I've been waiting for."

What he'd been waiting for. Of course it was what he'd been waiting for. He hadn't made any secret of that. Bedford Creek was just a stop on the busy highway of the life he'd mapped out for himself.

"Yes, I see," she said at last. "It's all right. Don't worry about it. I'll manage somehow."

He didn't look particularly satisfied with that. "I'm sorry, Rebecca. I don't want to leave you on your own, but I had to take the appointment they gave me. If I don't show up on Monday—"

"No, of course you have to be there Monday." She forced something she hoped resembled a smile. "It will be fine. They'd be foolish not to offer it to you."

They'd offer it. Brett would accept it. She watched her dreams disintegrate into ashes. He'd go back on his fast track to success, leaving her and Bedford Creek behind. And somehow she had to figure out a way to live with that.

The rehearsal dinner was being held at a restaurant that was new since Brett's time. He found his way to the side street, perched precariously on the edge of the hill. The Blackburn House sat flush with the sidewalk, its front windows lined with flower boxes. He spotted Rebecca, whisking inside just as he pulled up.

He'd expected to drive her from the church, but she'd slipped away before he had a chance to stop her.

And now she looked just as determined to avoid him at the restaurant.

This was ridiculous. Why should Rebecca make him feel guilty? His medical career depended on this crucial opportunity. The timing of the interview was unfortunate, but it couldn't be helped. His whole future was at stake.

He followed Rebecca inside. He had to find a chance to talk with her. He wanted to assure her it would be all right. He'd only be gone for a few days, and then he'd come back and intensify his search for a solution to the clinic problem. If Doc wouldn't agree to let the hospital take over, there had to be a young family-medicine specialist somewhere who'd want the job.

The tiny restaurant held round tables just big enough for the wedding party. Rebecca had managed to put herself between Anne and Anne's friend Helen.

"Here's a seat, Brett." Alex pulled out the chair next to him. It was opposite Rebecca, but she refused to glance his way when he sat down.

Something ached inside him at the sight of her averted face, so familiar and yet so distant. How had she become this important to him in such a short period of time? He hadn't intended anything to happen—but it had in spite of him.

He leaned back in his chair as the server put a bowl of tortellini in chicken broth in front of him.

"Looks great, Jessica." Alex's comment earned a

smile from the server as she moved swiftly around the table.

Brett took a spoonful of the soup and lifted his eyebrows. "Wonderful."

Alex nodded. "Jessica's brother is quite a chef."

Brett remembered Mitch telling him she and her brother were dropouts from the corporate world who'd moved to Bedford Creek a year ago to open the restaurant. A risky future, he'd thought, but apparently the one they wanted.

He pictured his own future, pursuing the fellowship in Chicago. It would be exciting, challenging, fulfilling. It would also be lonely until he'd made a few new friends.

Rebecca turned her head to say something to the woman serving her. The pure line of her neck caught his gaze, and he wanted to touch it. To hold her in his arms again.

Who did he think he was kidding? He would be lonely in Chicago not because he didn't know anyone, but because he'd be missing Rebecca.

Alarm bells sounded in his mind. What did he imagine he wanted to happen between them?

He didn't know. He just knew he didn't want it to be the end between them when he left Bedford Creek. And he had to find a way to tell her so.

"Brett? Something wrong?" He realized Alex was looking at him, realized, too, that Alex had probably said something to which he hadn't responded.

"No, nothing." He turned to Alex with what he hoped was an interested look. "You were saying?"

Before this night was over he was going to have a private talk with Rebecca, if he had to trap her in a corner to do it.

The moment, when it actually came, was just about like that. Rebecca had slipped out of the restaurant first, but he'd been prepared for that and hurried after her. He reached her just as she got to her car.

"Rebecca, hold on a minute. I want to talk to you."

"Here?" She started to open the car door.

He put his hand firmly over hers. "What's wrong with here?"

The others were still inside; the narrow street was silent. Moonlight slanted down between crooked roofs, painting pale shadows on the old brick sidewalk.

She shrugged, pulling her coat a little closer around her. "All right. What is it?"

Now that he had the moment he'd wanted, he wasn't sure how to begin. "About the fellowship… I want you to understand. Rebecca, I don't want there to be hard feelings between us."

She looked up at him, her face a pale oval turned by the moonlight into an ivory cameo. "You want my blessing, is that it? You want me to be like Doc and tell you everything's fine."

"No, I—"

"Well, I won't." She swept on, carried on a wave

of emotion he wasn't sure he understood. "You always want everyone to approve of you. You expect to turn on the famous Brett charm and have everyone smile. But sometimes it doesn't work that way."

The words cut, startling him by how deeply. "I'm not looking for everyone's approval. Just yours."

She turned away, staring down at the car keys in her hand as if they held a secret. "Don't ask me that now, Brett. I'm too angry that you're leaving."

He took her hands in his, half expecting her to yank them free. But she stood so motionless that only the pulse under his fingers assured him she was there.

"I need to know, Rebecca. Are you angry because you're losing a doctor or angry because you're losing me?" He could hear the strain in his voice. Could she hear it, too?

She looked up then, but it was too dark to read her expression. "I don't think I can separate the two. Either way, you're going."

"Rebecca, I don't want—"

The restaurant door burst open, flooding light and noise onto the sidewalk. The others came out in a chattering group. Before he could say anything, Rebecca pulled her hands free and slipped into the car. In a moment she was gone.

Goodbyes echoed along the still street as people got into their cars.

Mitch stopped beside Brett, giving him a quizzical look. "Something wrong?"

Brett shrugged. "Woman troubles." He watched the red taillights of Rebecca's car vanish around the corner. "You feel like offering any good advice?"

Mitch held both hands up in a gesture of surrender. "Not on this one, old buddy. This time you're on your own."

Mitch's words echoed in his mind as he drove toward home. He was on his own. His future was entangled with his feelings for Rebecca, and he was on his own.

There was someone else on his own tonight. Doc. He glanced at his watch. It wasn't that late. He'd better swing by Doc's house and make sure he was all right.

When he got there, the lights still shone from Doc's windows. Maybe, now that Rebecca wasn't around, Doc would be a little more forthcoming about what the specialist had to say. He strode quickly to the door and knocked.

"Brett." Doc didn't look especially glad to see him when he opened the door. "I didn't expect you."

"Just checking." Since Doc didn't invite him in, he walked in. "How are you feeling?"

"Fine." The testy answer had a slightly tremulous ring to it. "I'm fine. You go on home now."

"That's not very welcoming." Doc could be brusque, but he was never rude. What was going on?

Doc shut the door, then rubbed his forehead with

a hand that wasn't quite steady. "Sorry, son. I'm just tired, that's all."

Brett put his hand on Doc's shoulder, feeling the fragile old bones. "That's what you keep telling us. But it's not just fatigue, is it?"

"You calling me a liar, boy?" Some of the old fire reappeared in his faded blue eyes.

Brett met his gaze steadily. "I'm not saying you're not tired, Doc. But there's more to it than that. If the neurologist leveled with me, what would he say?"

Doc stiffened, holding out against him a moment longer. Then he shrugged. "TIAs. That's what I've been having. TIAs."

Transient ischemic attacks—maybe the forerunner of a stroke. It was one of the possibilities that had been in Brett's mind for days.

"Doc, I'm sorry." He patted the old man's shoulder, wanting to comfort him but knowing there wasn't much he could say. "What are you going to do?"

Doc shrugged. "I'm started on meds. Nothing much else to do but carry on."

"Carry on?" Somehow he wasn't surprised. "Doc, you could be on the verge of a stroke—you know that. You've got to slow down and let them take proper care of you."

"No way. I've got patients to take care of. I can't be sitting around, doing nothing."

"If you work yourself into a stroke, who's going to take care of them?"

Doc's face set in stubborn lines. "Leave it, Brett. I'm too old to change my ways."

For the first time in too long, Brett found himself praying for the right words. *Please, Lord.*

"Is that really what you want, Doc? To have a stroke at the office, have Rebecca be the one to find you? Have her blame herself for not saving you, the way she blames herself for not being there sooner for her father?"

Doc winced. "You know how to hit where it hurts, don't you."

He forced himself to speak calmly. "Tell me how you'd deal with a stubborn patient who wouldn't listen to your advice."

"The same way." Doc rubbed his hand over his face and managed a faint smile. "You're right. I know you're right. I just haven't been able to face it. To decide what to do about the clinic."

Brett hated to push, but he knew he had to. "I think you already know what the answer is for the clinic."

"Guess we're out of options." He nodded tiredly. "I guess Lincoln Medical Center will be taking over, like it or not."

"Doc…" His heart hurt. He wanted to make this better, but he couldn't. This really was for the best, whether Doc could see that or not. "People will get used to it. They'll be taken care of, that's the important thing."

"I guess so." Doc sagged into the nearest chair.

"Tell you the truth, I'm almost too tired to worry anymore." He looked up at Brett. "You think you could help with the details? Make it as smooth as possible?"

"You know I will, Doc."

"And Rebecca. Rebecca's going to take this hard."

Rebecca would take this hard. And Brett couldn't think of one single thing that would make it any easier.

Chapter Fourteen

Each time she saw him might be the last. That was in Rebecca's mind as she waited at the church the next day. He could leave, and the final words between them would be harsh. Whatever else she felt about Brett, she didn't want that to happen.

She smoothed the silk skirt of the aqua bridesmaid's dress and watched the door nervously. She'd gotten there early, ahead of the bride, to make sure all was in readiness. And to try to catch Brett for a few private moments before the wedding overtook them.

She had to apologize. After a night of agonizing, that was the only thing clear in her mind. It seemed she'd been arguing with God the entire night, and no other answers had emerged.

She closed her eyes for another swift, silent prayer. *I thought Brett's return was Your answer, Lord. I guess I was wrong. I've tried my best to make it work out, and it hasn't. Please show me what to do.*

Now if she could just resign herself to waiting for God's answer… Unfortunately, she'd never been very good at that. Maybe that was why God kept giving her so many opportunities to practice.

The door swung again, and everything inside her constricted. Brett? No, it was the florist, carrying an arrangement of white mums.

She held the sanctuary door open for the man, and when she turned back, Brett stood behind her in the vestibule. Her breath caught.

Brett, she'd long since decided, looked good no matter what he wore. In a tuxedo, he was gorgeous.

She managed to take a breath. "Brett. I was hoping to catch you before everyone else got here."

He eyed her with what seemed to be wariness. "Did you think of something else you wanted to say to me?"

"No. I mean, yes." She felt the warm flush in her cheeks. "I did want to say something else. Just…I'm sorry for the way I talked to you."

He stared at her for a long moment, his green eyes unreadable. Then he shook his head. "If that was what you felt, Rebecca, you had every right to say it." A faint smile flickered. "Friends ought to be honest with each other."

"I was angry." She shook her head. "God must get tired of hearing my repentance every time I lose my temper and say more than I should." She hesitated. She couldn't really say she hadn't meant it, because even in her anger, she believed it. She just shouldn't have said it. "I don't want you to go away thinking I'm angry with you."

"Thank you." He held out his hand to her. "Friends again?"

She couldn't hesitate, or he'd think she didn't mean it. She put her hand in his, trying not to let her feelings show in her face. "Friends."

They stood there, hands clasped. Could he feel the way her pulse was racing? She hoped not. But he was frowning down at her, his usually open expression closed.

She had to say something. "Are you... I guess you're taking the commuter flight tomorrow?"

That was a foregone conclusion. If you were flying anywhere from Bedford Creek, you took the once-a-day puddle jumper to a larger airport. She slipped her hand from his, still seeming to feel the warmth of his grip.

He nodded. "That's the only thing that will get me there in time, unless I want to drive all night."

There ought to be a graceful way to get out of this conversation. She just couldn't seem to think what it was. She'd said what she wanted to say, made her apologies, prepared to part as friends. Now the only way to hold on to her composure was to beat a hasty retreat.

The organ sounded beyond the double doors to the sanctuary. Ellie was warming up.

Rebecca gestured toward the sound. "I'd better go. Anne should be here by now."

His hand closed on her wrist again, stopping her. "Wait a second, Rebecca."

His frown made her heart skip a beat. "I really have to go."

"We've got another minute, surely." He shook his head impatiently, a lock of dark gold hair falling onto his brow. "There's something more."

Only the fact that I love you. Her throat went dry as she thought the words she'd never be able to say. She stared at him mutely.

"I wanted to tell you—"

The outer door swung open, and Alex popped his head in. "Brett, come on. Mitch is getting nervous."

"In a second." Brett looked harassed. "I wanted to say—"

Helen rushed into the hallway from the parlor and beckoned urgently to Rebecca. "We need you. I can't get Anne's veil to hang right."

Escape beckoned from both directions. She managed a smile for Brett.

"It looks as if duty is calling us. We can catch up with whatever it is later."

He nodded reluctantly. "All right. Later. But I really do need to talk to you."

"Are you sure Anne is here?" Mitch started toward the door, apparently intending to check for himself.

Brett grabbed him and grinned at Alex. "She's here, she's here. And they'll clobber you if you try to see her before the ceremony."

Mitch subsided, yanking anxiously at his bow tie. "What do you think? Do I look right?"

Alex straightened the tie. "You look like a nervous wreck. Calm down. You're marrying the woman you love. You can't ask for better than that."

"You're right." He smiled, looking from one to the other of them. "Who would have thought this day would come?"

Brett put his hand on Mitch's shoulder, knowing what lay behind the words. Who'd have thought the boy from the wrong side of the tracks would end up the chief of police, married to a bright, elegant attorney?

"We did," he said firmly. "We did."

It was Mitch's day. He wouldn't cast a shadow on it by telling him about Doc, even though the idea of sharing that particular burden was overwhelming. He wouldn't tell Mitch today, but he had to tell Rebecca—and the sooner, the better.

He'd tried. No one could say he hadn't tried. But he'd been caught off guard when he saw her, and the moment had slipped away.

Later. At the reception, there'd be a moment when he could have a private word with her. He'd find a way to break it to her gently, although given the way she loved Doc, she'd have trouble with this.

He'd just have to stress the positive. If Doc followed his physician's orders and took proper care of himself, there was no reason why he couldn't have a long, happy retirement. But he couldn't possibly carry the burden of the clinic any longer, and Rebecca had to realize that.

Nothing about this was easy, because there simply weren't any good answers. Only acceptable ones. Well, maybe sometimes in life "acceptable" was the best you got.

Alex touched his shoulder lightly. "Brett? Something wrong?"

He shook his head. This was no time to tell Alex, either. "Everything's okay." He took a second look at his friend. "How about you? I see you're not using your cane today."

"Maybe I'll need it later, but not for the ceremony." Alex hesitated, his lean face grave. "Brett, if I didn't seem enthusiastic about the therapy, I was wrong. And you were right. I probably never would have pursued it if you hadn't pushed me into it. And I can feel it helping already." His grip tightened. "Thanks, buddy."

For a moment Brett couldn't trust his voice to speak. He cleared his throat. "That's okay. Any time."

He'd told himself he needed to repay the debt he owed Alex in order to feel things were right between them. Oddly enough, now that the moment had come, that seemed pretty unimportant. He'd helped his friend. That was what mattered. Maybe he couldn't help Doc, but he'd helped Alex.

Good news, bad news, all piled on top of each other. That was what life was like for a small town doctor. Where you knew people this intimately, you couldn't stay detached. You got to celebrate the good things, like Alex's hope of recovery. But the bad things cut you to the heart. How had Doc stood it all these years?

He knew what the answer would be if he asked Doc that question. Doc wouldn't trade the life he'd had here in Bedford Creek for anything. He'd never wanted it to change.

Unfortunately, change was inevitable. Brett straightened his tie, buttoned his jacket. In another hour Mitch would be married, changing their relationship forever. In a few weeks the town would get used to the Lincoln Medical Center clinic caring for its needs. Change came, like it or not, and usually it ended up for the better.

Would it? A niggling little doubt crept in. Alex could have gone to the medical center for treatment. They'd have provided him with an up-to-date therapy program. But they wouldn't have tracked him down and insisted on it.

Pastor Richie opened the door and winked at them. "Looks like it's almost time. Everyone ready?"

"You bet." Mitch spoke quickly. "Brett, better get your skates on. You're supposed to be seating people."

"Right." No more time for worrying about the future. He had to get on with the job of seeing his friend married. The rest of it would have to wait until later.

More people than he'd have expected came to see Mitch wed his Anne, but few of them insisted on the formality of having Brett escort them down the aisle. Finally they were all tucked into their pews.

Mitch's elderly friend and neighbor, Kate Cavendish, sat in place of the groom's family, with the baby on her lap and Mitch's foster son next to her, wearing what was probably his first suit. On the opposite side of the aisle, Anne's parents looked elegantly turned out and uncomfortably aware of being out of their element.

The organist swung into the processional, and Brett went quickly down the side aisle to join Mitch and Alex at the chancel. Whatever nerves Mitch had felt earlier had apparently been banished. He divided a smile between his friends, then focused on the back of the church, where Anne would appear.

Rebecca would come first, Brett knew, so he was prepared for the sight of her as she started down the aisle. At least, he thought he was prepared. Then, as a ray of sunlight through stained glass gilded her bronze hair with gold, he realized he wasn't prepared at all. He looked at her, and his heart stopped.

She was beautiful. He already knew that, of course. She was dear to him. He knew that, too.

And he was in love with her.

The thought nearly knocked him over. He was in love with her. How could he have worked so closely with her over these past weeks and not realized it? Why hadn't he known it the instant he looked at her?

He knew it now. She reached the chancel and took her place opposite him, giving him a small, private smile. And he wanted to step right across the space between them, snatch her into his arms, and tell her he loved her, that maybe he'd always loved her, and that he'd never love anyone else as long as he lived.

He couldn't do that, of course. The maid of honor moved into her place, the music changed with a sound like the heralding of trumpets, and Anne started down the aisle.

Only something as strong as the expression on Mitch's face when he saw his bride could have distracted Brett from Rebecca. Mitch looked like a starving man shown to the banqueting table. And when Anne joined him at the chancel, the love shining between them was almost too bright to watch.

Brett's mind leaped ahead, seeing himself and Rebecca standing here together, holding hands, repeating the same vows Mitch and Anne were saying.

Funny that all his adult life he'd run at the first suggestion of anything permanent. Maybe, on some level, he'd been waiting for Rebecca.

"Now, don't forget to try some of the wedding cookies I brought." Rebecca's mother hugged her and then fluttered away, preoccupied with her serving duties. Mitch and Anne had decided on a simple reception in the social room, but that hadn't kept the women of the church from putting together a repast suitable for a royal garden party.

Rebecca hovered near the buffet table, scanning the crowd that filled the room. Brett had said he had to talk with her, and as little as she wanted another private chat, it probably couldn't be avoided. She'd seen Doc come in, but hadn't had a chance to corner him yet to see how he was doing.

Doc veered away from elderly Mrs. Carlson, who undoubtedly wanted to tell him her latest symptoms, and joined Rebecca. She looked at him with concern. He looked dreadfully tired, as if he hadn't slept in days.

"Doc, what's wrong?" She took his arm, drawing him back into a quiet corner. "You look exhausted. Are you sure you should be here?"

He shrugged. "Couldn't miss Mitch's wedding, could I? Guess you've talked to Brett."

"Talked to Brett?" she echoed. "About what?"

Doc looked at her for a moment, then shook his head. "No, I guess you haven't. Maybe he's waiting for me to tell you."

A cold hand seemed to grab her heart. "Tell me what? Doc, what's going on?"

He rubbed a hand wearily across his forehead. "I didn't exactly tell you the truth about what the neurologist had to say. It's not as simple as fatigue. Brett guessed, and he made me face it. I've been having the warning signs of stroke."

"Oh, Doc." The jumble of feelings threatened to choke her. She put her arms around him. "You…but you'll be all right. We'll take good care of you. We will." *I can't lose you, too. I can't.* "What are—"

Doc cut her off with a shake of his head. "Not now, Rebecca." He glanced around. "You've got a reception, and I think I'll just go home and rest a bit. We'll talk later, all right?"

He was right, of course, but she didn't want to let him out of her sight. "I should drive you home."

"Absolutely not." That sounded more like Doc. "I'm fine." He patted her hand. "We'll talk later."

He slipped away, leaving her to choke down her fears and try to paste a smile on her face. She had to get through the rest of the reception. She couldn't let anything spoil that for Mitch and Anne. Then she and Brett…

Her thoughts stopped there. She and Brett would do what? Brett knew about Doc's illness, and he was still planning to leave the next day for his interview. What did he intend to do?

There was only one way to find out. Ask him.

She found him trying futilely to refuse the mound of potato salad one of the ladies insisted on putting on his plate.

"Brett?" Her smile had to look as false to him as it felt to her. "Can I talk to you for a minute?"

He put the plate down on the nearest flat surface, which happened to be the piano. "Let's find a little privacy, okay?"

He took her hand and led her quickly into the hallway. The door swung closed behind them, shutting out the noise of the reception. He turned to face her, green eyes intent. "I thought we'd never get a moment alone."

She nodded, her smile crumpling. "I know. What you were trying to tell me before about Doc...he told me."

He captured her hands in his. "Rebecca, I promise it's not as bad as you might think. There's no reason why he can't have a long, healthy retirement if he just takes care of himself."

"Retirement." She shook her head. "I don't know how he'll cope with that. I know he doesn't have a choice, but I'm so afraid he'll shrivel up and die when he doesn't have his patients to take care of." Her voice trembled, and she swallowed hard. Poor Doc. What was he going to do? What were they all going to do?

"He's stronger than that." Brett sounded as if he were trying to convince himself. "You'll see. He'll be fine, and now that he knows the clinic will be taken care of…"

She looked up, startled. "What do you mean? How is the clinic going to be taken care of?" For an instant hope blossomed in her heart.

"The medical center is taking it over." He said it in

a rush, as if he wanted to get it out before she could object. "Look, I know it's not a perfect solution, but we can't wait for perfect. It answers a lot of problems at once."

She grappled with the idea, trying to assimilate it. "But…you sound as if it's all decided. I didn't even know Doc was talking to the medical center. He's always opposed that idea in the past. And anyway, I thought we were too small for them to want."

Brett's grip on her hands tightened. "Doc hasn't been talking with them. I have. They're willing to take over the clinic and merge it with the one in Townsend. Doc can retire and know his patients are being cared for."

"You've been talking to them." This was all too much to absorb. "But Doc would hate the idea of merging the clinics. He's always said Bedford Creek needed its own doctor. He'll never go along with that."

"Rebecca, Doc doesn't have a choice anymore, don't you understand?" He took a deep breath. "Look, this really is best for everyone. The clinic is taken care of. If I get the offer in Chicago…" He shook his head. "This isn't the way I intended to say this. I wanted flowers and moonlight."

She stared at him. "What are you talking about?"

He touched her face, brushing her hair back gently. "I love you, Rebecca. That's what I'm talking about. I love you. When I leave, I want you to come with me. I want us to build a life together."

The words pierced her heart. She'd waited all her life to hear them. Now he was saying them, but it didn't seem real. It was all jumbled up with everything else that had been happening.

"Rebecca?" His eyes darkened, questioning her. "What is it? Am I wrong? Don't you love me?"

"Love you?" A little laugh escaped her. "I've loved you always. I could never love anyone else."

"Then what's wrong?" His fingers moved restlessly against her cheek, as if he wanted to draw her closer but didn't quite dare. "I love you. You love me. The clinic is taken care of. We can go to Chicago and start our new life. Together."

It was everything she'd always wanted, everything she'd dreamed of all her life, held out to her like a gift. All she had to do was reach out and take it.

But it came at too high a price. Slowly she shook her head. "I can't."

"Can't?" Brett looked stunned. "Rebecca, you don't mean that."

"I can't," she repeated, feeling her heart break in two. "I can't just walk away. Doc still needs me. The people of this town need their clinic. I won't desert them."

His face tensed. "Rebecca, you're not making any sense. You can't manage the clinic by yourself. You've got to accept it. That kind of medicine is gone for good. What do you think you can do by staying?"

"I don't know." Could a heart really go on beating

when it hurt this much? "I just know I have to stay. No matter what it costs."

For a long moment he stared at her, hurt and baffled. Then he turned and walked away.

Chapter Fifteen

Rebecca stood in the hallway, hand pressed to her chest. It had never occurred to her that the phrase *a broken heart* meant actual physical pain.

She choked back a sob. She wouldn't cry. She wouldn't.

Her treacherous imagination insisted on picturing what it would have been like if she'd said yes to Brett—a wedding in the sanctuary she loved so much, a cozy apartment just big enough for two, laughter and kisses and shoptalk over a candlelit table in the evenings.

She wiped away a stray tear with the back of her hand. She had to sacrifice that lovely image. She'd stay in Bedford Creek because anything else was unthinkable. Too many people depended on her, and she wouldn't let them down. And Brett didn't want this life. She couldn't use their love to try and trap him in a life he didn't want.

She forced herself to look steadily at a future without Brett. Even with so many people around who loved her, it would be lonely.

She took a deep breath. Enough. She couldn't stand here grieving over what wasn't meant to be. She had to get moving if she intended to save the clinic.

No matter how sick Doc was, she couldn't believe he had given in to the medical center.

A change in the pitch from beyond the door suggested the bride and groom were about to leave. Time to force a smile and see Mitch and Anne off on the one-night honeymoon that was all they'd allowed themselves away from the children. Then she'd talk to Doc.

"There has to be something we can do." She paced across Doc's small living room, the silk skirt of her bridesmaid's dress swishing against her legs. "Doc, there has to be something."

Doc leaned back in his chair, his face drawn and defeated, and her conscience stabbed at her. She shouldn't be bothering Doc—not when he was dealing with so much himself. But if she didn't talk to him, who would advise her?

"I wish I knew." Doc made a small, defeated gesture. "This is all my fault."

"Doc, no." She hurried to him, skirt fanning out around her as she knelt next to his chair. "It's not your fault at all. I didn't mean to make you feel that way. I just want to find some other solution."

"I know." He patted her hand. "But even so, it is my fault. I should have agreed to take in a partner years ago."

"You were waiting for Brett." Fresh pain struck as she said his name.

"No, I was being a stubborn old man. I thought I could do everything myself, and now we're all going to pay the price for that arrogance."

"But Brett…"

He gripped her hand, his faded blue eyes suddenly fierce. "No. Don't blame Brett. He has a right to go where he feels called. We can't make that choice for him, Rebecca. No matter how much we love him."

Did Doc guess just how much that was? Probably. He seemed to know everything else.

But he wasn't going to know she'd turned down her chance at happiness, or why, because she'd never tell him. And Brett certainly wouldn't.

"I still think he owed it to you to stay." She suspected she was beginning to sound just as stubborn as Doc claimed he'd been.

He shook his head. "There weren't any strings attached to the money I loaned him. I wanted to help him become a doctor. If I had other hopes…well, that's all they were. Just hopes. If Brett had come back, I'd have been happy. But I won't blame him for his decision, and neither should you."

He promised me. That was what she wanted to say, crying like the five-year-old child she'd been.

But Doc was right. No one could hold Brett to a childhood promise.

"All right." She took a deep breath, pushing down the hurt. "Forget about Brett. He's leaving. Isn't there anything else we can do to save the clinic?"

"When the clinic board finds out about my health, they'll have to take action immediately—you know that." He looked as if the thought left a bitter taste in his mouth. "And right now, the medical center's offer is the only one on the table. If we had more time, maybe we could find someone, but we don't."

Time. That was what they needed, what they didn't have. She gripped Doc's hand as an obvious solution struck her.

"What about trying to get a temporary physician? There must be someone out there who'd like to spend a working vacation in a beautiful mountain town."

"Do you really believe that?" Doc looked at her gravely. "Rebecca, think about it. Even if we could get a temporary, which is a big if, we'd still have to find someone willing to take over the clinic on a permanent basis. And we'd probably only have a couple of months at most to do it."

"You're saying it's a forlorn hope."

"Just about."

She got up, patting his hand. "Right now, I feel as if a forlorn hope is better than none. Do I have your permission to talk with the board members?"

He sighed tiredly. "Tell them I'm behind you, one hundred percent. And, Rebecca—"

She'd started to turn away, but his voice brought her back.

"Don't blame Brett, you hear me?"

She nodded, her throat too tight to speak.

"I thought you might come by." Doc looked up from his desk as Brett opened the office door at the clinic. He seemed to be spending Sunday afternoon as he often did, catching up.

"And I thought you might be here." Brett discovered it was difficult to talk around the lump in his throat. "You ought to be home, taking it easy."

"Plenty of time for that after I retire." A shadow crossed Doc's eyes at the words, but he didn't betray any other emotion. "I wanted to have a look through some of these old files."

Brett suspected much of Bedford Creek's life was contained in those files, if one knew how to read them. Births, deaths, tragedies borne bravely or railed at— all of those and more were hidden in Doc's terse notes.

Doc nodded at the briefcase in Brett's hand. "You about ready to go?"

Brett nodded, unable to speak for an instant. He cleared his throat. "Doc, I wish I could see my way clear to being what you want."

"Nonsense!" Doc barked the word, sounding for a moment like the gruff doctor of Brett's childhood.

"This life was right for me, but I'm not fool enough to think it's right for everyone. You've got to follow your own calling, no matter where it leads you."

Follow your own calling. The words echoed in his mind. Before he came back to Bedford Creek he'd been so sure he knew exactly what that calling was. Now…well, maybe now he wasn't so sure.

"I just wish…" He realized he'd spoken that wistful thought aloud. He stopped, then knew he could say just about anything to Doc. "I just wish Rebecca felt the way you do."

Doc looked at him steadily. "You haven't hurt her, have you, boy?"

The words stung him. "I didn't intend to. And if I did…well, she's hurt me about as much."

"So that's the way it is." Doc seemed to understand all the things Brett didn't say. "Well, I'm sorry. I'm afraid Rebecca was born stubborn."

"She won't even consider leaving Bedford Creek." He wished the words back as soon as they were out. He shouldn't tell Doc or anyone else what had passed between them.

"No, I guess she wouldn't." Doc got up, came around the desk and put his hand on Brett's shoulder. "I'm sorry, son. Rebecca's got a pretty big bump of responsibility. Maybe she just needs to be needed. And she's needed here."

Was he thinking that Brett was needed here, too? Was that what he felt but would never say?

The shriek of tires spinning into the parking lot stopped whatever Brett might have said. He turned to the window and saw the police car with Mitch behind the wheel.

"Looks as if the newlyweds are back. Mitch probably just stopped to wish me luck."

He headed for the back door and flung it open. But any joking words about newlyweds vanished when he saw Mitch lift a small form from the back of the police car. Angela stumbled out of the car after him, weeping.

"Kristie!" He reached them in seconds, feeling for a pulse as Mitch carried the child inside. "What happened?"

Doc threw open the exam room door, already reaching for his stethoscope, as Mitch put the child down.

"I don't know." Mitch sent a harassed glance toward Angela, who was crying and clutching Brett's arm at the same time. "I haven't been able to get any sense out of Angela."

Doc grabbed Angela by the arms and shook her. "Stop that at once," he ordered. "Tell us what happened."

The treatment worked. Angela gulped, swallowed and gasped a little. "She was in the backyard, playing." A sob escaped her. "I heard her crying, but by the time I got there, she couldn't tell me what was wrong."

"Did she fall?" Brett's hands moved as he fired the question, assessing possible injuries. If she'd been in the tree house…

"No! No, I know she didn't fall. She was picking flowers one minute…" Angela's tears started again. "I told Rebecca I'd watch her, and now look what's happened. It's all my fault."

"It's nobody's fault." Doc's voice was stern. "Stop blaming yourself and help us figure out what happened."

"I think I know." Brett pushed back the sleeve of Kristie's shirt. "Look at this." The welt swelled even as he looked at it. "Angela, is Kristie allergic to bee stings?"

"I…I don't know." Angela's voice faltered. "Quinn never said anything. Is that what it is?"

"Pale, wheezing, swelling around the lips." He cataloged the symptoms, and Doc nodded. "I think so."

"He might not have known." Doc's voice was low. He glanced at Mitch. "Take Angela into the outer office, will you?"

Mitch nodded, took her arm, then paused. "You sure you don't want me to drive Kristie to the hospital?"

Forty miles over mountain roads. Brett shook his head. "No time for that. Take Angela out, and try to find Rebecca." Rebecca was the closest thing to a mother Kristie had. She was the one the child would want.

Doc had already prepared the epinephrine. He handed it to Brett.

They worked silently, each anticipating the other's needs, but Brett's anxiety rose. Kristie wasn't responding. There was a bluish tinge to her small face. They'd wasted precious moments getting her to the clinic, more trying to figure out what was wrong.

Brett snatched the smallest endotracheal tube from the cabinet. "We've got to get a tube down her." He moved swiftly, trying not to think of the child who'd leaned against him, telling him how much she missed her daddy.

But a moment later he was forced to throw the useless tube down. "Can't get it. The swelling must have closed her throat."

Doc shook his head. "She needs a tracheotomy. Now."

The words echoed between them. The two men were frozen, staring at each other across the child's limp form.

"You want me to do it?" Brett could hear the doubt in his own voice.

"You're the surgeon." Doc held out trembling hands. "You want to trust these with a scalpel?"

In that single moment, Brett knew why he'd fought so hard against coming back to Bedford Creek. This was exactly what he'd dreaded since the day he'd set foot in the clinic—the moment when the life of someone he loved would be in his hands.

No choices. There were no choices left. He had to do it. He couldn't let Kristie down the way he'd let Alex down all those years ago.

Guide my hands, Lord. Don't let me lose this precious child.

He took a deep breath and picked up the scalpel.

Rebecca leaped out of the car, not bothering to slam the door, and ran toward the clinic. *Please, God, please, God.*

She hadn't been able to find any other words, not since the call reached her while she was talking to a member of the clinic board. Maybe she didn't need any other words. At a time like this, surely God knew what she wanted.

She ran full tilt into the waiting room and collided with Mitch's solid frame.

"Easy, Rebecca. Take it easy. They're working on her now."

"What happened?" She looked at Angela, who burst into tears.

"A bee sting, apparently. Looks like she's allergic to it," Mitch answered for her.

"It's my fault." Angela sobbed the words. "But I was watching her."

"Oh, honey, I know you were." Rebecca put her arms around her sister, holding her tightly. "You aren't to blame." She looked at Mitch over her sister's head. "How bad?"

Mitch looked uncomfortable. "I don't know, Rebecca. There wasn't time to get her to the hospital."

"No, of course not." Her answer was automatic.

She pushed her sister gently into Mitch's arms. "Take care of her." She started toward the treatment room and opened the door.

Doc moved quickly to intercept her. "Rebecca, it's all right. I promise. We had to do a tracheotomy, but she's going to be fine."

"You're sure?" She looked at him searchingly, heart in her throat.

He nodded. "I'm sure. You can see her, but don't upset her."

He let her go, and she went softly to the table. Kristie looked very small on the white sheet, even her carroty hair exhausted and limp. But the child managed a sleepy smile.

Rebecca stroked her cheek, heart overflowing with prayers of thanksgiving. "It's all right, sweetheart. Don't try to talk. You're okay now."

The sight of the trach tube made her heart stop all over again. It had been life-threatening, and none of them had even known she was allergic.

She looked up at Doc.

"You saved her." Her voice trembled.

"Not me. I couldn't have done it." Doc nodded toward the one person she hadn't expected to see here. "Brett saved her."

Chapter Sixteen

Rebecca stared at Brett, unable to find any words. If he hadn't been here at the right moment…well, it didn't bear thinking about.

"I'll go talk to Angela," Doc said, and the door closed behind him.

"You—" She stopped, swallowed, and started again. "You saved her life. If you hadn't been here…"

"Don't. Don't start imagining things." He sent a warning glance toward Kristie, but she'd drifted safely off to sleep. "She's fine, that's what counts."

"I should have been there." She blinked away the tears that welled in spite of her best efforts to suppress them. "I didn't even know she was allergic. If I'd been there, at least I'd have known what to do."

Brett raised an eyebrow. "Do you want to get into a contest with Angela about whose fault it is? Make sense, Rebecca. It's nobody's fault. No one knew. Now that you know, you can take precautions. But don't start blaming yourself for something that was pure accident."

His tart common sense dried up her tears better than sympathy would have. "You're right. I know." She looked down at the sleeping child, and her heart contracted with love. "I guess I just want to make everything perfect for her."

Brett came to stand on the opposite side of the table. He adjusted the blanket gently. "You can't do that, and even if you could, it wouldn't be good for her. You can't play God in the lives of people you love, Rebecca."

"I'm not trying to take over for God." The anger that flared surprised her. She'd thought she was past being angry with Brett. "I just want what's best for everyone."

"And are you so sure you know what that is?" His normally expressive face didn't give anything away this time. He might have been talking about Kristie, but he might also have been talking about himself.

"No." The anger slid away as she thought of everything that had happened in the past few days. "No, I'm not sure." She looked at him. "But I still have to go on doing what I think is right."

"Staying here. Trying to save the clinic." Emotion flickered in his eyes. "No matter how futile it is."

She crossed her arms, hugging herself to keep the pain away. They were right back where they'd been. Probably nothing could bridge that chasm now.

"I'm not ready to give up yet," she said. "We're trying to get a temporary to fill in while we look for someone to take over the practice."

He looked at her intently. "Is that really what you want?"

"Not just me. That's what Doc wants, too."

She thought another spasm of pain crossed his face at Doc's name, but she couldn't be sure. He turned away, face averted, and picked up his jacket.

"Then I wish you luck, Rebecca. I hope you find someone."

He was going, and there was nothing she could do to stop him. She tried to find the words that would let her say goodbye without falling apart.

"Have a good flight." She tried to smile, but the effort failed.

Brett glanced at his watch. "I'm afraid it's too late for that. The commuter's already gone."

He'd missed his flight to the interview that would take him away from them, and all because he'd been needed here. But he didn't seem to appreciate the irony.

"What will you do?"

He shrugged. "Drive through to Pittsburgh and try to pick up a flight. If I can't, I'll just have to keep driving and hope I can make it in time."

"But you can't—"

"Sure I can." He glanced at Kristie. "Take good care of her. And of yourself." He pushed the door open and was gone.

* * *

It was Wednesday, and Brett had neither returned nor called. Rebecca frowned at the sheaf of papers on her desk—leads to a possible temporary physician for the clinic. Well, Brett didn't have to stay in touch with them. They didn't have any claim on him.

Pain clutched her heart. She ought to have gotten used to it by this time, but she hadn't. It was still just as sharp as the moment she'd told him she couldn't go with him. And tears welled just as readily. She blinked fiercely, willing them back.

"How is it coming?" Doc poked his head in the door, looking at her questioningly.

"It's coming." She closed the folder. There was no point in telling Doc just how slowly. "What are you doing here? I thought you were taking the afternoon off."

She and Doc between them had hammered out an agreement. He came in mornings only; she handled the routine cases as much as possible; and anything that looked serious was sent to the clinic in Henderson. It seemed to be working, but she still worried that Doc was doing too much.

"I'm leaving in a few minutes. Stop fussing at me." Doc glared at her, but there was no anger behind it, just affection.

"See that you do," she retorted, mock seriously.

Actually, Doc had looked better the last few days. It was as if once his condition was out in the open, the strain had been removed. He seemed more relaxed, and his color was better.

"How's Kristie doing?" Doc leaned against the door frame. "You want me to stop by the house and check on her?"

"No, I want you to go home and take it easy. Kristie's fine. Quinn wanted to fly home, but we told him she's doing fine. We practically have to tie her down. Come to think of it, that might be a good solution for you, too."

He held up his hands in surrender. "Okay, okay, I'm going. But you'll have to take care of the applicant in my office."

"Applicant?"

Doc had already started down the hall, and she had to chase after him. "What do you mean? What applicant?"

Doc shrugged, opening the door. "Young fellow who's interested in the position. Looks pretty good to me. You talk to him and let me know what you think."

"Wait, Doc…"

It was no use. He'd closed the door behind him, apparently content to let her deal with the unknown applicant.

Well, she was doing most of the searching anyway. She'd have to talk to the person in any event, so she might as well do it now and get it over with. And she would not start comparing the poor man unfavorably with Brett Elliot. That wasn't fair to either of them.

Donning a welcoming smile, she went into Doc's office. The person waiting turned from the window, and the afternoon sun outlined him in gold.

"Brett." His name came out in a gasp. She stopped as suddenly as if she'd run into a wall. It couldn't be. "What are you doing here?"

His eyebrows lifted. "The interview's over. I'm back. Did you think I'd stay in Chicago indefinitely?"

"No, I mean—" Her mind whirled, then fastened on to one solid thought. "I'm sorry. Doc wanted me to talk to someone who's here about the position. I thought he was in here, but I guess I misunderstood."

"No."

She stared at him blankly. "What do you mean? No what?"

"No, you didn't misunderstand. The applicant is here. I'm the one applying for the job."

She shook her head, hoping to clear it. It didn't help. "I don't understand. You mean you didn't get the fellowship, so you want to work here temporarily until something else comes up?"

And then they'd have to go through the trauma of parting all over again. She didn't think her bruised heart could stand that.

He shook his head. "They offered me the fellowship. I turned it down."

The words lingered in the air. She considered them, hardly daring to hope. "Why? I thought it was just what you wanted."

"I thought so, too." He took a step toward her, his eyes steady. "I was on the verge of saying yes when something stopped me." He shook his head. "Chicago isn't where I want to be. It isn't where I'm meant to be. I belong here, in Bedford Creek. With you."

"But you—"

With a long step Brett closed the distance between them. He pulled Rebecca into his arms and stopped her words with a kiss.

"I love you, Rebecca," he said. "I love you. I don't want a life that doesn't include you."

She tried to force herself to think rationally, but that wasn't easy with his arms around her and his breath warm against her lips. She forced herself to draw back a little in the circle of his arms so that she could see his face.

"Brett, don't. I can't ask you to make a sacrifice like that."

"You're not asking. And it's not a sacrifice." He lifted an eyebrow. "Or have you decided you don't love me, after all?"

"I love you." The words came out in something between a laugh and a sob. "I've loved you all my life, I think. But I don't want you to make a decision because of me and then regret it later."

"No regrets," he said gently. He stroked her cheek, and her skin warmed at his touch. "Remember when you said you couldn't separate the man from the doctor? Well, I can't separate you from Bedford Creek. And I want the whole package."

"But your surgery fellowship…"

He was shaking his head. "That long drive gave me time to think about things. About why I thought I didn't want a position where I'd care too much about my patients as people. About why it was so important to me to stay detached." His voice choked a little. "I was so convinced God gave me my skills for success. Maybe He really gave them to me so I'd be in the right place at the right time to save Kristie. I've been trying to figure out what God wants for me, and now I know. This is where I'm meant to be."

He drew her close against him, and his breath whispered across her ear. "Now will you please stop arguing and say you'll marry me?"

She was in his arms, and that was the place she was meant to be. Funny, that once they both stopped trying to make things work out the way they thought best, God took care of everything.

She looked at him, seeing the love shining in his eyes, and knew they were both home to stay. "Yes," she said softly. "I will."

Epilogue

"**O**pen one more present, and then I'll serve the dessert." Anne handed a gift to Brett, and he put in it Rebecca's lap.

"Rebecca's in charge of opening engagement gifts," he said.

"Can I help, please?" Kristie leaned against his knee. "Please, Uncle Brett?"

He nodded, drawing her closer so she could help Rebecca undo the ribbon. Colorful paper fluttered knee-deep in Mitch and Anne's living room, echoing the spring flowers blooming outside. It looked as if Anne had invited half the town to their engagement party. His parents had come back from Florida earlier than usual to be there, and his mother couldn't stop smiling.

Kristie and Rebecca bent together over the package. She was so excited about being a flower girl in the wedding that she hadn't been still all day.

Rebecca held the card out to him. "This one's from Doc."

"He didn't need to do that." He grinned at the beach scene on the card. "It's enough that he's coming all the way from South Carolina for the wedding."

"He insisted." Alex leaned across to help balance the package. "He's called me three times to make sure it arrived."

Brett glanced from face to face in the circle of friends as they watched Rebecca open the box. How could he have thought he'd be content any place else in the world?

Rebecca turned to show him the seashell lamp, her laughing face so inexpressibly dear to him, and his heart swelled with love.

"Can you believe this?" she said. "They've practically given us enough to furnish the house."

"Not bad for a woman who planned never to marry." He dropped a light kiss on the tip of her nose.

"Never marry?" She looked startled. "When did I say that?"

"At Mitch and Anne's engagement party. You told me you were content to always be the bridesmaid, remember?"

Mischief twinkled in her eyes. "That's because I was waiting to find Prince Charming."

"And did you?"

"Oh, yes." Her fingers closed over his. "I found him in the doctor next door."

* * * * *

Dear Reader,

Thank you for choosing to pick up this book. I hope you enjoy the love story of Dr. Brett and the woman he remembers as a pesky kid sister. Perhaps you'll relate to the struggle Brett and Rebecca experience as they try to find God's will for their lives.

Have you ever noticed how being aligned with God's will for your life puts everything else into perspective? I thought about that as I wrote this story, but I didn't find the perfect Scripture verse until I taught a lesson to my fifth- and sixth-grade Sunday school class. After hearing the Scripture, one of them said, "You mean God already has good deeds picked out for us to do? But what if we aren't there to do them?"

Yes, I thought! That's exactly the question Brett has to ask himself.

Please let me know how you liked this story.

Best Wishes,

Marta Perry

In the exciting new FITZGERALD BAY *series
from Love Inspired Suspense, law enforcement siblings
fight for justice and family when one of their own
is accused of murder.*

Read on for a sneak preview of the first book,
THE LAWMAN'S LEGACY by Shirlee McCoy.

Police captain Douglas Fitzgerald stepped into his father's house. The entire Fitzgerald clan had gathered, and he was the last to arrive. Not a problem. He had a foolproof excuse. Duty first. That's the way his father had raised him. It was the only way he knew how to be.

Voices carried from the dining room. With his boisterous family around, his life could never be empty.

But there *were* moments when he felt that something was missing.

Some*one* was missing.

Before he could dwell on his thoughts, his radio crackled and the dispatcher came on.

"Captain? We have a situation on our hands. A body has been found near the lighthouse."

"Where?"

"At the base of the cliffs. The caller believes the deceased may be Olivia Henry."

"It can't be Olivia." Douglas's brother Charles spoke. The custodial parent to his twin toddlers, he employed Olivia as their nanny.

"I'll be there in ten minutes." He jogged back outside and jumped into his vehicle.

Douglas flew down Main Street and out onto the rural road that led to the bluff. Two police cars followed. His brothers and his father. Douglas was sure of it. Together, they'd piece together what had happened.

The lighthouse loomed in the distance, growing closer with every passing mile. A beat-up station wagon sat in the driveway.

Douglas got out and made his way along the path to the cliff.

Up ahead, a woman stood near the edge.

Meredith O'Leary.

There was no mistaking her strawberry-blond hair, her feminine curves, or the way his stomach clenched, his senses springing to life when he saw her.

"Merry!"

"Captain Fitzgerald! Olivia is…"

"Stay here. I'll take a look."

He approached the cliff's edge. Even from a distance, Douglas recognized the small frame.

His father stepped up beside him. "It's her."

"I'm afraid so."

"We need to be the first to examine the body. If she fell, fine. If she didn't, we need to know what happened."

If she fell.

The words seemed to hang in the air, the other possibilities hovering with them.

Can Merry work together with Douglas to find justice for Olivia…without giving up her own deadly secrets?
To find out, pick up
THE LAWMAN'S LEGACY by Shirlee McCoy,
on sale January 10, 2012.

Love Inspired

SUSPENSE

RIVETING INSPIRATIONAL ROMANCE

FITZGERALD BAY

Law-enforcement siblings fight for justice and family.

Follow the men and women of Fitzgerald Bay as they unravel the mystery of their small town and find love in the process, with:

THE LAWMAN'S LEGACY by Shirlee McCoy
January 2012

THE ROOKIE'S ASSIGNMENT by Valerie Hansen
February 2012

THE DETECTIVE'S SECRET DAUGHTER
by Rachelle McCalla
March 2012

THE WIDOW'S PROTECTOR by Stephanie Newton
April 2012

THE BLACK SHEEP'S REDEMPTION by Lynette Eason
May 2012

THE DEPUTY'S DUTY by Terri Reed
June 2012

*Available wherever
books are sold.*

™

www.LoveInspiredBooks.com

LISCONT12

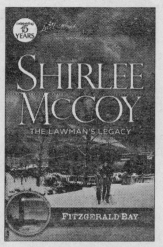

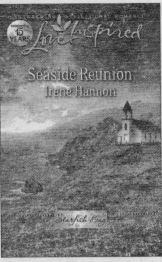

Love Inspired

After surviving a devastating tragedy, combat reporter Nate Garrison returns home to Starfish Bay. But his reunion with lovely Lindsey Collier is nothing like he's dreamed. Lindsey is now a sad-eyed widow who avoids loss and love. Knowing he's been given a second chance, Nate sets out to show her faith's true healing power.

Seaside Reunion
by Irene Hannon

Available January wherever books are sold.

www.LoveInspiredBooks.com

LI87715